A TALE MAGNOLIOUS

A TALE
MAGNOLIOUS

Suzanne Nelson

ALFRED A. KNOPF

NEW YORK

THIS IS A BORZOI BOOK PUBLISHED BY ALFRED A. KNOPF

Visit us on the Web! rhcbooks.com

Educators and librarians, for a variety of teaching tools, visit us at RHTeachersLibrarians.com

Library of Congress Cataloging-in-Publication Data is available upon request.

ISBN 978-1-9848-3174-3 (trade) — ISBN 978-1-9848-3175-0 (lib. bdg.) — ISBN 978-1-9848-3176-7 (ebook)

The text of this book is set in 12-point Adobe Garamond Pro.
Interior design by Jaclyn Whalen

Printed in the United States of America
June 2019
10 9 8 7 6 5 4 3 2 1

First Edition

In loving memory of my grandfather George W. Tallman,
a magnolious farmer who believed in luck and dreaming big
and who always embraced the great unknowable with joy.
And for the many farmers in my family, loved one and all.

—S.N.

A girl,
an elephant,
and a dust storm.
That's how it all began. . . .

CHAPTER ONE

IN WHICH A THIEF AND A PACHYDERM VANISH

Nitty Luce wasn't born a thief. She wasn't born to rescue elephants. Or to make miracles. Nobody ever told her that, though, so she never had reason to doubt. If she'd doubted, none of the bamboozling goings-on in Fortune's Bluff that spring might ever have happened.

But they *did* happen.

The morning started much like any other, with Nitty's empty stomach. It was near on two weeks since she'd run away from Grimsgate Orphanage, two weeks fighting pigs for the slop in their troughs and waiting for breadlines to empty out to scrounge a few dropped crumbs. She wouldn't stoop to begging, not after Headmistress Ricketts's stories of police tossing street urchins into lockup. Just yesterday she'd caught sight

1

of her reflection in a store window, and oh, was she a shambles! Her tumbleweed hair poked out in all directions, crispy with days-old dust. There was a film over her sun-toasted skin and her flour-sack dress, so in the glass she appeared more as a dirt smear than a ten-year-old girl.

"You'll bunk in prison with the likes of Cutthroat Cob," Miz Ricketts had told them at the orphanage. She always gave this sinister warning before lights-out, in case any of her wards got ideas about running away at night. "Or worse, Fang-Toothed Lou."

Nitty didn't believe a word of it. At least, not during daylight hours. Still, she didn't like the idea of fangs of any sort, so whenever she caught sight of police officers, she kept her distance.

But this particular morning, she was doing battle with her hunger again, and it was being a downright bully. When she wandered into the heart of a city, a solid piece west of Grimsgate and north of nowhere, she was too light-headed to worry over police. In fact, on reading the poster nailed to a lone withering tree on Main Street, Nitty had to steady herself against a nearby lamppost.

COME ONE, COME ALL!
WITNESS THE DEATH OF A MURDEROUS FOUR-TON BEAST!
PUBLIC HANGING IN THE SQUARE AT HIGH NOON.
A GUSTO AND GALLANT SPECTACLE NEVER TO BE FORGOTTEN.

Below the words was a gruesome cartoon drawing of a circus elephant trampling a man, with a small caption: GREAT MAGNOLIOUS KILLS TRAINER IN COLD BLOOD.

Nitty leaned closer, studying the fangs and claws drawn on the elephant, the steam pouring from its mouth and trunk, the smoldering rage in its eyes. The picture was nightmarish, the sort of sensational rubbish Miz Ricketts loved to read about in the *Daily Tattler*. Nitty didn't think too harshly of the *Tattler*, though. In fact, she often rescued old editions from the fireplace before they became kindling. They offered the most entertaining reading at Grimsgate.

Now the crowd gathered about the poster was nodding and whispering, heads bobbing like the wind-up tin clowns Nitty had once seen in a toy shop.

"Savage business," one man declared, while two young women fretted about needing to procure smelling salts before the hanging. "The Gusto and Gallant Circus is well rid of the monster. I feel its devilry in my very bones. It would kill again, mark my words."

"Yes," one woman twittered. "I heard its eyes are red as Beelzebub himself."

Nitty frowned. What did these people know about this elephant? Not a speck more than she did, probably. She'd never seen an elephant before, and she doubted any of them had either. She'd once read an account of an elephant in the *Tattler*, a "Just So" story by a man named Rudyard Kipling, that said the animals had an "insatiable curiosity." "Insatiable" made her think of eating chocolate, which would be delicious and wonderful, if there were any chocolate to be had. Which there was not. But if "insatiable" made her think of the delicious and wonderful, then an elephant's curiosity must be those things as well.

Elephants must surely be like orphan girls, she decided: creatures sorely misunderstood and blamed for a host of troubles they had nothing to do with.

She nudged her way through the crowd, glimpsing food carts and tinkers' wagons lining the edges of the square. A barbershop quartet sang at one corner while a clown at another sold balloons. The square had the jaunty atmosphere of a carnival, which seemed even worse than backward to Nitty, given the occasion—especially once she spotted a towering crane rising up from its center. The crane, she guessed, was how they meant to hoist Magnolious from her feet. It was every kind of awful. A chain fashioned into a noose hung from its arm, swaying as a forceful gust of wind hit it.

Nitty shielded her eyes from the grit blasting her face, and others around her held kerchiefs to their mouths and scanned the sky. They were worrying over a dust storm, waiting for the telltale mud-colored clouds to barrel down on them with the force of a bison stampede.

Nitty held her breath, scoping for alleyways where she might take shelter, but the gust soon wheezed out.

She turned away from the crane. She wouldn't watch the hanging, a gawker like the rest. It would be too cruel. But—her stomach whined at wafting scents of roasted peanuts and cotton candy—she would stay close by, in case somebody spilled popcorn or dropped one or two precious peanuts. Most any food had a sandy aftertaste these days anyway, so it wouldn't much matter if she got it from the ground.

She was heading toward the peanut cart when a sudden spark of green caught her eye. She swiveled her head and spotted a wooden wagon. A slatted board in its side was propped open to display an array of colorful oddities. Puppets dangling from strings, jewel-toned bottles full of mysterious potions or exotic perfumes, glass globes holding miniature kingdoms so real-looking that Nitty half expected to see ant-sized people popping out of their cottages and castles. The sign painted along the wagon's side read THE MERRYTHOUGHT WINDOWSHOP.

Nitty stepped closer, and again a twinkle of green flashed. She traced it to a small open pouch full of the strangest objects she'd ever seen. Shaped like question marks no bigger than a fingernail, they were the greenest sight in town. Maybe in the whole county—or state, for that matter. Their bright hue was so cheerful, so incandescent, that Nitty had the urge to climb into the pouch with them.

Her heart reached out to them, rising snugly and pleasantly into her throat. Being inside that pouch would be like being in a proper jungle—a jungle so full up with trees and plants that she could wrap herself in hammocks of leaves and weave herself a home of vines. Nothing would be brown in that jungle. Even dirt and rocks would grow lovely, fuzzy moss.

"I know that look, girl." The tinker—mostly hidden by a threadbare cloak—leaned out over the window. Nitty couldn't see the eyes appraising her, but she felt them spinning her stomach like a whirligig. The voice inside the hood echoed like water over stones. "That's a hungry look," it continued. A knotted hand passed over the pouch. "If it's food you're after, I have none to offer."

"I don't want food," Nitty blurted. She had wanted it, badly, only a minute before, but now . . . she couldn't take her eyes from the green glow of the pouch. "That there in the pouch—"

"These?" The tinker's eyes glittered from the cloak's shadows. "These are seeds. They came from the very first garden on earth. The one that grew before anything else. Before people or animals." The tinker leaned closer. "Before hate and cruelty, before kindness was forgotten. Back when there was only love. And hope. Before time itself."

"There wasn't any such garden," Nitty scoffed.

The tinker smiled, a smile that despite its toothlessness was strangely buoyant. "Oh, but there was, and it was greener than spring grass after a rain, so green that being in the garden was like sitting inside an emerald. It held every dream and every promise of what could be, of what the world wanted to become." The tinker's voice was lullaby soft now, and Nitty felt it again, the urge to be sitting in the midst of that green.

"How much? For the seeds?"

The tinker huffed. "You can't afford them. Few people can."

"But . . . what do they grow?" She couldn't stop staring at the shimmering pods. The longer she stared, the more they looked like they were quivering in the pouch, wanting to be free.

With a crooked finger, the tinker beckoned her closer. "That, girl, depends on the farmer. What do you *need* them to grow?"

Nitty stalled, her thoughts a tangle. She hadn't been thinking about planting them, only keeping them. She felt her Gleam Jar pressed against her side, tied around her waist with twine, and thought how lovely the seeds would look inside. It was only a plain mason jar she'd filched from the Grimsgate kitchen on canning day, but what was inside it . . . well . . . those objects gleamed in all the ways, and with all the colors, that the world—in these days of dust and doldrums—didn't. If Nitty had a second heart, her Gleam Jar was it.

Nitty felt the tinker's hooded gaze, and wanted to be out from under it. She lifted her chin and fixed the tinker with a glare. "I don't need anything."

The tinker straightened with a crowlike cackle. "Ah, but you do. More than you know." Just then, a wisp-thin woman with a passel of knee-high children approached the wagon, asking about cough tonics, and the tinker's focus shifted to her.

Nitty's fingers tingled, itching for that pouch. The wind picked up again, and there was a static hum to the air, the sure sign of a dust storm brewing. Murmurs of excitement suddenly rippled through the crowd, and Nitty turned to see a path being parted by police officers in the square as an enormous creature ambled down the street.

"Great Magnolious!" one of the knee-high boys near her cried out. He yanked on his mother's hand, trying to pry her away from the Merrythought wagon. "Hurry up, Mama, or we'll miss the hanging!"

Nitty stretched onto tiptoe for a better view. The elephant was shackled in chains that gave her a shortened, awkward gait. Her folds of skin bore crisscrossing scars, some puffed and gray like the rest of her, others pink, raw, and fresh. Her head hung low, her long-lashed eyelids half closed in tiredness, or sadness. For no logical reason at all, Nitty longed to go to her, to take that enormous head in her hands and press her face against that trunk. She imagined it feeling tickly with bristles, wrinkled as a raisin but altogether lovelier to touch.

Nitty's fists clenched as jeers and taunts burbled in the crowd. *Poor Old Mag,* she thought, *there's nothing beastly about you.*

"Mama!" the boy beside Nitty shouted. "Come on!"

Nitty's attention turned back to the Merrythought wagon and to the seed pouch. She'd had enough of this town and would be on her way. Any town about to kill such a strange- and wonderful-looking animal was too ugly to stay in, even if there were food pickings to be had. But . . . she hesitated. The seeds. She couldn't leave them. She reached out her hand, fingers buzzing with yearning.

A small dirt devil swirled through the square, making everyone lower their heads just long enough for Nitty to snatch the pouch and scurry into the crowd.

She glanced back once, and she could've sworn the tinker's hood swiveled toward her in a knowing way. Seconds passed, without anyone coming after her. She slowed, wrestling a jab of guilt. The truth of it was, she wasn't cut out for stealing. No more than that elephant was cut out for cruelty. Nitty had goodness in her, she was sure of it. Even if nobody else was.

"Nothing but a scrappy, selfish babe you were, from the moment I set eyes on you," Miz Ricketts liked to remind her. "No wonder you were dropped at Grimsgate's doorstep. Who else would have you? What, with that rat's-nest hair and those peculiar eyes?"

Nitty didn't think her eyes were peculiar. They were simply *very* green. Greener than the seeds she'd just stolen. Greener than the tree frog that Nitty had once hidden atop Miz Ricketts's best Sunday hat. (This might've been the best trick Nitty had ever played on the headmistress, except she wasn't positive the poor frog had recovered from the broom beating Miz Ricketts gave it afterward. Nitty herself had been sore for a week from that broom, and she was much sturdier than a frog.)

"Highly suspicious," Miz Ricketts said whenever the subject of Nitty's eyes came up (and she made sure the subject came up daily). "Suspicious and very probably dangerous."

Miz Ricketts expected nothing but the worst from Nitty,

and that disapproval stuck faster than a bur to a bear. It had spread through the Grimsgate staff and the other orphans until Nitty was blamed for every turn of rotten luck that happened at the orphanage. When the children took sick, it was Nitty's "contagion" that had caused it. If a mouse was discovered in the pantry, it was because "that impish child" had put it there. (Of this offense, Nitty was often actually guilty.) Even if Miz Ricketts's bunion took to swelling, it was because Nitty had given it the "evil eye."

For ten years, Nitty had taken the blame when she was (mostly) blameless. Ten years nearly to the day, and now she hurried through the square with the stolen pouch of seeds. Maybe she'd give up on goodness altogether, since it wasn't being generous with offering her chances to claim it. But then she'd be proving Miz Ricketts right.

Nitty stopped mid-step in the swirling dust, deciding to return the seeds to the Merrythought Windowshop, when an eerie whine rose up from the north. She lifted her eyes to the sky. A telltale wall of toast-colored clouds was charging toward them. Within minutes the square would be choked in dust as thick as pudding. No matter how you tried to catch a gasp of clean air during one of these dusters, none would come. Every breath felt like sucking up a mound of chimney soot.

A shudder passed through the crowd, and some hurried for motorcars, carriages, or storefronts, searching for shelter. Nitty's eyes were scouting for someplace to wait the storm out when a police whistle shrilled the air.

"Stop that girl!" An officer across the square jabbed his stick in her direction. "She's a thief!"

Nitty sprang, darting jackrabbit quick between elbows and legs, slipping through grabbing hands. There was only one spot in the entire square where no crowds dared gather. She headed straight for it, heart clattering. Magnolious stood under the crane with two dozen officers surrounding her. Encircling her neck was a chain as thick around as Nitty's leg. The elephant's feet alone were twice the size of Nitty's head. She remembered the poster, and the man crushed under those feet.

Then another thought struck her. This animal was friendless, as was she. This animal was unloved, as was she.

Surely Magnolious wouldn't hurt a body so like herself?

"Mag!" Nitty cried out, when what she really meant was *Help me.*

The words flew to the elephant's ears. Her drooping eyelids opened; her head lifted. She'd been called many names in her life and remembered all of them. There'd been Great Magnolious, which she'd never liked, because it was usually followed by unnerving cheers and applause. There'd been "beast," "cow," and some others that didn't bear repeating, and, most recently, "murderer." That last was the most loathsome because it was said with tones of such anger, such hatred. She'd never, until this moment, been called Mag. It was the way the name was spoken, in desperation and in kindness, that made her raise her head to see the scrawny girl pushing her way through the crowd.

"Mag," Nitty said again as she broke through the circle of officers surrounding the elephant. A collective gasp swept over the onlookers, and whispers broke out.

"The girl's mad."

"She'll get herself killed."

"Girl! Get back from that beast!"

Nitty ignored them, lifting her eyes to Mag's.

The girl and the elephant regarded each other for a long moment. Then Mag gave the smallest toss of her head and lifted her trunk, and Nitty scooted between her front legs and into the safety of Mag's underbelly.

Stillness fell as everyone watched, waited, and feared the worst.

Mag shifted and straightened her legs over Nitty's crouching form, feeling a new purpose and an odd but not unwelcome responsibility for the charge beneath her.

From under Mag, Nitty peered out at the officers. Would any of them get up the gumption to come after her now?

None did.

Not ten seconds later, the duster hurtled into the square, bellowing heat and spitting grainy sand that pricked the skin and blinded the eyes.

The world turned russet, and Nitty could only see the crowd as ghostly shadows passing through streams of flying earth. Mag's body loomed large above her. Shielding her eyes, Nitty crawled out from under the elephant and to her side, then reached for her ear.

Mag bent her head low in response.

"You're good, Old Mag, aren't you?" Nitty said quietly, holding an open hand out to the elephant. "Nothing like they say you are."

Mag blinked, and the tip of her trunk swung to Nitty's hand, flexing as it explored her fingers and palm.

The trunk brushed ticklishly against her hand, and Nitty felt strangely comforted by it.

"I'm leaving here," Nitty said. "Come with me."

Dirt churned around them, growing thicker. At last Mag gave Nitty the gentlest nudge with her giant head, as if to say, *Step back*. Once Nitty was well clear, Mag rose onto her hind legs and, without much effort at all, pulled the chains that bound her from the ground. Then, with her chains loose and dragging, she lowered herself until she rested on her back haunches with her belly nearly brushing the ground. She bent her front left leg at the knee, as if it were a stepping stool, then stilled. Nitty thought she understood, and she stepped onto Mag's awaiting knee and used it for a boost to clamber behind Mag's head. Mag's spine beneath her was hard, her skin rough and prickly, and Nitty's legs stretched so far across the immensity of Mag's neck that her feet stuck out comically. Nitty took hold of the chain about Mag's neck so she'd have something to keep her steady.

As the sky darkened and dust rained down, Mag began walking. Nitty pulled the collar of her shift up over her mouth and scooted farther down on Mag's back, leaning slightly to one side so that her head was behind one of Mag's flapping ears. The ear shielded her from the worst of the dust.

She felt the pouch of seeds hanging on her twine belt, safe alongside the Gleam Jar; she felt the long, lumbering strides of Old Mag beneath her. She felt the dirt pelting her back, legs, and shoulders. She felt a welcome easing in her feet. They were tuckered out from weeks of running. So was she. In fact, she was sapped from living as a stray.

She'd never go back to Grimsgate, but . . . where *would* she go?

What she needed right now, and maybe what Old Mag needed, too, was for this day to turn out differently from the others that had gone before it. To turn out better, for once.

She pressed her cheek against the bumpy ridges of Old Mag's back and closed her eyes, wanting to believe that something wondrous could happen. Maybe even something miraculous.

CHAPTER TWO

IN WHICH AN ELEPHANT SHOWS GREAT PROMISE AS A COMPASS

It is said that elephants have an extraordinary sense of direction, that they can follow the scent of water from miles away, that they can remember places they've never been, places their ancestors visited before they were ever born.

Nitty didn't know this. Neither did Mag.

As it turns out, thousands of years of elephant instinct come in handy during dust storms. Mag plodded through the squall in much the same way feet might sink into sand at the beach, with dirt heaping and spilling around her, pouring over her head, shoulders, and back. Under other circumstances, the dirt might have felt pleasant, cool and soothing against her skin. *This* dirt felt like a battery of stinging wasps about her eyes and trunk. Not pleasant at all.

She suspected it was much worse for the girl on her back, which was why she kept going, pushing her forehead against the wind, flapping her ears to and fro in hopes of fanning the heaviest blasts of dirt away from the girl's face. The girl was so small, without a trunk to plug from the worst of the grit. Really, such a slight creature wasn't meant for weather like this.

Mag had taken a liking to her the minute she'd seen her running through the square, the minute her trunk had taken in the girl's scent—untamed and sweet. These days, all Mag sniffed on people's skin was the rotten-egg smell of suspicion. Worse than that was the smell of fear and blame—bitter and distasteful as the moldy hay that made up her meals. Meanness, too. Her trainer's skin had stunk with sour-smelling meanness whenever he'd swung the bull hook across her flank. He seemed to think her skin didn't feel hurt the way his did.

He was wrong.

This girl, though, was different. Her eyes were open like a stretch of unbroken grass, with a pinch of wild about them. Mag's sight had grown tired and blurred, but she had been able to see those bright eyes clearly. She liked those eyes. She especially liked that they seemed to understand that Mag didn't want to die, that she shouldn't die.

So Old Mag carried the girl through the storm, all the while listening to the whispers inside her that led her on, this way first and then that way; right, then left; north, then east; and hoping the girl had the sense to keep holding on.

ᏨᎥᏨ

Nitty's throat felt like someone had taken a cheese grater to it, and when she coughed, a gritty mud coated her mouth. Old Mag's sides ballooned outward each time she inhaled, and Nitty's legs hugged tight to them as the elephant's muscles rolled beneath her fingertips.

It seemed like Mag had been walking for hours. In the disorienting vacuum of the storm, though, it might only have been minutes. Nitty couldn't be sure. What she could be sure of was that her own chest was hurting, filling up with dirt.

She opened her eyes a crack and saw nothing but a cyclone of blowing silt. They could be in the middle of towering buildings or on a vast, empty prairie. There was no way to tell. If they stopped, the dirt would be up to Mag's knees in a matter of minutes, and then up to her chest, and then . . .

Nitty swallowed and bent her head closer to Mag's ear.

"We're lost," she whispered.

Then her hand brushed against something solid and run through with ridges. She squinted until she saw planks of wood and hinges.

"Down, please, Mag." She waited, wondering if the elephant would understand.

Mag stretched her body out and down then, like she had before, and offered her bent knee to Nitty.

Nitty climbed from her back, then placed her palms firmly against the object before her.

A door, she thought, and opened it.

⟨⟩

The barn was dark but welcoming, smelling mustily of hay, damp wool, and warm animals. Nitty heard a cow's lowing, the bleating of sheep, and the comforting clucking of chickens. A mare whinnied nervously at the sight of Old Mag's giant head coming through the door, but Mag must have been used to the animals of the circus, because she didn't give the horse a second glance. Instead she headed for the watering trough on the far side of the barn.

Rust-colored light filtered in through slats in the wood, and after Nitty's eyes adjusted, she glanced at Mag and laughed. "Look at you." The elephant was caked in so much dirt that it rained down to form anthill-like heaps on the floor.

Nitty's laugh was gravelly, and the sound of it made Mag raise her head from the trough and look at Nitty as if to say, *You think* I'm *a mess? You should see yourself.*

"I know." Nitty didn't find it at all strange to be addressing an elephant. So far, Old Mag had proven to be the most well-mannered conversationalist Nitty had ever met. She was certainly an improvement over Miz Ricketts: much less opinionated, for one, and far less critical.

Nitty shook out her dress, but the fierce dirt seemed to have burrowed itself under her very skin. She leaned over the trough, only to find nearly all the water gone. After scooping some handfuls into her mouth, she straightened, placing her hands on her hips and eyeing Mag.

"You didn't leave me much to work with, did you?"

Old Mag swung her head toward Nitty, until her right eye was in line with Nitty's face. She brought her trunk within inches of Nitty's skin, moving it purposefully through the air, seeming to trace the outline of Nitty's body, hovering but not touching. Up and down, front to back, Mag's trunk explored, with such thoroughness that Nitty felt compelled to blurt, "Do you mind? If you haven't found something likeable about me by now, it's a hopeless case."

The tip of Mag's trunk dared to push against Nitty's belly button then, and slid its way up until it had reached the top of Nitty's head.

Nitty stood stock-still, feeling the muscular power in that strange strawlike feature and wondering if she'd been foolish to trust an animal of such immense strength. The trunk ruffled her hair, and then blew a powerful shower of water right over Nitty's head.

Nitty sputtered and gasped, laughing as thick red mud ran off her in rivers. There was only enough water in the trough for one more trunkful, and even after that Nitty stayed sticky with mud.

Mag sniffed the empty trough, seeming disgruntled, and Nitty nodded in agreement. "We're going to need more water." She didn't know where they'd get it from, or how. "We'll worry about that later."

She had no idea where they were, whose barn this was, or where they'd go from here. She only knew that she was too tired to run anymore today, and from the looks of things, Old Mag wasn't going anywhere either.

With a huff that sent flurries of dust into the air, the elephant settled onto a nearby mound of hay.

Nitty sat down a safe distance away, then took out her Gleam Jar and held it up to the dim light slanting through the barn's siding. She did this every day with the jar, taking stock of its contents and comfort in its presence. The light bounced off the objects in the jar, sending flecks of blue, yellow, and red spinning about the room. Blue, yellow, red; ribbon, button, marble. These three objects—so small—to a stranger might've seemed unremarkable. To Nitty they were her only link to family, and to a world brimming with color that she'd never seen. *The jar needs green,* Nitty thought sleepily now. *The tinker's seeds.* The barn creaked in the wind, more dust spilling through the wooden slats.

The whole world needs that sort of green, she thought at the sight of the dust.

She'd heard there'd been a time when green had grown up

on its own, straight from the ground. When food and jobs had been as plentiful—even commonplace—as the dust was now. That was before she'd been born. Before jobs and crops had dried up. Before folks had taken to breadlines and bleak stares. Still, she hungered for that green of better times. How much more would others hunger for it, those who'd once seen it coating the bluffs and prairies? There couldn't be much worse than having something so wonderful only to have it taken from you. She knew about that.

Green was wonderful. So were mamas and daddies. Families. Maybe like the one she'd been supposed to have but didn't. It was terrible missing something you didn't remember but knew you'd once loved.

She hugged her Gleam Jar tighter, yawned, and slumped to the floor, several feet from Old Mag. In the hours that passed, in the shifting and turning of slumber, the distance between Nitty and Mag closed. They'd found each other through happenstance, but already being apart seemed unnatural. Soon Nitty's head was cradled in Mag's trunk, girl and elephant curled together.

CHAPTER THREE

In Which an Event of Life-Changing Enormity Befuddles Windle Homes

Windle Homes was stuffing an oil-soaked rag under his front door when the heart-shaped freckle behind his right ear took to itching. He straightened, the way a birch tree might after bowing to the wind, slowly and with a measure of grace. His arms and legs branched from his lean trunk at sharp angles, and it was easy to imagine a timbery creaking accompanying their movements.

The dust kept seeping in around the rag as Windle scratched his freckle.

Strange, that freckle. It had only itched four other times in his life. The moment he'd fallen in love with his sweetheart, Clara; again the moment he'd lost her; a third time when his darling daughter, Lillah, had entered the world; and the fourth time. Well, he didn't like to think about the fourth time at all, so he didn't. Nevertheless, each itch of the freckle had heralded an event of life-changing enormity.

But what could possibly be life-changing about another duster?

The storms had become so commonplace that folks no longer took two lumps of sugar in their tea, but two lumps of prairie sod instead. Some even took to attributing flavors to the different sorts of dirt that blew into their homes and seasoned their every meal. Chokeberry Silt blew down from the Dakotas and left a fruity aftertaste on the tongue, while Oily Loam blazed up from Texas with a sticky stubbornness and tarlike tang. Bison Sward barreled in from Wyoming and left a burly sourness in eyes, mouths, and noses. The worst was the Toeter Grime from Iowa, blowing in with the storm today. Sadly, this particular soil tasted very much of sweaty, unwashed feet, which was why Windle had been trying particularly hard to block it from coming through the door. His itchy freckle distracted him. It made him dread and hope, fear and anticipate.

It made him glance out the window, searching for a sign.

He saw an elephant. Or an elephant-shaped and -sized form. With the storm howling as it was, and whole fields' worth of dirt blowing sideways across the windowpane, it was difficult to tell what, exactly, was lumbering across Windle's yard. But as it drew closer to the barn, he became certain. It was an elephant, and . . . a person. A small person.

It was an elephant and a little girl.

From what he could make out, the girl was a ragamuffin, so toothpick thin that, if the elephant hadn't been there for her to brace against, she would have been blown halfway to Canada by now.

Windle watched the two of them disappear into his barn. Such a pair appearing in his yard during a dust storm could only mean one thing. They were running away.

But from what? Or whom?

He frowned. Windle wasn't keen on runaways. They meant trouble, and he already had enough of that.

He sat down in Clara's empty chair. In his experience, there was no better place for pondering than a rocking chair, and Clara's chair was a fine rocker. He knew. He'd built it. And he needed to ponder for a bit.

What did he know about elephants? Very little. About young girls? Nearly as little. That had been Clara's specialty. His had always been farming. Not that he could do any farming right now.

Windle rocked and pondered, pondered and rocked. His freckle quit itching, and he knew. An event of life-changing enormity *had* happened, and it was—no, *they* were—waiting for him in his barn.

He didn't like it. Not one bit.

↞✧↠

Nitty woke beneath the shade of a tall but scrawny tree. She blinked and looked again. It wasn't a tree but an old man. He was peering down at her, his thin lips teetering on the edge of a frown.

"Who gave you permission to house a pachyderm in my barn?" The question was demanding, but the rumbly voice didn't sound nearly as stern as she'd expected. In fact, it sounded like a voice trying hard to be something it wasn't. It gave her courage, and as she tucked herself tighter against Old Mag's side, she jutted out her chin and narrowed her eyes, hoping this made her look fierce.

"Who gave *you* permission to be so rude to guests?" she countered.

He lowered his head, his narrow, beaky nose making her think of a crane dipping its head into a creek to nab a fish. "Guests are usually invited by their host *before* they arrive. If I had invited an elephant onto my property, I would've remembered."

"Maybe not." She stared at him, unflinching. "Old folks forget heaps of things." She didn't want to sound hateful, but fear was making her cagey. Not to mention, being woken by a cranky old man right in the middle of a wonderful dream about riding Mag through a lush green meadow struck her as plain unjust.

"*I* am Windle Homes, and rumors of my demise have been highly exaggerated." The man straightened, and when he did,

Nitty realized he might not be quite as age-old as she'd originally thought. His wrinkles sat lightly about his tawny face, as if they were only perched there and could flit away whenever they fancied. Those wrinkles, Nitty guessed, had come on quick. Maybe from some unexpected sadness.

She glanced around and noticed that the light streaming in through the barn's slats was brighter now, more golden than brown.

"Yes, the storm passed hours ago," Windle said, as if reading her thoughts. "Which means you two can be on your way."

"We will be, too." Nitty gave Mag a pat on her side, and they both got to their feet. Mag dipped her trunk into the watering trough and gave a sulky snuffle when it came up empty.

"Come on, Mag. We've got places to be." Nitty held her head high and hugged her Gleam Jar close against her chest, trying her best to ignore the moaning of her stomach and the parched ache in her throat. Mag was surely as thirsty and hungry as she was. But this old man wasn't offering up any cordiality, and Nitty wasn't the begging sort. She nudged the back of Mag's left foreleg, and Mag reluctantly galumphed toward the barn door.

Outside, the sky was a cloudless blue sliding into a fuzzy ocher along the horizon. That fuzziness was leftover dust that hadn't yet settled. It probably wouldn't have the chance to settle before another storm blew through. For now, the day was clear and bright, but drier than a horned toad's tongue. Beyond the barn was a small plank house, its whitewash streaked with dirt and peeling, its window boxes empty and crooked, one half-unhinged and swinging in the breeze. Planters lining the porch still held the remains of bent, shriveled flowers. As far as Nitty could see was nothing but fields of dirt and sand dunes, with a few brittle, mostly dead shrubs poking up here and there.

Nitty had never set eyes on anyplace so withered, so downright lonesome. *Lovelorn* was the word that popped into her head. She'd read that word in the *Daily Tattler,* too. She remembered the sentence perfectly: *Her lovelorn heart searched for solace in starlight.* She thought it must mean a kind of pining for love—maybe love lost, or forgotten. This land had a lovelorn feeling to it, and she didn't think starlight could provide the comfort it needed. That thought made her tighten her grip on her Gleam Jar, wanting to check up on it, as she had a tendency to do, and be reassured by its presence. She imagined it wasn't near as soothing as the kiss of a mother, or the hug of a father. But it was all she had, so she made do with it.

"This is your farm?" she asked Windle, who was standing behind her in grudging silence, as if he'd been taking in the view from Nitty's vantage point and wasn't at all happy with what he saw.

What came from Windle's throat started as a cough and ended as a growl. "It *was* a farm. Once. The finest soil around these parts, some said. Before dusters blew it to bits. Just good-for-nothing dirt now, like every plot of land around the town of Fortune's Bluff."

"Fortune's Bluff!" Nitty blurted. "What a woeful tribulation of a name to have these days!"

Windle's eyes widened. "I suppose that's true." For a second, the corners of his mouth drew upward, though the smile never broke open. "But the place is so dog-eared by dusters it hardly matters what it's called."

"Course it matters. It's your town."

A shadow darkened Windle's face. "It belongs more to Mayor Snollygost than to anybody else now. And it's a sorry sight." He pointed into the far distance at the town—a small, humble brown smudge in the bleak landscape.

"I'm not about to call it that." Nitty stuck her hands on her hips. "It hardly seems fair to harbor such low expectations of a place I've never been. A raindrop's not much to look at either, till it's a river."

"Bah." Windle scowled but then chuckled, a soft, low sound like distant thunder wrapped in velvet. He cleared his throat with a no-nonsense rumble. "Right, then. You *do* . . . have somewhere to be?"

"Oh yes, sir." Nitty made her voice rock-steady. "I mean, as soon as we find it, we'll have it."

His lips flattened, and he drew a hand through the graying shock of hair across his forehead, pacing and mumbling, "Jab-bering Jehoshaphat."

"Jumping," Nitty corrected.

He quit pacing and glared ferociously at Nitty. "Listen here, girl. I don't know how you came by this elephant—"

"Her name is Magnolious," Nitty blurted defensively, "and I'm Nitty Luce. But I prefer just Nitty, and *she* prefers Mag."

" 'She prefers . . . ,' " Windle muttered, and took up pacing again. "The girl knows what the pachyderm *prefers*. Confound it all." He shoved his hands into his pockets, giving Nitty side glances every turn he took. "What I'm saying is that you can't stay here." He trudged toward the house while waving one hand behind his back in farewell.

Nitty stared after him. With its cockeyed porch and squeaking window boxes, the house didn't look like it could stand up to anything stronger than the gentlest breeze, but there was something snug about it that made Nitty want to step inside. She turned her eyes to the fields of dirt stretching toward the horizon. If she started walking with Mag through that dirt, she might never reach the end of it.

Nitty looked deep into Mag's eyes, so deep she thought she could see all the way inside Mag's chest. She placed her hand against Mag's side. The elephant's great heart pounded, slow and steady, a comforting strumming beneath Nitty's palm. Mag's heart was surely the size of a watermelon, maybe even a very large pumpkin. How much love could a heart that size hold?

"Wait!" She ran after Windle, with Mag following, and lifted the seed pouch to his face. "We can help you plant crops. Mag and I." Her words tumbled and tripped. "I bet an elephant works twice as fast as any horse and plow. She'll be a good worker. Won't you?"

Mag nuzzled Windle's neck with her trunk, right at the freckled spot behind his ear. Windle pushed her trunk away. "No seeds'll sprout in this dirt. The wind blows them all away. The wind steals everything."

"I have different seeds," Nitty argued. "They'll grow anywhere, in anything."

Windle eyed the seed pouch, the corners of his mouth deep furrows curving down to his stubbled chin. "Argle-bargle."

"It's true!" Nitty persisted, even though she wasn't sure any of what she was saying was true. Still, if wanting made any difference in whether something was true, then this had to be true.

She'd make it true.

"The only plant that grows anywhere and in anything is a weed." Windle dismissed Nitty with another wave. "Keep your seeds."

"They'll grow." She remembered what the tinker had said. "Whatever you *need* them to grow." Nitty jabbed a finger at the green seeds, which juddered in the sunlight like they wanted a chance to prove themselves. "That's the promise of them. That's my promise to you. Just say what you need."

"I need . . . I need . . ." Windle glanced toward the barren fields and back toward the empty house. "I need you . . . I need you and that beast . . ." After a pause, he threw up his hands. "*You* should be the one telling *me* what I need, girl. You're so certain of yourself."

Nitty stiffened. Well! If he wanted to put her to the test,

she'd pass it and then some. She narrowed her eyes and studied him—the drawn lines of his face, the emptiness hanging about his spindly limbs. And she thought she knew. "You," she said matter-of-factly, "need a remedy for a broken heart."

"Bah!" he cried, but there was no anger in it.

What Nitty didn't admit (and never would) was that she hadn't the faintest idea what the remedy for a broken heart was. If she'd known, she'd have swallowed down a dose when she'd been left on the doorstep of Grimsgate as a bawling baby.

"At least let me try to help!" Nitty ran in front of Windle, blocking the path between him and the house. "Let us stay for a handful of days. We'll plant the seeds, and then do whatever work you have for us."

"I don't have any work."

"You do! That windmill needs mending, and . . ." Nitty scanned the farm, ideas fizzing and flashing about her brain like lightning bugs. "And your fields need plowing, and . . . and . . ." She huffed in a breath as Mag nudged her with her trunk. The nudge had a bossy feel, like Mag was trying to tell her something. Nitty swiveled to face her. Mag swung her head from side to side, giving a few short trumpet calls, the first true sounds she'd made so far.

"What is it, Mag?" Nitty asked.

"What's this, now?" Windle groused. "Don't tell me you can understand that beast."

It was true that Nitty had had no experience conversing with elephants. Well, except for the last few hours, and that had been all her own talking and Mag listening. But Nitty wasn't the type to remind herself of what she couldn't do. She'd heard about her can'ts her whole life. Can'ts could chip away at a person's core until she was worn down to a stub of nothingness. She'd never put a lick of credence in them, and she wasn't about to now. So she stared long and hard into Mag's face, watching the elephant's eyelashes brush against the wrinkles bordering deep, black eyes, and she listened. Not with her head, but with her heart, its door wide open and waiting.

She understood then what Mag was telling her.

Windle shuffled his feet impatiently until Nitty turned back to him.

"Mag knows what needs to be done around here," she announced, her voice sure and even. "She'll set everything to right."

"An elephant?" Windle's eyebrows jumped skyward.

"Why *not* an elephant?" Nitty folded her arms.

He shook his head. "I'll give you three nights. But if anyone comes asking after an elephant and a runaway, I'll turn you in quicker than a blink. And I don't have an extra bed in the house either."

"I'll sleep with Mag in the barn," Nitty blurted, not wanting to give him a single reason for changing his mind.

He nodded. "Well, then. Better ask your elephant where she'd like to start first."

CHAPTER FOUR

IN WHICH A COUGH HERALDS A FRIENDSHIP

It was all well and good for Nitty to declare her faith in the face of Windle's doubts. But once the door to the plank house was shut and she and Mag were left standing in the yard alone, that faith seemed a lot less dependable. It seemed downright flimsy.

But that was the truth of faith, Nitty supposed. The only way to get it to stick fast was to grab it firm by the fist and set it to work proving itself. She planted her hands on her hips and eyed Mag.

"Well?"

Mag lifted her trunk until it formed a perky S shape. Then she set out, with Nitty alongside her, plodding in a westerly direction past the house with what was left of her chains dragging behind her. Her head swung in a wide arc, side to side, as her trunk explored the air. When they reached the windmill, Mag stopped, tracing the walls of the nearly empty water tank at its bottom with her trunk.

"Nothing but a dribble." Nitty shook her head at the water spout. The windmill, missing all but two of its blades, wobbled weakly in the breeze. Nitty scooped a few handfuls of silty water into her mouth before Mag drained the rest. Nitty frowned at her. "What'd you go and do that for? It'll be hours before there's even a puddle in that tank again!"

Mag snuffled Nitty's hair in response, and Nitty heard a deep rumbling that she thought might be elephant laughter. Only it wasn't coming from Mag. It was coming from behind an empty, rotting corn pen. She turned just in time to see a flash of bright blue disappearing behind the corner of the pen.

The sound came again, louder and longer this time.

"Who's there?" Nitty called. When no one answered, she added, "You might be near invisible, but you sure as stars aren't quiet."

Now, Nitty had read about spacemen in the *Daily Tattler,* and the creature that rounded the corner of the pen bore a striking resemblance to one (well, according to *her* imagination, anyway). Ill-fitting, enormous goggles perched on a small, noseless, mouthless head covered in a cheesecloth mask. The creature carried a narrow, rectangular, bright blue box in its arms, with the Morton Salt girl and umbrella printed across the front. So, thought Nitty, *not* a spaceman. Because surely a spaceman wouldn't be carrying something as ordinary as salt.

"Rats and darnation! My stealth is always thwarted by this cough!" a boyish-sounding person mumbled from the depths of the mask, then seemed to remember that he was talking to a stranger and straightened his twig-thin frame. He pulled a notepad and stubby pencil from the back pocket of his dungarees, dropping the blue box along the way.

Nitty scooped up the strange contraption, but the boy snatched it back just as quick. "Hey! Don't you bust my periscope! It took me months to collect enough Morton Salt labels to mail away for it, and it's the finest surveillance equipment I have."

"I didn't want to see it anyway," Nitty huffed, even though she did. Desperately.

The boy tucked the periscope under his arm, then cleared his throat in a no-nonsense way. "Detective Higgler's the name. I have a few questions about the elephant." He bounced fast and light on the tips of his toes, like he was itching to run, or maybe even spring clear into the air the way a cat would, pouncing on a mouse.

"Detective?" Nitty snorted. "You're no more a detective than I'm a princess." She gave Mag a stroke on her trunk and, after a moment's reflection, added, "Not that I'd *want* to be a princess, mind you, always in distress and waiting to be rescued. But that's beside the point. The *point* is . . . I'm not answering questions about Mag. Especially to a stranger I can't look dead-on in the eyes. So. Go snoop someplace else."

He shook his head. "Can't. It's my job, see. Sniffing out danger and foulsome, rotten villainy." He jerked his head toward Old Mag. Now his fingertips were tapping in addition to his toe-bouncing, until soon his entire body was wibbling in jumping-bean fashion. "Old Mag, you say?" He peered around Nitty at Mag, and Mag took the opportunity to inspect his mask and goggles with her trunk. The boy quit wibbling, stood stock-still, and gulped. "Is . . . is she? Dangerous, that is?"

Nitty laughed. She was beginning to enjoy this. "Not with *me.* But then, I don't know what she'll do to boys in frog goggles."

"Criminy!" The boy relaxed then and resumed his wibbling. "I've told Ma a thousand times that nobody could ever take a detective seriously in this getup. But she never lets me leave our house without it. And I barely get out as it is, on account of the mud in my lungs. Doctor says they're so full up with it I could grow a crop on the inside. He says one day corn might bust right out from my ears and belly button. And I told him I wouldn't even mind, as long as it was sweet corn." His laugh was a burbling brook. "But the dusters make it worse, so I wear the mask to keep from breathing more dirt in. It's hot as a skillet inside it, and it itches like the dickens." He yanked off the goggles and mask, revealing walnut eyes set in a face of the very same brown shade. He grinned and shrugged. "Better. There won't be any duster this morning anyway." He stuck out his hand for a shake. "Full name's Angus Higgler, but folks call me Twitch."

Nitty didn't need to ask where the nickname came from. A hummingbird stayed stiller than he did. She introduced herself then, saying simply that she was visiting from out of town. When Twitch asked how she knew Windle, she stiffened. "I don't see how that's any business of yours."

Twitch was undaunted. "I'll uncover it in good time. Always do." He nodded to Mag. "Are you positive she's not dangerous? Even a little?" His voice stretched toward hopeful. "If she were, she could prove invaluable to my operations. My agency's in sore need of a strong-armed interrogator. Er, strong-trunked, in this case."

Nitty stiffened. How dare he leap to offer Mag a job without a second's thought to Nitty's own interrogation experience? Why, she'd set Miz Ricketts to trembling with questions plenty of times—mostly about how Miz Ricketts could eat roast chicken and bread pudding for dinner while Nitty and the other children ate cold porridge. "Mag's not yours to use for whatever you like, you know, and you might've thought to ask about *my* qualifications. I have buckets full! But that's no matter, because *we*—the both of us—are extremely busy and can't be bothered with detectiving nonsense." She spun on her heel to walk away with Mag, but the boy hurried after them.

"Wait! Oh, don't be sore with me." His face was eager and regretful. "You could help, too! I didn't mean for you to think you couldn't. I was overcome by excitement is all. It's not every day a person stumbles on an elephant."

Nitty had to admit this was true.

He turned his periscope in his hands. "I don't leave my house much, you see. Hardly ever, really, unless I manage to sneak by Ma. And even when I do get out, Fortune's Bluff is as exciting as a plank of wood." He paused. "Excepting the dastardly deeds of Mayor Snollygost, of course."

Nitty stopped mid-step, Mag beside her. "What sort of deeds?" She'd learned from the *Daily Tattler* that anything labeled "dastardly" was tremendously interesting.

Twitch's face turned instantly animated at the question. "That's exactly what I'm trying to find out. I heard Ma and Pa say once that Snollygost was never elected mayor square and fair. He owns the loans on most folks' land in Fortune's Bluff. Heck, these days he owns most every corner of Fortune's Bluff. No one ever says it out loud, but they whisper that he forced folks to vote for him. He'd take their land otherwise."

"Whispers about a person don't make truth," Nitty said, thinking about all the whispering Headmistress Ricketts had done over her, and how that whispering had always been just loud enough to be heard.

"Suppose not," Twitch agreed. "But I'm guessing you haven't met Mayor Snollygost yet. Once you do, you'll see it."

"What?"

Twitch leaned closer. "His air of malevolence," he whispered. "Every villain has one. Says so right here in the *Detective*

Comics." He pulled a rolled-up comic book from the back pocket of his dungarees and opened it. The pages were so worn a few loose ones tried to slip out, but Twitch pushed them back into place. He pointed to the top of a page. "'Ten Ways to Be a Villain, number five: Exude an air of malevolence.'" He nodded once, authoritatively. "Snollygost does that for sure. It sneaks into his smile every once in a while. Nobody else notices. But *I* do. And you will, too."

"If nobody else notices it, why do you think I will?"

He shrugged. "You noticed me, didn't you?"

Nitty didn't think it would be kind to point out that it would be hard not to, what with the cough and the spaceman goggles.

"You're not worn out like the rest," Twitch said decisively, inspecting her from head to toe. "I was watching you. Good detectives get hunches. My hunch tells me you're different." He scrutinized her, then nodded firmly. "I figure it's the elephant. An elephant is exceptional, so maybe you are, too."

Nitty grinned. She was beginning to like Twitch. She appreciated a decent snoop. (She'd been one herself at Grimsgate. That was how she'd discovered that Miz Ricketts wore a wig, and how she'd successfully hung it from the dining hall chandelier.) She liked the words Twitch used, too. Twitch sounded like a living, breathing *Daily Tattler*. It was very entertaining . . . and handy. She'd love to add some more words to her vocabulary. Besides, Twitch had a periscope. A periscope *and* an inspiring vocabulary—those were powerful enticements.

"All right, then, Detective Higgler," she said to Twitch. "Old Mag and I are fixing up this farm. We've got seeds to plant and plants to grow. If you want to get to know my exceptional elephant, how about you give us a hand?"

Twitch opened his mouth, but Nitty held up a finger and added a quick "And *don't* say it can't be done."

Twitch stuck out his chin. "I wasn't about to. But one thing you can't do is use the tractor. The Homes tractor has been clogged with dust for months, same as ours. I helped Pa on our farm plenty before my lungs turned muddy. I was going to point out that for farming these days, you're going to need a horse-drawn plow. That's all."

Nitty smiled. "What about an elephant-drawn plow?"

With that, Nitty and Twitch turned toward the field's edge, where a plow lay on its side, half buried under dirt. Nitty looked at her elephant, then pointed to the plow. She was pleased to see Mag turn in the direction she pointed. "What do you think, Mag? Would you be willing to try it?"

Mag snuffled the abandoned plow and the yoke that lay a few feet from it. She'd seen the likes of that yoke before. She'd worn one to drag stacks of poles through fields and dirt, then to pull the poles to standing to raise the big top, as she'd learned the humans called it. It was pleasant to be out from under that big top, which blocked the sky and snuffed the breeze. It was lovely to be far from her trainer's angry bark and bull hook. Here, alongside this girl, she could see bright blue overhead and feel soft dirt underfoot. Here, alongside this girl, she could move without being commanded; she could do as she pleased without obeying. This made her skin tickle, her trunk swing, her old bones feel young again. It made her want to stay near the girl. And not only that. It made her want to thank the girl, too. She sensed a need in this girl, a canyon of need deep enough to cut a river. She wanted to help fill it. There wasn't anyone barking at her to do it. Just herself, deciding to. That made it feel right.

So Mag bent, slowly, and lifted the yoke with her trunk. Nitty looked at Twitch, and they both grinned.

"Couldn't tell a plow from a pickle, those two," Windle grumbled as he watched Mag and Nitty through the window. And how in darnation she'd finagled Angus Higgler into the mix, Windle didn't want to know. That boy's lungs couldn't handle a sneeze, and he was puffing alongside Nitty trying to fit the yoke onto Mag. Because Mag was roughly five times the size of a horse, it wasn't going at all well.

Windle frowned. He'd banked on the certainty of their failure, sure enough. He just hadn't banked on caring.

This girl couldn't have ever farmed a day in her life. She was walking around the plow, eyeing it from every angle, a riddle she needed to solve.

"She'll give up," Windle said decisively. He knew a thing or two about giving up. Oh, he'd battled that infernal dust, all right. He'd plowed and sown his crops each spring, first with a sturdy hope, then with a seesawing one, and finally with one that had dwindled down to diddly. Each April he'd watched shoots spring from the ground, only to watch them shrivel without rain or be blown to kingdom come by the dust storms.

Despair didn't come naturally to Windle. As a younger man, he'd been brimful of dreams about what he'd do with his farm, how it would grow grain and corn so healthy and tall the tips would sweep the very clouds above. He was certain of his knowledge in farming. He was certain of his future success. He was certain of the path before him.

"Certainty never sticks, not with the world changeable as it is," Clara had told him, resting her head under his chin and patting his hand. "But there's joy to be found in the unknowable, too."

Windle had laughed, for he *knew* soil and crops and farming. He planned; he planted; he grew himself the finest crops for hundreds of miles around. The crops brought the best prices at market, year after year. A "master farmer," the folks of Fortune's Bluff took to calling him. None of them (with one exception) had minded that the Homes fields outshone all others. Instead they'd been proud to claim Windle as their neighbor and as a citizen of Fortune's Bluff.

And Windle had found joy in the certainty of knowing how each and every day would pass, of the path his life was sure to take. He'd found joy in their snug white house, in Clara's peach cheek pressed to his shoulder, in their little girl, Lillah, who had run giggling through the cornfields. But then came the fourth event of life-changing enormity. And on its heels? The dusters.

There was no joy in the dusters. There was no knowing when, or if, they'd ever stop. There was no knowing how much longer the savings he'd stuffed under his mattress with such great care would last. There was no knowing when, or if, he might set eyes on his Lillah again either. There was no certainty at all. Which was why despair stopped in to visit Windle and decided to stay for a spell.

Despair was what made him say again now, "Yes. She'll give up. We all do in time. And the better off she'll be for it, when I haven't a smidgen to offer her."

That's when his eyes fell on the photograph of Clara and Lillah—the one in the smack-dab center of his rickety kitchen table. Clara was smiling, holding a little laughing Lillah in her arms. Their sweet eyes struck Windle as suddenly beseeching.

Windle frowned. He knew confiding in a photograph might strike most as a daffy pastime, but what else did he have to turn to besides a house full of emptiness? "I know what you'd have me do. You two and your sympathetic notions. But somebody's bound to be looking for them. An elephant's not your everyday sort of stray."

The photo said nothing, as photos are prone to do, which was no help at all to Windle.

He glanced back out the window, his wiry paintbrush eyebrows tipping skyward. Nitty Luce did not look like a girl about to give up. With her lips puckered in concentration and her eyes fixed on the plow, she looked like a girl with an uncommon store of pluck. Why, at this very moment, she was trying the yoke on herself, nearly buckling under its weight but still digging her heels into the dirt to try to pull.

He yanked his work hat onto his head, casting a glance back at the photo on the table. "I'll go. Just because I don't want to see my plow broken to pieces by that elephant."

His pronouncement was met by silence. The very same silence he'd heard for near on ten years. He wondered, as he had many times before, if he'd ever get used to it. With sinking spirits, he feared, just as he had so many times before, that he would not.

He stepped onto the front porch and, without a glance in Nitty's direction, headed for the barn. He'd start with fashioning a proper harness for that beast. But that wouldn't mean he was helping. Not a speck.

CHAPTER FIVE

In Which Dirt Discovers Its Potential

It only took the span of a few short minutes for Nitty to discover that Windle Homes didn't want her thanks, or her questions. In fact, he didn't want to be paid any attention at all. When she tried following him into the barn, he waved her away. When she asked if he needed anything, he snapped, "Yes. I need you to leave me be."

"He sure is cantankerous," she said, returning to Twitch, who sat wheezing beside the immovable plow. "Is there anything in your detective manual about villains being remarkably bad-tempered?"

Twitch gave her a sideways look. "You're suspicious of Mr. Homes?"

Nitty shrugged. "Just trying to unpuzzle his moodiness is all."

"It's no puzzle." Twitch jerked his chin toward the white house. "It's on account of his being a hermit. Least, that's the reason Ma gives for it. First, Mrs. Homes passed, and then their daughter, Lillah, traipsed clear across the globe. She sings, and travels for her performances. Windle hasn't seen her in near on ten years. And Ma says when a body's been alone for that long, it's bound to turn ornery. Like a stray cat."

Nitty shook her head, dropping her voice to a whisper. "Hoo-wee. If I had the likes of that sort of sorrow, I suppose I'd be moody, too."

Just then Windle loped out of the barn, carrying a tangle of leather and rope in his hands and a bolt cutter under his arm.

"Shhh," Twitch commanded, nudging Nitty. "Best not talk about it in front of Mr. Homes. It would only worsen his mood."

Windle stopped in front of them, his eyes stern under the shelf of his brow. "Angus?" He bent over Twitch. "Does your ma know you're out of the house? I won't have you suffering any attacks on my account. I know how she frets over your breathing. . . ."

Twitch sent Nitty a quick plea with his eyes. *Don't tell,* his eyes said.

Nitty wouldn't, she decided. She was enjoying his company far too much for that.

"As long as I keep my mask on, Ma says it's fine." Twitch looked Windle dead in the eye.

Nitty felt a stirring of admiration. Twitch was a solid fibber. Not as good as she was, mind, but he could hold his own.

"I'll take your word, then. Man to man," Windle said. "I never did like the idea of you cooped up in that house all day. But the moment you start feeling poorly, you tell me and I'll take you home."

"Yes, sir," Twitch said.

Windle busied himself with the bolt cutter, snapping the chains from about Mag's ankles and neck. When the ankle cuffs thudded heavily to the ground, Mag raised her head higher, as if in relief. Windle gave a nod of satisfaction at his handiwork, then faced Nitty. "This harness won't work." He held it out to Nitty. "That beast'll break through the straps in no time. Don't know why I bothered."

Nitty grinned. "Being bothered is better than being bored."

Windle grunted. "Never said I was bored."

"Well, if *I* was a farmer without fields, I'd be bored as a pirate without a ship." Before Windle could say another word, Nitty scooped the harness from his hands and, as Mag bowed down of her own accord, slipped it over Mag's head and around her chest. She could feel Windle watching her, which only made her more determined to fit it into place to show that she knew a thing or two about harnesses. (She didn't, of course, but who needs expertise when you have confidence?) The harness was fashioned with a broad leather band at Mag's chest and straps running from it along Mag's sides to the front of the plow. Mag seemed comfortable in it, and within seconds she was plodding through the field, pulling the plow behind her.

"Come on, Twitch!" Nitty said triumphantly, hurrying to

catch up to the plow to hold it steady as it churned up dirt. "Let's get to work." She glanced back to see Twitch scrambling toward her and Mag with a wide grin. Windle looked after all of them, frowning and shaking his head.

Nitty paid him no mind, and within minutes she and Mag had plowed two long rows across the field. They weren't straight, but they were better than nothing. She and Twitch followed Mag as she tilled each new row, but every half hour or so Twitch would make for home.

"Got to pester Ma for something or she'll suspect that I'm on the lam," he told Nitty. "The trick is in my cunning. A skilled detective gets your guard down without ever lowering his. See?"

Nitty saw, all right. Twitch darted to and from his house and Windle's with the quick craftiness of a fox. He'd be beside her one minute and gone the next, doing his best to run on those gangly stalks of his. She didn't have the heart to tell him how often his muddy cough gave away his whereabouts.

He helped as much as he could, until his breaths came out in thundery rumbles and Nitty made him quit to rest on the porch. By that time, she'd forgotten all about Windle and his frown until Twitch managed a puffing "Doesn't seem bored anymore, does he?"

Nitty followed Twitch's gaze to the windmill, where Windle, balanced atop a rickety ladder, was hammering on the last of the new blades. The windmill slowly turned in the breeze, then spun faster, and within minutes, water was pouring from the spout at its base into the water tank, filling it up.

"How about that?" Nitty patted Mag's side. "You've got yourself some fresh water." She looked into Mag's right eye, where she could've sworn she saw a glimmer of satisfaction. "All right, all right. I'll never doubt you again." Mag tossed her head, and Nitty laughed. Then Windle whirled on his ladder to face her.

"Are you three going to lollygag or make yourselves useful?" Windle asked.

Nitty turned back to the field, and Twitch stood up from his seat on the porch and returned to the plow.

"He sure is demanding," Twitch said.

But there was something new in Windle's tone that made Nitty feel encouraged. He had expectations for her, accomplishments he was banking on her making.

So she did. She and Mag and Twitch (when he could breathe). They plowed until sundown that first day. Windle studied the half-finished field for a long time before muttering, "Hardly worth the work when a duster's sure to blow it all away. But still . . ." His voice lifted a pinch. "Still . . ." And the cloudless sky stayed dust-free.

After Twitch walked home (for the last time) and Windle busied himself feeding the other animals, Nitty and Mag staggered into the barn, where they found hay and a sparse serving of chipped beef on toast waiting for them.

Nitty was licking the last bits of beef from her fingers when Mag's stomach gave a mighty rumble. She turned to see Mag snuffling the dirt floor, every last morsel of her hay gone.

"I'm still hungry, too." Nitty patted Mag's belly in sympathy. "But I've a suspicion he gave us all he could for tonight. I snuck a peek through the kitchen window a bit ago, and his dinner plate was just as meager as mine."

She sat down and set her Gleam Jar in her lap, and not a moment later, Mag settled down beside her. Nitty rolled the jar in her hands, and the contents chimed quietly against the glass. Blue, yellow, red. Ribbon, button, marble. Nitty closed her eyes and focused until she could see them all—her family—before her. The ribbon twining through her mother's hair, the button tucked into her father's pocket, the marble rolling between her brother's fingertips.

Her chest tightened with the all-too-familiar pains of missing them, but then she felt the strange, bristled softness of Mag's trunk pressing against her chest, in the very spot where it ached.

Nitty opened her eyes to find Mag's enormous head so near her own that winding gullies of gray wrinkles filled Nitty's vision. Mag's right eye was watching her intently, her trunk still pressing against Nitty's chest, right over her heart, as if Mag was wanting to take measure of its beating.

"You had a family once, too," Nitty whispered to her. "Do you remember them?"

Mag blinked and blinked again, never shifting her gaze from Nitty's face. She didn't know what the girl was saying, but her tone was quiet, and more than a little lost-sounding. And her heart . . . her little heart was pounding in a lonely way, like Mag had once heard an injured horse's do after a big-top show. But the longer Mag stayed near, the longer she held her trunk to the girl's chest, the stronger and steadier the little heart sounded. It made Mag feel needed, more than she'd ever been needed before, and that was a feeling that made *her* feel less alone.

Just as Mag thought this, Nitty raised her hand to rub under Mag's chin. When Mag sighed and tilted her chin toward her, Nitty laughed.

"You like that?" Nitty asked, then laughed harder when Mag opened her mouth to expose her pink tongue. "I'll rub your chin as much as you want. *Not* your tongue."

Mag seemed to accept this and let her head sink back against the ground, then flopped entirely onto her side, every ounce of her mountainous self limp. This gave Nitty her first up-close glimpse of the welts Mag bore along her belly and legs. Nitty touched the scars gingerly, tracing her fingertips along their ridges. Then she placed her palms against Mag's rough, thick skin and rubbed her underbelly and sides.

"They'd no right to do it," Nitty whispered fiercely. "And as long as I'm with you, no one will hurt you like that ever again."

Whether from this pledge or from the feel of the hands caressing her, Nitty didn't know, but Mag heaved a contented sigh. Her great eyelids fluttered and half closed, and as they did, Nitty yawned, too.

She tucked her Gleam Jar tight against her belly, then lay down in the curl of Mag's trunk.

Mag, close to drifting off to sleep herself, felt the small, still warmth of the girl pressed against her, and made her own pledge. That she'd protect the girl's lost and lonely heart with her own for as long as she was able.

Then, almost at the same moment, the two fell into a heavy, woolly sleep.

⌒⚬⌒

The next morning, Nitty woke with a crisp apple under her nose, cans of white paint beside her head, and Mag tickling her toes with her trunk. Nitty could see the scant remains of the fresh bale of hay that had been left for Mag, which the elephant had already made neat work of finishing.

Rise and shine, Mag's trunk insisted.

"All right already." Nitty sat up, stretching. "I'm getting there."

Still, a spray of cold water from Mag's trunk made certain.

Nitty sputtered, jolting awake. "You could've asked more politely."

Mag patted Nitty's head, once, twice, and then, tucking her trunk under Nitty's armpit, pulled her gently to her feet. Nitty smiled and rubbed under Mag's chin. "I take it you like it here, then?" she asked, leaning her head against Mag's chest. "I do, too," she whispered. "But don't let on just yet."

Nitty and Mag emerged from the barn to the sight of Windle scraping the last curl of old peeling paint from the house. Twitch was there, too, his nose (out of the dust mask, for the time being) stuck in a *Detective Comics.*

"Morning, Twitch," Nitty said.

"It says here that villains can go easily undetected. 'Ten Ways to Be a Villain, number eight: Disguise yourself as a patron of philanthropy and good citizenship.'" He tapped his comic with a finger. "Neezer Snollygost is the *mayor.*"

Nitty yawned.

"Don't you see?" Twitch's knees bobbed up and down so violently that the comic threatened to slide off his lap. "Posing as mayor is the perfect disguise."

Windle quit scraping, his limbs stiffening. "No time for comics and villains today. Mask on, Twitch. We've work to do." He slapped paintbrushes into both their hands as soon as Twitch reluctantly donned his mask, then led Mag toward the field. "You paint while the pachyderm and I finish plowing."

Nitty and Twitch painted until Nitty's face and Twitch's mask were covered in white freckles. Nitty's arms burned like she'd gotten into a patch of fire ants. By sundown the house shone clean and bright against the endless toasted landscape, and the field was plowed into expectant rows.

"Waste of paint, this, when a duster's going to turn it brown in a blink," Windle said. "But still . . ." And the sky beamed down blue over the glowing house, which, from the sky's vantage point, must've looked like a perfect white egg, waiting to hatch.

On the third day, with no dusters in sight, Nitty woke well before sunrise. A biscuit sat under her nose, wrapped in a kerchief, but Nitty ignored it.

Her pouch of green seeds was juddering. She pressed the pouch against her heart, feeling the seeds' vim and verve warming her from the outside in.

"I know," she told them. "It's time you were planted."

She opened the barn door onto a still-purple sky. Last night's stars were waltzing with the sun's first rays, seeing who could outshine the others. It was the enchanted in-between time, when minutes hover without passing, when the universe holds its breath, waiting to see what will happen beyond the crest of the brand-new day.

The seeds juddered faster.

"Mag." That was all Nitty needed to say, because Mag felt it, too.

Mag felt the humming expectancy in the air, under her feet, in her heart. She nuzzled the girl's cheek and felt the girl's excitement rising from her skin. It had the scent of a fresh, clear watering hole. She stuck her trunk into the girl's bag of seeds and felt the tiny life inside them, whirring with wanting to get out. She understood what needed to be done.

The two of them walked to the edge of the field. Nitty picked up a pile of dirt in her palm and held it, wondering, worrying. The dirt was loose and dry as a desert, hardly fertile for planting. The smallest breeze might blow the seeds away, and a duster . . . a duster would . . .

"No it won't either," Nitty said aloud, wanting to make sure the dirt, the air, and the sky heard her loud and clear. Windle's glum thinking would never be hers. Not if she could help it. She knelt down and dug a hole in the soil with her finger.

Mag snuffled that hole and, using her trunk like a spoon, scooped out another small hole a ways down from it. She took a few steps into the row, then dug another, and another. While Mag dug, Nitty took the first seed from the pouch. Its newborn green shimmered beneath the sun and stars, eager and exultant.

She laid the seed into a hole and covered it with a blanket of dirt. She bent toward the earth. She was about to say *Grow,* but stopped. Growing seemed so . . . unimpressive. She wanted the seed to do more than grow. Much, much more. She thought for a long minute, then whispered, "Triumph," giving the dirt one more encouraging pat.

So they planted during the in-between time, Nitty and Mag, until the entire field was sown and all but a handful of seeds were snug under the soil. After considering for several minutes, Nitty tucked that last handful into the planters along the porch and under the windowsills. Maybe something bright and lovely would sprout in them—something to lure a hermit from his lonely lair. Soon enough, all the seeds were planted save one. That one seed Nitty tucked into her Gleam Jar, not able to part with its green. Blue, yellow, red, green. Ribbon, button, marble, seed. She smiled. The seed fit in perfectly.

Then she and Mag sat down at the field's edge.

Just about the time that the marigold sun finally bested

the stars, Windle appeared on the porch, coffee in hand. He nodded at the planted field.

"It'll need water, and we'll spread some hay over the top, to keep the soil from blowing." He took a sip of coffee, peering at Nitty and Mag over the cup's rim. "How is your elephant at irrigating?"

Nitty had no idea, but she answered confidently, "She's magnolious. How else would she be?"

Windle harrumphed, but the harrumph came out garbled. Nitty suspected there might've been a laugh corked up under it somewhere. "We'll see about that."

Nitty rubbed Mag behind an ear. "You're not going to let him offend you like that, are you?"

Mag straightened her legs and lifted her head. She most certainly was not.

"Good," Nitty said. "Let's draw some water."

At first Mag hung back, studying Nitty and her bucket intently. Then she went to the trough and mimicked Nitty's process, using her trunk. Nitty did her best to keep up, but there was no rivaling Mag. That trunk could draw twice as much water from the trough as the bucket and could irrigate six seeds to Nitty's three. The windmill kept spinning, water kept flowing into the trough, and Mag kept drawing it into her trunk and fountaining it onto the seeds. At some point, Twitch showed up to watch, but his cough was much muddier than in the days before, so watching was about all he could do. As Mag walked the rows, darkening the soil with damp, Windle spread the hay after her, until the sun was high overhead.

"It's on the verge," Nitty announced when the water trough had been emptied and refilled a dozen times and the last inch of soil was strewn with hay.

"On the verge of what?" Twitch asked.

Nitty stared at him, then sighed. "Of happening."

"What's going to happen?"

"Everything that needs to. Am I the only one who feels it coming? It has a certain smell, like . . ." She raised her head toward the sky. "Like the sweetness of morning dew."

Twitch paused over his *Detective Comics,* then grinned, nodding. "That is a fine smell."

"Hogwash and hornswoggle," Windle said. "I smell nothing but"—he sniffed the air—"unwashed feet." He grimaced. "Mark my words, there'll be a Toeter Grime duster here within the hour." They raised their eyes to the sky. Creeping over the horizon were the brown clouds—nothing but toadstools now, but soon they'd be billowing titans. The animals, too, seemed to sense what was coming, because the horses left the corral for their stalls and the chickens left their coop, fluttering to the safety of the barn's rafters instead. "Twitch, I'll take you home before it hits. Nitty, you and Mag head back to the barn and stay put."

"But the seeds," Nitty and Twitch said together.

Windle peered into their waiting, wide-eyed faces. His

common sense tolled a doomsday bell. But what came out of Windle's mouth wasn't doom. What came out of his mouth was "If the seeds are worth their salt, they will reveal their merits in a timely manner. For now, they would do well to dig in snug and hold on tight."

Nitty and Twitch stared at him.

"Are you *sure* you're a curmudgeon?" Nitty cocked her head at Windle.

Windle's frown was back before Nitty could blink, and then he stomped away to fetch the truck. Mag rested her trunk on Nitty's shoulder as they watched him go.

"He likes you," Twitch told Nitty. "And Mag, too."

"He's hardly said boo to either one of us." But Nitty's heart-strings pinged like wind chimes stirring in a breeze. "How do you know he likes us?"

Twitch nodded toward the repaired windmill and the freshly painted house. "He's fixing things. He's trying. Trying isn't a small thing. Especially when everybody around you is giving up." Twitch peered toward the barn. "I've got to hightail it before he comes with the truck."

Nitty's eyes settled on the horizon. The brown toadstools in the sky were taller, looming closer. "Twitch, let him take you home."

"And have Ma catch me?" He shook his head. "Nah."

"Doesn't she notice you disappearing?"

"Remember what I told you? About folks not noticing?" Twitch said. "It's funny about parents. They're the worst about noticing. Oh, they see the dirt behind your ears, or when your toenails could stand clipping. But they don't always see *you*." He stared down at his toes. "Ma's been different since Pa went west to look for work. She spends most of the time anymore fretting over money." His voice sank a notch, and his mouth sagged. "When she quits hearing my muddy cough for a spell, she's so relieved she never thinks to wonder why." He grinned. "I disappear, my cough disappears, too. Ma hardly comes to my room at all anyway. Besides, I'm mostly supposed to stay in bed, sipping the turnip soup she fixes." He wrinkled his nose. "Can't stand the stuff. I don't trust turnips any more than I trust Miz Turngiddy."

"Miz Who?" Nitty asked.

"Mayor Snollygost's secretary. She comes around our house most weeks wanting to know when we'll pay Mayor Snollygost what we owe him."

"What do you owe him for?"

"Our land, for one. And all the goods we buy from Snolly-gost General Store." He studied his feet. "Ma's pride doesn't like buying on credit, but she says it's either that or empty bellies."

Nitty nodded. There'd never been enough to eat at Grims-gate either, at least not for anyone besides Miz Ricketts. Plenty of times, late into the night, she'd heard whining stomachs echoing in the dorm. "Lately it feels like the whole world's emptied out. It needs to be filled again, don't you think?"

"With what?"

Nitty shrugged. "I'm not sure. But Mag and me. We're going to try to fill it up."

"Me too," Twitch added, and Nitty nodded. He tucked his comic under his arm and waved to Nitty. "See you tomorrow," he hollered, then took off, trotting and wheezing.

A moment later, the slight breeze turned into a proper blow. Squinting against the wafting grit, Nitty and Mag reached the barn door just as Windle drove up. He frowned when she told him that Twitch had already gone.

"I have a mind to speak to Mrs. Higgler about the boy's ramblings," he groused. "His lungs can't take it."

"You don't know that," Nitty said. "Maybe they can."

Windle stared at her, his dark eyes sorrowful. "Limitations are as plentiful in this world as the air we breathe. You think you can beat them. We all do, at one time or another. But we can't." He sighed. "Might as well get used to it now."

Nitty stared right back at him. "If I wanted to get used to that kind of thinking, I would've stayed back at—" *Grimsgate,* she finished in her head. She wasn't about to let that slip. But she knew all about limitations.

"You would've stayed where?" Windle peered down at her.

"Nowhere." She stuck out her chin. "All I meant was, if you're going to live expecting nothing but letdowns, might as well not live at all." He harrumphed, and she added, "I bet you never said such a thing to your daughter. I bet you used to tell her that she could do anything—"

"And she left, confound it! That's what she did!" Windle paled, his body ramrodding. "Enough. I've heard enough." He got out of the truck, adding gruffly, "You had your three days. Time's up in the morning." With that, he turned toward the house, ushering Nitty and Mag into the barn's shelter as he went.

Nitty sighed as the barn door banged shut and the wind took to whining through its cracks. She glanced at Mag, who bobbed her head up and down, like she was already agreeing with what Nitty hadn't yet said out loud. Then it came.

"Three days isn't near enough time to change his mind."

⌒ᵔ⌒

As the dust barreled through Fortune's Bluff that evening, the residents of the Homes farm dreamed.

A curmudgeonly farmer dreamed of corn sweeping the clouds above, of his sweet Clara resting her chin on his shoulder, of their young girl who used to giggle as she ran through the fields. He dreamed that, at long last, the infernal freckle behind his right ear quit itching.

An elephant dreamed of mountains of fresh, sweet hay and of the snug warmth of the girl whose head rested against her belly. She dreamed of a world without bull hooks or sour-smelling trainers. She curled her trunk around the girl as a blanket.

And the girl. The girl dreamed of walking with Mag through

a flourishing garden, a stalwart farmer and a twitchy detective beside them. Her hands tightened around her Gleam Jar, where, even though nobody noticed, a single green seed glowed.

Dreams are forces in themselves, strong enough to leave footprints behind in the imagination. But there was another, greater force at work. A force stirring beneath the dirt where the green seeds lay, damp, contented, and juddering. Some might call it magic. Whatever it was, it woke a long-forgotten feeling in the earth that moved her to her very core.

The world felt the green seeds tickling her surface. She felt them juddering. She felt the wind and dust pulling and tearing at her soil, wanting to rip the seeds away from her. She held them closer. They reminded her of something. A garden. An ancient garden that had once belonged to her. A garden greener than spring grass after rain, so green that being in it was like sitting inside an emerald. A garden full of *her* dreams.

Then, all at once, the world remembered. She remembered every dream and every promise of what could be, of what she—the world—wanted to become.

She whispered her memories to the juddering seeds, and they dug in and broke open. Their roots, tiny tendrils fine as angel hair, curled into the damp earth. The seeds began to grow.

CHAPTER SIX

IN WHICH A SPECTRAL SMILE
PREVENTS AN UNTIMELY DEPARTURE

There was no breakfast under Nitty's nose in the morning. No hay for Mag either. Nitty sighed.

She tucked her Gleam Jar into the pocket of her flour-sack dress and then slid a hand onto the end of Mag's trunk. Mag's trunk curled gently over it. If Nitty had to face defeat, she reasoned, it was best to do it while holding tight to another living being. If that living being happened to be an exceptional elephant, so much the better.

They stepped out of the barn together, blinking into the sooty sunlight. Everything—the newly painted house, the windmill, the silo—was smudged in brown all over again. Everything, that is, except for one field. Every inch of that field was covered in sproutlings of such an astonishing green that Nitty had to squint at the sheer radiance of it.

"It's happening!" Nitty whooped and hugged Mag's trunk. She ran to the edge of the field with Mag galumphing close behind.

She brushed her fingertips over the curling tops of the little plants, feeling tiny hairlike fibers covering each one. Mag did the same, running the tip of her trunk over the sproutlings and sneezing with great gusto.

Nitty grinned. "They tickle like a caterpillar's fuzz." She tilted her head. "I haven't seen them around in ages, but I just love the way caterpillars scoot across a hand. They have a determined air. It must be on account of all they want to accomplish before turning into butterflies." Nitty leaned over to get a closer look at the sproutlings. Like their seeds, they had a question-mark shape and, every few seconds, juddered from root to tip. They were bigger than the seeds, of course, and—strange—seemed to be growing taller even as Nitty looked on. "These sproutlings have that determined air, too. They're aiming to go places."

The moment she thought of going places, a knot clogged her throat. She reached for her Gleam Jar, turning it over and over in her hands until the colors swirled inside. Ribbon, button, marble, seed. Blue, yellow, red, green. She hugged the jar, wishing a family could sprout whole and loving from it the way the seeds were sprouting from the ground. Even if that never happened, her Gleam Jar would never leave her side.

It would never tell her she wasn't welcome, or that she wasn't loved.

At least she had that. And Mag.

"We'd best be on our way," Nitty whispered to her now, standing on tiptoe to rub Mag's leathery ear. "He doesn't want us here."

She cast a final glance at the sproutlings, her chest wrenching with the pain of walking away from all the glorious green. Then she cupped her hand under the tip of Mag's trunk and turned her back on the little farmhouse to face the wide expanse of barren brown land ahead.

"Come, Mag." She stepped off, head high, expecting Mag to follow.

Mag did not. She lifted her trunk into the air, snuffling. The air around her smelled sweet, alive with chickens and horses, water and sproutlings. The air ahead, in the direction the girl was walking, smelled bitter, parched and lifeless. Ahead there would be nothing but hunger and thirst. Ahead there would be no place to hide herself from those who spoke in hard, hateful tones, who called her "murderer." There would be no place to hide the girl from the dust.

She could not take the girl to such a place. She would not. Her enormous feet rooted firmly in the spot.

"Mag, come!" Nitty said again, louder this time. Mag did not move, but instead lowered her head to the ground, trailing her trunk through the dirt. Nitty wrapped her arms about Mag's right foreleg and gave it an experimental tug. But while a determined ten-year-old is one thing, a determined elephant is quite another. "Suffering sardines! You're immovable as a mountain."

Nitty planted her hands on her hips, staring Mag down. Her pulse sprinted, and for the first time since she'd arrived on the farm, Nitty felt scared. What if Mag didn't want to follow? What if she didn't want to stay with Nitty after all? Nitty swallowed, the knot in her throat tightening. She stepped nearer Mag and took her trunk in her hands, stroking it. "I'm not happy about it either," she said to her, "but he didn't give us much choice. We're leaving—"

"What's this about leaving?" Windle's gruff voice interrupted. Nitty spun to see Windle standing in the farmhouse doorway. His paintbrush eyebrows pulled into a V above his nose, but his eyes . . . Nitty tilted her head to get a better view. Yes, she'd thought as much. His eyes *were* a smidge less curmudgeonly than they'd been yesterday, and something in them calmed her sprinting pulse a bit.

Windle stepped onto the porch, surveying the field, his twiggy fingers wrapped around his tin coffee cup.

"I told you they'd grow," Nitty said.

Windle grunted. "The question is for how long? Our well water's turning muddy, which means it's running low. If the well goes dry—"

"No ifs," Nitty pronounced as she moved to stand beside him, with Mag following. "Not today. Not with *that*." She pointed to the field. "That's some kind of viridescent splendor, right there." Windle's left eyebrow arched in her direction, so Nitty clarified. " 'The emerald necklace nested in her bosom, a viridescent bird I longed to cage.' That's from the *Tattler*'s serial *The Countess and the Convict*. I read every installment but the last one. You'd be astounded by the number of times the word 'bosom' appears in the *Daily Tattler*. Once I counted over fifty in a single Saturday-morning edition!"

Windle sighed, keeping his eyes on the field. "First, I much prefer your use of 'viridescent' to the *Daily Tattler*'s. No doubt I'd find plenty to astound me in its pages, but I'm partial to the works of Robert Louis Stevenson. I expect you'll have your own opinion about *Treasure Island* once you're finished reading it."

Windle pulled a frayed edition of the book from his back pocket and handed it to Nitty.

"Second," Windle continued as Nitty clutched the book to her chest, "if you're coming to town with me, you best take a bath directly. And . . . here." He cleared his throat, reached around the kitchen door, and retrieved a girl's dress, which he pushed awkwardly toward Nitty. His cheeks reddened. "It belonged to my daughter, Lillah, back when she was about your age. It's a mite musty, but more tolerable than burlap, I reckon."

Nitty's heart jumped. Hoo-wee, what a dress! It was a proper one of red-and-white gingham, with a wide ribbon at the waist and a pleated skirt. It was fancier than anything anyone at Grimsgate wore, and certainly looked much less itchy than Nitty's own flour-sack shift.

"Thanks for the dress," Nitty offered, then searched her

mind (and her *Daily Tattler* reserve) for a word that would show her manners and smarts all at once. When she decided on one, she used it alongside her most gracious smile. "It's utterly resplendent."

Windle sputtered into his coffee, and Nitty thought she caught the specter of a smile peeking from behind his cup.

A remedy for a broken heart, she'd guessed Windle needed, that first day. No doubt about that, Nitty thought now, hanging newfound hope on that specter of a smile. If there was a specter of a smile, a real one might follow. And then perhaps a broken heart mended. Not unscarred, mind you. Never that. But maybe stitched up enough to carry the beat of the living. The question now was: Would one sprouting field be enough?

Windle straightened, and the spectral smile faded as quickly as it had come. "Third, there's a cot in the kitchen. *You* may sleep in it. *Not* the pachyderm. She sleeps in the barn."

A twizzle of emotions, light and ticklish as confetti, whirled inside Nitty. Windle was offering her a cot, a book, decent clothes (how delicious!), and a bath (not quite as delicious, but, even she had to admit, a necessity). That meant she was staying put, at least for the time being. Three words hummed happily in her head. *From now on . . . from now on . . . from now on.* Didn't they have a forever sort of ring to them? No, Nitty scolded herself. She'd make do with day-by-day gladness. Better to do that than hang hopes on a future nobody could pin down.

"Thank you." She took a step toward Windle. She wasn't

sure what she planned to do, but something along the lines of hugging crossed her mind.

He held up his hands before she reached him, backing against the door. In recent years, hugging for Windle had become a risky business. You never knew when a hug might soften a part of the heart that couldn't stand any more weakening. "No thanks needed," he said hurriedly. "This is strictly a business arrangement. You'll be working for your room and board, you understand."

Nitty grinned. "I do understand."

"Fine, fine." Windle finished his coffee. "We're wasting daylight. Setting foot in Neezer Snollygost's store always tilts my axis, but we'll need hay for your elephant." Windle eyed Old Mag, then sighed. "A lot more hay."

Well, Nitty thought, at least he hadn't called Mag a beast this time. This was progress. In the meantime, however, a new worry had presented itself. The last time she'd set foot in any town, she'd stolen an elephant and some rather unusual seeds. It seemed like she and Mag had traveled a fair piece from that city to find Windle's farm, but what if someone here in Fortune's Bluff had heard of what she'd done? Even more worrying was the possibility that the police were searching for her and Mag. She instinctively hugged Mag's trunk, thinking of how Windle had called Mag *her* elephant. As if the two of them were a pair and went together as well as salt and pepper.

"Maybe it would be more prudent for me to stay here?" Nitty suggested to Windle now.

The sound that tunneled up through Windle's throat might have been a laugh, or a growl. Nitty couldn't be sure. "Prudence doesn't seem to suit elephants, or crops that sprout overnight in dusters. I'm inclined to overlook it today."

He paused, watching Nitty for long enough that Nitty wondered if he was waiting for her to confess. She wouldn't, though her tongue (which had as much potential for goodness as the rest of her) was itching to tell the truth.

"We'll leave your elephant here." Windle stepped off the porch and toward the barn without another word.

Whether his decision was based on suspicions he had about Mag's origins or on convenience, Nitty didn't know. Whatever his reason, she was grateful. Besides, from the keen way Mag's trunk was exploring the nearby chicken coop, it didn't look like she had plans to go anywhere soon. In fact, it looked for all the world like she might be hoping to make some friends of the feathered variety.

Don't worry about us, Mag's long-lashed eyes seemed to say as she snuffled the clucking chickens. *We'll be busy getting acquainted.*

So with that settled, Nitty jumped off the porch, running after Windle.

"Mr. Homes!" she called first, but when he didn't turn, she blurted, "Windle!"

He stopped at that, and Nitty waited for him to scold. He didn't. Instead, he arched an eyebrow. "And what leads you to believe you may call me by my first name?"

"Well, seeing as we're going to be sleeping under the same roof, I thought it would be cozier. And besides, it's a friendly sort of name and should be used whenever opportunity arises. Don't you agree?"

His eyebrow rose higher. "I've never given it a thought."

"You should." She grinned. "In the meantime, I'll try it out on a trial basis, to see if it strikes your fancy." When he didn't argue, Nitty straightened with the sense she'd made commendable progress. "Now . . . about *Treasure Island.* I could stand to improve on my elocution." It was another line she'd taken from the *Daily Tattler,* this time from *The Education of Miss Valancy.* She'd fancied it because of the smart-sounding manner in which "elocution" rolled through her lips. "I'd like to read it aloud. To you and Mag. If you don't mind."

Windle gazed down at the girl before him, at her earnest eyes the very color of the field sprouting behind her. "I don't mind." His heart galumphed.

CHAPTER SEVEN

In Which a Nose Exhibits a Peculiarly Worrisome Talent

To call Fortune's Bluff a proper town would've been an embellishment bordering on an out-and-out falsehood. Nitty supposed it had been a proper town once. There were signs here and there of the care it had been given in years past—a swath of peeling blue paint curlicuing down the front of the Palace Nickelodeon, storefronts with hand-painted signs that were now faded and dangling, crooked and broken. There was a boarded-up schoolhouse, too, bearing a sign that read: CLOSED. TEACHER LEFT TOWN.

The townsfolk looked just as poorly, dragging themselves through the streets, heads hanging low.

Most windows were layered so thick with dust that they

were impossible to see through. The window of Crispin Sigh's bakery, however, was busy getting scrubbed into spotlessness by a half dozen children. It offered a view of dangling ropes, strung like curtains across the glass, and empty shelves, save two, which were lined with the sorriest, saggiest loaves of bread Nitty had ever seen. The children weren't any better off either, their clothes so threadbare and flimsy that Nitty was suddenly embarrassed by her red gingham dress. She'd washed the stubborn dirt from her limbs and combed the weeks-old knots from her hair, and she'd been secretly pleased with the result, even if the washing and combing had been a nuisance. On seeing the children, though, she wished she hadn't. It was nothing more than sheer luck that she wasn't still wearing her own flour-sack dress.

A slight, olive-skinned man with a mass of tousled black curls walked out of the bakery to hold up a trembling hand to Windle, and Windle stopped the truck at the curb.

"That'd be Crispin. Waiting on me." Windle plunked a nickel into Nitty's palm. "Fetch us two loaves of bread."

Nickel in hand, Nitty crossed the street. As she got closer to the bakery, she realized that what she'd thought were ropes in the window were, instead, the skins of snakes. Her palms turned butter slick, but when she glanced over her shoulder at Windle, he only nodded her onward.

Nitty didn't hesitate again. When she reached the bakery door, Crispin was already holding out the loaves, wrapped in newspaper. His hands shook so badly the loaves slipped from the paper. Nitty caught them seconds before they hit the ground. Then, when she saw that they were covered in a pale green fuzz of mold, she nearly dropped them for a second time.

"You're new." Crispin's voice shook as badly as his hands.

The way he said it, Nitty could've sworn he was accusing her of a crime. In her defense, she said simply, "I'm just Nitty." She glanced sideways at the children, who were beginning to whine about being hungry.

The tallest of the girls glowered at Nitty. Crispin took no notice. His eyes were fixed on the ocher sky overhead.

"Rain? Rain? Where is the rain?" he muttered, then tapped the side of his temple. "Rain wears the marble, you see. Worry and rain, rain and worry." He pulled a rolling pin from his back pocket and shook it, then held it up to his ear. He seemed both discouraged and relieved to discover that the rolling pin remained mute.

He leaned toward Nitty, his eyes red-rimmed and watery. "The yeast won't rise; the air's too dry. I need a recipe. A rain recipe!" He disappeared into the back of the shop, tapping his temple and mumbling, "Flour, stratus, sugar, salt, cumulonimbus . . ." He broke into waves of laughter.

"Thank you for the bread!" Nitty called after him.

He didn't seem to hear.

"You!" The frowning girl stepped in front of Nitty, blocking her way back to Windle. "Just to be clear, Papa didn't do any wrong. No matter what anyone says." The hardness of the girl's expression made Nitty think of a clenched fist, ready to throw a punch.

Nitty recognized the look. She'd given it plenty of times herself at Grimsgate. "It's no business of mine what your papa did or didn't do," she said quietly. Then she left before the girl had a chance to change her frown into a fistful of action.

Back at the truck, she handed Windle the bread. "Only . . . it's molded through and through."

He nodded, not the least bit surprised. "It'll do just fine as chicken feed."

How many times, Nitty wondered then, had Windle bought Crispin's bread knowing it would only do for the chickens?

"Windle," she whispered, "why is Crispin's bakery strung with snakeskins? And why does he shake so awful?"

Windle cast sharp eyes on her. "Desperation." Then he set the bread in the truck's cab and turned abruptly down the sidewalk. Nitty followed, knowing well enough that he wouldn't say another word on the matter.

"What a mumpish shadow this town's under!" she blurted.

"It's under a shadow, to be sure." Windle motioned beyond the north end of Main Street, and Nitty gaped into the distance, at what she hadn't noticed before. An enormous building towered over all else, blocking out the morning sun with its bulk. The word SNOLLYGOST blazed across the front in swirling copper letters. It was the only building in sight that wasn't decrepit with shabbiness. In fact, it looked so well cared for, it had a sheen to it, as if someone took pains to polish it daily. From the building came a periodic and reverberating *WHUMP,* exactly like the sound Nitty imagined a giant's foot might make as it struck the ground. *WHUMP! WHUMP! WHUMP!*

It was an ugsome, ominous sound. It was a sound, Nitty thought, foretelling misfortune.

She stared. "What in the indecipherable cosmos *is* that?"

"*That*"—Windle's eyes darkened under his brow—"is the headquarters and warehouse of the Snollygost Institute. The mayor built it some ten years ago."

"What for?"

Before Windle could answer, a small child being toted down the street by her mother paused to answer with dutiful somberness, "For community progress, fulfillment, and the betterment of all." The little girl, pressing her hands over her ears to dampen the whumping, continued on her way while her mother praised her for remembering "the Snollygost motto."

"There you have it," Windle mumbled. "It didn't always make that cursed rumpus. The noise started up a few months ago."

Nitty's eyes flitted from the Snollygost Institute to the rest of the main street. "There's nothing but melancholy as far as the eye can see. Where is the betterment and fulfillment?"

"According to Neezer Snollygost, we're awaiting its imminent arrival."

"And according to you?"

Windle worked his jaw, contemplating, before finally responding with "That is a matter I keep to myself. And you'd prove wise to do as I do and pay that institute no mind."

But Nitty's eyes lingered on the Snollygost Institute. As she watched, a line of dust-covered trucks drove up to the imposing structure and then disappeared through two enormous doors, open and waiting, at its side. The doors swung shut just as Nitty and Windle reached the front of the Snollygost General Store.

Nitty vowed to ask Twitch about the institute when she saw him next. Especially its whumping. It was simply too peculiar to ignore, and she was sure that, unlike Windle, Twitch would be raring to share an opinion on it.

She stared at the general store's window displays. They were gleaming with pyramids of canned goods, sacks of grain, and bottles of fresh milk. It was more food than Nitty had ever seen in one place—in fact, more food than she'd ever seen at all.

"Hooooo-wee and codswallop!" Nitty exclaimed. "You could live off that for years."

"Not at Snollygost's prices," Windle muttered. "Let's be quick about it. Remember our objective."

"We have an objective?"

Windle nodded. The freckle behind his right ear was itching something fierce, as was its habit whenever the fourth event of life-changing enormity crossed his mind. (It was the very decade-old event Windle preferred never to think about, but often *did* think about at Snollygost General Store.) "Mind our business. Buy our goods. Leave before we're called on to converse."

"What's wrong with conversing?" Nitty asked, at the same

time wondering why he kept scratching at that spot behind his ear.

"Conversing leads to questions. Questions lead to chinwagging, and I've had enough of that to last my lifetime. Besides, people could mistake a simple, unassuming hello as friendliness."

"Better than mistaking you for friendless." Nitty cast a sidelong glance at him.

"Humph," Windle said in response, and then he was loping through the doors of the store with Nitty scrambling to catch up to him.

It took less than a minute for Windle's objectives to be compromised. During that minute, an anguished howl rang out, and something that bore a striking resemblance to a small rodent flew over Nitty's head and hit Windle with a squelch, sticking to the front of his shirt.

"Is it a bat?" Nitty asked excitedly. Bats were the one creature that had eluded her capture at Grimsgate, although she'd often thought that letting one loose in Miz Ricketts's bedroom would've been great fun.

"Could be a rabid mole," a shopper remarked, giving Windle a wide berth as she passed with her children.

Windle raised his eyes to the ceiling as he pulled the strange object from his shirt. "It's a mustache."

"Without a face?" Nitty only had a moment to inspect the drooping, furry thing dangling from Windle's fingers before it was snatched away by a bearish fist.

The fist belonged to a squat, barrel-shaped man with apple-red cheeks. He had a mustache, too, one lying limp and droopy across his upper lip, full of bald patches and shedding more strands of hair even as Nitty watched.

"Without a face indeed!" the man bellowed. "And therein lies the calamity. What face would want to be seen wearing such a travesty as this? I ask you." He shook the mustache clenched in his fist at Nitty, then pressed it against his eyes, his head sagging. His own face took on the shade of an overripe plum.

"Having trouble with the mustaches again, Ferdinand?" Windle asked, then introduced Nitty to the man, explaining, much to Nitty's relief, that she was a visitor passing through town. Windle added as an aside, "Mr. Klempt owns the Schnurr-bart Emporium down the street. He's a mustache maker."

"A pogonologist, in fact," Ferdinand said somberly, his shoulders straightening. "A student of beards, and, more importantly, an avid admirer and creator of that most superb and refined of all hairs." He paused, bowing to the word he was about to say, which was uttered reverentially. "The mustache. The walrus, the pencil, the handlebar, the imperial. But it was my father who was the true mustachio virtuoso. Papa's mustaches were like no others. Beauteous creatures, crafted of the finest corn silk in these parts."

"But . . . why make mustaches when people can grow their own?" Nitty asked.

"Pah! And what of the poor soul who can't? Must he lead a mustacheless existence?" He shook his head with such violence that the right side of his mustache slid down over his lip. He quickly pressed it back into place. "Of course not! The Schnurrbart Emporium sells mustaches for all. You see?"

Nitty could only nod as Ferdinand rushed on: "There is so much in this confounded existence that is beyond our reach. Lonely hearts want company but remain alone; loving couples want children but remain childless; kindly people want great suffering to cease, but cease"—he sighed—"it does not." He peered into Nitty's eyes. "Why, then, should anyone want for a perfectly groomed mustache, if we have the means to provide it? Don't you agree that it's our duty to use our talents to bring what's beyond reach into being?"

Nitty thought of the seeds sprouting back at Windle's. "I do. Only I had no idea people suffered over mustaches."

Ferdinand closed his eyes. "There are tremendous sufferings and trifling ones. It's all suffering just the same. As my dear papa, inventor of the Super-Duper Triple-Crimp Mustache, used to say, 'Who is to judge one person's dearest wishes against another's?' For some, a mustache is as defining as a fingerprint. There is quite a demand among funambulists and ringmasters. Why, only last month I sold Papa's best horseshoe mustache to Gusto and Gallant's ringmaster. Mr. Percival Gallant himself."

Nitty froze at the mention of Gusto and Gallant. That was the circus troupe Mag had been a part of. She remembered seeing the names on the poster announcing Mag's hanging. Her muscles clenched. Nitty trained her eyes on the floor, avoiding Windle's hawkish gaze, as Ferdinand kept talking.

"Even Windle here wore one of Papa's walrus masterpieces when he was courting Clara." He smiled at the memory. "Do you remember, my friend?"

Nitty dared a glance at Windle, but his gaze now seemed suddenly lost in some far-off place. "She fancied it dashing," he muttered, "until it fell into her glass of iced tea." He arched an eyebrow at Ferdinand, but Ferdinand dismissed the look with a wave of his hand.

"A mere malfunction with the glue." Ferdinand scrutinized Nitty. "Tell me, young lady, what is your opinion of the mustache?"

Nitty thought on that. "It depends entirely on the person wearing it."

Ferdinand Klempt clasped his hands together and nodded until his thick brown curls bounced about his head. "Ah . . . just so! An unworthy scallywag can ruin the effect of a respectable British upper lip, while a respectable gentleman might never live up to the pointed shiftiness of a scallywag's pencil. But—oh! None of that matters now." His eyes dulled; his face crumpled. "All is lost! Lost! Papa's mustaches are in ruins. The dusters have withered them all, and my own creations are only sorry imitations. Dear Papa, forgive me! I've failed you again." He lifted his eyes to the ceiling, and then issued a series of mutterings that very well might've been German, but to Nitty sounded like "Embittered ants should eat me!"

"Oh no, Mr. Klempt." Nitty laid a hand on his arm. "Surely you don't deserve such an awful fate as that."

Ferdinand sniffed and blinked through streaming tears. "Do you know what it's like to *be* someone's disappointment? There is no fate more awful." With that, he gave Nitty's hand a squeeze and rushed from the store with the droopy mustache pressed over his eyes as a kerchief.

Nitty looked at Windle, who was shaking his head as he watched Ferdinand leave.

"Darn these dusters and what they're doing to all of us."

"What did Mr. Klempt mean just then?" Nitty asked him. "Was it his papa he disappointed?"

Windle rubbed at the stubble caught in the cleft in his chin. "Mr. Klempt's father was a hard man. Upstanding, surely, but hard. Sooner notice a stain on your collar than a smile on your face. And Ferdinand . . ."

"Was a stain." Nitty saw it clear as day. If Miz Ricketts had ever thought to add "stain" to the long list of inflammatory remarks she'd made at Nitty's expense, Nitty surely could've counted herself as one, too. "It sets my innards scalding to think on it."

Windle fixed her with a warning glance. "It's not for us to think on at all."

Nitty shut her mouth while deciding firmly that she could think on it as little or as much as she fancied. How was Windle to know as long as she kept those thoughts to herself? Except, she feared, that might prove a trial.

"Time's wasting and we have supplies to get," he said briskly, straightening. Then he strode to the back of the store, heading for the sign marked FEED.

Nitty followed at a much slower pace.

There was far too much of interest to see along the way. If she was going to stay in Fortune's Bluff for the time being, she wanted to understand it. Understanding a place and its people, she reasoned, was the best way to stay out of mischief when you didn't want it and to find it when you did.

"Only one can of tomatoes today," a mother was saying to her nearly grown daughter, who was struggling with two sobbing babies in her arms. "And some bologna to fry up for dinner."

Mother, daughter, and babies all wore earmuffs, much to Nitty's bafflement. With cold weather having left some time ago, Nitty couldn't figure why, except that the earmuffs quieted the incessant whumping from the Snollygost Institute. Nitty could hear it even from inside the store. She'd only had to endure it a little while, but it was already becoming annoying.

A little farther down the aisle, a man and his earmuffed son debated between canned beans and Spam, but when they checked the prices, they put them both back and left empty-handed, with the man saying, "We'll make do with milk toast for another few days."

While every shelf in the store was piled with food, most people (some earmuffed, some not) chose only one or two items. One little girl let her fingers trail across the food as she walked the aisle, as if touching it might satisfy her hunger. Nitty guessed she was probably imagining tasting it, too. But with empty pockets, imagining was all folks could do.

The wrongness of it pestered like a giant skeeter bite on Nitty's spirit. Weren't times hard enough without having mountains of canned peaches rubbed in your face? It made her want to march right out of the store, but the sound of a muddy cough stopped her.

Twitch, she thought. She followed the sound down an aisle until a hand grabbed her, pulling her behind a pyramid of canned condensed milk.

"Hiya—" Nitty started, near to bursting with all the questions she wanted to ask him about mysterious trucks and whumping and moldy bread. Twitch pressed a finger to his lips. He motioned to her to join him as he hunkered down behind the cans.

"Don't blow my cover," he whispered. "I'm doing reconnaissance." Twitch was on his hands and knees, crawling toward the back of the store, his lungs wheezing accordions. He paused for only a second in his crawling to eye Nitty's dress suspiciously. "What happened to you?"

"It was Lillah's, but Windle let me borrow it." She shrugged as she fell into a crawling stride beside him. "It's tolerable." Nitty tried to keep her pleated skirt from dragging along the floor, not ready to admit how much she relished the dress's crisp fabric and the softness of it against her knobby knees.

"So he's warming to you, then." Twitch nodded knowingly. "I figured as much, alone as he is all the livelong day."

Nitty nodded. "It's not me so much as the seedlings."

Twitch would've made a fine fish, right then, the way he was gawking. "You mean—"

"They're sprouting dandy." Nitty smiled. "You have to come see . . ."

Her words died as Twitch yanked her unceremoniously through a partially opened doorway into darkness. "Twitch," Nitty hissed, making out the gray silhouette of a mop and bucket in the corner of the tiny room. "Why are we in a broom closet?"

"It could be a secret passage disguised as a broom closet," he said, pulling a cord dangling from the ceiling to illuminate a dim bulb overhead. He pressed against the walls with his palms, and when that revealed nothing, settled to inspecting the supply shelves. His head disappeared deep into the recesses of one shelf, then reappeared with a triumphant smile. "Eureka!" He wrestled to keep hold of the shiny brass contraption (nearly half his size) in his arms. "Does *this* look like a broom to you?"

"Hoo-wee! It looks like a euphonium," Nitty said admiringly, already searching for a mouthpiece so she might give it a try. She'd seen a picture of one in the *Daily Tattler*'s "Music from Around the World" edition and thought it a marvelous-looking instrument.

Only on closer inspection did Nitty see that the contraption before her had no mouthpiece, but instead was shaped into an enormous funnel at the top, narrowing to a spoutlike opening at the bottom. "What *is* it, exactly?"

"I've never seen the likes of it," he said, "but I'd wager it's a gadget made by the mayor himself. Pa used to talk about how Snollygost built all manner of oddities, back in his boyhood. He recalled that most resulted in mishaps of one sort or another." Twitch studied the instrument, and his eyes lit up. "Look here! There's a red button on its side."

"Push it," Nitty urged without a moment's hesitation, because buttons, of any sort or color, always begged to be pushed, if only to see what unexpected event might unfold as a result of the pushing.

Twitch did, and they both jumped as a vacuous *sssslurp!* filled the closet. Nitty didn't jump far enough away from the contraption, which wasted no time in sucking a substantial amount of her hair right down its funneled gullet.

"Get! Off! Me! You! Diabolical! Entity!" she said through clenched teeth as she gripped its neck (or what she surmised was its neck) and attempted to choke it into submission.

Twitch clamped a hand over Nitty's mouth and jabbed a finger at the door in warning, even as he grappled with the wriggling contraption. Strangely, the air in the room seemed to be getting sucked into the funnel's great mouth, and Nitty and Twitch soon found themselves gasping for breath. At last Twitch found the red button again and, once more, pushed it. As quick as it had started, the vacuum inside the closet died, and Nitty and Twitch were left breathless, staring at the brass instrument with a mixture of awe and trepidation.

They had no chance to examine it further, because suddenly voices sounded outside, approaching the closet door. Twitch opened the door a crack and peeked through, then opened it wider and motioned for Nitty to follow him as he headed for the safe haven of a stack of canned tomatoes.

"Here comes Miz Turngiddy with Mayor Snollygost. Listen," he hissed, once they were hidden to his satisfaction. "Observe." His eyes darkened somberly. "Probe."

Nitty pressed her head against Twitch's, and together they peered through a narrow gap between the cans.

A woman scurried into Nitty's line of vision, walking in the shadow of the burly man beside her. Miz Turngiddy was short and stooped, wearing a dreary dress the same mud shade as the Fortune's Bluff landscape. The notepad she scribbled on was held so close to her squinting eyes it nearly brushed the tip of her narrow, pointed nose, giving her the impression of a studious weasel.

On the other hand, Neezer Snollygost, broad-shouldered, with a neck and forearms as wide around as telephone poles, put Nitty in mind of a buffalo.

"Henshaw, Higgler, Hilder," Miz Turngiddy muttered as she scribbled. "Late, late, late. Jackford, Jenson, Johnson." She jabbed her pen against the notepad. "Late."

"All of them late with their payments, you say?" Neezer's voice had a stuffy-nosed, bagpipe quality. He shook his head slowly. "A shame, a shame. *Such* a shame." He patted his brawny hands against his purple waistcoat as if he'd just finished a most satisfying meal.

"There's more, sir. Many, many more." Her lips quivered as she murmured a string of numbers under her breath. "Eighty-five percent of Fortune's Bluff, to be exact."

People paused in their shopping upon hearing that troubling news.

Neezer looked at the shoppers watching, and his teeth spread a crescent moon across his face. "Well, we must determine how best to help our struggling townsfolk." He bowed his head to the shoppers deferentially. "We must do our civic duty."

Miz Turngiddy nodded. "About that, sir . . ." Her voice lifted enthusiastically. "I'm anxious to do my part, and I've been studying the newest advancements in farming techniques." She flipped through the pages of her notebook. "I've done some calculations, and—"

"No time to waste on that at the moment, Miz Turngiddy. Now is the time for a stoic commander to listen to the needs of his citizens."

"Of course it is." Miz Turngiddy's voice sank, but she waited, pen poised, for the citizens in the Snollygost General Store to speak their needs.

Nitty waited, too. Would they protest the exorbitant prices in the store? Or that whumping that surely kept them up nights?

Not a single citizen spoke.

"Thank you. Your silent contentment speaks volumes." Neezer nodded appreciatively, breathing slowly in and out. As he breathed, his nose whistled. Softly, at first, and then not so softly.

The whistling began to take on a familiar tune. Nitty tilted her head to get a better listen. "Is that 'My Country, 'Tis of Thee'?"

Twitch nodded. "We hear that one when he gives speeches in the town square, too." His eyes narrowed at Neezer. "I don't trust a nose that makes music. See here." He whipped a *Detective Comics* from his back pocket. " 'Ten Ways to Be a Villain, number three: Develop a signature peculiarity or mannerism that easily distinguishes you from other villainy.' "

Nitty listened to the whistling. "He can't help what his nose does."

Twitch didn't look convinced. "If you ever hear Beethoven's Fifth whistling from that snout, clear out quick. The last time I heard it whistle that tune was the day Crispin Sigh was packed away to—"

Twitch's words were cut off as he was abruptly yanked from the floor by his suspenders.

"Angus Higgler! What did I say about busybodying?" The voice was low, silk smooth, and commanding. The woman it belonged to was only as tall as Nitty, and nearly as thin. She clutched a blue bottle of Mr. Moop's Cough Tonic in her hand. Her heart-shaped face and tired—oh, so tired—eyes seemed far too delicate for such a voice. But from the speed with which Twitch was shuffling his feet, Nitty understood that that voice was made to be minded.

"A great detective's always on duty, Ma," Twitch said, as Miz Turngiddy and Neezer turned their eyes toward them.

"Angus Higgler!" There was a dash of menace in the way the mayor boomed Twitch's name. "Show yourself." He swept his lapels aside to put his hands on his hips as Mrs. Higgler brought Twitch to stand before him. All eyes were on Twitch now, especially Neezer Snollygost's.

He loomed over Twitch with a too-bright, too-white smile. "What's this I hear about you playing detective?" His smile stretched wider. "I do so admire an individual with aim. Ambition is the fortress on which to build success." He clapped Twitch on the back, and the nose's "My Country, 'Tis of Thee" shifted into "Puttin' on the Ritz." "And what sort of sleuthing might you be up to, my young friend?"

Twitch stood tall, staring into Neezer's face. "I am suspicious of evildoings in Fortune's Bluff."

The nose emitted a whinny of laughter. "As mayor, it's my duty to make sure our town is safe and snug as a turtle shell."

"That noise," Twitch persisted, "coming from the institute. What are you hiding that makes such a noise?"

Neezer laughed again. "That noise, my boy, is the sound of progress. The sound of an innovation the likes of which no one has ever seen." He bent nearer Twitch, until they were eye to eye. "That is the sound of this town's salvation."

Mutterings arose from the shoppers.

"That's right, citizens," Neezer continued. "As we speak, I am hard at work on a solution to our woes. A machine to end the dusters." Hopeful gasps winged about the room, and folks clasped hands in gratitude. "You've heard the music of its inner workings for some time now. A few of you besides Angus here even broached the subject with me before, only I thought it best not to divulge details until I was sure of the machine's success. Now, you can let the sound of it soothe your worries." Neezer nodded encouragingly. "And know that all will be revealed in good time." He clamped a hand on Twitch's shoulder. "And thank you, young Angus, for your inquiry. Rest assured that if there *were* evildoings in our beloved town, I would be the first to uncover them."

"Unless . . ." Twitch sucked in a gurgled breath. "Unless you—"

A cough stopped him before he could finish, and within seconds he was bent over, gasping. Mrs. Higgler held up the bottle of cough elixir. "All right, Twitch, honey. Doc Grant says this tonic will do you wonders. Just let me go put it on our account—"

"Mrs. Higgler, one moment, if I may." Miz Turngiddy placed her hand over the blue bottle. "Your account, as I was just informing Mayor Snollygost, is overdrawn."

Twitch's mama twisted the bottle in her hands. "Yes, yes, I know," she said quietly. "Only I thought . . . I was hoping . . . if we could have an extension on our credit . . ."

Folks paused around them, busy trying *not* to look like they were eavesdropping as they hung on every word. Mrs. Higgler continued, "A few more weeks and a little rain . . . When my husband returns, we can get another crop to seed—"

"No need for that, no need at all," Neezer interjected. "Times like these we must keep the wells of kindness overflowing." He swept Miz Turngiddy's notepad into his fist and turned a circle, including each person in his gaze. "The Snollygost General Store will waive payments on credit accounts through the end of the month."

Murmurs of relief and applause swept the room. Miz Turngiddy's applause was the last to come, but come it did. Rather stiffly, Nitty thought.

"Your magnanimity knows no bounds, sir." Miz Turngiddy's face puckered as if a sour grape were stuck to the roof of her mouth. She motioned to Twitch and his ma to follow her to the front of the store.

As they left, Twitch waved to Nitty over his shoulder, wheezing out a barely audible, "Remember. Beware Beethoven's Fifth!"

Nitty might've giggled, but now that Twitch and his ma were gone, Nitty found Neezer's eyes focused entirely on her. Peering into those wily eyes drained the cheer right out of her.

"Who do we have here?" Neezer's nose-whistling rose an octave. "Am I to surmise you are new to Fortune's Bluff?" A single clap of his enormous hands and the floor beneath Nitty's feet shuddered. "Welcome! Welcome!"

"Thank you." Nitty suddenly wished Mag were beside her,

and then, seconds later, wished Mag were even farther from Neezer than she already was. "I'm Nitty Luce. I'm . . . I'm . . ."

"She's with me," Windle said, rounding the corner of the aisle to join her.

"Windle." Neezer gave him a single nod, and Windle did the same.

"Neezer."

For a long moment, the two men's eyes locked in a staring duel. Watching them, Nitty wondered how many unspoken words were piling up behind those stares. Months of them, maybe. Even years. What the words were, Nitty couldn't tell, but one thing was certain from the eyes keeping them at bay. Those words had heaps of things to say, and not all good either.

"Nitty's a guest at my place," Windle said. "For the time being."

"A guest, you say?" Neezer's eyebrows rose. "I don't recall the Homes farm ever entertaining guests before."

"Haven't had any reason to before," Windle replied.

"And what reason have you now?"

"None that I care to divulge," Windle said simply.

Neezer's cheek twitched for a hairsbreadth, and then he clapped a hand on Windle's shoulder. "Well, knowing how you've suffered from my niece's absence, I'm certain having a visitor will do you good."

Nitty stared at him. Was it possible? "Your niece? You mean you and Windle are—"

"Brothers," Neezer finished for her. "Indeed we are."

"Brothers-in-law," Windle corrected quietly. He was scratching his freckle again, rather furiously this time.

"No point quibbling over semantics," Neezer barreled on. "Alas, we two don't spend nearly as much time together as I'd like. Do we, Windle? And where has dear Lillah's singing taken her now?" Then he added as an aside to Nitty, "Did you know my niece is an accomplished opera singer?"

"Last I had word, she was in Spain," Windle said.

"Serenading the bullfighters with her arias, no doubt." Neezer smiled as Windle scratched at his freckle. "Well, it's understandable that a person of her great talent would grow weary of your little farmhouse. Don't you agree?"

Windle said nothing.

"But you've become downright reclusive since Lillah's departure!" Neezer mopped his brow as his nose swung into a jaunty "When the Saints Go Marching In." "I've been sick with worry. Simply sick!"

"You don't look sick at all," Nitty blurted.

"Sick at heart, child." He ruffled Nitty's hair, spoiling its careful combing.

Nitty ducked out from his hand. *After all that effort, too!* she thought grumpily.

"Well. A visitor to ease your solitude. This *is* splendid news!" Neezer's teeth blazed at Nitty. "And how are your crops coming? I heard from Miz Turngiddy that a duster swept away the corn seed you planted last month. A travesty, that. But perhaps now you'll consider my offer to buy the farm?"

Windle was on the cusp of frowning, but then he looked at Nitty. Nitty thought of the green sproutlings. *Their* sproutlings. And—she couldn't help herself—she grinned. She waited for Windle to tell Neezer that nothing could grow in Fortune's Bluff but weeds. She waited for Windle to tell Neezer of the host of reasons why the crop they had growing might fail. Instead Windle grinned back at Nitty.

"My crop," he finally said, "will be something to behold. And I am not a man who considers. I am a man who does."

Neezer bellowed out a chuckle, and his face purpled to the very shade of his satin vest. "As am I, Windle! As am I."

Windle turned to Nitty. "We'd best get the hay home before a duster blows it off the truck." He started down the aisle with Nitty beside him, then paused. "Oh, and Neezer." He grinned again. "You'll be needing more hay directly."

Neezer blinked. "More? We stocked forty bales yesterday!"

"Yes." Windle winked at Nitty. "I bought them all."

CHAPTER EIGHT

In Which a Hand Is Taken and a Great Gulf Crossed

As Windle's truck slogged along under the weight of the hay, Nitty asked the question that had been pestering her since back at the store.

"If Neezer's your brother—"

"In-law," Windle added.

"Why don't you get along?"

Windle glanced at her, his brows exclamation points. "You didn't see us arguing, did you?"

"Your mouths might not have been feuding, but your eyes sure were."

He stared out the window. "It was a long time ago. Hardly worth the words it would take to explain it."

"Seems like no fight should take that long to fix."

Windle gave a single, hard "Ha!" then added, "I see I'll have to teach you about the Hundred Years' War in addition to Robert Louis Stevenson." He stared through the windshield. "There was a time when Neezer and I were friends." His voice softened. "Good friends. Then . . . we weren't."

"I imagine Lillah didn't like that. The two of you fighting." A grimace flickered across Windle's face. "Is that part of why she left?"

"She left to sing." He glowered over the steering wheel. "Now let that put an end to your inquisition."

"But—"

"That is all."

A million questions buzzed in Nitty's brain. Like why Windle's face had suddenly sunk in on itself with sadness. Like what had caused Windle and Neezer to fight in the first place. Like how two people could fall into and out of friendship, when friendship was such a rarity to begin with. At least, it had been a rarity in *her* life. She had a million questions, but Windle's stony face said he wouldn't be answering a single one of them today. So she resigned herself to living with the mystery for now, and thought instead about how happy Old Mag would be with the hay they were bringing home for her. Nitty couldn't help giggling.

"What's given you a case of the twitters?" Windle asked with relief at the change of subject.

"Did you see Neezer's face when you told him about the hay?" She giggled again. "Wasn't he just stupefied?"

She grinned at Windle, but he only shook his head, muttering, "I was a fool to say such a thing. Next he'll be wanting to know what the hay is for, instead of leaving us to our own affairs. Next he'll be asking how we came by an elephant in the first place."

"Oh," Nitty mumbled as this sank in. Then she sat up straighter as a simple solution presented itself. "We don't have to tell him about Mag at all." She swallowed and studied Windle, hoping for a sign of solidarity. "Do we?"

Windle frowned. "Anybody who knows more than Neezer is somebody who knows too much. And your elephant . . . well . . . she can't be kept secret for long."

"I *know* that. Only . . . she can't go back to . . . to where she came from either." She hoped that was all she'd have to say on the matter, but Windle looked at her long and hard.

"Why not?" he asked.

"She wasn't happy with her old way of life." The crane, with its dangling noose, came to her mind, and then an image of Grimsgate, with its barred windows and storm-gray stones. She shivered and reached for her Gleam Jar, which today she'd tied about her neck with the old twine from her flour-sack dress. How many nights at Grimsgate had she only had her Gleam Jar to ward off her loneliness or Miz Ricketts's harsh words? Mag had never had a Gleam Jar—or anything, probably—to offer her comfort. "No one thought much of her. Back where she came from."

Windle harrumphed. "I suspect Neezer may take issue with an elephant in Fortune's Bluff."

"Why?" Nitty asked.

"Because she wasn't his idea." He sighed.

They drove on a piece in silence, and then Windle slowed the truck and turned toward her, his eyes grave knots in the grain of his face. "Your elephant. How do you know she wasn't happy?"

"Because . . ." Nitty's voice was wind-through-a-cornfield soft. "She wasn't loved."

"Elephants don't need love."

Nitty glared at him then. "What sort of catawampus idea is that? I believe everything needs love."

Windle cleared his throat gruffly. "Best not believe too deeply. Better to protect your heart."

"What's the point of that?" A heart wasn't like a canned good, meant to sit on the shelf of some darkened cupboard for years, shut up tight. No. Hearts were meant for opening.

Windle blinked, then studied the steering wheel for a long minute. "After love comes loss. And loss brings more unhappiness."

"Until?" Nitty asked. "There *has* to be an 'until.'"

She waited, but Windle returned his eyes to the road and drove on without another word. Maybe he didn't know what was on the other side of loss, Nitty decided then. Maybe he didn't know because he hadn't reached the other side yet.

That thought made her lean across the seat to take his hand.

He turned stock-still, the tips of his ears reddening. "Thanks for the hay." Her hand sat pint-sized in his great, furrowed one.

A muffled growl rose from his throat, which Nitty understood to mean, *You're welcome.* A second later, he released her hand to grip the steering wheel.

But not without first giving it the smallest, fleetingest of squeezes.

Nitty had to admit that a cot was much preferable to a barn floor when it came to comfort, but still, as she lay among the slanting shadows of the farmhouse kitchen that night, she decided that a cot was not at all preferable to the curl of an elephant's trunk.

She rolled over on the cot for the dozenth time, but it was no use. All she could think about was Mag in the barn, without her. She slid the cot across the floor, opened the kitchen window, and, propping herself up on her elbow, peered out at the darkened barn. Was Mag lonely without her? she wondered. Or worse, was she frightened?

Nitty flopped onto her back with a sigh, pangs of missing Mag needling her heart. She'd just about made up her mind to go to her when, suddenly, slinking through the open window came an inquisitive trunk. Its tip swished at the air for a moment and then, as if it had managed to determine its exact location, lowered itself onto Nitty's forehead to deposit a damp, snouty kiss.

Nitty giggled, and Mag's head appeared at the other side of the kitchen window, peering in.

"There isn't much point to Windle latching the barn door, is there?" she asked then, guessing that Mag had unlatched it with her trunk (which, in truth, was exactly what she *had* done). She smiled into the dark as she rubbed Mag's trunk. "Were you missing me, too?"

Mag blew a puff of air across Nitty's forehead, and a rolling rumble—almost like a purr, only much louder—sounded from deep in Mag's throat. It was a pleasant sound, lulling and rhythmic, like water lapping on a shore, and Nitty noticed that it grew the longer she rubbed Mag's trunk.

"I'm glad you're here," she whispered. "I was having a time of it trying to get to sleep without you." She turned on her elbow to face Mag's blinking eyes. "Would you . . . stay here with me? Until I fall asleep?"

Mag's trunk eased the open window higher so that she could squeeze the bottom of her head and chin through. Nitty, laughing, obliged the effort with a chin rub.

"I've never had anyone to tuck me in properly," Nitty went on, feeling herself settling more comfortably into the crook of her cot. "I always imagined it would be lovely." She studied Mag's patient face, her dark eyes. "I suppose you never had either."

She thought on this a spell, trying to discern what might be the best way to tuck in an elephant. "I could tell you a story. One of my own, if you like. Maybe about my time at

Grimsgate? It'd have to stay our secret, mind, because no one here can know where I came from. But I don't suppose you'll tell anyone, will you?"

Mag trilled a soft *Brrt* with her trunk, and that was enough to satisfy Nitty.

"All right, then." Nitty nodded, cupping her palm around the tip of Mag's trunk. "One of my favorites is about the time I dumped an entire inkwell into Miz Ricketts's tea, on account of her locking me in the attic for a week. . . ."

Mag's ears lifted as the girl began talking. The rise and fall of the girl's voice was pleasant. She'd missed that voice tonight in the darkness of the barn. She liked it here well enough, but mostly she simply liked being near the girl. No one—animal or human—had ever treated her so gently, or ever spoken to her in such soft tones. It almost made her forget about her trainer. Almost.

Now the girl's voice sounded heavy with sleep, and Mag herself felt a drowsiness stealing over her. Still, she stayed, not wanting to leave the girl's side.

At last the girl fell silent, calm, and peaceful.

Ever so slowly, using her trunk, Mag pushed the blanket up to the girl's chin. Then, with deep satisfaction, she plodded slowly back to the barn and latched the door behind her.

CHAPTER NINE

In Which the Nature of Bottomless Hunger and Whumping Is Explored

Neezer Snollygost was musing over Nitty. And hay. And the Homes farm. And the whumping, which sounded at regular intervals from behind the locked door beside his office. In fact, as he sat behind his desk at the Snollygost Institute with his nose whistling "I'm a Jolly Banker," Neezer was musing over a great many things.

He leaned back in his chair, his hands drumming his chest. Musing had a habit of making him hungry.

"Miz Turngiddy!" he bellowed over the whumping.

Seconds later, Miz Turngiddy scampered through his office door. "Yes, sir?" she shouted. "What can I do for you, sir?"

Nearly every conversation between Neezer Snollygost and

Miz Turngiddy involved shouting, because of the incessant whumping.

"I am in need of sustenance," Neezer said.

Someone other than Miz Turngiddy might've been surprised by this declaration. Especially someone glancing at the top of Neezer's desk, as Miz Turngiddy was doing now.

On this desktop, spread before Neezer, was a lavish meal of more than a dozen courses. A feast the likes of which no other soul in all of Fortune's Bluff had ever seen. Steak and potatoes, watermelon, a platter of corn piled two feet high, fritters, sweet cakes, pies. It was enough to feed an entire Fortune's Bluff family. Four or five families, in fact. But Neezer Snollygost was dining alone.

Miz Turngiddy was *not* surprised by Neezer's declaration. Her skills of observation were much keener than Neezer understood them to be, due to the fact that the mayor didn't fancy thinking of anyone's skills except his own. This was fine by Miz Turngiddy. She was not in the habit of revealing the whole of her impressive intellect to her supervisor, as she always suspected he would dislike it. And Miz Turngiddy needed to keep her job so that she might use this intellect to help alleviate the dire circumstances she found her beloved town of Fortune's Bluff facing. She needed her job, too, for its pay, which she mailed out west to her son and grandbabies. But if Fortune's Bluff could be revived, then her grandbabies, with their sweet-cream scent and apricot-fuzz curls, might someday move back to town. It was this hope that kept Miz Turngiddy's skills keen and her wit sharp. And it was with these keen skills of observation that she had come to understand one inexorable certainty about Neezer Snollygost: his hunger was as bottomless as his hubris was great.

From the moment he'd arrived in the world with a demanding holler, Neezer had hungered. One bottle of milk was never as good as two, two never as good as three. It might've been because he was born early and small and he needed to gain strength and girth. It might've been because just as Neezer was brought into this world, his mama passed from it.

Even though Neezer had a loving older sister in Clara, his mama's passing carved a hollow in his heart. And when his papa passed, too, and Neezer and Clara were taken in by their grandfather, the hollow deepened.

"No need to be as big as a mountain to move one," his grandfather told him when Neezer's small size made it impossible for him to fetch water buckets or push the plow.

Whatever chores Neezer couldn't manage, Clara did for him, and he loved her all the more for it. Clara had a way of making him forget his hunger with her kindness. But Neezer had his share of tormentors, too—schoolmates who chided him for his smallness and his unusual ideas. Where Clara's love filled a portion of the hollow in Neezer's heart, others' misjudgments made it impossible for the hollow to heal entirely. It remained, and so did Neezer's cravings, growing as he did.

It wasn't simply food that Neezer craved. Neezer Snollygost craved admiration. What he couldn't achieve with physical strength, he tried to achieve with innovation.

He was eight when he locked himself in his grandfather's barn and emerged, two days later, with the Speedy Seed-Spitter, his first brainchild. "Guaranteed to plant seeds faster than any man or plow."

When the Speedy Seed-Spitter delivered the battery of seeds into the chicken coop instead of the field (where the hens promptly ate the would-be crop), Neezer's grandfather smiled and squeezed his shoulder, saying as gently as he could, "Perhaps farming isn't your calling."

But Neezer wanted it to be. Oh, did he want it to be! So at nine, Neezer built the Self-Propellant Plow. The plow propelled itself right through the side of the barn, which delighted the horses, who promptly escaped to spend a week gallivanting with the mares across town. At ten, he created the Refracting Rain-Catcher, which flooded the fields.

And so it went as the years passed. One calamitous invention after another.

"Someday you'll succeed," his grandfather told him. "At something besides farming."

Neezer refused to give up, and when he met Clara's beau, Windle Homes—Windle, with all his confidence and certainty and great farming talent—his heart buoyed. For Windle was a man who understood what it was to aspire to greatness, a man who would put his faith in Neezer's farming inventions as Neezer's grandfather never had.

Neezer didn't mind that it was to Clara and Windle that his grandfather left the farm, because they still offered him a partnership in it. He believed that, in time, his inventions would convince them of his worth, and then he might buy a portion of the farm for himself. He loved them and Lillah, too, when she came along. His hunger, in the face of friendship, family, and newfound possibility, began to fade.

But then came the Fantastic Farm-O-Matic catastrophe—a failure of such enormity there could be no recovering from it. It was after this that Neezer finally saw he would never succeed at farming. It was after this that he saw he had been wrong to put his faith in friendship and family. It was after this that his heart's hollow—which had been ever so slowly healing—ruptured into an unconquerable chasm. His hunger—which had been fading—grew exponentially in size and ferocity.

It was after this that Neezer, at last, found success.

First he succeeded in banking. He succeeded at lending farmers money to buy land and seed, and then at collecting the money they made. Next he succeeded in gaining their trust. As he grew in stature and strength, his smile grew, too, widening until it drew in just about every person in town. Which was how, finally, he succeeded in becoming mayor.

Neezer's successes, though, didn't satisfy him. Perhaps they had come too late, and at too great a price. Perhaps it was watching Clara and Windle continue to grow their farm and family without him. Or perhaps the irreparable rupture to Neezer's heart had made it that he was never satisfied with anything, that he was always seeking an idea of happiness that could never exist. No matter whether it was all or none of those reasons, or some other reason entirely, Neezer hungered and hungered.

And since his hunger was not an ordinary one, it could never be satisfied by ordinary means. Miz Turngiddy suspected this, which was why she considered the tending of Neezer's bottomless hunger one of her most pivotal tasks. The cogs and wheels of Miz Turngiddy's mind were in constant motion, striving to learn as much about civic service and mayoral duties as she could.

Truth be told, Neezer's hunger frightened her. It had frightened her son, too, enough to send him, with the grandbabies, out west. But Miz Turngiddy, like so many other folks, remembered Fortune's Bluff in its glory days, long before Neezer, and she loved it as much now as then, even in its decrepitude. It was the home of her own childhood—a place she couldn't leave. She vowed to stay behind to help it, so that someday her grandbabies could come home to it as it used to be: green and welcoming. Helping Fortune's Bluff, she believed, meant curtailing Neezer's hunger.

She thought she might curtail it if she could only succeed in finding that most elusive of foods that could satisfy it.

Which she set about doing now, flipping the pages of her

notepad, her pursed lips quivering. "Oranges!" she cried hopefully above the whumping. "You said yourself that a delivery arrived earlier today, sir, and one truck was full to the brim with oranges. Straight from California! Perhaps a freshly peeled orange, then, sir?"

"Oranges, you say? Hmmm." Neezer mulled this over as he finished a second helping of rhubarb pie. "It *has* been several weeks since I've had an orange." He nodded. "I will have oranges, then, Miz Turngiddy. Bring me half a dozen."

"Very good, sir!" Miz Turngiddy hollered over the whumping.

For Neezer Snollygost, the whumping was symphonic in its sweetness. It was a sound like no other. A sound that brought him one step closer to community progress, fulfillment, and the betterment of all. A sound that meant he would be remembered forever. A sound that, at long last, one day very soon, might sate his bottomless hunger.

On the other hand, the whumping was a source of annoyance for Miz Turngiddy. How could it not be, when, for months now, it had whumped its eternal *WHUMP* every minute of every hour, day and night? At times the whumping seemed no better than a mallet striking at Miz Turngiddy's temples. In fact, she secretly hoped that one day it would stop altogether, once Neezer's machine was, at last, complete. This was why she asked now, "Mr. Snollygost, how is progress on the Whirlybog coming?"

"Exemplary! Couldn't be better," Neezer said between bites

of mashed potatoes. "It is only the briefest matter of time now. A mere twinkling away from stopping the dusters, I should say."

Miz Turngiddy had come to understand that to Neezer, the "briefest matter of time" could mean days, or months, or—worst of all—years. Neezer had already been toiling over his invention for ten years (although it was only in the last months the *WHUMP* had started), and he was forever making promises of its nearing completion. She stared at the locked door as the whumping rattled her teeth. Behind it lay the Whirlybog, something she had yet to set eyes on but guessed was as enormous in its size as its sound. The machine was not seen by anyone other than Neezer himself. Ever. Those were his strict orders, and, to keep her job, Miz Turngiddy obeyed. Still, she longed to set eyes on it, to study it, to put the cogs and wheels of her mind to work improving it. For she was sure she could improve it, as she was sure she could improve so many things in Fortune's Bluff, if only given a proper chance. She took a deep breath. "It's heartening to think that your invention could save Fortune's Bluff. I wonder if we might, too, think of securing the soil itself? To prevent it from blowing away? Perhaps by plowing terraces in the land?"

"Terraces! The very idea is absurd!"

Miz Turngiddy pinched her lips together at that. She tried again. "Mr. Snollygost, if you'd permit me entrance to your workshop, I might examine the machine and help—"

Her words were cut short by Neezer's chuckle, a disquieting

sound somewhere between sneezing and blowing one's nose. "No need to tax yourself. My efforts are nothing more than the humble fruits of an inspired mind. I'm only doing my duty."

Miz Turngiddy had her response ready, as she always did, although it tended to taste like rotten cabbage on her tongue. "You do much more than that, sir. So much more!"

Neezer shook his head. "To business, Miz Turngiddy, before you embarrass me further. Have you made an inventory of today's deliveries?"

"Of course, sir. Potatoes, canned peas, corn, peaches, Spam . . . oh, and some chocolate." Miz Turngiddy checked off each food on her list as she read it. Of course she had not been present for the deliveries. She never was. They arrived both day and night, but Neezer always insisted on taking care of them himself, always while Miz Turngiddy was out. Miz Turngiddy was only able to inventory the items *after* the delivery trucks had come and gone.

There were questions Miz Turngiddy could not ask Neezer, though she often wanted to. Questions about why the machine he promised was taking so long to complete, when it managed to whump very completely and successfully already. Questions about why dusters seemed to be getting worse in Fortune's Bluff but not, according to her recent research, anywhere else. Questions about where their food deliveries came from, and why she never saw bills of sale for them.

"Not matters to trouble your mind," Neezer had said once, when she'd posed these questions to him.

She was suspicious of his answer, and of the offhand way in

which his nose struck up "It Don't Mean a Thing" afterward. She was suspicious, in general, of Neezer Snollygost himself. Often she wondered about the sincerity of his smile *and* his whistling nose.

But since the biggest trouble of Miz Turngiddy's mind was keeping her job to help Fortune's Bluff and to bring back her grandbabies, she vowed to stifle her suspicions and her questions.

"Well." Neezer sat back in his chair now, smiling. "Folks are bound to be tickled by the chocolate. I can't remember when anyone in Fortune's Bluff last saw chocolate! Can you?"

She shook her head. "You must have paid a fortune for it." Neezer kept his accounting ledgers locked in his workshop alongside the Whirlybog. Miz Turngiddy would've loved to study those as well.

Neezer waved a hand. "Think nothing of it, Miz Turngiddy. I live to be of service to our community. I'm just thankful there's still food to be had." Neezer tapped the tips of his fingers together.

"Only . . ." Miz Turngiddy consulted her notes. "We do seem to have a shortage of hay at the moment. As a result of Windle's visit to the store today."

"Hay! Yes. I was aware of that, of course."

When she was sure Neezer wasn't paying attention, Miz Turngiddy raised her eyes to the ceiling.

Neezer's nose changed its tune to "Worried Man Blues." "A peculiar purchase, that enormous amount of hay. And a peculiar girl, that Nitty Luce, with those odd green eyes. Do you agree?"

Miz Turngiddy had noticed Nitty's eyes, to be certain, as she noticed everything else in Fortune's Bluff. For her part, she'd found Nitty's eyes refreshing in their greenness—cheery, even. She didn't dare say so to Neezer. What she did say was, "Decidedly odd. Most certainly."

"I do wonder how Windle came by his guest. This Nitty Luce." He chewed thoughtfully on a roasted leg of chicken. "We must keep a watchful eye, Miz Turngiddy. To ensure that Windle shares our goals of community progress and fulfillment, as all our citizens should." He focused his eyes on Miz Turngiddy with the gravity of a colonel giving his soldier a mission. "Can I entrust you with this task?"

"You can," Miz Turngiddy assured him.

"But first. The oranges?"

"Oranges, oranges, yes, yes." With that, Miz Turngiddy scurried away. It might've been her feet's way of trying to keep pace with her whirring mind, but Miz Turngiddy, as it happened, was a very adept scurrier.

As she scurried, Neezer returned to his musings. He abandoned his feast, much of which was still untouched, and focused his attention on the locked door beside his office. *WHUMP! WHUMP! WHUMP!* The Whirlybog was calling him.

With a few adjustments to the Dustometer, some tightening of screws here and there, it could be more powerful. The Whirlybog, indeed, would be the solution to all the problems of Fortune's Bluff. Neezer smiled. Then he unlocked the door and disappeared behind it.

CHAPTER TEN

IN WHICH SLEUTHING AND SNAKESKINS COLLIDE

By the time sleep overcame Nitty and Mag that night, the sproutlings had already grown a foot tall. By the next day, they brushed Nitty's shoulder, and by the day after that, they were taller and fuller than any cornstalk ever seen in those parts. Soon stalks as big as Nitty's arm branched into leaves as wide and round as umbrellas.

Windle didn't know what to make of it. He stood on the porch every morning, bewildered, while his coffee turned cold in its cup.

"It can't last," he'd finally mutter. Especially with the well turning muddier every day, and not a drop of rain in sight.

But it *did* last. Dusters came each afternoon, howling and nipping, sometimes bending the stalks to the ground with their winds. But once the storms were over, the stalks sprang up, determined and sprightly, juddering until the dust was shaken from each and every leaf.

Nitty liked to watch the stalks in the evening hours after the storms, when it was safe for her and Mag to take up their stations on the porch again. It was at this time of day, with chores done and supper over, that Nitty would read aloud from *Treasure Island* while Mag rested her trunk on her shoulder.

More often than not, Nitty discovered items waiting for her and Mag on the windowsill beside the front door, left there as if by some mysterious hand. One evening, Nitty discovered a peppermint. The next, she found a hairbrush and two barrettes that she suspected Lillah had once worn as a young girl. An old croquet ball appeared one evening for Mag, and she spent the better part of an hour rolling it across the porch with her trunk.

Only once, Nitty tried offering thanks to Windle for a spinning top he'd left for her, but she was met with such a formidable stare she vowed never to say boo about it again.

Instead she made sure to pronounce her admiration for the offerings aloud to Mag, knowing Windle would hear it, even if he wouldn't acknowledge it. "You're one lucky elephant today," Nitty would say when Mag found peanuts or apple slices on the sill. "And nobody ever asks you to share," she added teasingly. "Even luckier."

Of course Mag always shared, dropping a peanut or apple slice in Nitty's lap before returning her trunk to Nitty's shoulder. There her trunk would stay, until a page in *Treasure Island* needed turning. Mag, Nitty was delighted to discover, was both an eager listener and adept page turner. The moment Nitty paused at a page's end, Mag's trunk would slowly push the page upward until it flipped. This never failed to make Windle's specter smile appear as he sat in his rocking chair just inside the screen door.

When Nitty stumbled over a word, Windle called out the correct pronunciation instantly. His corrections were gruff, but they pleased Nitty all the same, for that was how she was sure he was listening.

When Nitty paused in her reading to gaze out on the juddering emerald field, when she whispered to Mag, "You know what I think? I think those stalks are dancing, that's what. They're dancing because they're strong, they're tended, and they're here," she knew Windle heard, too.

It was far better, she thought, to have him listening to a book than staring forlornly at the photo on the kitchen table. She'd noticed him doing this often, and she'd even, at times, overheard him murmuring to it when he thought her out of earshot. Seeing him like that—so sad, and scratching at his freckle—made her more determined than ever to help him.

Even as she waited on Windle's change of heart and the field's triumph, she discovered that there was no lack of tasks for her to accomplish. This was partly due to Windle's belief in productivity, but mostly due to Twitch's belief in mischief. Each morning, Twitch appeared on the front porch, pacing, a

Detective Comics issue under one arm, his Morton Salt periscope under the other, and his notepad and pencil in his pocket.

As he posited theory upon theory about Neezer (so far, he'd considered that Neezer was building a torture chamber, a speak-easy, and an oubliette), Nitty hurried through chores, knowing that, all too soon, Twitch would get antsy for town. She only paused long enough to laugh at Mag, who'd assigned herself the morning chore of rousing the chickens from their roosts. Mag accomplished this by slyly sneaking up on the chickens with her trunk and blasting them with a stream of hot air. The chickens would explode from their coop, squawking, as Mag puckishly swung her trunk at them. Then Twitch would turn too fidgety, and he and Nitty would go in search of Windle.

"Can we run any errands for you in town today?" Twitch would ask Windle impatiently. Nitty knew that what he really meant was *Can we go sleuthing today?*

"Mind you don't fribble the time away," Windle always warned sternly after he'd finished listing the errands. "Be back before noon so you steer clear of dusters."

Nitty promised they would. Windle's errands, Nitty came to realize, were less errands and more acts of kindness. Some days she and Twitch delivered the one or two eggs Windle's chickens had laid to the Johnsons or the O'Reillys. Other days they took a fresh pail of Bessie's milk to the Steins. Each and every day they left another handful of wilting corn silk (scrounged from Windle's rotting corn crib) for Ferdinand Klempt, who could always be found sagging over his worktable at the Schnurrbart Emporium, crying over another failed mustache.

Whatever meager offerings the Homes farm still produced, Windle gave away.

"Leave it on the doorstep" was Windle's instruction for each delivery. "No need to call attention to yourselves."

This was fine by Nitty and Twitch, because the less attention they were paid, the greater their chances of sleuthing success. Together they'd spotted a half dozen more mystery trucks coming and going from the Snollygost Institute, though these trucks were so coated in dust it was impossible to decipher any signage on them that might offer a hint as to their purpose. Twitch had also observed Neezer carrying a book under his arm titled *Sublime Skyscrapers: The Beauty of a Metropolis.*

"I've never seen him reading anything before, let alone a book," Twitch had said. "Why would he want a book on skyscrapers?"

Neither of them knew, but afterward Twitch vowed to double their visits to town *and* their sleuthing efforts.

Nitty didn't like leaving Mag behind for these errands, but Mag didn't seem to mind, and knowing it was for Mag's own good helped ease the pain of it. As Nitty walked down the road away from the farm, she'd look back to see that Mag, with a chicken or two in tow, had taken up post beside Windle.

Windle never discussed what he and Mag did while Nitty and Twitch made their daily rounds about town. From the repairs and improvements that were made, slowly but surely, to the Homes farm, Nitty decided they made a productive team.

Window boxes were rehung and straightened, broken railings mended, and splintered porch stairs replaced. She suspected that it suited Windle just dandy to work with an elephant, since hours could pass without so much as a single word spoken between them.

On the other hand, there was never any shortage of words passing between Nitty and Twitch, especially on the particular day their errands included a stop at Crispin's Bakery.

"I've been waiting for this for ages." Twitch's breaths were coming in excited, whining puffs like a steam whistle. "Ma won't get within ten feet of those snakeskins. Nobody in Fortune's Bluff will." He grinned. "I bet they're rattlers, too, with fangs near a foot long!"

"Sure as bats in a belfry they are," Nitty affirmed as they reached Main Street, where she fought the urge to plug her ears against the incessant noise coming from the Snollygost Institute. The *WHUMP* was whumping, louder and longer than it had yesterday or the day before. "I saw them up close myself. After the first shock of it, they didn't bother me any. I was far more worried about getting pummeled by Crispin's daughter. The oldest one."

"You mean Bernice." Twitch said her name quietly and with guarded respect, as if the simple act of saying it might incur Bernice's wrath. "If only she'd commit a crime, she would make a stellar villain."

"Bernice didn't strike me as a villain. But she sure struck me as angry."

"Well, she only meets one of the villainous criteria so far. 'Ten Ways to Be a Villain, number one: Suffer an alleged wrong or injustice that leaves you embittered of the world and its every occupant.'"

"What sort of wrong did she suffer?"

"It was Crispin who suffered it, not Bernice, but she's angry enough for the whole Sigh family. It was a while back, maybe two or so years ago. Right after the last Sigh baby was born and Mrs. Sigh passed. Fortune's Bluff was in a sorry state. Crops blown away, no food to be found. And then the Snollygost General Store opened and offered everyone free store credit. Only, Crispin didn't think anybody should be beholden to Neezer. He didn't trust him. Same as me." Twitch patted the *Detective Comics* rolled up in his back pocket. "Intuition, see." He tapped his temple knowingly, then broke into a coughing fit.

As Nitty waited for it to pass, she shook her head. "What does any of this have to do with injustice?"

"I'm getting to that!" Twitch blurted, breathless, glowering at her. "So Crispin starts giving his bread away for free, and for a while people quit shopping at Snollygost's, just eating bread and whatever else Crispin mustered up to offer them. Neezer never said a word about it, but everybody knew he was fit to be tied. Then, one day, a duster blew through and brought a twister with it. And wouldn't you know, that twister touched down right on Crispin's storehouse, taking almost all his flour, eggs, everything he needed for his bread. Then it left, without touching another building in town." Twitch leaned toward Nitty, whispering conspiratorially, "*Almost* like that twister was planned."

Nitty stared at Twitch. She might've been tempted to laugh, but the gravity in Twitch's eyes made her think twice. "A twister can't pick where it's going to land."

"No, but what if a person could tell it where to land?"

"That's imposs—" She caught herself. To say that one mysterious happening was impossible meant that others were, too. Wasn't the crop growing on the Homes farm mysterious? Nitty didn't want to be a skeptic. A skeptic could take something mysterious and squelch the magic right out of it. Instead she said, "That would be bewildering, to be sure."

"Well, that's what Crispin believes. After the twister, Crispin took to wandering outside the Snollygost Institute at all hours. He was convinced that Neezer was behind the twister. That the proof was hidden somewhere at the institute."

"Did he find anything?"

"No one knows for sure. Miz Turngiddy never would let him inside, so finally one night Crispin broke in. Neezer caught him, of course, and sent him to the Kickapoo Asylum, saying Crispin was imagining things, making up stories."

"An asylum." Nitty swallowed. Asylums featured in some of the *Daily Tattler*'s most sensationalistic stories. Nitty imagined them as dismal places haunted by the moans and cries of the wronged and misjudged. Asylums were the sort of places that only belonged in made-up stories, never in real life. They were far too terrible for that. "How long was Crispin there for?"

"Two months." Twitch nodded slowly. "And when Neezer saw Crispin loaded into the asylum's wagon, his nose whistled Beethoven's Fifth. I witnessed it myself. Swear on my muddy lungs."

Nitty gasped. "And that whole time Bernice and the other Sigh children were alone?" She shook her head, brushing her hand over her Gleam Jar for reassurance. "How awful." She felt a sudden surge of anger toward Neezer Snollygost. What right did he have to turn children into orphans?

Twitch nodded. "It was awful. Whatever Crispin saw inside the Snollygost Institute changed him. Now he rambles on about whirlybogs and wind. Mostly, though, he talks about rain. Why, last month he launched a balloon full of lit dynamite over Fortune's Bluff to see if it could make rain. It didn't." Twitch grinned. "But it sure made for some dandy fireworks."

"Twitch!" Nitty scolded, but she could hardly blame him for his enthusiasm. It would've been a sight!

"It's not just dynamite either," Twitch said. "That's why Crispin hangs those snakeskins. He chants to the sky, too. All for rain."

"And I bet nobody believes a word he says about the Snollygost Institute," Nitty guessed.

"Oh, some wondered when Crispin got taken away, and

then again when the *WHUMP* started up months back. But they only whispered over it. They didn't dare speak up to Neezer for fear of him demanding payments on their loans and store credits. And now Neezer's got everyone hoodwinked with promises of that invention to stop the dusters."

"What makes folks think Neezer's ideas are so much better than Crispin's, anyway?" Nitty asked.

"Power." Twitch nodded knowingly. "That's what Pa used to say. Mostly, I think folks are too worn for questioning anymore. 'Cept me." He shrugged. "If I could make heads or tails of Crispin's words, I would, but others think he's gone balmy. Neezer's told everyone to steer clear of the bakery. He says it's dangerous, that Crispin's a threat. And the snakeskins and dynamite spook people."

Nitty stopped mid-step. "So nobody eats Crispin's bread anymore?"

"Crispin can't bake much these days. He won't buy supplies from the Snollygost General Store, so I don't know where he gets his ingredients. Windle buys what little Crispin bakes, but he . . . he's the only one." Twitch turned suddenly sheepish. "I told you Ma doesn't let me go near the bakery!"

Anger fizzed in Nitty. "Isn't that just the way! A person devises an uncommon solution to a problem, such as snakeskins or dynamite, and folks turn a cold shoulder." Here she was, all this time thinking that Miz Ricketts might be the only one suffering from a stagnant imagination! When really it was a voluminous horde! She stalked toward the bakery now, tripling her pace.

"Nitty?" Twitch was running to keep up, huffing beside her. "What are you going to do?"

"I'm going to rid Bernice Sigh of her pricklies, that's what."

Nitty found Crispin standing in the bakery's doorway, scanning the sky, holding his rolling pin up to his ear.

"Rain. Rain. Where's the rain?" Crispin's hands trembled fiercely. "Cans of sauce, from the cross; hide them all, says the boss."

He blinked his red-rimmed, watery eyes at Nitty. "Do you have a recipe for rain? I need a recipe for rain. The dough's too starched; the sky's too parched."

"No recipe today, Mr. Sigh." Nitty smiled. At the sight of his trembling and sad eyes, her anger started fresh. She didn't know for certain if Neezer Snollygost was truly to blame. It hardly mattered in the face of Crispin's torment. "I've come to buy some bread."

Crispin blinked, then blinked again. At last he nodded and turned toward the bakery's shelves. "Only one loaf today. My barrel's near empty, and I've nothing to grind."

Nitty couldn't make any sense of that until Bernice stepped from the back of the bakery, trailing three sniffling, smudge-covered little Sighs from her tattered apron.

124

"He means the flour," Bernice said. "We've only one barrel left."

Nitty thought Bernice looked like a sentry when she stepped protectively in front of Crispin. She folded her arms and glared from Nitty to Twitch and back again, as if daring them to make a wrong move.

Nitty eased to the left of Bernice and gently took the loaf from Crispin's outstretched arms, depositing the nickel Windle had given her in its place. Crispin clutched the coin to his chest, then disappeared with it into the back of the store, the littlest Sighs trailing behind him. Bernice stayed where she was.

"The bread looks delectable. Doesn't it, Twitch?" Nitty nudged Twitch in the ribs, which prompted his enthusiastic "Yes!"

Bernice glared harder. Her hands curled into fists. "Are you poking fun? If you are—"

Nitty didn't give her time to finish. She chose not to think about the spots of fuzzy mold she'd seen on the loaf. It wouldn't be the first time she'd eaten food that had turned. Instead she closed her eyes and sank her teeth into a sizable chunk of the loaf. It was hard as stone, but after chewing for some time, she swallowed it down.

"Perfectly palatable," she said. She opened her eyes and saw Bernice. She wasn't glaring anymore, just staring.

"You don't really like it." Bernice's tone was more surprised than angry. "Any fool knows it tastes like dirt."

As Nitty saw it, she was faced with two options. The first was to construct a lie, hold her breath, and await Bernice's fist in her nose. The second was to confess to the truth, hold her breath, and await Bernice's fist in her nose. Since the outcome of either option seemed inevitable, she decided to try her hand at the truth.

"Well." She took a deep breath, then glanced at Twitch for some sign of encouragement. He nodded her on in stalwart detectiving fashion, but edged toward the door, probably in case there was pummeling and they needed to run for it. "If you want to know," Nitty pressed on, "the bread could do with a little more seasoning and a little less Toeter Grime."

A long silence followed this pronouncement, and then Bernice snorted. It was a hiccup of a snort. Bernice quickly stopped it, covering her mouth with her hand. Only it was too late.

"You laughed," Nitty proclaimed.

"Did not." Bernice's face turned flinty again.

Twitch narrowed his eyes at her. "We're onto you. You are *not* what you seem."

Bernice spun on her foot and made to stomp away, but Nitty called after her. "We're detectives! We don't put any credence in gossip."

"But we believe in papas," Twitch added. "And in the possibility of evildoings in Fortune's Bluff."

Bernice stopped, whirling to face them. "What do you know about any of it?"

"Not much," Nitty said.

"Yet," Twitch added. "But we're on the case. And the case involves Neezer Snollygost."

"He's got everyone in this town fooled except for Papa." At the mention of her papa, Bernice's voice turned soft around its jagged edges. "He's the only one who knows the truth. Or knew the truth." She dropped her eyes. "These days he only talks in gibberish riddles."

Nitty thought of the poems and riddles she'd read in the *Daily Tattler.* No matter how hard they were to decipher, in the end they always said *something* that mattered. "Maybe he's trying to tell you something with the riddles. Maybe he wants you to solve them. He said one just as we walked in. Twitch, do you remember?"

"It had to do with cans and crisscrosses, I think."

He pulled his notepad and pencil from the front pocket of his dungarees and wrote as much of it down as they could remember. As he was scribbling, a movement outside the bakery window caught Nitty's eye.

"It's Neezer!" she hissed, then ducked under the window, pulling Twitch down alongside her. Bernice stood with her arms crossed before her, glaring down at them, unmoving.

Nitty didn't dare yank on her the way she had Twitch, but she did glare back. "You may not like us any yet, but at least don't hamper our gumshoeing!"

At that Bernice grudgingly dropped to her knees beside them.

Twitch put his notepad away and lifted his Morton Salt periscope up to his goggles, directing it at the Snollygost General

Store. He lowered it a second later with a frustrated sigh. "Can't ever see a thing through these goggles."

As he took off his goggles, Nitty raised the periscope to her own eyes, delighted, as she always was, by the sheer sneakiness of such an instrument. Her breath hitched as Neezer came into focus. He was standing outside the store, loading a crate of mason jars into the back of his automobile.

"What do you see? What do you see?" Twitch was tugging on her arm, apt to pull it off entirely if she stayed mum a second longer.

"He's got jars full of something . . . I can't tell what. But . . ." She shifted the periscope slightly to get a better look. "Whatever's inside the jars is murky-colored . . . and *moving*!" Bernice scoffed doubtfully, until Nitty handed her the periscope for a turn.

Bernice was silent for a long moment as she stared through the eyepiece, and then she mumbled, "There's writing on the jars, but I can't make out what it says." Her voice was less guarded, but only for the second before a dark shadow descended over them.

As Bernice shoved the periscope behind her back, Nitty glanced up to see Miz Turngiddy, her arms full of newspapers, peering at them from the other side of the bakery window.

"It's Neezer's cloak-and-dagger," Twitch whispered. "Beware."

Miz Turngiddy strode into the bakery just as Neezer drove away in the direction of the institute, taking the mysterious crate of jars with him.

"Good morning." Miz Turngiddy nodded to the three of

them, setting down her newspapers on the counter and pulling her notebook from her pocket. She scanned the bakery's shelves. "And how is your father today, Bernice? Is he making any progress on his weather studies?"

Bernice stared at Miz Turngiddy. "I wouldn't tell you if he were." Her words were as impenetrable as a wall. *Impressive bravado,* noted Nitty silently.

Miz Turngiddy, though, was not impressed. She frowned, and her pen shook over her notebook—whether in fury or disappointment, it was hard to say. "No matter," she said briskly. "Mayor Snollygost considers it his duty to keep abreast of the health and well-being of each citizen. He'll look in on your father personally. Another day."

With that, she was through the door and scurrying up Main Street toward the institute.

"She's going to give a report to Mayor Snollygost," Bernice said drily.

"About your father?"

"About you. Being here." Bernice shrugged. "Neezer won't like it, just you wait and see. He doesn't like anyone paying visits to the bakery."

"Well, well, well." Twitch had turned his attention to the bakery's tall counter. "Look what she left behind." He held up the pile of newspapers.

Bernice rolled her eyes. "They're just a bunch of papers, Twitch."

He gaped in horror at the remark. "There is no 'just' in

detectiving. Papers might seem insignificant, but they *could* turn out to be irrefutable evidence. I don't ever take what looks ordinary for granted." He folded them under his arm with great formality. "I'll read through them for clues later. In the meantime, our next step is to get inside the Snollygost Institute. Whatever's in those jars, whatever Neezer's hiding . . . we'll uncover it." He held out his hand to Bernice for a shake. "If your papa says anything else of import, you'll inform us at once?"

Bernice's eyes slivered. "How can I trust you won't snitch to the mayor and Miz Turngiddy?"

Nitty and Twitch looked at each other, then back at Bernice. "We'll be as silent as a sarcophagus," Nitty vowed solemnly. "The sort without an accursed, moaning mummy inside." *That* tale in the *Daily Tattler* had kept her up plenty of nights.

At that moment, a child's cry rang out from the room over their heads, and Bernice glanced up wearily. "I don't have time to concern myself with mummies." She frowned. "That'd be Verna wanting her rattle. Papa never remembers where he sets it down." She started to walk away, then turned back to Nitty. "I can't believe you ate the bread."

Nitty grinned, then shrugged. "I can't believe you didn't pummel me."

Bernice grinned. "I can't either."

CHAPTER ELEVEN

In Which the Pogonologist Tells a Tale of a Mustache and Its Nits

Nitty had barely put a single foot outside Crispin's door, but Twitch was hurrying down the street, already a dozen steps ahead of her.

"Where are you going?" Nitty ran to catch up with him.

"Where do you think?" His march was full of purpose. "The Snollygost Institute. We're going to figure out a way in and—"

A cough overtook Twitch before he could finish. He reached into his pocket for the bottle of Mr. Moop's Cough Tonic he'd taken to keeping there, for just such occasions. He swallowed down a gulp as Nitty looked on, worry niggling her insides.

She wanted to investigate the institute as much as he did, but what if his lungs couldn't take it? The building sat atop the bluff in the distance, and getting there would mean they'd have to walk through the rest of town and then uphill until they reached the institute's formidable iron gates. Just the walk into town had left Twitch wheezing worse than usual. But pointing that out to him would only make Twitch sore at her.

Nitty grabbed his arm, stopping him mid-step. "We can't go up there. Not in the middle of the day like this. We'll be too easily spotted."

Twitch opened his mouth to protest, but the sound Nitty heard was the distant rumble of wind galloping over prairie.

"A duster's coming." She glanced up at a towering wave of dust, its first gritty blasts already stinging her face. She'd seen plenty like it before, barreling past the windows of Grimsgate. "A bad one, by the looks of it. We need to get back to the farm."

Twitch was coughing again, this time doubled over with the effort. As fast as this duster was moving, it would consume Main Street in minutes. The sky darkened to near night as clouds blocked the sun, and dirt hurtled against their skin in frenzied, stinging bites. She tugged on Twitch's arm, aiming to take him back to Crispin's, but then she heard Ferdinand Klempt calling to her.

"Come, come!" He beckoned to them from the doorway of the Schnurrbart Emporium. "Before you're blinded by the storm."

It was with some effort that the two of them reached Ferdinand's door, and by the time they did, the rest of the buildings and houses on the street were hidden. They shook the dust from their clothes as Ferdinand fetched them water.

While Twitch recovered his breath, Nitty used the opportunity to study the inside of the emporium. On previous visits she'd found Ferdinand sobbing and not in any mood for company, so she hadn't yet been able to take in the shop properly.

Now, upon inspection, she found it fascinating. Corn-silk mustaches by the dozens—dyed brightest silver to darkest obsidian and every shade in between—adorned the walls and workbench, giving Nitty the impression that there were countless faces hidden in the woodwork, their upper lips the only parts of themselves they were brave enough to show.

When she said as much to Ferdinand, he sighed. "It is only one face I see watching me . . . Papa's. And his lips are forever frowning."

"But these mustaches are beautiful," Nitty said encouragingly.

Ferdinand howled, his head dropping to his worktable. "They are! Because I didn't make them. Papa did! But look." He lifted one of his father's mustaches from its place on the wall and set it in Nitty's open palm. "See what the dusters have done."

As Nitty cautiously took the corner of the mustache between her fingertips, the corn silk crumbled to dust. "Oh," she said quietly.

Ferdinand nodded. "And this . . ." He cupped a droopy, moplike bunch of corn silk in his hands. "This is *my* craftsmanship. Another failure."

"Have you never sold a single mustache of your own?"

Nitty asked gently, suddenly wishing she had money to buy one herself.

Much to her relief, he nodded, holding up a single finger. "One. Just one. Months ago, to an elephant trainer passing through town with the Gusto and Gallant Circus."

Nitty's heart twittered at the mention of the circus, and she lifted her water cup to her mouth to mask whatever emotions might be showing on her face. She discovered she'd been too late to escape Twitch's notice, however. She hadn't breathed a word about Mag's origins to Twitch, but it became clear from his wide, knowing eyes that he'd just figured it out. He coughed over his own cup—a little too loudly, Nitty thought—and she gave him a hefty pat on the back as a warning not to say a word about Mag. When he gave a nearly imperceptible nod, Nitty felt awash with relief and gratitude.

"It could hardly even be considered a mustache," Ferdinand went on, oblivious to Nitty and Twitch's exchange of glances. "It was the most pathetic toothbrush mustache—uneven and riddled with nits."

Nitty paused over her cup, wondering if she'd heard right. "Did you say . . . nits?"

Ferdinand nodded. "I couldn't help myself, you see. Not after he told me what he'd done to his elephant. He was a braggart, and went on and on about how he had to keep his beast in her place. 'A bone-breaking wallop every few days does the trick,' he said. 'To remind her who's the master.'"

Nitty's hands were shaking, and she set her cup down on the

worktable before she sloshed it over herself. She felt Twitch's eyes on her face, and when he came to stand beside her, Nitty saw that his eyes looked as sorrowful as her heart felt. *Oh Mag,* she silently cried, *how they hurt you.*

"So . . . you sold the trainer a lemon?" Twitch said to Ferdinand, because Nitty couldn't find her voice to speak.

"I did. I gave him the moldiest, most nit-infested mustache I could find in my trash bin. One I never would've sold to a decent soul. I should've had the gallantry to give him a wallop instead, but . . ." Ferdinand shook his head. "I never could stand up for myself. Let alone anyone else."

Nitty wondered if Ferdinand was thinking of his own father, instead of the trainer. She laid a hand on Ferdinand's arm. "Well. I for one hope those nits itched him to kingdom come and back." No sooner had the words left her mouth than Nitty felt a nudge of guilt, wondering if it was wrong to say such a thing about a person no longer living. Maybe it was, but it was also wrong to treat any living being the way he'd treated Mag. She sighed.

Ferdinand stared at his pile of failing corn-silk mustaches. "How do you make peace with certain sorts of cruelty?"

"Maybe you never do," Twitch said.

"Maybe you bury them with your own better doings," she said, thinking of Mag's sweetness. She handed Ferdinand one of his works in progress.

His eyes filled, and Nitty feared he'd start crying again and possibly *never* stop, so she grabbed a handful of corn silk and motioned for Twitch to do the same. "Twitch and I can't go anywhere until the storm's passed, so why don't we help you with your work?"

Twitch's eyes lit up. "Could you fashion me one for detectiving? One that says I'm hard-boiled and meant to be taken seriously?"

Ferdinand hesitated, then scanned the mustaches covering the walls. "You don't want one of my disasters. And now the dust is making Papa's masterpieces fall apart at the slightest touch. The corn silk can't withstand it."

"Of course he wants one of your mustaches." Nitty exchanged a look with Twitch that was meant to stifle any protests. "He needs an original worthy of his investigating genius."

Twitch grinned at that, as Nitty had guessed he would.

Ferdinand looked hesitant, then nodded slowly. "All right, but I'd be obliged if you'd keep your expectations low." He inspected the shape of Twitch's face, jotting down some measurements. "A chevron for you, I think. Sober, intelligent, and, when need be, intimidating as well."

"Yes," Nitty said enthusiastically. "That sounds exactly right."

As dirt screeched past the store's window panes and the wind howled, the three of them set to work, with Ferdinand trimming and shaping corn silk, Nitty gluing it into place on a felt band, and Twitch applying a finishing sheen with warm wax.

At last Twitch's chevron mustache was finished, and so was the storm. Once Ferdinand glued it into place beneath Twitch's nose, he and Nitty scrutinized it.

"I loathe it," Ferdinand moaned. "It's yours at no charge. Papa would say the curl of the tips is askew and that it's poorly trimmed."

"He's not here, though," Nitty replied, "and *I* say it looks dashing and inspective."

Twitch admired his reflection in the emporium's mirror, turning this way and that. "It says 'sleuth' from every angle!" He grinned at Ferdinand. "Thank you."

The red of Ferdinand's plum cheeks deepened, and Nitty thought he looked almost happy. She was about to say as much, but only a moment later the emporium's door flew open, and Windle stormed in, pale and windblown.

"*Here* you are!" he cried breathlessly. "The duster blew in, and I thought you'd been caught out in it, but then the truck wouldn't start . . ." He ran a hand through his mussed hair. "I've been searching creation for you two."

"Ferdinand took us in," Nitty said. "We were safe."

"This may have been the worst one yet," Ferdinand said to Windle. "And to come so early in the day. There's no rhyme or reason to any of it at all."

"There is, too," Twitch blurted. He turned to Nitty. "Did you notice that the duster sprang up right on the heels of Miz Turngiddy spotting us at Crispin's?" Nitty nodded. "I'd call that more than coincidence. There was conniving involved. . . ."

Windle's brow furrowed. "Twitch, you don't mean to say that Miz Turngiddy summoned the storm, do you? That's as far-fetched a theory as I've ever heard."

"Not Miz Turngiddy, but maybe Neezer himself." Twitch's eyes narrowed. "I'd say this storm's reeking with shiftiness."

He said it with such conviction that Nitty had to smile into her sleeve. Windle, however, didn't seem the least bit convinced.

"That's enough flapdoodle for one day, Angus," he said. "Your ma is beside herself. She came looking for you before the storm hit, and she was none too happy to hear you were in town." He raised an eyebrow at Twitch. "I suppose you forgot to tell her about the errands I've been sending you and Nitty on?"

"Forgot." Twitch fidgeted with his periscope. "Y-yes."

"Well." Windle clapped a hand on Twitch's shoulder. "I didn't see any harm in the errands either. But I fear we're all in a heap of trouble now."

"She's not right blaming you for my disappearing," Twitch said. "She can't coop me up forever, and I'll tell her so."

"A word of warning." Windle held up a finger. "It's never wise to start an argument with a mother when she's spent hours fearing for her child's life." Twitch groaned at that, but the groan turned into a cough, which only made the worry lines on Windle's forehead deepen. "I'm under strict orders to get you home and to bed," Windle went on, "and I won't hear any buts about it."

So, with the sinking feeling that their adventures were at an end, Nitty walked to the door with Twitch beside her. Still, she'd have plenty to relay tonight when Mag paid her nightly visit to the kitchen window to tuck Nitty in for the night. They'd made a habit of it, the two of them, and Nitty looked forward to their nighttime conversations all day long.

"Adults can find more ways to ruin a decent caper . . . ," Twitch mumbled now, but he didn't look too downtrodden as he stroked his chevron mustache. "It's a fine mustache, isn't it?" Even as the words were spoken, a few strands of corn silk loosened and fell from his upper lip.

"It is," Nitty whispered as they walked to Windle's truck, "only, it may not last the day." She put a finger to her lips. "Don't tell Ferdinand or he'll likely give up altogether."

"Not a word," Twitch whispered back.

CHAPTER TWELVE

In Which a Motorcar Is Driven by Two Loaves of Bread

Mag might've been kept a secret for at least a bit longer if it hadn't been for the sheer immensity of green that overtook the Homes farm during the next few days. Out in the field, fuchsia-colored buds, still shut tight, clustered under leaves like bright lanterns waiting to be lit for a party. Under the house's windowsills, great fuchsia flowers bloomed in petaled clouds of such profusion that the window boxes bulged and strained under their weight.

One morning upon waking, Nitty opened her eyes to find Windle sitting at the kitchen table, staring at the photo of Clara and Lillah, gripping a postcard in his hands. She guessed, without needing to ask, that it was from Lillah.

"Hoo-weee! Paris!" Nitty exclaimed when she caught sight

of the picture on the front of the postcard. "The *Daily Tattler* says Parisians are 'the very zenith of sophistication and creativity.'" Windle's harrumph was so melancholic that Nitty quickly added, "I have my doubts about that, mostly on account of folks there eating snails and liking them."

She wrinkled her nose, and one corner of Windle's mouth curled, but that was as far as his smile ventured.

Nitty couldn't help herself then. She snuck a peek at what Lillah had written. "But, Windle! Lillah writes that she hasn't heard from you in months!" She held tight to her Gleam Jar, thinking of all the calamities Lillah might be imagining had befallen her father. "Why haven't you written to her?"

"Haven't had anything to say," he muttered, and when Nitty glared at him, opening her mouth to argue, he stopped her by adding, "At any rate, I had no news to share besides dusters and drought."

"But you have *good* news now," she said in a rush. She *almost* added, *Tell her about me and Mag,* but caught herself. Because . . . what if he didn't think her worthy of mentioning? That thought made her breath hitch. Instead she ventured, "Tell her about the new crop growing."

Windle thought on this. There was a world of wanting in his eyes. The difference between wanting and doing, though, is the difference between a paintbrush and a masterpiece.

Windle's silence stretched, a rope pulled taut with sadness. "Can't."

Nitty saw then, plain as day. The problem was that Windle

was scared—scared to pen his hopes for the crop onto paper. Even now, with the crop growing prettier and sturdier each day, he was scared of losing it.

His voice was gruff as he stood abruptly. "I'd best go feed the animals."

Nitty knew better than to try to dissuade him. She figured a person could be on the brink of change for some time. Maybe even a long time. His heart could only tiptoe around its fears for now, but sooner or later it'd have to stomp all over them. He'd write to Lillah when he was good and ready.

Still, Windle's gloom was a nut that wouldn't crack. It usually brightened by the daily appearance of Twitch. But since their visit to Crispin's Bakery and the Schnurrbart Emporium, Twitch hadn't been back to the farm. Nitty suspected it was more the persistence of his ma than his cough that was keeping him away, especially when Windle had word from Mrs. Higgler on the matter.

"Another fever," Windle muttered with a shake of his head. "Best hope it's not dust pneumonia."

Nitty thought it wasn't, mostly due to a note she'd found wedged in the slat of the barn door addressed to "Detective Nitty and Her Exceptional Sidekick." The note made no mention of fever or pneumonia.

I come under cover of darkness. I've eluded my captor for now, but time is of the essence. I've unearthed some information of import. But it's too risky to divulge on paper. As my official assistant, you must be my eyes and ears. Upon my return, I expect a full report on any developments in the Snollygost Case. Remember: A villain is a keen observer who seeks out and preys on the weakness of others. (Ten Ways to Be a Villain, number four.) PS. Keep a sharp lookout for spies.

Mag, Nitty soon noticed, suffered from Twitch's absence on the farm as much as Windle did. She'd gotten into all manner of mischief of late, tickling the horses' haunches with her trunk until they whinnied in annoyance and spending inordinate amounts of time around the chicken coop, hoping for the hens to perch on her ears (which they'd taken a fancy to doing). Nitty missed Twitch, too, and especially missed their sleuthing trips into Fortune's Bluff. It might've been only three days since their last visit to town, but that felt as spun out as an eternity to Nitty.

It wasn't often—or ever, really—that people passed by the Homes farm. It sat on the farthest outskirts of Fortune's Bluff, and there was nothing between the farm and California except fifteen hundred miles of desert-dry dirt. If you happened past the farm, you were either going to Fortune's Bluff or getting as far away from it as possible. Nitty couldn't bank on passersby, and this was both a curse and a blessing. A curse because it only compounded her loneliness for Twitch; a blessing because it meant no one had yet caught on to the fact of Mag's existence.

So when, early one morning, a dilapidated Tin Lizzie

sputtered down the lane leading to the Homes house, Nitty was torn between burning curiosity and an inclination to hide and be quick about it. She eyed the driver's silhouette suspiciously, thinking that if Miz Ricketts had found her out, she still stood a chance at escape, if only she could wrangle Mag away from the chicken coop.

She was mid-jump off the front porch when a shaft of sunlight exposed the face behind the steering wheel. Nitty skittered to a stop, staring. The driver was none other than Bernice Sigh!

"Flabbergast and render me thunderstruck!" Nitty cried as Bernice brought the automobile to a jerky stop. "You can drive an automobile?"

"Course I can." Bernice faced Nitty's stare with an indomitable one of her own. "Have ever since Papa . . ." She stiffened in her seat as the younger Sighs tumbled helter-skelter from every corner of the motorcar. "How else were we supposed to get to Kickapoo and back for visits?"

Nitty guessed then what she meant. Bernice must've driven to Kickapoo to visit her papa in the asylum, maybe even with the passel of young Sigh children in tow. This, compounded by the novelty of her driving a motorcar at all, made Bernice instantly rise a thousand times higher in Nitty's estimation.

"It's rumbustious," she uttered appreciatively. "It could be a getaway car, like in *The Swashbuckler's Plunder*."

"The what?" Bernice snorted. "Never mind. I just did what needed doing is all." She stepped from the car, revealing a pile of Sears, Roebuck catalogs on the driver's seat and two thick loaves of bread strapped to her feet for reaching the pedals. Her eyes fell on the sprouting field, where the younger Sighs were marveling at the fuchsia buds. Bernice barely gave the crop a second glance. Her mind seemed to be somewhere else entirely. "I need to see Mr. Homes."

A thousand questions tickled Nitty's tongue: Was Bernice here with news of Neezer? Had Crispin said something of import? But Bernice's stony expression warned against any questions.

"He's in the barn." That was all Nitty had the chance to say before Bernice was marching to the barn, loaved feet and all. Not a minute later, Windle was hurrying out the barn door for his truck, calling out to Nitty that he'd be back in due course and that under no circumstances was any other youngster to drive Crispin's motorcar until further notice.

Nitty's disappointment at this dictum (for she'd been wondering how she might convince Bernice to let her do just that) was squelched as soon as she saw Bernice sag onto the front-porch steps, chin in her hands. It was difficult to tell by her swallowed-a-bug disgruntlement if she was angry or sad. It hardly mattered, Nitty decided, because Bernice looked, most of all, in need of a lending ear.

She wasn't the only one who sensed this, because just as Nitty took a step toward Bernice, Mag rounded the corner of the barn, heading straight for her. Nitty had already witnessed firsthand Mag's ability to make an impressive entrance, but today Mag outdid herself. All twelve of the Homes chickens roosted on her back and atop her head, ornamenting her with a feathered headdress. Nitty thought it beautiful, but Bernice?

She shot from the steps with the speed of a rattler striking, and within seconds had baby Verna hoisted onto her hip and the younger Sighs herded up behind her.

"An elephant!" they squealed in astonishment and delight, peeking around Bernice even as she tried to barricade them.

"I can see that," Bernice groused, then stared, with unbridled suspicion, as Nitty greeted Mag with a rub under the chin.

"I know you're eager to make the Sighs' acquaintance," Nitty whispered in Mag's ear. "Only give them a chance to get used to the idea first."

Mag swung her trunk to and fro, then raised its tip into the air, as if she was taking in the Sighs in the best way she knew how, with a proper and thorough sniffing.

To Bernice, Nitty added, "This is Magnolious. She's enormous, to be sure, but gentle as a baby."

Bernice didn't seem convinced, until Mag plucked a fuchsia bud from the field's edge and, ever so slowly, tucked the bud into Bernice's hair.

Just as slowly, Bernice raised a hand to touch the bud, blushing as she did. "She's all right, I guess," she finally mumbled. At that the other Sighs whooped and sprang from behind Bernice's back, each eager to greet Mag themselves. Within minutes, Mag had curled her trunk into a swing for the younger Sighs while Nitty, Bernice, and Verna watched from the porch steps.

"You could ride her," Nitty offered. "If you wanted."

Bernice shook her head as she bounced Verna on her knee. "And leave these five running wild?" She nodded toward the younger Sighs. "A duster'd likely blow them to the moon without me keeping watch." She stared down at the loaves on her feet and shook her head, as if she'd only just remembered she was wearing them in the first place. She slid Verna to Nitty's knee as she undid the twine holding them in place. "Papa . . . he had a bad spell this morning."

Nitty held her breath. Bernice might be skittish as a deer, but if Nitty stayed still and patient, she guessed Bernice would say more. Sure enough, after near-torturous minutes of silence, Bernice kept on.

"Neezer paid us a visit, first thing, saying he needed to inspect the bakery. To check on its cleanliness, for the sake of customers, he said." She scowled. "He really came to threaten Papa with closing the shop. And after he left . . . Papa flew into a frenzy. That's why I came to fetch Mr. Homes. He looks in on him from time to time. He might calm him, like he's done before."

"I'm sure he will." Nitty expected nothing less of him, even with all his grousing. Windle's kindness was the sly sort that shied from acclamation. She felt the stirrings of a pride in it, and wondered if this was how a daughter might feel about her papa, if he was a good, upstanding papa. She tucked the thought into a cozy corner of her heart, for safekeeping.

"I haven't seen Papa like that in . . ." Bernice swallowed and pressed her lips into a fixed line. She held up the loaves for

147

Nitty to see. "He baked these, and I can't make heads or tails of what it means."

Nitty passed Verna back to Bernice and took the loaves. For the first time, she noticed their unusual design. On top of each loaf was a starlike shape etched into the bread, with a round knob set in the dead center of the star.

"This reminds me of something." Nitty traced the lines of the star with her finger, noting how the two lines running through the center, horizontally and vertically, were longer than the others. Her mind whirred with *Daily Tattler* stories of pirates, conquistadores, pioneers. . . . "A compass!" she cried exultantly. "This looks exactly like the lines on the face of a compass that show direction." She clutched the bread. "Did your papa say anything about it? One of his riddles, maybe?"

Bernice nodded as she set the fussing Verna on the ground. "He said . . . 'North is silt; south is oil. Turn the dial; pick the soil.' "

"The dial?" Nitty repeated.

"I want to believe he's talking sense, but . . ." Her words were drowned by the earsplitting hollers of two of the Sigh boys, who were now tussling on the front porch, each with a firm grip on the other's hair and ears. Bernice was on her feet in an instant, looming over them with a scowl. "What in the crab apple are you two fighting over now?"

Between shouts of "It's mine!" and "I saw it first," Bernice dauntlessly dove into the fray of punching fists and kicking feet, and soon had a hand firmly atop each of the boys' moppy heads, holding them apart.

She nodded to a small brown object lying at her feet, saying to Nitty, "They told me they found it under the porch." She glared at both boys. "But that does *not* mean it's yours. And it's only a rusty key, besides."

Disappointed at the loss of their prize, the boys scooted from the porch while Nitty picked up the object. She knew from the *Daily Tattler* that rusty, old keys were always emblematic of some great secret. Her pulse pranced at the pure romance of it. "Horsefeathers, Bernice, keys like this unlock secret chambers and mummies' tombs, not to mention treasure chests! This key is a clue!"

Bernice, who'd turned to tending a fresh scrape on Verna's knee as the baby clung to her ankle, paused just long enough to frown. "Don't have time to waste deciphering clues when there are noses to wipe and squabbles to quash." But she cocked her head, looking more closely at the key.

That was when Nitty caught the tiniest spark of curiosity light Bernice's eyes. She snatched at it.

"What if this key proves a help to your papa? Would you snub it then?"

Bernice stared at Nitty. She stared at the key. She snorted.

Nitty took this as a sign of her open-mindedness in the matter. She grinned, an idea hatching as she did. Twitch could prove a fine remedy for Bernice's melancholy over her papa, if only she could spring him from his convalescence. And besides, she and Twitch and Mag were overdue for some muckraking for certain.

Nitty leaped off the porch, beelining for the Higgler farm. "Stay put!" she told Bernice. "I'll be back with Twitch in a wink."

Bernice hollered after her, "Just what is it you plan to do?"

Nitty wondered at such a question. If Bernice had read even a single issue of the *Daily Tattler,* the answer would've been obvious. Didn't the poor girl have a speck of mischievery left at all? Or had the wiping of all those little noses worn it out of her? Whatever the case, Nitty decided then and there that Bernice could benefit from some adventuring.

Nitty called over her shoulder as she ran, "We're going to find the lock to fit that key."

CHAPTER THIRTEEN

In Which There Is Much Cogitation on Secrets and Speedy Seed-Spitters

"This is *exactly* the sort of key to hide a fiendish secret," Twitch confirmed the moment Bernice laid the key in his hand.

"I knew it." Nitty grinned as she sat down on the porch, motioning for Twitch to do the same. The walk from his house back to the Homes farm had winded him, and she wanted to give him a chance to catch his breath.

As he sat, Twitch lifted the key to his nose and sniffed. "Smells like criminality."

Bernice guffawed at that. She set Verna down on the ground, letting the baby crawl to her brothers, who were rolling the croquet ball back and forth to Mag, whooping raucously each time Mag returned it with a shove of her trunk. "Don't go spouting that criminality has a smell."

"It does, too," Twitch said indignantly. He fingered the chevron detecting mustache he had insisted on wearing over his cheesecloth mask. As soon as he touched it, a substantial chunk of its silk fell into his lap. Twitch shrugged at the mishap, and Nitty guessed he was determined to wear the mustache until it deteriorated entirely. "*Detective Comics* calls it 'the repellent stench of treachery.' *I* think it bears the distinct odor of rotten eggs and turnips."

Bernice shook her head. "I don't give a weevil's snout what odor it bears. What do you plan to do, dig up every scrap of dirt from here to Fortune's Bluff in search of some hidden bunkum?"

Twitch hopped up, puffing, and within seconds was nose to nose with Bernice, bouncing on his tiptoes like a boxer. "I am a seasoned detective, and seasoned detectives do not go on wild-goose chases."

Bernice stuck a hand to her hip. "What *do* they do, then?"

"Look here." He pulled a pile of papers from where they'd been tucked into the waist of his pants.

"Aren't those the newspapers Miz Turngiddy left at the bakery?" Nitty asked, peering over Twitch's shoulder.

He nodded. "I told you I had information of import, didn't I?" With no small measure of satisfaction, he spread the papers onto the porch, jabbing his finger at several headlines. "These articles all say the same thing: that dusters are dying down in plenty of places."

Nitty read the headlines. DUST STORMS DIMINISHING read

one, while another exclaimed DUSTERS IN NORTH DAKOTA ARE GONE WITH THE WIND. She frowned. "How can that be? When they're getting worse here by the day?"

"I don't know. There's got to be an explanation, and I bet it has to do with Neezer Snollygost. I bet there's an explanation for why Miz Turngiddy had all those papers in the first place, too." He held up the key. "Neezer used to live on this farm, and now we have this key. It's bound to reveal something, and I—"

Twitch tried to finish what he was saying, but no sound came except a bubbling cough. Nitty cringed. It had taken all her powers of persuasion, and Twitch promising not to remove his cheesecloth mask, to convince Mrs. Higgler to let Twitch venture outside. She'd been none too happy about him having to forgo her fresh batch of turnip soup, but she'd finally relented.

"Mind you stay quiet," she'd said. "Read your comics. *Calmly.* No running or horseplay."

Twitch had promised, but instead of keeping him quiet, the matter of this mystery key had increased his twitchiness tenfold. Nitty could hardly blame him. She was feeling twitchy herself, itching to look for the key's lock.

She went to Twitch now, and stood by his side while she waited for the coughing fit to pass. She had a mind to holler at Bernice for provoking him in the first place, until she saw that Bernice looked as worried over Twitch's coughing as she was herself. Mag, too, had forgotten her ball (and abandoned her chickens, flapping her ears to set them aflight) and was lumbering toward Twitch.

She issued a scolding *Brrrt!* as if to say, *He has no business being up and about.*

"Don't look at me like that," Nitty mumbled to Mag, dropping her eyes. "It's the key he's worked up about. We can't force him into invalidism if his mind's set on capers."

Once Mag reached Twitch, she stroked his back with her trunk until his cough subsided, then calmly snuffled the key for a moment and perfunctorily plucked it from his hand. She turned and headed confidently, and without hesitation, toward the barn. Nitty looked on in satisfaction as Bernice's mouth fell open.

"You and Mag are still getting acquainted, but you should know, she has a habit of proving that elephants, as a whole, are a rather spectacular species." She started after Mag, saying over her shoulder, "Come on. She wants us to follow her."

Twitch caught up to Nitty as quick as he could, but Bernice hung back, hesitating, arms crossed. Twitch shook his head at Nitty. "She wants to be ornery about it, so leave her be," he wheezed. He added, loud enough for Bernice to hear, "If she wants to let her papa be defeated by a charlatan like Neezer, that's her decision."

Nitty snuck a glance at Bernice, aghast at Twitch's rebuke and sure that Bernice's swift retribution would follow.

Bernice clasped and unclasped her fists, her face revealing

her quandary. Then, using the twine she'd discarded from her loaf pedals earlier, she quickly tethered baby Verna by her bitty waist, then tied the other end of the twine to the front-porch railing. She leveled a stern gaze at the other Sighs. "Keep watch over Verna, or I'll make you change her next diaper." After issuing that command, she fell into step alongside Nitty and Twitch. "I'll not stand by one more second watching Papa suffer his fits and my brothers and sisters go wanting. Daft as these hijinks strike me, if this ends up having anything to do with Neezer, I'm coming."

Nitty didn't let on how pleased she was by this development, especially when she noticed a new liveliness to Bernice's step that had been missing when she'd first arrived. Instead she turned her attention to Mag and her unwavering stride.

"That's the way, Mag." She smiled up at her as they moved into the shadows of the barn. "You know where you're going."

Mag didn't hesitate a moment, but plodded to a far corner of the barn Nitty hadn't yet explored—a corner where cobwebs veiled a menagerie of discarded hoes and scythes, a dust-riddled tractor, and even an old rocking horse. Tattered sheets covered other objects, and Mag made for one sheet in particular. After setting the key down beside it, she drew the sheet back with her trunk to reveal a large, weather-beaten chest underneath.

She swiveled her head toward Bernice, her mouth curling upward into what might've been an elephantine smile.

"You're better than a bloodhound," Twitch said. "The most indispensable sidekick I've come across." He patted Mag's side appreciatively.

"The *only* sidekick you've come across," quipped Bernice, to which Twitch offered her an impressive glower.

Before another argument could break out (and she expected one any second), Nitty snatched the key from the floor and slid it into the tarnished keyhole in the chest's front. The lock protested with a tinny groan but then gave way, the chest spewing dust as it rasped open.

" 'And so the cavernous gateway to enigmas opens,' " Nitty whispered. It was a quote from *The Cursed Treasure of Captain Blackbeard,* one she thought most fitting for the occasion.

There was nearly a collision of heads as Nitty, Bernice, and Twitch bent over for a look inside. The chest brimmed with musty items: books, a moth-eaten quilt, a yellowed pair of delicate crocheted gloves. There was a smattering of tatty photos, most of people Nitty didn't recognize. She was the first to dare reach a hand into the chest, but soon Twitch and Bernice were sifting through its contents, too.

Nitty spotted a photo that struck her as familiar somehow, and she held it up to a shaft of sunlight. Three figures stared out from it: two young men with a petite fair-haired lady seated between them. The lady Nitty recognized as Clara, but a younger Clara than the one from the photo in Windle's kitchen. Nitty peered closer at the taller of the two men, then sucked in her breath. There was Windle—a younger Windle, as spindly as ever but with a shock of dark hair and merry eyes—his hand resting on Clara's shoulder. And on the other side of Clara . . . Could it be?

"Neezer!" she blurted. He was younger and scrawnier, no sign of his brawn about him yet. Twitch and Bernice crowded around the photo, staring.

"Neezer looks different. Not like the puffed-up peacock he usually does." Bernice tilted the photo in the light, studying it from different angles.

"He's smiling." Twitch shook his head in confusion. "Almost an honest smile, too."

"All three of them look happy." Nitty slid the photo back into the chest. "What happened that ruined it all?"

"Keep digging" was Twitch's response. "We're hot on the trail. I feel it."

"What about this?" Bernice pulled a ragged leather-bound notebook from the chest's depths. "It's full of notes and drawings. . . ." She flipped through the dog-eared pages.

"A . . . Refracting Rain-Catcher?" Nitty read the handwriting from over Bernice's shoulder. "And . . . the Speedy Seed-Spitter? Here's another one . . . a Fantastic Farm-O-Matic. The oddest contraptions, by the looks of them. It's a journal, I think."

"May I?" Twitch held out his hand for the notebook, his tone suddenly the epitome of an investigative professional. He opened the cover to the first page. "The dates are from long before any of us were born." His eyes widened. "'An account of the inspired ideas and inventions of Neezer Snollygost,'" he read from the first page, "'as written by the creator himself.'"

Bernice snorted as Twitch skimmed the pages. "So he never was one for humbleness, then. Even before he was mayor."

Twitch froze, staring, then turned an open page toward Nitty. "He calls it the Wind Whiffler, but what does that look like to you?"

Nitty scrutinized Neezer's sketch, and as she did, her blood surged. "That's the brass contraption that nearly balded me in the Snollygost broom closet!"

"Indubitably." Twitch nodded an affirmation. "But what is its purpose?"

"I'll tell you what it is!" Nitty exclaimed, the unpleasantness of the incident in the closet returning to her full force. "It's to cause all manner of scalp suffering to unsuspecting girls!"

Twitch was too consumed with the journal to respond, and a moment later he shouted, "Rats and darnation!" He jabbed his finger at the page. "There's a drawing in here titled 'Whirlybog.'"

The sketch was of the strangest machine Nitty had ever seen. Dozens of blades resembling windmills jutted from the top of the machine, and at its center was an enormous, clear canister labeled HOLDING TANK. None of those peculiar features, though, caught Nitty's attention. What did was a large dial in the middle of the machine's control panel, labeled DUSTOMETER, with lines spreading from its star-shaped center.

"Bernice." Nitty pointed to the dial. "What does that Dustometer remind you of?"

Bernice stared, eyes widening. "It's the compass lines Pa baked in the bread."

Nitty nodded. "Your pa was baking a copy of that dial, which means—"

"He's seen it before," Bernice finished. "When he broke into the Snollygost Institute." She sat back on her heels, relieved and exultant. "The Whirlybog that Papa talked about actually exists."

"But Neezer's admitted as much," Nitty said. "He's already told everyone himself that he's building something that will save the town from dusters."

Bernice scrutinized the sketch in the notebook. "He hasn't written anything here about what the Whirlybog does. But with a Dustometer, it's got to involve dust in some way or other."

Twitch coughed, then sputtered, "There's a shadiness to it. Make no mistake. We have to see this Whirlybog. The real one. For ourselves."

While each of them thought on this, Mag snuffled her trunk past the chest and into the deepest reaches of the shadowy corner of the barn. She rummaged with such enthusiasm that the old rocking horse and scythes toppled, and Nitty and Bernice were unceremoniously pushed to the side.

"Mag," Nitty scolded, "if you want to share in the snooping, use better manners."

But Twitch, seeing an opportunity for further investigating, crawled between Mag's forelegs and into the corner to inspect some newly unearthed objects, while Bernice kept paging through Neezer's journal.

Nitty, thinking that maybe Twitch was onto another flummoxing discovery, followed him. She scooted under Mag's chin and through the narrow space to find Twitch, his back to her, kneeling before a small wooden trough.

"What did you fi—"

Twitch turned to her, and his look stopped her cold. It made her think of Grimsgate, of the looks on the orphans' faces whenever they weren't chosen for adoption. It was a look she'd seen so often before. On Windle's face, on Crispin's, on Ferdinand Klempt's.

It was a look of loss. But what had Twitch lost, and why had he never told her?

It made an ache start inside Nitty's chest, and she pressed her Gleam Jar closer. Blue, yellow, red, green. Ribbon, button, marble, seed. It should've made her feel better, but this time it didn't.

Mag's trunk swung worriedly back and forth from Nitty to Twitch, touching her shoulder, then his. It was as if she sensed a darkening mood, but wasn't sure whom to comfort first.

Nitty started to ask Twitch what was wrong, but he leaped up before she could get the words out. "I'm going outside."

Nitty sank onto her heels, entirely stumped. Then she saw,

and her heart wilted in dismay. What Twitch had found wasn't a trough after all. It was a little wooden cradle.

"Twitch, wait!" Nitty jumped up to follow him, her chest wrenching, but Windle caught her by the arms. He stood before her, a fence post of rigidity.

"What have you done?" His voice was thunderous as he looked from her to the open chest before him, its contents strewn on the floor. Bernice stood behind him, her face the very portrait of entrapment and misery. "You had no business opening this. No business at all."

Nitty could scarce meet his eyes, so icy with anger were their depths. Still, she needed him to know it hadn't been entirely her fault. Or Twitch's and Bernice's either. "We found the key by accident," she explained quietly. "Under the porch."

"Confound it." Windle scratched the freckle behind his right ear. "I lost it years ago and was none too sorry for the loss."

"But there are photographs in there of Clara. Of you. Why would you lock those away?" It seemed incomprehensible to her to have something of a real family and want to be rid of it. Clara's fingers must've touched that quilt. Lillah must've worn those gloves. The chest was better than any Gleam Jar. Much, much better. Why didn't Windle understand that?

He glowered. "It should've been left alone. All of it. Some things are better off locked away. Do you understand?"

Bernice started at his words, and Nitty watched as the flintiness returned to her eyes. Bernice spun and ran from the barn, and as she did, Mag swung her trunk toward Windle, trumpeted one short but definitively cross *Brrrt!* and lumbered after Bernice and Twitch. Windle's anger wilted into regret.

Nitty glanced down at the photographs and the notebook. There were stories that needed telling here, secrets that needed sharing. She locked eyes with Windle. "I don't like saying so, because I've taken a liking to you, crabbiness and all. But . . . you're wrong."

With that, she straightened her shoulders, set her jaw, and marched from the barn.

CHAPTER FOURTEEN

In Which an Accomplice Prophesies Calamity

The ride back to the Homes farm from the Sighs' shop was a quiet one.

Ever since Windle had stomped from the barn declaring that it was time for the Sighs to be on their way home, the collective mood of the entire group was nothing short of wretched. Windle insisted on driving Bernice and the other Sighs back to town, saying he'd return Crispin's Tin Lizzie to the bakery later, but Nitty wasn't about to let Bernice endure Windle's brooding without her. After all, Bernice could hardly be blamed for anything except the gumption to drive a motorcar. Twitch must've shared Nitty's sentiment, because, though he said not a word, he piled into Windle's truck for the ride, too.

But even after Bernice had offered him a bracing shoulder nudge and a whispered "Don't quit the case, whatever you do" as her encouraging goodbye, Twitch remained mute.

Now he sat beside Nitty in the truck's bed, staring straight ahead, producing a tired, leaky balloon of wheezing from underneath his cheesecloth mask. Even the pages of his *Detective Comics* couldn't entice him. Nitty hugged her Gleam Jar tightly as the truck rumbled, thinking about Windle's ire and worrying over Twitch, although her Gleam Jar wasn't a balm this time.

She tried to be patient with Twitch. She spent approximately four minutes trying. For the first minute, she counted the number of times Windle harrumphed (five). For the second minute, she counted the number of times Twitch's muddy lungs squeaked (twelve). For the third and fourth minutes, she decided counting was an entirely futile distraction that did nothing except create *impatience.* After this revelation, she gave up trying altogether.

"Well?" she blurted to Twitch. "If you're sore at me, I wish you'd come out and say it!"

Twitch's shoulders scrunched in surprise. "I'm not sore at you." His voice sounded far away with sadness.

Nitty swallowed, knowing she'd have to bring up the topic sooner or later, but dreading what might come of it. "Was it . . . was it something to do with the cradle in the barn?"

For the first time since she'd met him, Twitch went entirely still. Not a single muscle moved. "That cradle . . . it belonged to our baby." His voice turned so quiet now that Nitty had to stop her own breath to hear proper. "Windle carved it for my sister. Anna."

"You had a sister?" Nitty's insides were suddenly slick and nervous. She wasn't sure she wanted to hear any more. But if Twitch had the courage to tell it, then she'd have to have the courage to listen.

Twitch slid his mask and goggles from his face. His mouth crumpled at its edges. "She was born in the middle of a duster." He cupped his hands together. "She was no bigger than a teacup. Seemed like her lungs were muddier than mine before she even took her first breath. She only lived a day."

There it was again. The look of loss.

"That's why Ma frets over me. And why Pa didn't stay. He loves Fortune's Bluff, or the way it used to be, anyway. Before the dusters. He was set on keeping us here. Sure things would get better. But then last year, Anna . . ." He sighed. "That was when Pa left to look for work out west. I believe he just couldn't bear the melancholy. I suppose he could come back once he forgets." Twitch looked at Nitty. "Only . . . I don't think he'll forget."

"It's the worst kind of funny, isn't it? If I had any memories of my family, I'd give anything to keep them. But your pa . . . he has his memories and wants to lose them."

"Anna was beautiful," Twitch said. "I would never want to forget that."

Nitty couldn't think of a single thing to say to this. She took Twitch's hand.

"The worst villains are the ones you can't see," Twitch whispered then. " 'Ten Ways to Be a Villain, number ten: Strike silently, swiftly, and ruthlessly.' "

Together they watched ocher clouds mushrooming along the horizon. Windle frowned as he looked through the windshield. A duster was coming.

When the truck at last reached the lush green stalks of Nitty's crop, Nitty nearly cried with gratefulness at the sight of Mag lumbering from the barn to greet them. If ever there was a time when she needed the comforting warmth of Mag's trunk resting on her shoulder, it was now.

Then a movement at the edge of the field caught Nitty's eye. At first Nitty mistook it for a walking tumbleweed. But, suddenly, the tumbleweed jumped. "An elephant!" it yelped.

"Miz Turngiddy," declared Nitty.

"Miz Turngiddy," lamented Windle.

"Spy," said Twitch. The sadness in his voice was replaced with sudden keenness, and he nodded toward the spot where Miz Turngiddy had parked her automobile, nearly out of sight among the field's forest of stalks. "An intriguing development in our case."

Nitty jumped from the bed of the now-stopped truck, moving to stand between Mag and Mayor Snollygost's rapidly approaching secretary.

Mag's ears lifted into stiff flags. Her heart became a cannon, booming in her chest. This human's scent was sickly sweet with nervousness, but Mag didn't understand why. The woman wasn't afraid of *her*. But she *was* afraid of someone. And that made Mag cautious and put her on alert for danger. She was ready to protect her girl. Her girl, though, seemed to want to protect *her*.

"It's all right." Nitty patted the underside of Mag's trunk. "She can't do a thing to you." Nitty hoped she was right about that.

"Afternoon, Miz Turngiddy," Windle said slowly, looking even broodier than he had minutes before (if that was possible). "What brings you from town?"

Miz Turngiddy stopped some distance away from Nitty and Mag, gripping her notepad in both hands. Her eyes darted from the field to Mag and back again. "I was making rounds on Mayor Snollygost's behalf. Paying friendly calls to neighbors and their lands."

"Demanding people's money." Twitch coughed. Loudly. It wasn't his muddy cough, but a scornful one.

Miz Turngiddy looked momentarily injured by Twitch's words, but her expression quickly transformed into a frown. "Young man, I am merely doing what my job requires of me. And Mayor Snollygost does not demand that debts be repaid today, or even tomorrow. Only that we work toward community progress, fulfillment, and the betterment of all." She leaned over Twitch, her eyes looking more beseeching than threatening, as if she were about to give him a test she hoped he'd pass. "You *do* know the Fortune's Bluff motto, don't you?"

"Nefarious deeds are afoot." Twitch was stiff as a soldier,

staring at Miz Turngiddy. "And *you* know that dusters are disappearing everywhere but here, don't you? Tell me. Do you know *why*?"

Nitty felt a rush of pride. Horsefeathers, her friend was brave! Possibly foolish, too, if the disappointment on Miz Turngiddy's scarlet face was any indication, but definitely brave.

Miz Turngiddy's mouth fell open, but no sound came from it. Finally she blustered, "I don't know what you're implying, but—"

"Miz Turngiddy." Windle placed himself between Miz Turngiddy and Twitch, diverting all her attention to him. "I'm afraid we've only just returned from an outing to town. I wasn't expecting you to pay a call—"

"Of course not!" Miz Turngiddy seemed to recover herself, and redirected her focus to the field. She touched one of the field's green stalks, as if to test its sturdiness. "I was only passing by your farm, and your field stopped me short. Why, nothing's grown in Fortune's Bluff in a decade! It's simply fascinating. And now this." Her weasel eyes squinted up at Mag's approaching form. "Mr. Homes! You are in possession of an elephant!"

"So it would seem."

Miz Turngiddy's nose twitched. She scribbled furiously in her notebook. "What is the purpose of this elephant?"

"I would think the answer to that would be obvious." Windle glanced at Nitty, and to her astonishment and relief, she saw his broodiness weakening. There was the hint of a twinkle in his eyes. A genuine twinkle! Nitty's heart lifted. "Farming."

168

"I thought as much."

There was something feverish in the way Miz Turngiddy eyed the field and Mag, her pinprick eyes glinting zealously. It made Nitty's palms gummy with sweat.

"How very unconventional," Miz Turngiddy continued. "Ingenious, really. And your crop. Its root system must be unusually sturdy to withstand the dusters. It will be of great interest to the mayor." Miz Turngiddy cupped one of the bulbous pink buds in her hand. "I'm not familiar with this particular . . ." Her voice faltered. "What is it, exactly?"

Windle glanced at Nitty again. "I couldn't rightly say."

"Well." Miz Turngiddy scribbled. "Well." She scribbled some more. "I'd love to obtain a sample, if I might—"

"You might not." Windle glanced toward the dust clouds building to their east. "Miz Turngiddy, there's a duster coming, and our elephant is in need of watering."

"Of course, of course." Her hand still cupped the fuchsia bud, but now tightened, as if it could barely stand letting the bud drop. "I will stay abreast of this. Such an anomaly for a crop to survive duster after duster," she mumbled to herself. "Such a streak of luck. I'd calculate the odds of it continuing to be one in a thousand. Time will tell."

As Miz Turngiddy's automobile rattled back toward Fortune's Bluff, spitting dust in its wake, Mag trumpeted. Rather indignantly, Nitty thought.

"I agree," Nitty responded. "I don't trust her either."

"We haven't heard the end from her," Windle said morosely.

Twitch looked at Nitty. " 'Ten Ways to Be a Villain, number two: Rely on a shrewd accomplice to be your eyes and ears.' " When Nitty looked at him blankly, Twitch added, with some chagrin, "She'll be telling Mayor Snollygost about Mag before the day's out."

"What should we do?" she asked him.

"Crack the case. As soon as possible."

Yes, thought Nitty. *Very soon.* Because one thing was sure: Miz Turngiddy was not entirely at ease with an elephant in Fortune's Bluff. And Neezer Snollygost, Nitty suspected, wouldn't be either.

CHAPTER FIFTEEN

In Which an Eggplant Is Mistaken for an Elephant

"An elephant!"

Those were the words spoken by Neezer Snollygost that evening as he sat in his office at the Snollygost Institute, only moments after Miz Turngiddy informed him of the unusual happenings at the Homes farm. Because of the ever-present *WHUMP! WHUMP! WHUMP!* resonating at regular intervals from the Whirlybog in the locked room beyond Neezer's office, because Neezer's mouth was full of steak and potatoes as he spoke, and because his nose was whistling "How Many Biscuits Can You Eat?" what Miz Turngiddy heard him say was, "An eggplant!"

Miz Turngiddy's frazzled hopes lifted. Could it be that eggplant was the answer, at last, to Neezer's bottomless hunger? If it was, perhaps Neezer would see reason at last and allow her to help restore Fortune's Bluff to its former glory. Then she might be able to write her son that all was again right and well in Fortune's Bluff. Her grandbabies, with their sweet-cream scent and apricot-fuzz curls, might come back.

If eggplant was the answer, perhaps Neezer, having been satiated, would see the logic in Miz Turngiddy's studying weather patterns and soil erosion. Perhaps he could be persuaded to visit other towns to find out why dusters were dying down everywhere but Fortune's Bluff. (She knew, as Angus Higgler had correctly and embarrassingly guessed, that this was undeniably the case.) Perhaps, most pressingly, he would let her into his Whirlybog workshop, where she was confident that, if given the opportunity, she could fix the machine so that, at last, it stopped the dusters. And what she wouldn't give to stop its infernal whumping!

If eggplant was to prove the solution to all, then—by gum!—Miz Turngiddy had her mission.

"Of course, sir," she said. "Right away, sir. If you're craving eggplant, I'm sure one can be found in the warehouse." She began to scurry from the office.

"Miz Turngiddy!" Neezer bellowed over the incessant *WHUMP!*

Miz Turngiddy stopped mid-scurry.

"It is a perilous thing, confusing an eggplant with an elephant when one is much more likely to cause turmoil than the other." He took another hefty bite of steak and potatoes, dipping it in the gravy boat beforehand to ensure that every morsel dripped with thick, rich sauce.

"No eggplant, then, sir?"

"Not as of yet, Miz Turngiddy." Neezer's nose swung into "I Heard the Voice of a Pork Chop" as he moved on to the next course of biscuits and grits. He motioned to the chair across from his desk. "Have a seat. Notes should be taken."

Miz Turngiddy sat, her notepad perched in readiness on her knees.

"We must ask ourselves some questions about Windle's elephant." He dabbed at his mouth with the napkin tucked under his chin. "For instance, how does the elephant work toward the betterment of all? Is this elephant contributing to our community's progress?"

"The answer is simple, sir. The elephant is helping Windle with his farming. Windle is part of our community."

Neezer propped his elbows onto the table and pressed his fingertips together in what he thought of as a pose of stately wisdom. Miz Turngiddy noted (silently, of course) that it was a pose that put his elbows into gravy. "Windle is one of many. Is it fair for him to prosper while others suffer?"

Miz Turngiddy paled at the idea of what she was about to say, but decided it would not put her job in too much jeopardy to venture this one truth. "Excuse me for saying so, sir, but I did not see him prospering. Only trying, which he can't be faulted for."

"Can't he?" Neezer tapped his fingertips together. "You say

his crop is flourishing. How is it, do you think, that his crop flourishes when everyone else's fails?"

"It is most unusual," Miz Turngiddy admitted. "But then, we *do* want crops to grow."

"We want Fortune's Bluff to reach its potential. To reach the pinnacle of fulfillment." Neezer's nose struck a fittingly high note of triumph, as if it agreed. "The people of Fortune's Bluff have every manner of food available to them already. What Fortune's Bluff craves, the Snollygost General Store provides, does it not?"

"Of course, sir," Miz Turngiddy said. "Except . . ."

"Yes?"

"Except many can't afford the food."

"Because folks are stuck on farmland that will *not* be farmed. Fortune's Bluff doesn't need more failing crops. What we need is progress of a concrete sort. Invention. Expansion." Neezer's stomach growled. "Fortune's Bluff could be a place of renown. Is it too much to ask that others share my vision for its evolution?"

"Of course not, sir. Here." Miz Turngiddy, whose own stomach stirred uneasily at this "evolution" he spoke of, offered him a chocolate éclair from the remnants of his feast. "Eat this."

Neezer bit into it, then heaved a weighty sigh. "I strive. I toil. I give. My mission is to serve Fortune's Bluff." His nose struck up the piteous first notes of "Swing Low, Sweet Chariot." "I've been patient, have I not? Extending loans and credit? Waiting for folks to realize that their debts can't be paid with farming? Waiting for them to turn to me for solutions? And I have solutions, Miz

Turngiddy! Indeed I do." He tapped his temple knowingly. "But now this. An elephant! A crop that serves one but not all." His head sank to his desk. "It is exhausting, Miz Turngiddy, bearing the shoulders on which an entire town rests."

Miz Turngiddy, for her part, was beginning to feel exhausted from bearing Neezer Snollygost. "I am sorry, sir." Her teeth clenched. "But if you'd permit me to at least help with your accounts, sir, and perhaps write to some other towns to learn *their* methods for preventing dusters—"

"You think other towns have solutions we lack?" Neezer's eyes blazed. "Solutions better than my Whirlybog, which I labor over day and night?"

Miz Turngiddy straightened, her doubts a battalion behind her clenched teeth. All she had to do was open her mouth and the words would pour forth. What a relief that would be! But she did not open her mouth. Neezer, instead, opened his.

"Take care that you don't forget yourself, Miz Turngiddy." His voice was slither smooth. "It's not like you. Not like you at all."

"Of course. Sir," she managed at last. "What I meant to say was that I hate to see you so burdened by the news of this elephant. With not a soul to ease your suffering."

Neezer offered her a renewed, albeit beleaguered, smile. "I'm relieved you understand my plight, Miz Turngiddy. Just as you understand the hazard of this elephant. Thus far, however, we have not asked ourselves the most significant question about the elephant." He folded his hands across his chest. Often he took comfort in the sheer strength and broadness of it, but tonight, he discovered, he could not. "*How* did Windle come by this elephant?"

"Ingenuity and skill, sir?" Miz Turngiddy suggested.

Neezer's face purpled. "Windle Homes? A possessor of ingenuity? I should think not." Neezer slapped a hand down onto the table. "No. This elephant came to Windle by dubious, conceivably unlawful means."

"How—how dismaying." Miz Turngiddy forced the words out, but in fact, she wasn't dismayed at all. She was electrified. Electrified by the idea of doing something as unconventional— as downright revolutionary!—as procuring an elephant by unlawful means. Not to mention, there was no end to the improvements an elephant might make to a farm, or even a town, for that matter. But her task, she reminded herself, was not to revolutionize. Her task was to keep Neezer Snollygost happy so that his hunger would stay confined to food and not turn to the whole of Fortune's Bluff. Although, with each day that passed, she doubted more and more that this was possible. With each day that passed, her misgivings and distrust of Neezer Snollygost grew.

Now the cogs and gears of her mind whirred until they produced a vision of an elephant—the very same elephant, in fact—standing behind the bars of a circus wagon. Even as it pained her to do it, she admitted, "I have it, sir. I remember. The Gusto and Gallant Circus. It passed through Fortune's Bluff a couple months ago, on its way to Kickapoo. Just before the horrible death of that elephant trainer."

A gradual smile slicked across Neezer's teeth. "Great Magnolious?" he mumbled to himself. "Could it be she?"

Miz Turngiddy approached Neezer's desk and pulled last week's edition of the *Kickapoo Gazette* from its top drawer. Neezer was not in the habit of reading the *Gazette*, or any other papers, for that matter, but he fancied that having a newspaper in his desk made him appear well-informed. Miz Turngiddy, on the other hand, regularly read over a dozen papers weekly, which was how she stayed abreast of stories surrounding dusters and their imminent extinction from everywhere but Fortune's Bluff. Her avid reading was a fact, of course, that she'd decided would be wise to keep to herself.

Now, with some reluctance, she opened the paper and read aloud the ad she'd remembered seeing some days before:

```
On the lookout for savage elephant!! Escaped
from Gusto and Gallant Circus caravan. Where-
abouts currently unknown. Extremely dangerous.
Last seen with runaway orphan. Girl approx. age
ten or eleven, average height, brown hair, ab-
normally green eyes. If seen, telegraph Percival
Gallant in Kickapoo, Kansas, immediately. Sub-
stantial reward if found.
```

Neezer's stomach gave a raucous growl. "Miz Turngiddy, what was the name of that girl Windle brought into the store a couple weeks past?"

Miz Turngiddy flipped through the pages of her notepad. "Nitty Luce, sir."

"Her eyes *were* curious, weren't they?"

Miz Turngiddy swallowed. "Greener than grass."

Neezer's smile widened. "Miz Turngiddy, a telegram must be sent. To Percival Gallant."

"Yes, sir." Despite Miz Turngiddy's hand shaking, she took up her notepad. "What should it say?"

Neezer dictated. Miz Turngiddy's pen trembled, but still did Neezer's bidding. When they were finished, Neezer's stomach gave a fretful rumble. Miz Turngiddy turned for the door.

"Before you go," Neezer said. "From what you saw of Windle's crop, do you think a duster could destroy it?"

She paused over this, recalling the sturdiness of those green stalks. "I suppose if the duster were bad enough, the crop could be destroyed. But it would have to be a very strong duster."

"Mmmm." Neezer nodded. "I see. The worst yet." His nose struck up "Oh! It's a Lovely War!" "Well done, Miz Turngiddy. Well done." He patted his stomach. "I'm ravenous. In fact, eggplant sounds delightful."

"Right away, sir." Miz Turngiddy scurried from the office, the wheels and cogs of her brain whirring. Given the fact that elephants in this part of the world were extremely rare, if not altogether unheard of, she calculated the probability of the Gusto and Gallant elephant and the Homes elephant being one and the same as 98.256 percent. Still, this statistic was not the reason for her mind's pinwheeling.

Miz Turngiddy's thoughts, instead, were consumed with how she might feel roaming free as a runaway elephant. Doing as she liked, saying what she liked. The elephant she'd seen at the Homes farm hadn't struck her as savage. On the contrary, that elephant had struck her as peacefully contented.

As Miz Turngiddy contemplated the nature of contentment, and how she might obtain it, Neezer was also contemplating. While the whumping serenaded his ears, Neezer rose from his chair, slid a large brass key from the top drawer of his desk, and walked to his locked workshop door. He slid the key into the lock, then slipped through the door, shutting it firmly behind him.

On a drafting table just inside the door sat a miniature model of Fortune's Bluff. Now Neezer leaned over it. With a feverish gleam in his eyes, he inspected the matchbox-sized buildings of Main Street, the smaller homes on the surrounding farms. His nose began whistling the *William Tell* Overture. Then he reached his fingers down and lifted the little white house from Windle's farm. He held it to his face, pinching it between his thumb and forefinger as he might a pesky fly.

He pinched until the house splintered into toothpicks. In the empty spot where the house had been, Neezer set an imposing building, a dozen stories high. Then several more beside it, until it looked as if a tiny city were rising on the exact spot where Windle's crop was flourishing.

"The pinnacle of fulfillment," he whispered. He smiled and turned from his model to the great machine whumping a few feet from where he stood. He had much work to do, and his Whirlybog was waiting.

When Miz Turngiddy returned to the office a little while later, holding a plate of delicious-looking eggplant Florentine in her hands, Neezer wasn't at his desk. From behind the workshop's door came sounds of hammering, clanging, and Neezer's occasional mutterings of "if I adjust this" or "if I raise the internal pressure."

Miz Turngiddy, who was still thinking, rather wistfully, about the benefits of doing and saying all she pleased, glared at the locked door. Her mind craved to examine what lay beyond it, but she was losing hope of Mayor Snollygost's ever allowing her access, just as she was losing hope in the mayor's promises about the Whirlybog itself. Now, to make matters worse, the eggplant Florentine she'd painstakingly made was growing cold. She set the plate down on Neezer's desk with a clatter, and as she did, she noticed one acutely annoying new development.

In the time she'd been gone fixing Neezer's supper, the whumping of the Whirlybog had grown considerably louder.

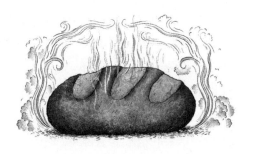

CHAPTER SIXTEEN

In Which a Confession Is Made and a Leap Taken

That night, not a soul at the Homes farm could sleep. It might've been on account of the duster, howling for hours, bringing with it a dark that felt sinister in its soupiness. Or it might've been the memories of each of the farm's occupants, roused from hibernation by the day's troubling events. Memories—particularly ones we'd prefer to forget—can be pesky this way.

Some memories tumbled, moth-eaten and fusty, from a closet in Windle's mind, and he took to scratching that freckle behind his right ear. One thorny memory pricked at Mag's pumpkin heart as she paced inside the barn, making her keen a low, resonant refrain.

Nitty's memories were of a different sort. Oh, there were the all-too-real memories of Grimsgate and Miz Ricketts. But the rest? Well, they weren't so much proper memories as long-ings for ones. These jangled, unfinished and impatient, in the Gleam Jar as Nitty wriggled wakefully on her cot. Before she'd found Mag, before Windle and Twitch and Bernice, the Gleam Jar was all she'd had in the whole wide world. Once, it had seemed like enough. Tonight, it seemed different. Tonight, it couldn't make anything right.

Windle had been remote and distracted since the afternoon, and even though he'd stood by Nitty and Mag in the face of Miz Turngiddy's scrutiny, Nitty worried she'd done irreparable damage to his opinion of her. Maybe she had tried too hard when she shouldn't have.

Mag's sad keening reached her ears on the blowing wind then, and Nitty's heart cramped at the sound. Mag was trou-bled tonight, too, and Nitty wondered why. She longed to go to her, to have Mag's trunk ruffle her hair from her forehead, to laugh when Mag startled a dozing chicken from her back by blowing a blast of air at it with her trunk. But there was no going to Mag now. Not with the dust nearly reaching the top of the windowsills.

Nitty flipped in her cot, and her Gleam Jar pressed into her rib, irritating her for the dozenth time in so many minutes.

"Oh, won't you leave me be!" Nitty cried out at last.

She never expected her outburst would startle Windle so badly that he would rush headlong from his bedroom, in his red woolen union suit, to come to her aid. Nitty stared in disbelief.

Her first thought was *Windle wants to protect me.*

This made her smile.

Her second thought was *Windle looks ridiculous in woolens.*

This made her laugh.

Then Windle, looking down at his union suit, laughed, too. A boisterous, donkey bray of a laugh that was as unlikely a sound as any to hear from a man who resembled a tree.

"Oh, Nitty girl." Windle slapped his knees, bent over as he was with laughing. "Here I thought you needed me."

Nitty looked at him for a long moment. Her heart chimed. "But I do." Nitty waited to let this sink in, waited to see if her saying that would turn Windle back into wood.

It didn't. Instead Windle wiped his laughing tears from his eyes and settled into Clara's rocker. He glanced at the photo of Clara and Lillah atop the kitchen table. What would they say, if they'd heard his laughter? He knew. Clara would declare that it was near on ten years since he'd laughed like that. Then Lillah would pronounce that *that* was ten years too long. And maybe, just maybe, they'd be right.

"Are you done, then?" Nitty asked him.

"With what?"

"Your brooding. I suppose you're entitled to a bit of it, since it was your property we rifled through. Still, the brooding's getting a mite tiresome."

Windle stiffened at this. He opened his mouth. He shut it again. He wished for the hundredth time that he could call on his Clara for consultation on how best to handle precociousness in little girls. A thought struck him. Maybe it didn't need handling at all. This thought was so alarming in its lawlessness that Windle nearly slapped the side of his head to shake it out. *Maybe,* said one of these lawless thoughts, *Nitty isn't the one who needs correcting.*

"I wouldn't say I'm done entirely," he finally uttered as he took up rocking. "But it's fair to say the worst of it has passed." He cleared his throat. "That chest in the barn's stayed locked for years. I wasn't prepared for its opening."

"Well." Nitty stared at him, unflinching. "You can't be prepared for everything all the time. And who wants that, besides?"

Windle harrumphed.

"And, like it or not, ever since we opened it, I've been pondering."

"A dangerous pastime." Windle rocked.

"Don't I know it." She sat up in the cot. "But I can't put a stop to it. Mostly I've been pondering the dangers of villains and accomplices. The difference between truth and wishing." She tapped her chin, wanting to make sure she'd remembered everything. "Oh. And muddy lungs, too."

"That is a sizable amount of pondering for one night." The floorboards whined under Clara's rocker.

Nitty nodded. "And what I want to know is: Why? Why do Mr. Klempt and Mr. Sigh have to suffer so? And why do you, with your lonely, broken heart?"

"Bah!" Windle blurted. "Who said anything about—"

"I'm not finished," Nitty interjected, then added for good measure, "And you do *too* have one."

Windle puffed his chest but stayed silent, after which Nitty, satisfied, continued. "Why did Twitch get a baby sister only to have her taken away?" Her Gleam Jar rattled in her lap, and she sucked in a breath. Then she asked the question that had been stuck like a nettle to her heart for as long as she could remember. "Why did I have parents who didn't want me?" She hated that her voice shilly-shallied over that last one, but there it was. Out of her mouth and into the world, where it hung in the silty air between her and Windle.

Windle quit rocking altogether. It was his turn to ponder. *So,* he thought, *it was as I suspected all along. The girl has no one but her elephant.* Then a loud, insistent voice inside him added, *And you. The girl has you.*

Windle clasped his hands, tucking them under his chin as he frowned at the floor. What had his craggy, brassbound self to offer up to her open, asking eyes? The truth. Windle Homes was a commendable truth teller.

"Sometimes," he said quietly, "there are no answers. People make choices. But that's never the whole of it. Life is as much happenstance and folly as decision. Chance, providence, fate—whatever infernal name you wish to call it—packs a mighty wallop."

Nitty thought on this as the wind screeched and fingers of dust stretched from under the front door. "I don't like it. Not one iota."

Windle nodded. "Didn't expect you to. I don't like it myself."

"So which was it, then? Choice or folly that made you and Neezer sworn enemies?"

Windle's freckle was afire now. For ten years he'd vowed not to dwell on Neezer and the fourth event of life-changing enormity. Only, tonight, with the wind and the memories and all this talk of folly and hearts, he *was* dwelling on it. Tonight it was not going to leave him be until he was out with it, once and for all.

"Neezer was never my enemy." Windle's voice was tired. "There was a time we ran this farm together. Neezer never had a knack for it, but he helped me with the business end of it, and I worked the land. We were partners. It gave my Clara joy to have us all together, with Lillah passed about from knee to knee each night. The crops grew; Lillah grew. We were happy. But Neezer wanted more."

"More of what?" asked Nitty. She understood wanting more. She'd wished for more so many times in the gray rooms of Grimsgate.

Windle sighed. "More success in his own right. We loved him as he was—Clara and I. But what he thought of most days wasn't the love. It was his failures. He wanted to prove himself, to show he could farm as well with his methods as I could with mine. He meant to help and thought he could make farming easier, better. He invented a machine. He called it the Fantastic Farm-O-Matic."

"I saw a drawing of it in Neezer's old journal."

Windle nodded. "He told me the machine would do everything a farmer could. Plant crops, irrigate them, even harvest. It would do it all. With the machine, anyone could be a farmer." His brow furrowed. "I had doubts, to be sure. But I saw the hopes Neezer pinned on that machine. Saw how badly he wanted to succeed, just once, at farming. So when he asked me to let him try the machine on my fields for an entire year . . ." Windle's shoulders sagged. "Of course I said yes. I hoped it would work, for his sake."

Windle's voice was so drenched in gloom that Nitty could already guess what had happened. "The machine didn't work?"

Windle harrumphed. "The machine tore up my fields one end to the other. What few crops grew failed in days, and worse, the soil turned rancid. It was two years before I could get anything to grow again." He shook his head. "Neezer was sick over it. Not just the machine's failure, but what it had done to the farm. He apologized over and over again, but I . . ." Windle's voice choked, and his face reddened. "I let my temper and pride overtake my common sense. I was embarrassed over what had happened, humiliated that I wasn't a master farmer anymore. I blamed Neezer, and minced no words telling him so. I spoke spiteful words that anyone would be ashamed to repeat. . . . I've never behaved so dishonorably. I called him a failure and broke off our partnership. He left the farm after that to go his own way."

"Oh," Nitty whispered. It wasn't easy to swallow, the knowing that Windle had brought on that sort of hurt. But Nitty could see from his drawn face how much he'd been hurt by *doing* the hurting, too. "And you never . . . you never set it right with him?"

"I tried, after I'd calmed down." His voice was hoarse. "I went to him with apologies, after the farm recovered and I grew a fresh crop. But by then he'd changed. He'd . . . turned ugly. His whole life, he'd wanted more. It started out with aspirations, but after our fight, it turned to greed. He took to hating farmland. Farming was too humble, he decided, and the town of Fortune's Bluff too small. Irrelevant, he called it. He said he wanted enterprise. A proper city instead of farmland. He offered to buy the land from me and Clara."

"For community progress, fulfillment, and the betterment of all," Nitty recited. "The Snollygost motto."

Windle's face was grim. "The betterment of all, fiddlesticks. It's the betterment of the Snollygost Institute that Neezer's concerned with now. Which is why we told him no when he offered to buy the farm. It should've stopped there. But then he turned on Clara, who'd never stopped loving him or hoping the two of us would make our peace. He called her greedy for wanting to keep the farm for herself. He accused her—both of us—of never having loved him in the first place. After that . . ." He sighed. "I had no use for him at all."

Nitty thought about the mystery crop just beyond the front door, the only speck of green for miles, maybe even for states. "I'm glad you kept the farm. Even if it *was* the cause of the kerfuffle between you and Neezer."

"I was glad, too, in the beginning. While Neezer ran for mayor and built his institute, I brought in the best crop I'd ever had. But I paid a painful price for it." Windle's face darkened. "Clara grew heartsick over what had happened. Lillah wanted us to make amends, for Clara's sake. But I refused to keep trying. I couldn't trust the man Neezer had become, even if I missed the man he'd been. Then the first duster blew through, right at harvest-time. It destroyed my entire crop." His voice quieted into a whisper. "Clara's health was already failing, and the dusters ruined what was left of it. Lillah left town soon after Clara's passing. She said she wanted to see the world, that she needed to travel for her singing. She just wanted to be out from under the sadness of it all."

"Well . . . Neezer was wrong to turn on Clara. You were only trying to protect her, and the farm." Nitty's heart panged at the sorrow in Windle's eyes, so bottomless there seemed to be no end to it at all.

"I said plenty that was wrong, too, and I've no excuse for it."

"But you could've tried making amends again and it would've done no good at all."

"Could've. Would've. Should've." Windle's freckle stung fiercer than a wasp on his skin. "Three words full of wasted wishing. There was much I might've done besides insisting on my own rightness. Was my stubbornness worth the grief of what was lost? Seems to me that humility might've served me better than pride."

Nitty and Windle sat together for a long time after Windle

finished talking. When Nitty spoke at last, it was with the certainty that she could never bring even an ounce more suffering to Windle Homes, that she had to do what she could to protect him, and that this began with absolute and total honesty.

She swallowed. "Windle?"

"Hmmmm?"

"I have some dire confessions to make."

Windle's paintbrush eyebrows drew together. "I'm waiting."

Nitty sucked in a breath and, in a headlong rush of words, listed every last one of her wrongdoings. Running away from Grimsgate seemed the least offensive, so she began with that, then moved on to her thievery and Mag's escape from the noose.

"I did steal the seeds, but I didn't steal Mag so much as rescue her," Nitty cried as she finished. "Just like she rescued me! And you can hardly blame me, can you? When she was about to be murdered? When she was so magnificent and in such great need?"

She sank back on her cot after that and waited. What if Windle sent her out the door and into the throes of the wailing duster? What if she never saw her crop, or Mag, or Windle again? But no. She would not cry. She set her mouth and shoulders. Whatever judgment awaited her, she'd meet it with as much mettle as she could muster.

Windle stood. Nitty's heart galloped.

"It occurs to me," he said matter-of-factly, "that at this late hour, there is only one sensible solution before us."

"I'm prepared," Nitty responded bravely, although, perhaps

truly, being only ten and on the verge of possible exile, she was not.

"A decent dose of sleep," he pronounced. "Won't be worth a hill of beans come morning without it."

Nitty blinked. "But . . . you're not frightened, then? Of me being a criminal, that is?"

Windle harrumphed. "To bed with you."

He turned for his room then, not wanting to let on that he was *plenty* frightened. For something uncanny was happening to Windle Homes. When he'd first set eyes on Nitty and Mag, he'd feared keeping them. Now, for the first time, he feared losing them.

He gave a backward glance to the photo of Clara and Lillah before shutting his door. He hadn't been able to keep Lillah from leaving, or his Clara from dying. How, then, could he protect anyone?

He lay down and closed his eyes. His heart clattered. *Try,* it told him. *Just try.*

And back in the kitchen, on her cot, Nitty smiled. She understood what Windle couldn't say.

Windle wanted her and Mag to stay.

CHAPTER SEVENTEEN

IN WHICH MOONLIGHT BRINGS BLOSSOMING

It had been many years since the little farmhouse had felt like a proper home—many years since it had been filled with anything other than Windle's despair. On this night, though, as Windle made his unspoken promise to Nitty, a change swept over the farmhouse. No longer was it forlorn, or "lorn" of any sort. While Nitty and Windle slipped into sleep, a newfound warmth—some might even have called it the beginnings of love—swept through the little farmhouse, then wound its way from house to porch and beyond.

The milky goliath moon felt it, and drew nearer, sending the few remaining tawny-brown clouds scudding away. The stars felt it, and shone so mightily over the farm that it was bathed in a silvery glow. The earth felt it, and gave the bending green stalks above her an encouraging prod that straightened them up and shook the dust from their leaves.

The warmth twined and twirled itself around the green stalks of Nitty's mystery crop. It paused over the lantern-like, fuchsia buds, giving each the gentlest of coaxing caresses. Then, like newborn babies opening their eyes for the very first time to gaze upon the world, the buds began to bloom.

Nitty sat up in her cot as the first bud unfurled. It woke her with its unexpected whisper—a tiny but jubilant *Whee!* as if there were nothing better than to be born among starlight and moonshine in a field of emerald green.

Nitty heard the second bud unfurl and went to the door. The third and she was off the porch and running to the field. Never, in all of her life, had Nitty seen moonshine like this. Bright as daylight but the palest, prettiest of blues, it made everything look freshly washed and new.

She found Mag at the field's edge, strutting happily with her trunk tickling the stalks.

"I can see your mood's improved." Nitty laughed, standing on tiptoe to rub under Mag's chin. "And I'm glad to see it. So has mine."

All around them now, the soft cries of the flowers' delight filled the air.

Nitty crouched before one bud, watching it tremble in antici-pation.

"Come on, then," she whispered to it. "Come see the world." As she did, the lantern of petals burst open into a cloud of pinks. At the center of the flower hung a cluster of round, fuchsia . . . What were they exactly? Fruits? Berries? Vegetables? Nitty had never seen the likes of them before. Each was the size of a cherry, with a pink frond like corn silk hanging from its top. Whatever they were, they shone sumptuously in the moonlight. And what a scent they had! A fresh-baked-cookie, fresh-picked-strawberry sort of smell that warmed Nitty's heart.

She was sorely tempted to pick one and taste it. Mag, too, was exploring one of the clusters with her trunk.

"Do they smell as heavenly to you as they do to me?" Nitty asked her.

Mag bowed her head to Nitty's height, and Nitty stroked her trunk, looking deeply into Mag's left eye. She thought she saw a glimmer of delight there, as if Mag were just as excited by this turn of events as she was.

Then, curious and hopeful, they walked straight into the stalks together. The stalks, for their part, didn't seem to mind the intrusion in the least, and sprang back up the moment Mag's enormous feet passed.

Nitty spread her arms like wings as she walked, rustling the stalks with her fingertips. Green was everywhere and everywhere was green, glowing in the moonlight.

Before long, the two of them reached the middle of the field. Then, because at that moment Nitty couldn't think of a single thing she wanted to do more, she lay down. Her bare toes and fingers tickled pleasantly from the cool stalks cushioned beneath her.

Seconds later, there was a momentous rustling and sighing as Mag lay down beside her.

Above their heads, the stalks formed a canopy with the cascading stars. Their green blazed, and Nitty sucked in a breath. *What would it feel like,* she'd wondered when she'd stolen the seeds, *to be in the middle of all that green?* Now she knew beyond any doubt. It was like being inside an emerald.

Nitty plucked one of the strange-looking clusters from a nearby stalk and pulled off three of the mystery fruits. Just in the last minutes, the fruits had grown bigger, and they were now the size of small plums. As she pulled each one from its cluster, its silky tassel came off in her hand, leaving a star-shaped opening at the top.

She held one of them out to Mag. "What do you think?"

Without a second's hesitation, Mag took the fruit with her trunk and scooped it into her mouth. There was a pulpy crunching, followed by Mag's single, short trumpet of satisfaction.

The taste of the fruit stirred an instinctive memory in Mag's heart—one that didn't belong to her but to her ancestors before her. A memory of sweeping gold grass that tickled the belly. Of a sprawling savanna dappled with other animals— animals that seemed foreign but familiar all at once. Animals that shared the open space with one another, roaming, hunting, living, dying. Everything in balance. Every creature free. The fruit tasted like all these things.

Mag picked a second bundle of fruit from the field and gently set it in Nitty's lap.

"You want me to eat it?" Nitty asked.

Mag nudged the bundle encouragingly with the tip of her trunk.

Nitty raised the fruit to her lips. Now that the fruit was right under her nose, its scent was even more enticing.

Nitty took a bite, and a tangy sweetness burst over her tongue. The outer skin of the fruit was thin but crisp. The inside was juicy, tart, and pudding smooth all at once. Its flavor was like nothing she'd ever known—as if every flower and fruit in the world had melded into every cookie, cake, and chocolate. It tasted like a found family. Like green growing in desert dryness. Like a smile. It tasted like everything the world should have been but often wasn't. There was something else, too. Something she couldn't quite pin down.

Nitty laughed. She took another bite, and another. As she ate, a strange feeling came over her, until she felt like one of those fuchsia buds before they'd opened—pent-up and near to bursting with everything she'd kept bottled inside her for these many years. She untied her Gleam Jar from around her neck and set it carefully between her and Mag.

"I know you can't tell me what happened to you in the circus," she said to Mag. "You might not want to even if you could, and I can hardly blame you. There are some things I don't talk about either. Like what's in this jar." She tapped the lid and opened it. "There's not a soul on earth who's heard about it. But tonight I'd like to tell you, because . . ." She rubbed Mag's chin. "Because you're the first friend I ever had. And you're a mighty fine listener."

Beside Nitty, Mag raised her head. Her girl's voice was soft and warbly. A bird's voice. She liked listening to it. She gently traced the lid of the Gleam Jar with her trunk, spending some minutes smelling its contents. The scent of her girl—a wonderful fresh-grass, cool-dirt scent—covered the jar. There was the scent of salt and sadness, too—the scent of tears. Mag moved her trunk from the jar to her girl's cheeks, searching for tears but finding none. The tears on the jar were old, then, but they were also many. What had caused her girl such sadness, and what could she do to take it from her? She moved the tip of her trunk over the girl's hair, sweeping it from her forehead. Slowly she stroked her girl's hair and listened to her story. It wasn't in a language she could understand, but that hardly mattered, for she could hear the yearning in it all the same.

The first object Nitty took from the jar was the satin ribbon of robin's-egg blue. She set it in her palm, where it lay like a curl of captured sky. "This ribbon was tucked into my blanket when I was left at Grimsgate Orphanage." She brushed it against her cheek. "I believe my mama used to tie her hair back with this ribbon. She would've had luminous hair, Mama would've, the cool blue-black of a river at night. Mama is tiger tough, and she fought to protect me from hunger and wanting as long as she could. That's how she lost her ribbon. Fighting to protect me."

The second object was the daffodil-yellow button, smaller than a penny.

"This button I found buried in the yard at Grimsgate. My pa left it there for me to find. To bring me luck. He is a man who believes in luck and dreaming big. Until the day he buried it for me to find, he carried that button in his own pocket, hoping his luck would turn so he could keep me."

Nitty reached into the jar again and brought out the third object—the cardinal-red agate marble. "This marble belonged to my brother. The day I left Grimsgate, I saw it in a roadside ditch. He was so upset about me being left at Grimsgate, he up and dropped his favorite marble. He's an expert at shooting marbles."

Nitty held the marble up to the moonlight, and its center glowed, skittering fractured red light across her face and Mag's.

"They're made-up stories," she said softly. "Course I know that." It was the first time she'd ever said that aloud, and it made a sadness steal over her as she did. "I used to tell them before I came here, when I was lonesome. The more I did, the more they struck me as true, until I could barely tell the difference between what was true and what I wished to be true." She stroked the blue ribbon with her finger. "Only, lately, I haven't had much use for the stories. In fact"—she heaved a sigh—"they've been causing me all manner of grief and consternation. They're nothing but mirages playing tricks on me. But I wanted to tell you about them, before they're gone for good."

Even though Nitty had given it specific orders not to, her

voice disobeyed her by wobbling. Mag paused in her stroking of Nitty's hair, and Nitty pressed her face into Mag's trunk, holding on tight.

"Did your family make you promises? Back before the circus?" Nitty whispered to her. "I bet they did. I bet they would've done anything to keep you from chains, if they could've."

Nitty turned the Gleam Jar in her hands, and as she did, its contents caught the starlight, sending a shower of color across the ground. She thought about her mama and daddy. Had they made promises to each other? To her, back before they left her at Grimsgate? Had they promised to keep her safe and warm and fed? Had they promised to give her the best life they could? Had Twitch's mama made that promise to his little sister?

Though she fought it, a single tear leaked from one of her eyes. Before she could move to brush it away, Mag, with a caress as gentle as any mother's, did it for her.

"Maybe," Nitty said, "there are ways of keeping promises that don't make much sense." She sniffled, then gave a little laugh when Mag did the same. "I'll tell you what else. Elephant or person, I don't think anybody, if she's honest and true, ever means to break a promise."

Mag gave a *whoomph* of a sigh and took up stroking Nitty's hair again for a long stretch of minutes as Nitty stared up into the star-freckled dark. Mag couldn't say it aloud, but Nitty felt she understood. She leaned against Mag's mountain belly. Mag's pumpkin heart drummed a rich, faithful beat against her cheek.

"I've been thinking," Nitty whispered. "That we could be family. Together." She stilled, turning to Mag. "So do you . . ." Her pulse skipped. "Do you like the idea?"

Mag lifted her trunk to Nitty, and in the moonlight it looked to Nitty like a welcoming, open arm. Nitty tucked into it, fitting snugly and seamlessly against its curled warmth. Sleep soon slipped over them, and for the briefest twinkling in time, the two hearts beat in unison.

CHAPTER EIGHTEEN

IN WHICH FRUIT IS GIVEN A MOST UNUSUAL NAME

"Rats and darnation! We have sleuthing to do, and I find you sawing logs in the middle of a field?"

Nitty blinked her eyes open to see Twitch standing over her, hands on hips, one foot hammering the ground loud and fast as a woodpecker's peck.

"Quit your grousing, Twitch." She sat up beside Mag, who was already stretching her trunk toward more fuchsia fruit, perky and alert in the early-morning light. Gone were last night's clear skies, replaced with a sooty, mustard haze. "Can't you see we've got our crop?" She picked a piece of fruit, which had tripled in size overnight. She tossed it to Twitch, who caught it against his stomach with an *oof.*

Twitch coughed, and Nitty winced at the sound, wishing

she hadn't been so careless. It wasn't a pebbles-tumbling-under-water cough anymore so much as a barking rattle-rasp.

Twitch's cough was getting worse.

He raised his goggles, and he stared at the fruit. "It's as big as your head!"

"Well, are you going to try it or not?" Nitty said impatiently.

Twitch didn't hesitate another second. Pink juice dribbled down his chin in syrupy rivers. He took another bite and another. Then he plunked down beside Nitty and Mag. His eyes glistened, and he swiped at them quickly. Nitty guessed he didn't want anyone to notice, so she kept her eyes on Mag's trunk, which was snuffling the rest of the fruit in Twitch's hand.

"It tastes like Anna's tiny fist, curled around my finger. Like Pa coming home." He laughed softly, but the laugh soon turned into a cough.

"Eat more," Nitty encouraged, a notion taking shape in her head. The fruit seemed to have a delightful effect on her, and Mag couldn't seem to get enough of it either. Mightn't it help Twitch's cough?

Twitch was poised to take another bite when a sudden rustling in the field made them all turn.

Windle burst through the stalks with phrases like "What in blazes" and "Pachyderm trampling my crop," but stopped short at the sight of Nitty and Twitch, their mouths and chins bright pink, grinning amid the abundance of fruit. Nitty stood to place a piece of fruit in his hand.

"Morning, Windle," Nitty chirped, as if this were a perfectly ordinary day and there was nothing at all unusual about a pink, melon-sized mystery crop ripening overnight. "Have some fruit."

There were a great many things Windle might've done in this moment. He might've cried with relief at his strange but bountiful crop—the first crop he'd grown in years. He might've laughed at Nitty, Twitch, and even Mag, with their chins and cheeks dribbling with fuchsia juice. He might've whooped and hollered and bounded for joy at his farm returning to life after being buried, for so long, in dust. In his heart, in fact, Windle *was* doing all of these things. But because his boggled mind hadn't quite caught up with his rhapsodizing heart, he was only capable of taking the simplest, easiest action. Windle ate some fruit.

He chewed slowly, solemnly. Nothing about his expression gave the slightest hint at his thoughts.

Nitty held her breath.

At last Windle harrumphed. It was a different sort of harrumph, puny with crankiness but robust with joy. "Tastes like the sight of my sweet Clara sitting in her rocker. Like a little girl giggling, running through cornfields."

A remedy for a broken heart, Nitty thought. "Do you see?" She grinned, because she suddenly understood what it was about the fruit that she hadn't been able to pin down before. "It tastes like triumph, sure as can be."

Nitty waited for Windle to argue. He didn't. No one did. Because they were beginning to see. Every one of them.

"It needs a proper name," Twitch said then.

"Yes. For when we take it to town." Nitty's eyes met Twitch's in a moment of unspoken understanding. She'd thought, too, about the mountains of food in Snollygost General Store that no one could pay for, about Miz Turngiddy's list of names. She'd had the very same idea that she saw forming on Twitch's face now.

Nitty held a piece of fruit under her nose. She breathed in its blissful scent. Then it came to her—a name as unexpected and singular as the fruit itself. "Froozle. It's froozle fruit."

"Froozle's a fine name." Twitch grinned, bouncing on his toes.

"Who said anything about taking it to town?" Windle's eyebrows were flapping wings, dipping and diving.

"Well, of course we have to take it to town!" Nitty stared at Windle. "Everyone in Fortune's Bluff needs it. Right away. Then they don't have to worry over food they can't afford."

Windle said nothing, but a light flickered on in his eyes. His gaze swept the field, and as it did, the hazy sunlight caught the green stalks in just a certain way, until the stalks' tips seemed to be sweeping the very clouds above. A lightning bolt of realization struck Windle. He had grown a crop worthy of his younger, braver self. A crop worthy of the land and the town he'd once loved. What good did any crop do a farmer unless it was put to proper use? Crops were meant for harvesting. Meant for eating.

"I'll get the truck," he said.

CHAPTER NINETEEN

In Which a Farm Takes a Trip into Town

Windle's truck hadn't made it halfway down the main street of Fortune's Bluff when its occupants started staring.

Windle stared at the roof of the Palace Nickelodeon. Or, rather, he stared at the hole atop the nickelodeon where the roof had once been. He stared at the broken windows of the homes lining the street. Nitty and Twitch stared at a dozen streetlamps that were snapped in half or uprooted entirely.

"Last night's duster," muttered Windle, shaking his head as he stopped the truck across from the Snollygost General Store.

Twitch started to lift his periscope to his goggles to assess the damage, then stopped, seeming not to have the heart for it. Instead he turned his head toward the Snollygost Institute, with its ever-present *WHUMP.* "'Ten Ways to Be a Villain, number seven,'" he wheezed. "'If something or someone stands in your way, destroy it.'"

Nitty climbed down from the seat, making a mental list of all the damage within sight. A portion of her spirit sank in on itself, like a cake falling after a violent noise. So much of Fortune's Bluff was broken now. It was hard to imagine anything beyond its splintered roofs and shattered windows. But Nitty tried, and as she did, she remembered the triumph of the froozle crop. After some time, her shoulders straightened. "Well. It has to be fixed, of course. All of it. We can help."

"No point in that." Ferdinand Klempt appeared in the doorway of the Schnurrbart Emporium, hoisting the corner of a slumping walrus mustache. "It will only be blown to pieces again with the next duster." He bowed his head, his sagging mustache trembling woefully. "All is lost. Lost, I tell you."

Murmurs of assent rose from dozens of earmuffed folks around them. There were sighs, too, and mournful tears trailing down countless cheeks. No one made a move to start fixing. Instead the people of Fortune's Bluff were staring, their faces perfect portraits of misery.

Folks walking by who hadn't worked in years but still wanted to appear as if they had someplace important to go; children who'd been hungry for so long their bellies had given up rumbling; children who hadn't slept in months on account of their teeth rattling all night from the whumping at the Snollygost Institute; parents who cried each night for their hungry, teeth-rattled children. All, each and every one, stared at the hurts of Fortune's Bluff. The only movement was a collective flinching—painful to watch—that came with each relentless *WHUMP* reverberating from the bluff overlooking the town.

This is what giving up looks like, Nitty thought.

"Notice anything unusual?" Twitch whispered to Nitty then.

Nitty frowned. "Nothing is usual about this dismal predicament."

Twitch jerked his head toward the institute. "The only two buildings untouched by the duster? The institute and the general store." He bounced on his toes. "Coincidence? I think not."

"You're right." Nitty's thoughts whirled. "But we can't investigate that now. Not with everyone in this state." She turned to Windle. "Why isn't anyone doing anything?"

Windle's brow furrowed. "There are limits to what people can bear. And when there's too much broken for you to see any clear path to fixing—"

"You clear a path yourself," Nitty blurted, unwilling to accept any other answer. The question now was, What did the town of Fortune's Bluff need?

Verve and vim and courage, and a great many other things besides, Nitty thought. But right now, she only had one thing to offer.

She scooped a mound of froozle fruit into her arms. Out of the corner of her eye, she saw Twitch and Windle do the same.

She held out a piece to a dust-smudged little girl who barely came up to her knee. "For you."

The little girl hesitated just long enough to get a nod from her mother, then snatched the fruit and took a hearty bite. She giggled. "Tastes like chocolate."

Murmurs of curiosity and eagerness rose from the crowd, so Nitty didn't waste a second. "It's froozle fruit. Help yourselves. Take as much as you'd like. There's plenty."

She held out more fruit, and within moments her arms were empty. So were Twitch's.

From all around them came the crackling of crisp froozle fruit being bitten into, and then contented sighs and gasps of wonder.

"Tastes like a bubble bath," said an old woman.

"Tastes like the smell of a new baby," said a woman whose belly bulged beneath her skirt.

"Tastes like finding a job," said a man.

"Tastes like respect," said another.

Faces that, a few minutes before, had been ashen and dull suddenly brightened. Children who'd been wailing for food all morning now laughed at their hearty, satisfied belches. As folks ate their fill of fruit, they glanced about Main Street, seeming to take it in with a fresh eye. There was talk of getting hammers and nails and paint buckets to fix what had been torn away by the duster.

There isn't a single soul who should be forgotten, Nitty thought. *Everyone needs the froozle fruit.*

Which is why, when Nitty saw Bernice and Crispin watching from the doorway of the bakery, looking out at all the happenings with yearning but reluctant to endure stares or questions, she didn't hesitate. Tucking a melon-sized froozle fruit under each arm, she hurried toward the bakery before the Sighs could retreat entirely.

Crispin greeted her with his usual "Rain. Rain. Where's the rain? Salt, nimbostratus, flour, altostratus . . ." He worried the knobs of his rolling pin in his hands. "The Whirlybog whumps, makes the sky gust. The nose sings out, 'Blow! And turn all to dust.'"

Nitty tried making sense of what he'd said, but when she discovered she couldn't, and Bernice's cheeks were growing brighter with embarrassment with each passing second, she plunked the froozle fruit into Bernice's arms. "I brought you a new ingredient. For your bread."

Bernice frowned. "We're out of flour. Used the last of it yesterday."

Nitty searched her store of ideas, not ready to let this small problem stand in the way of bigger prospects. "In that case, maybe you can make froozle flourless bread."

"Flourless," Crispin mumbled. "Froozle." He lifted the fruit to his mouth and took a bite.

At Nitty's nod of encouragement, Bernice grudgingly did the same.

"Tastes like not having to scrub dishes or change diapers," Bernice mumbled. "Tastes like having fun again." She snorted her snort-laugh.

Nitty ventured a smile. Then she and Bernice both stared

as Crispin stopped trembling and gazed down at the froozle fruit. "Tastes like rain. And fresh, rising dough." He looked at Bernice. "Baking. Today is a fine day for baking."

He turned on his heel and disappeared into the bakery with the rest of the froozle fruit.

"I don't understand it." Bernice looked after him, mystified. "Just this morning he swore he'd never bake again."

Nitty shrugged. "Maybe he should take more care with his swears." She caught Bernice's eyes, and Bernice snort-laughed again, louder this time.

"Would you like to help hand out the rest of the froozle fruit?" Nitty asked. "It's probably not the best fun you've ever had, but—"

Bernice was two steps out the door before Nitty could finish, calling over her shoulder, "I'll help. Long as nobody says boo about Papa."

Soon Nitty, Bernice, and Twitch fell into a rhythm at the truck, passing the heaviest of the fruits through their arms and out to folks eager and waiting. The only person in the crowd who wasn't bustling for the fruit was Ferdinand Klempt, who was hanging back, wringing his hands.

"Aren't you going to take some?" urged Nitty, offering him a fruit that gleamed with fuchsia splendor.

"How can I possibly? My father would say a man without creative vision cannot eat. A man without a muse is too pitiful for food." He waved away the fruit.

Nitty wasn't ready to give up. "Mr. Klempt, I've had such

verminous language used against me, you'd scarce believe it. My spirit might've been reduced to a measly dust mote." Nitty looked him square in the eyes. "It wasn't. Because my spirit is my own."

"My father—" Ferdinand Klempt started, his voice cracking.

Nitty dangled a fruit before his eyes, holding it by its silken, fuchsia tassel. Ferdinand Klempt stared at the tassel, his eyes widening.

"My father—" He stopped. He touched the fuchsia tassel, testing its texture with his fingers. He held it over his upper lip. His eyes took on the light of sun breaking through clouds. He smiled, grabbing as many froozle fruits as he could carry, and hurried into the Schnurrbart Emporium, slamming the door behind him.

"Is he all right?" Nitty asked Windle.

Windle nodded. "He will be. It's been years since I've seen that look on his face."

"What does it mean?"

"It means the muse is upon him." Windle stared at the Schnurrbart Emporium for a long minute, then grumbled, "He'll want me to try some newfangled mustache of his before the week's out. Just you wait."

Nitty placed her hand on his arm. "And you will, won't you?"

Windle sighed. "I suppose I'll have to." He didn't seem nearly as disgruntled about it as he was trying to sound. In fact, Nitty could've sworn she saw him smile as he turned back toward the truck bed to give out more fruit.

Bernice, too, was smiling, albeit warily and mostly into the sleeve of her shirt. Twitch was the only one, Nitty noticed then, who was not smiling.

Twitch's eyes were fixed on the Snollygost General Store, where two shadowy figures stared out from the window. "It's Miz Turngiddy and Mayor Snollygost," he whispered. "And Neezer's not happy."

Nitty looked again at the figures in the window and saw that Twitch was right. Miz Turngiddy was scribbling frantically on her notepad, her head bobbing like a doll's that had come loose. Neezer's expression—dark, turbulent, unpredictable— bore all the signs of a brewing storm. In a heartbeat, his eyes registered Nitty's and the storm lifted.

"He's coming." Nitty straightened her shoulders and set her jaw as Neezer strode toward their truck with Miz Turngiddy close behind.

"And what sort of merriment do we have here?" he asked.

With the booming of Neezer's voice, each person took a step away from the truck. Except Windle, Nitty, Twitch, and Bernice. They stood, unmoving, before the crop.

"The sort of merriment that our town should have but never does." Twitch narrowed his eyes at Neezer.

"Windle," Neezer began again, ignoring Twitch entirely, "what is all this ruckus?"

"Nothing to turn anyone's tide," Windle said slowly. "Only sharing our harvest."

"What a harvest it is!" Neezer picked up a piece of froozle

fruit, turning it over and over in his hands. "I've never seen the likes of this before."

"No one has." Nitty raised her chin in pride. "It's froozle fruit."

"Unorthodox, to be sure." Neezer's smile made a wide stretch of piano keys. He tossed the fruit up and down in his palm. His nose whistled "Conquering Now and Still to Conquer," the same song Nitty had once heard Miz Ricketts humming as she'd locked Nitty in the Grimsgate attic.

"Try it," she challenged, holding fruit out to Neezer and Miz Turngiddy.

"This froozle fruit . . ." Neezer eyed it. "There is much we don't know or understand about it as of yet. It is a crop never seen before, much less consumed before."

"It does look delicious." Miz Turngiddy lifted her piece to her nose and breathed deeply. "And what an extraordinarily fast growing cycle! Why, just the other day, this fruit was no more than a bud. A study of its internal structure might—"

"Delicious?" boomed Neezer, drowning out Miz Turngiddy. "We shall see." He took a froozle fruit from Nitty, and then, using a pocketknife retrieved from his purple waistcoat, cut himself a hefty slice of fruit and promptly popped it into his mouth.

He chewed some long seconds, then bent over with sudden, violent coughing.

"Mayor Snollygost?" Miz Turngiddy hovered over his bowed form. "What is it, sir?"

Murmurs of "Is he all right?" and "He's choking" rustled through the townsfolk as Neezer gasped and gripped his throat. "My tongue. It's . . . swelling. Need . . . water."

A flurry of activity and alarm erupted on the street as folks scattered to fetch water, but it was Miz Turngiddy who was quickest, hurrying into the Snollygost General Store to return mere seconds later with a cup.

Neezer gulped down several swallows of water, then leaned against Windle's truck for support until his rasping breaths calmed. He mopped his brow with a handkerchief but waved away the worried inquiries of the folks surrounding him. "I'll . . . recover momentarily," he managed with what appeared to be some difficulty. "Fortunately, I took only the smallest bite. Anything bigger and . . ."

He coughed mightily, and every person on Main Street stilled. Every mouth ceased chewing. Every face paled. Except for Nitty's, Twitch's, and Bernice's. They were studying Neezer intensely.

"It's a ruse," Twitch hissed into Nitty's ear. "A sleight of hand. I saw him do it with my own eyes. . . ."

"What do you mean?" Nitty asked.

Twitch didn't have a chance to respond before one young mother stepped forward, blurting, "It made the mayor sick." Several others nodded in agreement. "Did you see?" The woman dropped her fruit to the ground, where it broke open, splattering froozle juice over the sidewalk.

Neezer waved a dismissive hand. "Now, now . . . no need for alarm. I'll be all right in due course . . . I'm certain." He did not, however, *sound* certain. He straightened with effort, trembling slightly, his eyes sweeping the crowd. "It's only the slightest dizziness now, and numbness of the fingers."

"Look what it's done to him. What if the fruit's poison?" someone in the crowd cried out. "No one should eat it."

"No! The fruit's perfectly safe to eat!" Nitty blurted. "Twitch, Windle, and I ate stomachfuls this morning, and we're fiddle fit as can be."

"How can you be sure?" one father asked, shielding his children from the truck full of fruit.

"I'm sure." Bernice took another enormous bite of fruit.

"Me too," said Twitch.

Nitty gave them grateful smiles.

Worried mutterings spread through the rest of the crowd, however, and Neezer weakly nodded in sympathy. "Caution is sensible, friends," he said, seeming to rally as several families, with sadness, returned their fruits to the truck bed. "Better to get your food from trustworthy sources, and right now the Snollygost store has the most delicious oranges."

"Trustworthy as toadstools and turnips," muttered Twitch, and then he marched up to Neezer, heaving accordion breaths as he went. "You didn't taste the fruit. It never even touched your lips. I *saw* you slip it up your shirtsleeve—"

"Come now, Angus." Windle put his hands on Twitch's

shoulders, steering him back toward the truck. Twitch was panting heavily. "Save your breath before you have an attack."

Nitty scrutinized Neezer's sleeves then, and she was sure she saw an unidentifiable lump under Neezer's left cuff. Her pulse clanged in her ears.

Neezer, who'd paid no attention to Twitch's outburst, breezed past them, directing people toward his store. He seemed nearly recovered, save for the tentative way he was walking and massaging his fingers, as if to alleviate their numbness. "This way, friends. Herein lies the familiar. The trusted."

"Wait!" Nitty hurried after people as they walked away from Windle's truck empty-handed. "Froozle fruit won't make you sick. Come back."

Most folks did not come back. Parents began inspecting their children's mouths and throats and asking how their bellies felt. There were a few—a very few—who still went home with fruit, but their jubilation was gone, replaced with worry. Out of the whole of Fortune's Bluff, it was only Crispin and Ferdinand, in the end, who returned to the truck to stand their ground.

Crispin, unusually clear-eyed and calm, declared, "I'll take as much of the fruit as you can spare." Then he locked eyes with Neezer in a gaze that Nitty could only interpret as one of sheer defiance.

"And I'll take the tassels," Ferdinand said. "If you've no use for them."

"Take however much you need" was Windle's encouraging response.

For one small second, Neezer couldn't mask his surprise and annoyance, but he quickly covered both up with a smile.

Nitty stared at his smug smile and felt she might explode in fury. "How could you do that? How could you take this away from them?"

Neezer seemed not to hear, already turning to leave with Miz Turngiddy, who was frowning, eyes downcast. Nitty picked up a piece of froozle fruit the exact size of Neezer's head. She contemplated throwing it at him. She smiled at the thought of how the froozle juice would run down his purple waistcoat, likely staining it beyond repair.

"Nitty." Windle's voice broke through her thoughts, sparing her the loss of her temper and Neezer the possible loss of his head. "It's best that we go."

"But—" She looked at Windle, and her protests fizzled. His eyes were telling her it was no use, that no one would be back for more fruit. Slowly she said goodbye to Bernice, Crispin, and Ferdinand.

"I'll keep a staunch lookout from the bakery," Bernice promised.

Nitty was too angry to take much encouragement from this, although she appreciated Bernice's dedication to their cause. She climbed into the truck bed beside Twitch and a mountain of leftover froozle fruit. "That—that splenetic rap-scallion!" she blurted as soon as the truck pulled away from the curb. "I'd just as soon eat slug pie as look at him!"

"Haven't I been saying as much this entire time?" Twitch

coughed, and she handed him a piece of froozle fruit. "I know he was hiding that slice of fruit in his shirtsleeve. I should've wrestled him to the ground to prove it."

"Couldn't any of them see they were being steamrollered?"

Twitch shrugged. "Fear blinds folks from lots of wrongs they should see."

Nitty wanted to argue that it should be easy to step over that fear, or leap over it, if need be. Still, she knew that it wasn't an easy thing, dealing with fear. If it were, Mag might not have been sentenced to hang, Twitch's pa might never have left for California, and the whole of Fortune's Bluff might never have been caught in this predicament in the first place.

"I tell you what," she said then. "And I don't need to consult your *Detective Comics* to know it either. Fear is the very worst villain of them all."

"That's the truth of it," Twitch agreed.

They rode the rest of the way home in silence, the uneaten froozle fruit that surrounded them smelling ripe with deliciousness, but also with missed opportunity.

⌐↑⌐

Mag was sliding another bunch of the delicious pink fruit into her mouth when her girl came back to her. She expected Nitty to run to her, as she usually did, trilling in that chirpy voice Mag liked, offering a chin rubbing, which Mag liked even better. This time, the girl was quiet, and slow to come to her, her head down. It was so unlike her girl that Mag dropped the fruit in alarm.

She nuzzled the girl's hand with her trunk, breathing in her scent. There was still a green-grassiness to it, but there was also the bitterness of anger and—she sniffed more deeply this time—sadness, too. Something was wrong.

Mag sounded a low rumble of concern, and then the girl burst into a flood of words. The words were hard and clipped, like stones clattering over stones. Mag didn't like the tone of them, because there was pain to them. It was the same kind of pain she'd smelled yesterday, when the boy Twitch had come upon the small wooden trough in the barn.

Mag had gone to that trough because its scent had at first confused and then troubled her. It was not a hay or water scent, like the other troughs Mag had known. This trough held the milky-sweet scent of a baby—a human baby. It was a faint scent, an old one, and one that was tinged with sickness. The baby had been ill, and it hadn't been near the trough in a long time.

Now Mag wondered if her girl's sadness had to do with that trough, too.

Her girl began pacing, her voice louder, and Mag grew worried.

She'd seen pacing like that before. The lion had paced like that, in his cage, back at the big top. He'd paced day and night—restless, angry, not having anywhere to go or knowing what else to do.

Maybe her girl didn't know what to do now either.

Mag wanted to help. She thought of that trough, with its milky scent. She thought of filling it with something that might bring her girl comfort. Something that might make her girl's voice chirp happily, like before. She turned to the field and picked several of the biggest clusters of flowers that she could find. She pressed a cluster into her girl's arms.

At first her girl spoke, her tone rising in surprise, but then Mag slowly led her to the back corner of the barn, where the trough sat in shadow. Mag laid her flowers in the trough and waited. Her girl hesitated, then nodded. Slowly, quietly, her girl sat down beside the trough and laid her flowers in its bottom. She set the trough to a gentle rocking. Her girl's voice turned singsongy. It wasn't bird-chirp happy, but instead was whisper-soft and soothing.

Mag felt a rightness in what they'd done, and she stayed there with her girl for some time.

When at last she snuffled her girl's palm again, this time her girl answered the snuffle with an ear rub. Mag smelled some of the anger lifting from the girl's skin.

Mag offered her trunk, and her girl sat down in its curl, swinging. The evening wore on, but Mag didn't tire.

When her girl slid into sleep, Mag laid her down on a pile of hay and stood nearby to keep watch. It was only when the man Windle came in quietly to find the girl that Mag stepped aside. The man lifted her sleeping girl and gently carried her to the house.

He was the only one Mag would've let take her.

He wanted to protect her as much as Mag did. She sensed it in his strong, tree-bark scent, and in the low, rumbling tones of his voice—not threatening, but guarding. As long as he had care of her girl, Mag, at last, would sleep.

CHAPTER TWENTY

IN WHICH A TOWN AND AN ELEPHANT ARE PROPERLY INTRODUCED

Fear is a powerful oppressor, to be sure, but it is safe to say that, in all of history up to this point, fear had never encountered the irresistible allure of froozle fruit. All that night and into the next morning, the thoughts of the folks of Fortune's Bluff were consumed with that beautiful fuchsia bounty. For those who had tasted the fruit, its sweetness lingered on their lips, making them smile when they otherwise might have frowned. Those who had not yet tasted it saw the smiles on the faces of those who had and wished they had tasted it themselves.

As the hours passed and night turned to day, it became obvious that eating the fruit caused no ill effects. It was not poisonous. It was edible, delicious, and, in fact, exactly what the folks of Fortune's Bluff needed after so many long and cheerless years.

Which is why it was not at all surprising that at eight o'clock the next morning, Nitty opened the Homes door to find Crispin, Bernice, and the troop of little Sighs standing on the front porch. What *was* surprising was that Crispin didn't utter a single word or rhyme about rain.

Instead he smiled shyly and, with steady hands free of trembles, offered Nitty a perfectly fresh, crisp loaf of fuchsia bread. It was still warm.

"For you," he said, "in thanks."

"But I thought you had no more flour," Nitty said.

"We don't." Bernice's voice was airy light. She shrugged. "Turns out when we used froozle fruit in the recipe, we didn't need any."

The tantalizing smell of the bread reached Nitty's nose, and her mouth watered. "It looks delicious."

"Try it," Bernice blurted impatiently, an uncharacteristically optimistic grin spreading on her face. Before Nitty could do it herself, Bernice broke off a piece for her.

The bread zinged in Nitty's mouth, the perfect blend of cozy doughiness and tart froozle sweetness. "That . . . is some bread," she said. "A mouthful of mellifluousness."

That made Bernice giggle, which was so surprising that it brought Windle to the door.

"The Sighs brought us fresh bread." Nitty gave him a piece, and soon everyone was sitting on the porch, eating bread in companionable contentment. Everyone, that is, except Mag, who up until that point had been dozing with the chickens, horses, and cows in the barn.

When the scent of the bread reached her trunk, she ambled out from the open barn door, shaking roosting chickens from her head as she went, her trunk lifted playfully, following the trail of the scent.

"Magnolious!" the younger Sighs cried jubilantly, and they shrieked with delight when Nitty offered Mag a piece of bread and the elephant popped it into her mouth, then gave a short trumpet of satisfaction. Seeming to enjoy the attention, Mag soon settled herself into the dirt below the porch and rolled in it, spraying herself with a dirt shower that made the children laugh even more. Several of them sprang off the porch and ran to Mag, who happily lay there as they rubbed her ears and trunk.

Bernice was the only one who hung back, looking torn between longing to join in the fun and wanting to stay near Crispin in case he needed her.

"Ride her today," Nitty said. "Won't you?"

Bernice's eyes lit, but then she glanced at Crispin, doubtful.

Crispin, who'd been deep in conversation with Windle over the many culinary qualities of froozle fruit, smiled at Bernice. "Go on," he said steadily. "Have some fun for a change."

That was that. Nitty didn't wait for Bernice to hesitate, but instead pulled her from the porch toward Mag, as Bernice laughed in spite of herself. The other Sigh children looked on in awe and not a little jealousy as Nitty climbed onto Mag's neck, then helped Bernice up in front of her. There was a moment when Bernice gasped as Mag rose to her feet, but after Mag settled into a steady, plodding walk, Bernice relaxed and even ventured a tentative rub of Mag's ear.

The three of them took several turns around the froozle field. At some point during the ride, Nitty noticed that Twitch had arrived with Mrs. Higgler and was helping himself to a sizable hunk of bread and reading one of his comics aloud to the other Sighs. She called out to him that his turn with Mag was next, but Mrs. Higgler put a stop to that idea instantly, on account of the fragility of Twitch's lungs. Then Mag's chickens took to missing their perch, and they squawked and fussed until Mag came to a stop in front of the coop and knelt for Bernice and Nitty to climb down.

"What did you think of the ride?" Nitty couldn't resist asking.

Bernice stood, silent for a moment, watching as the chickens flew to Mag. She shook her head. "The ride was bumpy. But . . ." Her sulky mouth gave in to a smile. "Your elephant is great."

Nitty gazed up at Mag, whose ears, head, and trunk were covered in a fluttering, fluffing headdress of chickens. Yes, Mag was most certainly great. Not great because she befriended chickens, or because she offered rides to lonely, angry girls, or even because she showed a promising fondness for decent books. She was great because she was Mag—the elephant who'd carried Nitty through a dust storm, who'd planted the seeds of the greenest crop Nitty had ever set eyes on, who'd brought her to Windle Homes.

As for Mag, she was thinking that there was nothing greater than being an elephant covered in birds, standing near the girl she loved. She pressed her trunk into her girl's palm, breathing in her green-grass scent. There was a honeyed happiness about her girl today, so different from the sadness of yesterday, and Mag felt a relief at it. She remembered how rarely she'd smelled happiness on the other animals of the circus. Mostly they'd smelled prickly with pain or sadness. Mag hadn't been able to help those animals with their suffering. But she was here, helping her girl. She blew a blast of air against her girl's hair, just to hear her bird-chirp laughter, and was about to do it again when she felt a low vibration under her feet. Her ears perked, and she listened. Her girl stilled beside her, and Mag knew she heard it, too.

It was the echoing racket of a line of automobiles and wagons on the horizon, heading toward the farm. Nitty placed her hand against Mag's side, and together they watched the procession advance.

"What's this now?" Windle asked as the unusual parade came to a stop beside the froozle field.

Crispin walked over. "Seems half of Fortune's Bluff is paying you a visit." He wrung his hands, which gave the briefest tremble, the only one they'd had all morning.

Windle's brow zigzagged with worry. "What do you propose we do with your elephant?" he asked Nitty.

Nitty thought on this for a long minute. She thought on this as she watched Mag playing hide-and-seek with the Sighs, tapping them with her trunk when she found them hiding behind the corn crib and the plow. She thought on Mag, and the good she'd already brought Fortune's Bluff by helping to sow the seeds for the froozle-fruit crop. She thought on the fact that Miz Turngiddy, and surely Neezer, too, knew about Mag now. What would be the purpose of keeping her hidden? Maybe it was time to let Fortune's Bluff meet Mag.

Nitty went to her. "What do you think? It'll be a hullabaloo, no question. But they won't harm a hair on your head. I swear it. And if they can brave meeting you, maybe they'll learn to brave Neezer as well."

Mag swung her trunk up and down and offered a brief *Brrt!* as if to say she was of exactly the same mind and that a hullabaloo—if it was a happy one—was in tall order. Then she moved off toward the froozle field, not an ounce of uncertainty in her purposeful step.

"I propose we give Mag a proper introduction," Nitty said to Windle. "You'll be called on to converse. Quite a lot, by the looks of it."

"Jumbling Jehoshaphat," Windle mumbled reluctantly.

"Jumping." Nitty grinned as Windle harrumphed.

"There's not enough well water to brew coffee," he said. "And we don't have any food to offer."

While Nitty thought on this, her eyes fell on Mag, who at that moment was curling her trunk around one especially large froozle fruit. Mag squeezed, crushing the fruit and letting its liquid run into her mouth.

"That's it!" Nitty went to Mag and proudly patted her chin. "Mag has the simplest solution. She'll crush some fruit for us to make juice."

"Yes." Windle nodded, fortified. "Juice. We'll make do with that."

Mrs. Higgler turned toward the house. "I'll slice up some of the fruit for everyone, too," she said, stepping inside.

"And we have my bread," added Crispin.

"We should leave," Bernice said to Crispin then, her expression suddenly full of its old wariness. "I won't have them gossip over Papa," she whispered to Nitty. "And nobody will want us here."

"*I* want you here." Nitty squeezed her hand. "Stay." She nodded toward Mag, who was in the field crushing fruit as Windle collected the juice in a pitcher. "Besides, what are a few snakeskins next to a bona fide elephant?"

Bernice opened her mouth but found she couldn't argue with that. And then she lost the chance to argue altogether, because Ferdinand Klempt was leaping out from one of the automobiles, waving brilliantly fuchsia mustaches. "I've done it! I've done it! Behold the beauty!"

He ran to Twitch first, pulled what little remained of

Twitch's failing corn-silk chevron from his face, and stuck a full, lustrous pink handlebar mustache in its place. Twitch immediately hurried inside to show Mrs. Higgler while Ferdinand ran to the Sigh children next. He stuck them each with a mustache, laughing jovially as he did.

"Froozle mustaches for all!" he hollered.

Windle wagged a warning finger at Ferdinand when it was his turn, but Ferdinand was undeterred. "Windle Homes, you are a true and loyal friend who is in need of a mustache that mirrors the greatness of your spirit." He planted the mustache on Windle's upper lip and an enthusiastic smack of a kiss to each of Windle's cheeks. "Enjoy! Enjoy!"

"It does give you a daring air," Twitch said to Windle with a grin as he stepped onto the porch alongside Mrs. Higgler. He held a plate of froozle-fruit slices, which Nitty set out for the incoming guests next to the pitcher of froozle juice.

"Like a knight errant," Nitty seconded. "Though the effect would be improved by a sword and armor."

"Humph" was Windle's response to that, but it was the most half-hearted *humph* Nitty had ever heard.

It was at this moment that Mag, who'd been watching Ferdinand's mustache distribution with some interest from the shelter of the froozle field, burst from the towering green stalks and, with an excited bugle from her trunk, announced her presence to the crowd of folks just arriving.

Ferdinand turned, took a long, wide-eyed look at Mag,

then clapped his hands in delight. "Froozle fruit and elephants. Windle Homes, just how many marvels have you stowed away on this farm?"

Windle humphed again. "That's the whole of it." He paused, considered, then added, "That I know of. For now."

As Ferdinand beamed up at her, Mag wasted no time in taking the remaining mustaches from his hands and setting them all atop her head in a hairpiece of sorts.

"A magnificent coiffure for a magnificent creature!" Ferdinand cried gleefully. "Just so."

Without further ado, he hurried to his automobile for more mustaches. Meanwhile, a dozen other folks walked tremulously toward the Homes front porch, eyeing Mag and the froozle field with both cautiousness and expectation.

"Would you look at that crop!" a handful whispered. Many more whispered, "Would you look at that elephant!"

Nitty stood protectively at Mag's side, ready to defend her if anyone should so much as blink at her askance.

Mag raised her trunk, taking in the scents on the air. She lifted her ears, listening to these people's voices. Their tones were hesitant but also curious. She heard no blame in the tones, no anger. Her ears relaxed. She nuzzled her girl's neck with her trunk to let her know that all was well.

Nitty, taking the nuzzle as a vote of confidence, led Mag nearer. "If you'll offer it, she'd be pleased to snuffle your hand," she encouraged folks. "Even more pleased with a rub to her trunk. And if you've come for froozle fruit . . ." She smiled. "The field is full as full can be. Take as much as you want."

Relief passed over the faces of everyone present. There were plenty of people who greeted Mag then, and Nitty and Mag both were gratified to see their smiles and hear their laughter. Afterward, people took to the field, picking bundles of froozle fruit and filling aprons, arms, and pockets with as much as could be carried.

As folks harvested the fruit, Mrs. Higgler and Windle moved among them, offering froozle juice, while Crispin shyly followed, offering up his bread. Some initially eyed Crispin and his bread with suspicion, but then, as these few nibbled their fruit, suspicions eased into tentative friendliness. A few others persisted in refusing Crispin's bread entirely. These misguided souls, Nitty noted, were met with such vehement glares from Bernice that even they eventually offered Crispin polite, if not entirely comfortable, nods.

Folks whiled away the minutes eating fruit and talking, mostly about possibilities. Aspirations folks hadn't thought about in years burbled fresh in their minds, and a restful peace settled over the farm, as if each person there had been reassured, in some unspoken way, that all that was amiss could still be set right.

Nitty spent her time keeping close watch over Mag, making sure she was treated with the utmost respect and gentleness.

Mag felt the joy resonating in the air and heard the laughter of the children, and she, too, felt joyful. Her girl, she sensed by her scent, was happy, and the bustling, boisterous mood about the farm, though noisy, was different from the harsh chaos of the circus tent. Eventually she grew tired, and then she lay down in the midst of the froozle field and let the chatter around her fade into the background.

Everyone else, seeming to understand, left her alone there.

By then, morning had stretched lazily into afternoon, and everyone, young and old, had eaten their fill of froozle fruit and had enough to bring home to last them for days. Nitty smiled from her perch on the front porch, taking in the view. Crispin, Windle, and Ferdinand stood at the field's edge, cheerfully debating which of the froozle fruit's qualities—its pulp, its flavor, or its tassels—was the best. Mrs. Higgler sat on the porch steps with Bernice, sipping froozle juice and braiding Bernice's hair, as the other Sigh children rough-and-tumbled about their feet. Mrs. Higgler spoke to Bernice in low, soft tones, and a comfortable calm came over Bernice's face. Bernice, Nitty suspected, was warming to the notion of being mothered again, even if it was only for a little while.

Everywhere Nitty looked she saw contentment. So much so that it was on the tip of her tongue to declare the day a definitive success, until Twitch came bursting from the froozle field, goggles pulled down about his neck, panting and calling her over.

"Neezer's here," Twitch choked out as he pulled her into the field where no one else could hear. "I saw him. Just now."

Anger welled in Nitty as she remembered Neezer's behavior in town the day before. He'd already tried to turn folks against the froozle fruit. Did he have to ruin today's fun as well? "What's he doing?" Nitty asked.

"Leaving now, from the looks of it." Through a break in the froozle stalks, Twitch pointed into the distance toward the field's far edge, and Nitty could just make out the flash of Neezer's purple waistcoat as he climbed into his automobile and drove away, kicking up a cloud of dust as he went. "But he's been nosing about." Twitch frowned. "Likely masterminding sabotage."

"Sabotage!" Nitty repeated, disbelieving.

"Sabotage, to be sure." Twitch nodded soberly. Then he pulled a folded paper from his back pocket, and a mischievous glint shone in his eyes. "While Neezer was snooping around the froozle field, I did my own snooping. In his motorcar. And I found *this*."

"You stole something from his car?" Nitty was both impressed and worried by the idea.

"Borrowed. I'll sneak it back into the general store next time I'm there with Ma. I'll make it look like he dropped it. I'm always thinking one step ahead of him, outwitting him, see?" He grinned, then unfolded the paper and laid it flat on the ground. "It's a map of Fortune's Bluff, but that's not all. . . ."

He pointed to a dozen penned *X*s on the map.

Nitty took a closer look. "The *X*s are marked on buildings. The Palace Nickelodeon, the bakery, Ferdinand's emporium—"

233

"All buildings that were damaged by dusters," Twitch said victoriously. "More and more, it looks like those dusters were planned. Doesn't it?"

"Twitch." Before, she hadn't been sure what to make of his theory, but after yesterday it seemed possible, and the thought dampened her fine mood. What dampened it more, however, was the darkening of the horizon not more than fifteen minutes later.

"I told you so." Twitch jabbed a finger at the sky. "Sabotage."

Nitty frowned. "It *is* an unusually convenient coincidence. I'll warrant that."

Just then Windle called for them, and Nitty and Twitch met him on the porch, where he was worriedly taking in the rusty cast of the sky. "Let's help everyone get on their way before the duster hits."

Nitty didn't need to be told twice. She and Bernice were off the porch and helping folks load up babies and froozle fruit even as the wind turned from a breeze to a blow. Twitch was hurried away by Mrs. Higgler, who was pouring such copious amounts of Mr. Moop's tonic down his throat as they departed that Twitch could scarcely gurgle out a farewell.

There wasn't time for any proper goodbyes or well-wishes as folks turned their automobiles back toward Fortune's Bluff, but at least, Nitty knew, there had been time to fill bellies beforehand.

Bernice and the Sighs were the last to leave. Bernice approached Nitty with an uncommon shyness.

"That braid looks so picturesque on you, Bernice," Nitty announced.

Bernice blushed and scoffed all at once. "Won't last the day around Verna," she said as the baby yanked one of its tendrils loose. "But it's tolerable." She kissed the top of Verna's head, and Nitty saw how much she loved the baby, even as she groused about her.

Her pulse gave a sudden, expectant quiver. It struck her that, in the fading light, Bernice's hair was the blue-black of a river at night. And Bernice was tiger tough, fighting to protect the smallest Sighs, even though it was a job she might never have wished for. Nitty glanced down at her Gleam Jar, hung about her neck, and at the ribbon of robin's-egg blue curled at its bottom. She hadn't yet given up carrying the jar around, because she'd been waiting for the right moments to empty its contents. The jar's treasures had seen her through much, and they deserved new owners worthy of them. She unscrewed the lid, slipped her hand into the jar, and ever-so-gently lifted the ribbon from it.

Maybe it hadn't belonged to Nitty's *own* mother, but it could still belong to one, all the same. And wasn't that what Nitty had always wished for, besides? That the ribbon, button, and marble belong to a real, flesh-and-blood family? She held the ribbon out to Bernice.

"You could use it to tie your hair back, if you wanted. To keep it free from Verna's pulling," Nitty said softly.

Bernice looked to be on the verge of snorting, but she hesitated. "Pretty things aren't of any use to me."

Nitty laughed. "Well. How about if its use is just being yours? You wouldn't have to share it with anybody else."

Bernice's face turned eager at that. "One thing . . . that's just mine," she murmured.

Nitty nodded. "I think it suits you, too."

Bernice's eyes lingered over the ribbon for a long moment. Slowly she lifted it from Nitty's palm and tied it into her hair. A gradual smile spread over her face, and she turned to watch Crispin tickling the other children as they piled into the Tin Lizzie. "I haven't seen Papa this peaceful in ages." She grabbed Nitty in a quick hug, then jumped into the car, muttering "Thank you" before slamming the door shut.

Nitty grinned as the Sighs drove away, and kept on grinning as she took Mag to the safety of the barn, planting a kiss on her trunk as she did. She was still grinning later as, from her cot, she heard Windle tiptoe to the kitchen table. She pretended to sleep, but opened one eye a crack to see Windle seated before the photo of Clara and Lillah, a pen scratching across the paper under his hand. After all this time, Windle was writing a letter to Lillah. Which meant, Nitty suspected, that he finally had something worth sharing. Maybe something about the froozle fruit, or Mag. Maybe something about *her*. This, above all else, kept the grin on Nitty's face.

Even the duster that howled over the farm in the next hours couldn't dampen her mood. She—the contagion, the evil eye, the selfish, scrappy thing—had helped folks with her froozle fruit. She—Nitty Luce—*had* done good.

CHAPTER TWENTY-ONE

IN WHICH FRIENDS AND FOES COME TO BLOWS

The next morning, when Nitty sat up in her cot, she was greeted by a world smothered in dust. The windowpanes were layered in dirt so thick that the inside of the house was steeped in midnight shadows. A single shaft of light broke through one windowpane, and Nitty saw Mag's trunk on the other side of the glass, wiping at the dirt with a rag.

"Your elephant makes fine work of cleaning," Windle said.

Nitty opened the window, sending down a rain of dirt, and tickled Mag's trunk. "Good morning, girl," she whispered. Mag snuffled her palm in answer.

Nitty turned to Windle, who was busy sweeping foot-high mounds of dirt from the kitchen out the front door. Inches of fine rust-colored silt piled in every corner of the house. Beyond the open door, Nitty saw that the froozle field was still there, but the old corn crib and windmill were not.

"The well's bone-dry," Windle said softly, coming to stand beside her. "The storm yesterday blew the windmill to bits, and our water's gone."

"It'll be all right, won't it?" Nitty said. "Mag can crush more fruit for froozle juice. We'll fill pitchers with it first thing this morning. We can drink that."

"For now, but not forever. Fortune's Bluff is likely worse for the wear this morning, too."

Nitty stiffened as she imagined an even more tattered Fortune's Bluff than the one she'd seen two days before.

"At least folks have the froozle fruit now."

"Froozle fruit may stave off hunger, but it can't stop dusters." His voice was low and tired. "And there's no telling how much more Fortune's Bluff can survive."

Nitty wanted to argue but found she couldn't. Not this time. There was too much truth in his words. She'd seen it with her own eyes already. Beyond the froozle field lay a bleak landscape, brown and desolate. The world had grown drearier, and the cheery atmosphere of yesterday's froozle harvest suddenly seemed impossible to recollect.

Nitty spent most of the day working to clear the house of dust, but it seemed a bootless and never-ending task.

It was well on afternoon when she dumped the final mound of dirt into the yard, and that was when she spotted Mrs. Higgler hurrying down the lane, a kerchief pressed to her eyes. She called to Windle, who met the crying Mrs. Higgler just as she reached the porch.

"What's wrong, Rachel?" Windle asked her. "Is Angus ailing?"

"He's—he's home in bed with a fever again," Mrs. Higgler stammered, shaking her head. "But that's not why I'm here." She glanced up, her eyes red with tears. "Mayor Snollygost himself stopped by our house just now." Her voice cracked. "He's demanding total payment immediately on all loans. On store credits, too."

"What?" Windle's face paled to birch white. "But . . . there's not a person in Fortune's Bluff who can pay."

Mrs. Higgler nodded, crying softly again. "He says that anyone who can't pay will forfeit and their land will belong to Snollygost."

Windle scratched violently at the freckle behind his ear. "Why would he have a hornet in his hat over this now?"

Mrs. Higgler could only dab at her eyes with the handkerchief, shaking her head.

Windle sighed. "Come inside," he said at last. "We'll talk it over." Together, the two adults stepped into the house.

Nitty had a mind to run to Twitch's place straight off, but stopped herself, thinking that if he had a fever, it was best to leave him to his rest. Worrying over this wouldn't do his lungs a bit of good. Instead she tried to distract herself by taking up a game of hide-and-seek with Mag in the froozle field.

Mag trudged to the middle of the field as Nitty counted to

one hundred, and then waited, still as a statue, for Nitty to find her. Nitty never let on that Mag's head cresting the tops of the froozle stalks was a dead giveaway. What would've been the fun of that? Instead she made a big to-do over calling Mag's name and searching all around the barn and porch for her.

The first few attempts, the chickens found Mag well before Nitty, flapping topsy-turvy through the field to perch on Mag's back and squawk her whereabouts. But when the chickens tired of playing, Mag peeked the tip of her trunk above the field and, every few minutes, gave a clipped, tooting call, as if to hint at her hiding spot.

When it was Nitty's turn, she hardly offered any sort of contest, for when Mag gave chase, the elephant's pursuit was so loud, with pounding feet and excited trumpeting, that Nitty couldn't quit giggling.

Mag had just found Nitty hiding behind the barn door when, suddenly, she swung her head in the direction of the froozle field. Her ears lifted to attention as she listened intently, and then, after prodding Nitty with her trunk to follow, she took off resolutely for the far end of the field.

"What is it?" Nitty ran to catch up with her. But she soon heard the answer in Twitch's telling wheeze. He was crouched low among the froozle stalks, goggled and wearing an absurdly large suit jacket and fedora, along with Ferdinand's fuchsia mustache over his cheesecloth mask.

"What do you think?" He cocked his hat to one side, and it promptly slid down over his left eye. This caused his goggles and cheesecloth mask to slip, too, until his getup was in complete disarray. "Is my disguise convincing?"

"Twitch!" she hissed as he yanked her into the shelter of the stalks. "You're supposed to be sick in bed!" Without his goggles and mask on, Twitch looked sick, for certain, and Nitty was alarmed to hear his breath coming so short and fast.

Twitch, however, was impervious to her worry. "Nah. Detectives don't catch fevers. They catch outlaws." He muffled a cough in the sleeve of his jacket, then thrust a bundle into Nitty's hands. "Here. Put these on over your clothes. But take care. Ma will have your head if you tear her best Sunday dress."

Nitty held up a long blue lady's dress and a black-veiled pillbox hat. "Why am I putting these on?" she asked as she slid the dress over her clothes.

"Because . . ." Twitch glanced around, checking to make sure they weren't being overheard. "We're going undercover. When Neezer left our house, he drove straight to the old dried riverbed across the way." He nodded across the flat land that stretched from the Homes farm to Fortune's Bluff. In the middle of it, marked by the smallest outcropping of withered scrub brush, was a speck that Nitty could only assume was Neezer's motorcar. "His motorcar's trunk was full of mason jars, like the ones we saw him with at the Snollygost General Store. So full it wouldn't shut and was tied closed with twine. I saw it all from my bedroom window." He was so twitchy now that he was hopping from one foot to the other. "We have to find out what's in those jars, and then we've got to get to the Snollygost Institute."

Tiny droplets of fever sweat were forming on Twitch's forehead, and Nitty didn't like the glassiness of his eyes. Mag didn't seem to either. She was shifting from foot to foot, dabbing at his forehead with her trunk, sending small puffs of air across it. "Maybe we should wait till another day—"

"There is no other day. Ma took me to town this morning to see Doc Grant, and there wasn't a soul shopping at the Snollygost General Store. Mr. Klempt told me it's been empty two days now. Ever since we brought that truckload of fruit into town."

Nitty's heart was lifted by this news about the Snollygost General Store, but only for a fleeting moment. "So," she said, her face heating with anger, "no one is buying Snollygost's goods anymore, and he's going to make everyone pay."

"He's not either, because we're going to stop him. Today." He stood, then wobbled unsteadily for a moment before straightening. "We'll have him on the lam in no time."

Nitty looked at Mag, wishing she could give a sign of approval for the mission. Instead, Mag only warbled, soft and concerned, her trunk hovering protectively around Twitch. "I can't let him go alone," Nitty whispered to her. "You know that. And you know you can't come along. You keep watch here, all right?" Nitty pointed toward the house. "Go on."

Mag hesitated, offering a few snorts that sounded to Nitty like protests. Finally, after touching her trunk to each of their foreheads, Mag turned for the house.

The two detectives set out for the riverbed, eyes fixed on the target in the distance. "Onward," Twitch wheezed as they went, "to face the foe."

⸙

Facing the foe, as Nitty soon discovered, involved a good deal of lying facedown in the dirt. They'd walked a decent portion of the distance to the riverbed, but then Twitch had dropped to his belly, arguing they needed to shimmy the rest of the way.

"So as to remain unseen. Maintain our anonymity at all costs." Twitch explained this in halting whispers. Halting because of his wheezing, but also because when a body is facedown on the ground, it is extremely difficult to talk without ingesting mouthfuls of dirt. "Observe the skill with which I make my noiseless approach."

Nitty waited as Twitch wriggled across the ground. She observed two things: His approach was as skilled as a madcap three-legged lizard's. His approach was as noiseless as a harmonica played through a megaphone.

Nitty believed it was only because Neezer's nose was whistling "Buckin' the Wind" with as much vigor as Twitch's lungs were wheezing that they were able to go unnoticed. In fact, she heard Neezer's nose long before she saw his person. His motorcar sat at the crest of a small embankment flanked by pitiable bushes and tumbleweeds.

It wasn't until Nitty caught up to Twitch where he hunkered, behind the largest of the pitiable bushes, that she spotted Neezer down in the riverbed. Mason jars sat at his feet, and he held one in his hand. In the cradle of his other arm he held a brass contraption that Nitty recognized as looking uncannily like a euphonium.

She elbowed Twitch. "That's the Wind Whiffler! From the store's broom closet!"

Twitch nodded with an air of exasperation, as if he'd figured that out some time ago. Nitty, though irritated, decided now was not the time to say anything to him about it, as they seemed on the cusp of some significant discovery. Instead she lay down beside him, focusing her attention on Neezer.

There was an air of merriment to Neezer's demeanor as he scanned the sky, then stuck a finger in his mouth and held it up to the air, turning it this direction and that.

"Feels like a breeze today," Neezer said to himself. "Or, better yet, a blow or even a strong gust." Neezer opened the mason jar and set it on the ground, then positioned the Wind Whiffler directly over it. The Whiffler's bottom spout fit perfectly over the jar's opening.

"What is he doing?" Nitty whispered.

Twitch jabbed a finger to his lips for quiet.

Minutes passed, and Nitty's right shin took to itching something awful, but she dared not scratch it for fear the movement would incur Twitch's wrath. Then, suddenly, she felt it.

The slightest tickle of a breeze across her cheek. At the same moment, Neezer pushed the Whiffler's red button. A familiar *sssslurp!* sounded from the contraption as bits of fine dust from the air were sucked into its funneled top. When the breeze died abruptly, Neezer turned off the Whiffler and, quick as lightning, snapped a lid over the jar. He gave the jar a mighty shake, and Nitty and Twitch watched, bewildered, as the tiniest of tornadoes began spinning inside it.

"He caught it!" Twitch hissed, latching onto Nitty's arm. "He caught the wind."

Nitty could scarce believe it, and nearly said *Impossible,* but stopped herself. Who was she to think that, with the crop she'd grown? Instead she wordlessly followed Twitch, heart hammering, as he shimmied to Neezer's motorcar.

Together they rose to their knees to peek inside the open trunk. More mason jars sat in the trunk, all full of dusty air moving about in a mishmash of speeds and patterns. Each jar had a label scrawled on its lid.

DRAFT was a white haze drifting lazily around its jar. PUFF was a minuscule cloud that waxed and waned. There was a ZEPHYR, which spun (rather prettily, Nitty thought) about its jar. There was a GALE, a MISTRAL, and even a CHINOOK.

Nitty was so entranced by the vacillating brown, ocher, and white winds in the jars that she didn't notice Twitch unscrewing the lid on a jar marked BLAST until it was too late. A violent surge of air shot from the jar with a deafening howl, hitting

Twitch square in the face with such force that his cheeks ballooned outward like a chipmunk's.

Nitty might've doubled over laughing if not for Neezer's bellow from the riverbed.

By the time he shouted "Who goes there?" Nitty had grabbed Twitch's hand and they were running for the Homes farm, a discouragingly small speck in the distance.

"He'll never recognize us," Twitch puffed confidently.

Nitty was worried much less about that than she was about Twitch making it all the way back to the farm at all. He was panting already and they were only yards from the riverbed. The growl of a motorcar behind them made Nitty triple her pace, pulling Twitch along as best she could. But he was flagging, and soon Neezer would overtake them.

She expected Neezer's mighty voice to barrel over her at any second. Or for his hand to grab both of them by the collars and toss them into his motorcar, never to be seen or heard from again. What she did not expect was to see Bernice behind the wheel of Crispin's Tin Lizzie, screeching to a haphazard stop beside them.

"What a rip-roaring getaway car!" Twitch exclaimed dazedly between heaving breaths.

"Get in already," Bernice muttered.

In a fit of detecting melodrama, Twitch dove headfirst through the open window while Nitty scrambled for the door. With a spin of tires, a spray of dust, and great force applied to the two loaves of bread strapped to her feet, Bernice blazed away.

It was only after a solid piece of driving that Nitty dared a glance back at the riverbed. Neezer, his motorcar, and his jars of wind were speeding furiously toward Fortune's Bluff, where, Nitty had a dreaded hunch, the day of reckoning was at hand.

CHAPTER TWENTY-TWO

IN WHICH A NINCOMPOOP RECKONS AND IS RECKONED

"He nearly had us in his clutches! Did you see?" Twitch bounced on the seat of the Tin Lizzie with such exuberance, Nitty lifted off her seat, too. "But our retreat was swift, and the archnemesis foiled."

Bernice jerked the motorcar to a stop at the edge of the froozle field. "What I saw was you two about to be in a mammoth pickle." She snorted as she took in their clothes. "What sort of getups are you wearing, anyway?"

Twitch sniffed. "They were imperative to our covert operations."

Bernice raised a skeptical eyebrow. "Seemed like their imperative was to give you two left feet. What if I hadn't been there?"

"You saved our hides, no doubt about it." Nitty grinned at

her in thanks. "But what were you doing out there in the first place?"

"What do you think?" Bernice shook her head as if the answer were obvious already. "I was spying on Neezer, same as you. I've been tracking his movements about Fortune's Bluff, and let me tell you, he's in a state. Most folks lost their windmills in the last storms, but I could've sworn I saw him unloading a whole truckful of windmill blades at the institute."

"He's working on his Whirlybog," Nitty said.

"He's up to something. So today, when I saw him leave town, I followed in the motorcar. Only Verna lost her rattle again, so I was late leaving. Plus I had to sneak past Pa. Now that he's feeling better, he's laid down the law about my driving." She sighed.

Nitty sighed, too. Even just now she'd been admiring the authoritative way Bernice's hands rested on the steering wheel, hoping she might get a feel of the wheel herself. Oh, she'd wager she could put some speed into that gas pedal. "That is lamentable hard luck."

"I know it," Bernice responded gloomily. "Anyhow, by the time I got out of Fortune's Bluff, it was only to see you two running pell-mell from Neezer, and I guessed you might need a mode of escape."

"That's a fine use of deductive reasoning," Twitch said with an officiousness that had Nitty and Bernice *both* snorting.

Just then, Windle's voice rose up, calling Nitty inside and startling them all. Nitty scrambled out of her disguise and tossed it to Twitch, then opened the car door. "We'd all better hightail it home before they catch on to our delinquency."

"It's not delinquency. We're in pursuit of wrongdoers." Twitch climbed out, too, already turning in the direction of his house. He faltered, paling, and gripped the door for support. Nitty leaned toward him, worry hammering her chest, but he waved her off. "We have to corner Neezer. Apprehend him. At the stroke of midnight."

"Twitch," Nitty started, "you're not—"

"I'm fine. Keep alert, and await my signal." With that he took off, half staggering, half running toward home.

A second later, Bernice was squealing away in the Tin Lizzie, and Nitty was staring after them both, wondering what sort of scrape they were in for. She soon found out when she climbed the porch steps to find Windle waiting, his eyes dark with foreboding. Mag was quick to leave her antics at the chicken coop to join them, first emitting a joyous tootle at the sight of Nitty, but following it with an anxious whiffle as Windle began to speak.

"Do my eyes deceive me?" His voice was so grave, Nitty shivered to hear it. "Did I, or did I not, just see Bernice Sigh operating a motorcar?"

Nitty dropped her eyes, knowing there was no point lying. "You did."

"And did I, or did I not, also see an infirm Angus Higgler *running* for home?"

"You saw that, too." Nitty sighed, then added in a rush, "We only wanted to see what Mayor Snollygost was up to."

"That is *not* our affair."

Nitty glared at him. "It's everybody's affair."

Windle threw up his hands, stomping across the porch. "What do you propose I do with such bald-faced disobedience? Have you no care for that boy's lungs, or his mother's peace of mind?"

"Course I do!" Nitty blurted it loudly and angrily enough that Mag raised her ears and flapped them in concern. How dare Windle suggest she didn't care? Why, practically all she *did* was care! "That's why we're trying to stop Mayor Snollygost, before he takes everyone's land—"

Windle's hand pressed Nitty's shoulder, cutting her words short. "You'll do no such thing."

Nitty stared at him, wondering at the fact he didn't seem angrier about Neezer when he should've been absolutely inflamed. "We have to stop him! He's robbing folks of their land—"

"It's not robbing." Windle's voice was bone-tired. "Folks agreed to the loans. They signed the papers."

"They never had a choice." Nitty was looking to Mag now, wishing, as impossible as it was, that the elephant could argue her side. Mag only shifted worriedly from one foot to the other, snuffling Nitty's hair. "They had to feed their families and have a roof over their heads. And Neezer . . . he's cheating them. I know he is. Twitch does, too! We just need proof."

Windle looked at her. It was the look an adult gives a child when he thinks the child is fabricating stories. It was a look Nitty had received countless times from Miz Ricketts, but never from Windle. It was a look that made Nitty's very blood turn to fire.

"You don't believe me!" She locked eyes with Windle, wanting him to say something—*do* something—to prove her wrong. He only stood there, motionless.

Nitty directed the full force of a glare at Windle. "How can you let this happen?"

In the distance, a low rumble sounded, and Mag moved protectively to Nitty's side. *Another duster coming,* Nitty thought, scanning the darkening sky. That made two in less than twenty-four hours. The storms were getting closer together and more frequent. She caught the deepening concern on Windle's face and wondered if he was thinking the same thought.

Then his concern shifted into irritation. "There's nothing we can do."

"There is! But you're too afraid!" she yelled. "Too afraid of everything to do anything at all, you . . . you insufferable nincompoop!"

It wasn't exactly the biting insult she'd wanted to use, but she could see from the stricken look on Windle's face that she'd said it with an effective amount of wrath.

He turned toward the door, shoulders sagging.

"I'm tired of do-nothings all around," Nitty shouted after him. She whirled on her heel and, with Mag following, marched straight to the barn. She slammed the barn door shut with a clang that startled the horses and cows from their napping, then pressed herself against it. As an hour, and then another and another passed, she waited for Windle to come.

He didn't.

Even as the wind moaned fearfully, she risked a peek outside to see that night had fallen.

"Let him stew in his do-nothing juices!" Nitty hollered, kicking a pile of hay. "Suits me."

Mag huffed and tossed a pile of hay with her trunk, too.

Together they walked the length of the barn and back, throwing hay, hollering and trumpeting as they went, until Nitty's hair was tangled with yellow stalks. Nitty sank to the floor in a pile of dishevelment and dismay. Mag, in an effort to be helpful, loosened the hay from her hair and ate it.

Nitty threw up her hands. "How can you possibly eat while I'm in an abyss of despair?"

Mag swallowed and, with a flick of her trunk, dumped an entire mound of hay over Nitty's head.

"Hey! What'd you do that for?" Nitty's anger flared fresh, then fizzled as Mag set her trunk atop the crown of her head. Nitty could've sworn she saw a playful glint in Mag's eyes, and knew she meant well. But she couldn't bring herself to laugh. Not tonight.

Mag, who had been waiting, ears perked, for the bubbling sound of her girl's laughter, did not give up when the laughter didn't come. Instead she curled her trunk into an inviting hammock and waited. This, she noticed, made her girl's stomping feet quiet, the heat coming off her skin cool. Soon her girl curled into the hammock's curve, her small hands holding on tight.

Mag swayed her trunk, back and forth, back and forth, crooning a low rumble. She sighed. She had a memory of another of her own kind crooning this same rumbling song to her, long ago. Before she'd known her trainer, or any other human. It had made her feel warm and safe. This she could give to her girl now.

Nitty pressed her ear against Mag's trunk, listening. The elephant's susurrant rumbling had the soothing, drawn-out tones of a lullaby. It spoke to Nitty's heart and to all the disappointment she felt in that moment. Surely Mag was telling her she understood, that she'd always understand.

Soon the wind was screeching through the slats in the barn and dust was spilling through cracks and crevices. Nitty nestled against Mag, listening to that strange, gently thunderous lullaby and seeking the comfort of Mag's warmth. Only tonight, she had too many troubling thoughts for lasting comfort.

CHAPTER TWENTY-THREE

IN WHICH A SIGH IS A HOPEFUL SIGN

In the darkness of the barn, Nitty waited for midnight. When the duster's shrieking quieted, there came a certain suspense to the stillness. Then she heard a series of convoluted raps on the barn door, followed by a most uncanny "ca-caw, ca-caw," and a wheeze.

"Twitch." Nitty stood with relief as he peered around the door. "You sound like a tap-dancing, accordion-playing parrot."

"The sign's meant to confuddle. So only you and Bernice recognize it." His voice sounded small and pinched in the darkness. "I saw your cot in the kitchen was empty and figured you'd be out here with Mag." Before he could say anything else, he coughed.

Nitty stiffened at the sound. It was a horrible, drowning choke. "You're too sick," she whispered. "You shouldn't be here."

Emitting three short blats from her trunk, Mag began stroking Twitch's back. The cough took a full minute to end.

"Haven't sprouted any corn yet, so I imagine I'll get by." Twitch rasped. "The time for action is now."

A shaft of dust-mottled moonlight caught his face, and Nitty nearly gasped. His nut-brown skin was chalky, his forehead shining with a film of sweat. The hand holding his Morton Salt periscope trembled, even though the duster had left the air tepid. All in all, he looked even worse than he sounded. Nitty wished he would sit down to rest, but the sober determination in his eyes warned her not to even suggest such a thing. He'd likely march straight out the door in a rage.

Instead she asked, "What's the plan?"

Even as his teeth chattered, Twitch grinned. "We find a way into the Snollygost Institute. We witness firsthand Neezer's evildoings." He reached under his shirt and pulled a large burlap sack from it. "Then trap Neezer."

"In . . . a potato sack?" Nitty tried hard not to let her tone betray her reservations (and at the moment, her reservations were many).

"I know. It's a sorry substitute for handcuffs, but it'll have to do. And . . ." He pulled something from his back pocket. "I brought this, too. It's Ma's."

"A hairpin?"

"For picking locks, of course!" Twitch cried, incredulous. "It's in practically every issue of *Detective Comics.*"

"But how can we stop Neezer from collecting payments on loans?"

"We find proof of his villainy," Twitch answered. "We need to get up close to this Whirlybog, find out how it works and what it really does. We can search the institute for hard evidence of Neezer's deceit. That'll be enough to get folks to stand up to him."

Nitty hesitated. "I don't like Neezer any more than you do. But . . . what if we don't find any proof?"

Twitch stared at her, anger flickering across his features. "What if your seeds never grew?" he countered. "You had a hunch about those seeds, just like I have a hunch about this. I never doubted *you.*"

Nitty considered this, and her heart floundered. He was right, of course. He'd been there, beside her, those first few days of planting when Windle groused about the impossibility of her crop. He'd been beside her nearly every day, helping her and believing. No matter how ill he looked, or how worried she was for him, she had to see this through with him. "You're right." She locked her eyes on his. "Let's go."

They stepped toward the door but discovered that Mag had barricaded herself against it.

"Mag, you can't come with us." She tried to nuzzle Mag's trunk with her forehead, but Mag would have none of it. Her dark eyes were reproachful. *Don't go,* they seemed to plead, and this made Nitty's insides lurch.

What if this was Mag's way of warning her that, if they went, calamity would strike? But no . . . Twitch needed Nitty tonight.

"Mag. Please," she whispered. "For Twitch."

At last Mag moved from the door, her ears down, her trunk drooping, issuing a series of agitated blats. Then Nitty slipped around the door with Twitch, unable to glance at Mag for fear of seeing the elephant's distraught eyes staring back. Leaving Mag this way felt disloyal, but she had to see this through, no matter what.

⟨⎮⟩

The walk into Fortune's Bluff was painstakingly long. Twitch's staunch resolve was no match for his flagging lungs, and they could only walk in short intervals, stopping for Twitch to rest in between.

The moon shone dimly through the hazy brown clouds, and Fortune's Bluff itself lay in almost total darkness, making it difficult for them to find their way toward Main Street. Not for the first time, Nitty reflected with regret that Mag might've carried them to the institute in a quarter of the time. But it was too late for that now, she told herself, and better that Mag stayed safe.

When they were halfway down Main Street, Twitch doubled

over in a coughing fit so loud that it brought a shadowy figure running toward them.

Nitty's pulse drummed. "We're caught, Twitch." She wrapped an arm protectively around his shoulders. "Doomed."

There was no chance of running for it. The figure was moving too quickly, and Twitch was still hunched over, trying to catch his breath. Nitty braced herself and set her jaw, vowing that she'd stand her ground, an immovable force against tyranny.

"For cripes' sake, Twitch," the figure hissed, "some sign *this* is. You're liable to wake the dead with that coughing."

Nitty nearly whooped with relief as Bernice thrust a bottle of Mr. Moop's Cough Tonic toward Twitch.

"Take a swallow and hush already," Bernice ordered. As Twitch did as instructed, she glared at both of them. "What took you two so long getting here? The whole town's in a dither. Everybody's weeping. Folks are giving up." She wrinkled her nose. "And if Neezer has his way—"

"He won't," Twitch eked out, then swigged more cough tonic.

Nitty noticed a rolling pin protruding from Bernice's back pocket. "What's that for?"

Bernice slid it from her pocket and raised it like a baseball bat. "Defense."

Nitty grinned. "Resourceful. Wieldy, too. I like it."

Bernice stood a little taller at that. "Let's get this mission underway."

Another coughing fit shook Twitch, and Nitty had to help him keep standing. She and Bernice exchanged a glance.

"What will we do if he keeps on this way?" Bernice whispered over Twitch's stooped frame. "We can't carry him home."

"We can," Nitty answered firmly. She'd carry Twitch clear across the state if she had to. "But it won't come to that. Not if we hurry." She turned toward the looming shadow of the Snollygost Institute. Then, remembering one of her favorite lines from the *Daily Tattler*'s *The Countess and the Convict*—a line that, she felt, might instill anyone with greater bravery—she added, "'And onward they strode, not knowing the perils that lay ahead but believing that their unity could conquer all.'"

CHAPTER TWENTY-FOUR

IN WHICH FOULSOME ROTTEN VILLAINY IS AT LONG LAST REVEALED

A few minutes and a lot of coughing later, they stood before the imposing and dauntingly high iron-spiked fence surrounding the Snollygost Institute.

"How do you suppose we'll manage to climb that?" Nitty wondered aloud with floundering confidence.

"Why in blazes would you want to risk a limb climbing that?" Bernice scoffed. "Follow me." Bernice didn't wait to see if they were following but searched the length of the fence until she reached a spot where the iron bars had been warped into an opening big enough to slip through. Her teeth shone in a rare smile as she gestured toward the opening. "Pa mentioned this once in his ramblings. I suppose it's how he snuck into the institute himself."

"Fine work," Twitch said with an air of superiority, as if he were Holmes complimenting Watson, but his wheeze diminished the effect. Which was just as well.

The three of them crept low to the ground as they climbed the small knoll leading to the institute. The building sat in darkness, save for a faint glow from two small windows set high in its outer wall. It was, however, whumping its incessant *WHUMP,* loud as ever, and with what seemed like greater urgency and frequency. As they drew closer, Nitty saw several trucks parked beside the building.

"More of the trucks," Twitch said. "The ones that are always coming and going."

Nitty could barely make them out until the haze over the moon lifted for a moment. Dust clung thickly to the trucks, covering them all in a uniform brown, except for a strange, indecipherable red symbol on their sides, barely visible under the dirt.

"Hey." Nitty nudged Twitch. "There's some sort of symbol on those trucks. I'm going to get closer." Before Twitch could say a word (which, in his current state of breathlessness, was unlikely anyway), Nitty dropped to her stomach and shimmied.

She reached the first in the line of trucks, and, standing on tiptoe, brushed the inches-thick dust from its side. The symbol emerged, and Nitty gasped. It was a familiar bright red cross.

She shimmied her way back to Twitch and Bernice. "They're Red Cross trucks! Only . . . why are they here?"

Twitch shrugged. "Bet we'll find out when we get inside."

He nodded toward Bernice, who was eyeing one of the institute's windows.

"It looks to be open," she said. "Just a crack."

Nitty moved along the wall until she stood under the window. It was much too high for her to reach on her own, but then she spied the ivy—nearly dried out to the point of death—clinging to the wall beneath the window. She gave it an experimental tug and, when it held, pulled on it with the full force of her body. It seemed sturdy enough.

"This way," she whispered to Twitch and Bernice. She began to climb.

Once she reached the window's ledge, she was able to pry the window open just enough to squeeze through. It might've been a much greater drop to the floor inside had her fall not been broken by the sacks of flour piled beneath the window. Her landing sent a cloud of flour puffing into the air, but otherwise her arrival inside the institute was mostly silent. Even if she had made a sound, it wouldn't have been heard over the whumping, which was coming at regular intervals from somewhere nearby. Twitch and Bernice entered just as stealthily, although Twitch seemed to be holding his breath in an effort not to cough.

Twitch slid his goggles up onto his forehead while Nitty scanned the room from atop their flour pile, making sure they'd gone undetected. As she took in her surroundings, her mouth fell open.

"Would you look at all of this food!" she whispered. Canned

goods, sacks of flour, fresh melons, eggplant, corn—food by the ton was stacked from the floor to the ceiling. "There's enough here to feed an army!"

Bernice frowned. "This must be where Neezer keeps food before he takes it to the Snollygost General Store."

There was a sound, then, of voices approaching, and Twitch's wheezing quickened beside Nitty. Nitty scooted backward to take cover behind one of the larger sacks of flour, and Twitch and Bernice did the same. From the hiding place, if Nitty strained, she could just make out the voices above the whumping.

"There will be another truckload of donations delivered sometime next week," one voice was saying. "We want to make sure no one goes hungry."

"Speaking for all of Fortune's Bluff," came Neezer's familiar, nasal voice, "you and the Red Cross have our eternal gratitude."

As Neezer said his goodbyes to the deliverymen, Twitch gripped Nitty's arm.

"Those trucks," he whispered in Nitty's ear. His eyes looked wild, either with fever or excitement—Nitty couldn't tell which. "They're coming with donations!"

Bernice's eyes widened in understanding. "That's what Papa was trying to tell us with his rhyme. Remember? 'Cans of sauce, from the Cross . . .'"

"'Hide them all, says the boss,'" Twitch finished. "Neezer hides the donations here and then sells them at the store!"

"Papa wasn't talking nonsense at all." Bernice's voice was

more hopeful than Nitty had ever heard it before. "He was trying to tell everyone . . ."

"Only no one would listen," Nitty finished quietly. Her
chest was a furnace of anger. "Of all the pernicious, deceitful
escapades—"

"Shhhh!" Bernice hissed as Neezer—or rather the whistling
of Neezer's nose—drew closer. His footsteps, and his whistling,
breezed past them, and it was only then that Nitty dared peek
around the sack of flour. She saw Neezer unlock a door not
far from their hiding place. The door only opened a sliver, but
as it did, the sound of whumping intensified. Neezer slipped
through the door and shut it firmly behind him.

Nitty waited a moment, and when she was sure they were
alone in the storage room, she ventured a whisper. "The Whirlybog. It's got to be in that room."

Instantly Bernice stood and began picking her way carefully
down the mountain of flour, her rolling pin in her hand, ready
for battle.

Twitch still lay atop the sacks, heaving tired breaths, his face
pricked with sweat. "On . . . my . . . way . . . ," he sputtered.

Nitty frowned when she saw that he'd grown even paler since
they'd left Windle's barn. She hurried to Bernice. "Twitch . . .
he's getting worse. We should take him home."

"Not yet." Bernice looked back at Nitty and Twitch with
dogged determination. "Papa knew about the Red Cross. He
was right. He knew about the Whirlybog before anyone else,

too. And I'm not leaving here until I find out what it does. For Papa's sake."

"Bernice, wait." Nitty started after her, and saw that Twitch was struggling to get to his feet to do the same.

"I'm fine." Twitch gave Nitty a warning look. "Bernice is right. We came here to get hard evidence, and we can't leave without it. Otherwise no one will ever believe us."

Nitty hesitated as she watched Twitch moving unsteadily down the flour mound. *This is wrong,* she thought. But if Twitch kept going, the only thing she could do was stay with him.

Reluctantly, she followed him and Bernice as they snuck through the storage room, staying hidden behind the piles of food as much as they could. Nitty's heart hammered as they drew closer to the whumping.

The three of them got down on their knees and crawled the last few feet to the door.

Twitch handed Nitty the burlap sack, then slid the hairpin from his pocket. "Ready the instrument of capture," he said to Nitty, solemnly.

Nitty raised the burlap sack. Beside her, Bernice raised the rolling pin—prepared, Nitty guessed, to give Neezer a thorough pummeling.

With temporarily renewed energy and a true stealth Nitty found masterly, Twitch slid the hairpin into the door's lock. His eyes, though glazed, gleamed with exhilaration when he touched the doorknob and it turned under his grasp.

Silently, he pushed the door open a crack and lifted his periscope to his face. Together they peeked inside.

The Whirlybog was the oddest-looking machine Nitty had ever set eyes on—a massive structure of wood and metal covered in the blades of windmills. It was a large-scale replica of the sketch they'd discovered in Neezer's invention notebook. But the machine before them struck Nitty as much more ominous in reality than on paper.

"Look there." Bernice pointed toward the Whirlybog's control panel. There, at its center, was the very Dustometer dial Crispin had baked into his bread loaves. Each point on the dial had a name, and Nitty's pulse raced as she read them: Chokeberry Silt, Oily Loam, Bison Sward, Toeter Grime.

"Duster names," Twitch confirmed. "But what do they mean? And what is *that*?" He pointed to a drafting table, where a model full of miniature houses and taller buildings sat. His eyes narrowed. "Wait . . . that reminds me of the map I found in Neezer's car. It's . . . it's a model of Fortune's Bluff! But some buildings are missing—"

He swallowed the rest of his words as Neezer suddenly came into view, walking toward the giant clear holding tank at the center of the Whirlybog. He held three mason jars in his arms. He climbed a small stepladder, set the jars on the ladder's top step, and opened the Whirlybog's holding tank.

"A half a jar of Blast, I think," he mumbled as he opened one of the jars and poured a portion of its churning contents into the holding tank. "A third of a jar of Gale, and a full jar of Cyclone."

Down from the ladder, he turned the Dustometer on the Whirlybog to the Toeter Grime setting. Then he raised a large red lever to the side of the control dial, and as he did, the blades of the Whirlybog spun faster.

"More power." Neezer smiled triumphantly. "More wind. And we'll have the biggest duster yet!"

Nitty's eyes became saucers, and she glanced at Bernice and Twitch, who were both looking on with a mixture of anger and astonishment. "The Whirlybog's not ridding the town of dusters," she whispered. "It's causing them!" She'd seen enough—enough to tell Windle and everyone else in Fortune's Bluff what Neezer was doing. Now they could leave before they were discovered. "Let's go!"

Proof! Bernice mouthed then, pointing to one of the mason jars still sitting on Neezer's stepladder.

"Bernice. No!" But before Nitty could stop her, Bernice inched through the door, heading for the jar.

Nitty held her breath, not daring to move, as she watched Bernice's painstaking progress across the floor. Neezer's back was still safely turned to them, and Bernice's fingers were within inches of the jar when it happened.

Twitch covered his mouth with his hand.

Nitty braced herself against him, hoping she could muffle what she knew was coming. Twitch's cheeks ballooned with the effort of trying not to cough, but still, the smallest gurgle rose from his throat.

All three of them froze, because the gurgle had come in between *WHUMP*s, and, though small, it had been distinct. Nitty held her breath as she watched Neezer stiffen. She waited for him to turn around, but he didn't. Instead he reached for the red lever. The windmill blades spun furiously, and the whumping grew louder and faster. Much faster.

Then Nitty heard it. A sound much worse than the Whirly-bog's ominous whumping. It was the sound of whistling—a high-pitched, nasal whistling. But it was the tune being whis-tled that struck fear in Nitty's heart: a tune Twitch had once warned her must never be heard from the likes of the villainous mayor. Or else.

What Nitty heard was the sound of Neezer's nose whistling Beethoven's Fifth.

Nitty sprang to her feet as Twitch hollered to Bernice, "Run!"

Bernice, however, did not run. She lifted her rolling pin and brought it down with a conquering *crack!* against the Whirly-bog's holding tank. Nitty waited for a splinter, a shatter, any-thing. Bernice, eyes expectant and vengeful, waited, too. But the holding tank did what it was built to do. The holding tank *held*.

With the surprise and disappointment of her failure scored

on her face, Bernice snatched up Neezer's Cyclone jar and was through the door in seconds.

Nitty wanted to follow but was momentarily mesmerized by the sight of Neezer turning toward them, an impossibly congenial smile spreading across his lips.

She did the only thing she could think to do. She grabbed the burlap sack and launched it, with all the might she could muster, directly at Neezer's head. Then she too ran. She pulled Twitch, who had begun coughing as soon as he'd hollered his command and now couldn't seem to stop, along with her.

The Whirlybog's whumping had grown to a deafening bellow, and through the walls of the institute Nitty could hear the telltale whine of a duster brewing.

"He's making a duster!" Bernice cried. "With the Whirlybog."

Strange, thought Nitty, that Neezer wasn't yelling after them, or pursuing them at all. But that smile of his . . . Nitty shuddered. His smile could only mean one thing: he *would* get them, one way or another. She knew now that the beginning of Beethoven's Fifth had been the portent of an indomitable *end*.

They reached the bottom of the mound of flour, but Twitch was panting and weak. He'd never be able to climb up the sacks to the window.

Nitty's eyes flew about the room, looking for another exit, and they at last spotted a large door along the north wall. She could only hope it led to the outside.

"There!" she called to Bernice over the whumping, and

propping Twitch up between the two of them, they half stumbled, half ran toward it.

Nitty didn't look behind her as she ran. She couldn't hear footsteps. She couldn't hear anything over the Whirlybog. Every second that passed, she expected to feel Neezer's pawlike hand clamping down on her shoulder.

But then she was flinging the door open and barreling into the darkness of night with Twitch and Bernice beside her.

Safe was her first relieved thought. Her second was *Duster.*

A duster, already fierce in its violent winds and blinding dirt, was whirling around them. She tried to run into the wind, but it overpowered her, knocking her to the ground, wrenching her arms from Bernice and Twitch. Neezer hadn't let them go, Nitty realized. He'd sent the storm to catch them.

"Twitch!" She reached out in the darkness. Her words disappeared into the wind the moment she spoke them. "Bernice!"

She glimpsed Bernice for only a second, just long enough to watch Neezer's Cyclone jar get wrenched from her hands in the wind and fall to the ground, shattering. Her heart sank. Their proof was gone. Then a thick cloud engulfed Bernice, and Nitty lost sight of her.

She pulled the collar of her shirt up over her mouth and nose and shielded her eyes against the stinging grit. There— barely visible—was a shadowy form.

The dust swirled faster, flying into her nose and eyes, even through her shirt's fabric. She squinted, barely able to make out Twitch where he stood a few feet away.

271

"Bernice!" Nitty called. "Help!"

Bernice had disappeared completely into the darkness. And Twitch . . . Twitch couldn't stop coughing. He was hunched over, clutching his sides.

"I'm . . . not . . . breathing so good," he wheezed. He coughed again, and his bright blue periscope slipped out of his hand. It rolled the second it hit the ground, the wind making it spin and skitter in the dirt. A ferocious gust tore the periscope from the ground and into the air. Before Nitty could cry out, it was gone. Twitch, too, was gone, his form vanishing behind a black wall of dust.

"Nitty!" Twitch's voice was the tiniest mouse in the lion's roar of the storm.

"I'm here!" Nitty pushed the words from her open mouth, but as soon as she did, clots of dirt and dust choked her throat. She leaned into the wind, pulling her feet forward, step by step, reaching her outstretched hands toward the sound of Twitch's voice.

"Nitty." The mouse was tinier, weaker.

Bernice, Nitty was certain, would be fine. Wherever she was in the storm now, Bernice would find shelter, or some way to stay safe. But Twitch, with his fever and his cough . . .

Please, Nitty thought. *Please let me reach him.*

There was a crushing weight in Nitty's chest, as if a boulder were sitting atop it, and she fell to her knees, struggling to breathe. She began crawling. But which way to go?

She could hear no sound from Twitch. The only sound was the screaming wind. She tried, once more, to call out, but her voice failed her. She closed her eyes and reached out her arms, sweeping the piling dust through her fingers. She couldn't reach Twitch. She wouldn't find him.

She gathered all the thoughts in her head and stretched them toward the Homes farm, toward Windle. And even more toward Mag.

Mag! she thought then. *Mag, come to me. Help me.*

If there was ever a time for Mag to be magnolious, it was now.

⌒ᐟᜒ⌒

Through the miles of dust and wind, through the vastness of the wide, blowing world, Mag heard her girl call out to her.

She raised her head.

She lifted her ears.

Her pumpkin heart tolled a clanging alarm.

Her girl was in danger.

She lowered her head like a battering ram, and she ran.

⌒ᐟᜒ⌒

Nitty's breath was coming in shallow gasps. The dust was building a blanket, a heavy blanket smothering her. . . .

But then the blanket was yanked away by a sweeping trunk. A trunk that gave the briefest stroke to Nitty's cheek. A stroke that said, *I am here. I am here. I am here.*

Mag.

Nitty raised her head and, from the corner of her eye, saw the blur of a wooden plank tearing through the air. Then—*whack!*—it landed a jarring blow to her skull. The world spun with stars, but she fought to right it. Through the murky curtain of dust appeared the outline of the elephant, and a small, curled mound between Mag's legs.

The storm subsided just enough for Nitty to make out Mag's trunk lifting Twitch into the air, raising him up until he was umbrellaed under her enormous left ear.

Nitty sighed. Safe. Twitch was safe with Mag.

Now, at last, Nitty could sleep.

She closed her eyes.

But before she gave in to the warmth of her dust blanket, she heard a distant, nasal voice booming, "Beast! Murderous beast!"

CHAPTER TWENTY-FIVE

In Which Matters Are Complicated by Mayors and Missing Elephants

When Nitty next opened her eyes, she found herself under a willow tree. The willow was weeping, silently but stormily.

"Don't cry, Windle," Nitty whispered hoarsely. For it was Windle whose head was bent low over Nitty in grief. He was seated in Clara's rocker by her side. Nitty put out a shaky hand to touch the top of his uncombed hair. "Don't cry."

This only made Windle cry harder. "You're all right, then! All right." He brushed at his eyes to no avail. "You've been sleeping near on a full day now. Blast it if you didn't give this crotchety ticker a fright."

"But, Windle." Nitty's own eyes blurred. "You're crying for me."

Windle's paintbrush eyebrows knit together. He straightened

from a willow into a birch. "A momentary lapse of willpower, and I'll thank you not to make a fuss about it."

Nitty smiled at him, relieved to see that his crying had done nothing to diminish his terseness. She'd grown to like it (most of the time). Slowly she lifted her head to take in her surroundings. Why, she was back in the Homes kitchen in her cot! And—hoo-wee!—did she have a headache. Her throat was raw with grittiness, too, and she gratefully accepted the cup of froozle juice that Windle offered.

As she sipped it, she cautiously touched her forehead and discovered a sizable goose egg.

She raised her eyebrows, questioning, and Windle nodded. "You hit your head. Before we found you and Twitch. Probably hit it on some flying debris. The storm was a real whopper." He frowned.

Nitty's thoughts, which up until now had been fuddled and musty, turned suddenly sharp.

"The storm." She sat up in alarm. "Twitch and Mag! Bernice!"

Windle laid an arm across her shoulders, gently but firmly lowering her back onto the cot. "They're out of harm's way. Bernice ran all the way here in the storm to get help. She tried to drive—confound her—but Crispin's car was full up with dust. She got a lungful herself, and could hardly speak by the time she blew in the door, but she's safe with Crispin now. All I understood was that you and Twitch were caught in the storm outside the institute. I ran for my truck, but its engine was dust-plugged. By the time the truck finally started, Mag was already gone." He shook his head. "She broke down the barn door to get to you faster."

Nitty's relief lasted only until she noticed that Windle was skirting her gaze. Nitty glanced out the kitchen window, searching. The emerald green and fuchsia of the froozle field—still standing, if bowed—were marred by grimy layers of inches-thick dust. Nitty guessed it was getting on dusk. Still, it was hard to tell with the brown pea-souper hovering as a leftover from last night's duster. The porch, though shadowy, was clearly empty. If Twitch and Mag were all right, then Mag would be there at the window, looking in on her. Twitch would be here, too, likely reading her one of his *Detective Comics*.

Her limbs jellified.

"What happened?" Her voice was small. "Where are they? Twitch and Mag?" Windle stared at his toes, until Nitty grabbed the pillow from underneath her head, bursting out with "I swear I'll wallop you with this if you don't tell me right now!"

At that Windle's eyes widened, a near smile pulling at the corners of his mouth. Then he did something that surprised both of them. He took her hand. Not just for a second. No. He took her hand and held on tight.

"Oh, Nitty girl, you walloped me good and hard already, the very first day you showed up here on this farm. Me, Twitch . . . the whole of Fortune's Bluff." He shook his head. "Now we're all in a bind." He heaved a breath. "Twitch is ailing, but Mrs. Higgler's tending to him. She's fixed him some froozle soup, if you can believe that."

"His muddy lungs?" Nitty asked, and Windle nodded. She swallowed, remembering. "When we got caught out in the duster, Twitch couldn't breathe. He couldn't breathe at all."

Windle stared at the floor. "Nitty, he's got dust pneumonia."

Nitty's heart was a mallet, striking her ribs fast and fierce. "Well, he needs more cough tonic, that's all. And more froozle fruit. Rest, too, and then he'll be fine." She made her voice say the words, as a way of convincing her mind of their truth.

"Doc Grant has seen him already, but there's nothing much to be done for Angus. I'm afraid your froozle fruit won't cure him. His illness is too far gone for that. The fact is, his lungs can't bear any more dusters."

Silence fell between them. Nitty's eyes filled.

Poor Twitch. Poor, brave Twitch. Here he'd finally uncovered proof of Neezer Snollygost's villainy, only to have his muddy lungs betray him.

Nitty swung her legs over the side of the bed. "First I'll see Mag in the barn. And then I need to talk to Twitch. Right away. We discovered something at the institute. Something so shuddersome you'll scarce believe it."

Windle frowned. "I *thought* Bernice kept saying Neezer's name, but I couldn't understand much else through her coughing fits. What's he gone and done now? Built himself a throne?" Nitty shook her head, and she guessed she must've turned several shades paler, because Windle's eyes widened. "What is it?"

With halting breaths, she explained all she, Twitch, and

Bernice had seen at Neezer's institute. Windle's face, as she spoke, went through several stages of transformation—the bleached-bone look of shock, the grim acceptance of a difficult truth, and then, at last, the purpling bluster of anger. "No!" was his frequent exclamation, along with "He didn't dare!" and "He wouldn't," and, finally, a resigned "The scoundrel."

Nitty barely finished the dreaded recounting before a coughing fit overtook her. As she coughed, Windle shook his head, muttering, "How could I not have known?"

Nitty nearly blurted that he might've known earlier had he bothered to listen properly to Twitch's and her hunches. But his pained expression and trembling hands stopped her. She couldn't gloat at the sight of his suffering, not even if he *had* behaved like a thickheaded grown-up.

"All these years, right under our noses!" he said now. "And I saw the trucks coming and going. We all did."

"The dust did its job disguising them," Nitty managed to rasp. "It's not all your fault."

"More mine than most. I knew who Neezer had become. Better than anyone else. And I stuck my head in the sand and let Fortune's Bluff suffer through his skullduggery. I should've stood against it." He pounded a fist into his palm. "By balderdash, I should've stood for *something*!"

"We have to stop him," Nitty said. Then she coughed again, and the taste of sweaty, unwashed feet filled her mouth. Curse those Toeter Grime dusters!

Windle squeezed her hand. "You need to rest. You sucked up a mountain of dust yourself. Doc Grant was none too happy with the way your lungs were sounding either."

"I'm fine." Nitty gasped, straining to make her breath sound steady. "I'll be even better once I see Twitch and Mag. Once we have a plan."

Windle's mouth sagged. "About Mag. She's not here. Neezer—"

Suddenly the front door swung open and a voice boomed into the room. "Nitty Luce, alive and well!" Neezer Snollygost barreled through the doorway, his smile wide and slick as ever. "I thought I'd look in to see how the patient is faring today." The blazing purple of his waistcoat pained Nitty's eyes. "Just an amicable stop on my mayoral circuit of duties."

"You." Nitty frowned, suddenly wishing she had something more effective than a pillow for walloping. "What did you do with my elephant?"

"May I?" Neezer swept a box of chocolate out from behind his back, setting it beside Nitty on the bed. "A gift to brighten your convalescence."

Unbidden, Nitty's mouth began to water, but she turned her head away. "I won't touch one morsel of that contraband."

Neezer clucked his tongue. "Such a shame. Windle, I see you've had as much trouble imparting good sense to this girl as you did to Lillah. The both of them wild as lions."

Windle stood up, straightening. At his full height he was

nearly two heads taller than Neezer, but his newborn air of tenacity made him appear even taller. "On the contrary." His voice struck Nitty as suddenly impressive with authority. "Lillah had the sense to move on when I couldn't, and Nitty . . . well, the girl has more good sense than I've had in years."

Neezer's crescent-moon smile narrowed to a sliver. "Harboring a dangerous animal certainly doesn't strike me as good sense."

"My Mag wouldn't hurt a flea." A fire lit in Nitty's belly, then spread to her cheeks.

"Is that so? Well." Neezer moved to the foot of the bed. "Your Mag cost Angus Higgler dearly. She strangled him to within a hairsbreadth of his life."

"That's a lie!" Nitty's ragged breath came in hot, shallow gasps. "Mag was trying to help Twitch. She picked him up to keep him safe from the dust."

"The elephant's a gentle soul," Windle said. "I've never seen her behave with anything other than tenderness."

"Ah, but I have." Neezer's nose struck up a languid, morose rendering of Chopin's Funeral March. "She crushed the institute's fence in her fury, and then I saw her choking the boy with my own eyes. If I hadn't stepped in, tragedy surely would've struck. Miz Turngiddy witnessed the event firsthand. She can testify as to what happened. Can't you, Miz Turngiddy?"

Neezer nodded toward the doorway, and Nitty saw Miz Turngiddy hanging back on its threshold, her hands clasped tightly at her waist.

"She wasn't there," Nitty protested. "I saw as much for myself!"

"Miz Turngiddy?" Neezer prodded.

Miz Turngiddy looked pained. "I—I arrived just as the duster was waning. Truth be told, my view was obscured by the flying dirt—"

Neezer cleared his throat. Loudly. His nose struck up "Vigilante Man."

Miz Turngiddy paled. "It's true!" she blurted. "The elephant's trunk was wrapped around Angus. There is a ninety-nine-point-five percent probability that, with its strength, it could've done harm—"

"There!" Neezer's nose emitted a victorious *tweet!* "As I said, the elephant is a danger. A threat to us all."

Miz Turngiddy looked away, her expression drooping.

For a moment Nitty pitied the woman, as she'd pity anyone who blindly took up another's cause without, first, understanding the truth and, second, knowing her own opinion of it. Once the moment was over, Nitty maddened.

"Shame on you," she burst out. "Shame on both of you!"

Neezer ignored her. "Needless to say, the elephant is being kept in my custody, under the strictest of scrutiny, to assure the safety of everyone in Fortune's Bluff."

"You've locked her up, haven't you?" Nitty wanted to shout, but her voice was still weak, and all she could manage was a frustrated bark. "You can't chain her again! I won't let you. It's the worst sort of cruelty."

Dear Mag. Her heart wasn't meant to endure more deceit.

Nitty looked Neezer square in the eye and, with thoughts of Twitch in mind, said, "'Ten Ways to Be a Villain, number nine: Undermine all that is good, fair, and just with treachery.'"

"On the contrary, young lady, what is more just than making a criminal answerable to her crime?" Neezer sighed heavily and with great import. "I'm afraid this is what comes of stealing an animal from a circus. Misery all around."

Nitty glanced at Windle, worried what she might see in his face. He'd never asked for an elephant and a thief to descend upon him. He might easily regret it now. But he didn't look regretful. He looked proud.

"I had to steal her to save her," Nitty said then. "She was about to be hanged!"

Neezer pulled a telegram from his pocket and passed it to Windle. "Yes, I know all about it. The beast killed her trainer."

"She didn't! I'm sure it was an accident. You can ask Mr. Klempt if you like. He met her trainer. He swears the man mistreated Mag awfully. She bears the scars as proof!"

Windle, who'd been reading over the telegram again and again, lifted forlorn eyes from the paper. "Says here that Magnolious is lawfully owned by the Gusto and Gallant Circus. And . . . Percival Gallant will be coming to Fortune's Bluff to collect his property. Tomorrow."

"Tomorrow!" Nitty gasped. "We can't let him take Mag away. He'll kill her." She looked at Windle, imploring. "We can talk to Mr. Gallant. Maybe he'll let her go free as long as we promise she won't be a danger to anyone. We have to make him see."

"We'll do all we can," Windle said solemnly. He turned to Neezer. "We're going to put a stop to this, Neezer. We've had our differences, you and I, but this goes beyond the two of us. This is about doing right."

"Twitch knows what happened," Nitty continued. "He can explain how she rescued him."

Neezer shook his head. "I've just come from visiting Angus. The boy can barely breathe, let alone talk. Why, Mrs. Higgler is busy packing up their belongings as we speak."

At Nitty's blank look, Neezer added, "Oh. Didn't Windle tell you? Doc Grant has recommended a change of climate for Angus, as soon as possible. They leave for California at first light tomorrow. The best thing you can do for your friend now is to let him recuperate in peace."

The fire under Nitty's skin broke loose, burning her eyes until they watered. But no. If there was one thing she refused to do, it was to cry in front of Neezer Snollygost. She would not let him ever believe that he could reduce her to tears.

She lifted her chin. "The only person you know what's best for is yourself, Mr. Snollygost. I'll thank you to leave any other opinions about my friend *and* my elephant to yourself."

Neezer's nose commenced "The Battle Hymn of the Republic," and Nitty was struck with an almost irrepressible desire to stuff a sock up Neezer's nostrils.

"Regretfully," Neezer said, "as mayor I cannot allow a threat such as this elephant to remain in my town."

At that moment, Windle reached for the freckle behind his right ear. Then he stopped, for he'd had enough of the itching. He'd had enough of Neezer altogether. He lowered his hand and locked eyes with Neezer. "Know this." His voice was steady and strong. "You cannot stop us from keeping our elephant. She belongs here, with Nitty. With us."

Neezer might almost have looked startled by Windle's display of fortitude had he not remembered that enterprising swindlers, such as he, made a point of never looking startled. Instead he smiled. "Have you forgotten who owns Fortune's Bluff, Windle? Who owns the deeds on every parcel of farmland?"

"Except mine," Windle countered.

"Yes. Except yours. Such a shame, that. I could do wonders with this property." He clapped Windle on the back. "But I'll not let such a trifle stand in the way of our town's betterment. Indeed not. Other folks have seen reason these last few days. Why, just yesterday four families at last agreed to give me their land in return for the promise of new jobs."

"What jobs?" Windle scoffed. "You can't promise what you don't have."

Neezer waved a dismissive hand. "Once Fortune City is built over the ruins of Fortune's Bluff, I'll have jobs to offer. Bellboys, concierges . . . cooks for gourmet restaurants." His eyes glinted. "Imagine a high-rise hotel where the Higgler farm stands. Can you see it?"

Windle and Nitty said nothing. But Nitty understood now why Twitch had seen Neezer with that *Sublime Skyscrapers* book. Neezer had been plotting this all along.

"Fortune's Bluff, a metropolis," Miz Turngiddy whispered. She clutched her notebook, her knuckles whitening, and a sickly pallor swept her face.

Windle clenched his jaw. "You'll never have this farm."

"Oh?" Neezer tapped his chin, as if deep in thought. "And what would happen if a duster destroyed this farm? Would you still be so dead set on keeping it then?" Neezer's smile widened. He patted his stomach, which Nitty could hear grumbling.

"Now if you'll excuse me. A public servant's work is never done." He nodded toward Nitty in farewell. Then he and Miz Turngiddy left the room, and soon the dust-choked putter of Neezer's motorcar signaled their departure into the inky dark.

Nitty wasted no time in getting out of bed and starting to dress.

"Oh no you don't." Windle nodded toward the window. "It's six o'clock but might as well be midnight. The dust is still thick as tar. There won't be any rescue missions tonight."

"But, Windle—" She stopped short at his warning glance.

"I need to ponder and feed the animals. You need to sleep." He turned for the front door, and Nitty saw him eyeing Clara's rocker, and then the photograph on the kitchen table. He cleared his throat awkwardly. "I . . . posted a letter to Lillah."

His voice was a near whisper. "I told her about a young orphan girl whom she should like to meet, if ever she finds herself back this way. I told her . . ." His voice creaked like age-old floorboards. "How much you remind me of her."

Nitty's heart warmed through her sorrow. "Thank you. For showing me such kindness. I'd like to meet Lillah someday, too." Only now, she thought, this could never happen. But she didn't say so aloud.

Windle nodded and turned away, then hesitated. "I'm sorry about Twitch. And Mag. This is my fault. I . . . I never have known what to do with little girls, especially little girls with elephants." He sighed—a sigh so heavy Nitty thought it might drag him clear down through the floor.

"It's not your fault," Nitty whispered as he quietly shut the door. "It's mine."

She clenched her eyes shut, and a picture came to her of her own dear Mag, alone and frightened in a dark corner of the Snollygost Institute. Maybe Mag thought Nitty had abandoned her. Or worse. Maybe Mag thought Nitty didn't care what happened to her at all.

Nitty's heart wrenched. Then, at last, she began to cry.

CHAPTER TWENTY-SIX

In Which Tears, Large in Size and Amount, Are Shed

Elephants, it is believed by some, cannot cry. They may shed tears, but some say this is simply to wash dirt from their eyes. Neezer Snollygost was just such a skeptic, for that is exactly what he said when he and Miz Turngiddy walked into the Snollygost Institute to find their captive crying.

Mag stood in a dark corner, her head bowed, her ears drooping, her marble-sized tears rolling from her eyes to the tip of her trunk. The tears pooled around the chains binding her feet.

"Would you look at that elephant?" Miz Turngiddy shook her head, a redness creeping over her cheeks. "I believe she's crying!"

Neezer, who was preoccupied with brushing the dust from his coattails, chortled. "Pish! As if such a simple-minded beast could cry! It's just clearing the grit from its eyes." He gave her a stern look. "Really, Miz Turngiddy. What an unwarranted display of sentimentality."

"I—I'm sorry," Miz Turngiddy stammered, but she wasn't looking at Neezer when she said it. Instead her eyes were on Mag's. Mag's eyes, she discovered, were sweet and . . . even innocent. She did not like that the elephant was chained. Nor did she like all she'd witnessed of the mayor's behavior in recent days. She'd seen him hide that slice of froozle fruit in his sleeve. And though the elephant was strong, she did not truly think it would have harmed Angus Higgler. Nor did she think Neezer had seen the elephant do anything other than come to Angus's aid. She could not believe, after all she'd seen, that any of what he said was true, or that any of what he did was for good. But . . . her job. What would happen to Fortune's Bluff if she did not continue working to stand between it and Neezer?

For the first time in Miz Turngiddy's life, the cogs and wheels of her mind jammed, giving her an awful headache.

"I'll overlook it for now." Neezer turned his back to Mag and, with purposeful strides, headed for his office. "I have much work to do in preparation for the arrival of our guests."

"Guests, sir?" Miz Turngiddy consulted her notebook. "I thought it was just Percival Gallant coming."

Neezer smiled. "Percival Gallant is not the only individual interested in a return of property. There is also the matter of Nitty Luce. There are a host of individuals, myself and one headmistress in particular, who would be happy to have her returned to the orphanage."

Miz Turngiddy frowned. "Sir, I've researched such institutions in the interest of improving my knowledge of civic service. I doubt very much that one small orphan girl would be missed at an orphanage, when it means one less mouth to feed."

Neezer's smile widened. "She's missed exactly as much as I pay to have her missed . . . and returned."

Miz Turngiddy stared at him, her face paling. Her grandbabies appeared in her aching mind's eye, complete with their sweet-cream scent and apricot-fuzz curls. Her grandbabies, so far from her, their own kin. Nitty Luce . . . so far from her own kin. Miz Turngiddy's head pounded. "You won't send her away, not with Windle Homes having taken her in as his own. Why, he could be planning to adopt—"

"Remember the Snollygost motto, Miz Turngiddy. Know that all I do, I do for community progress, fulfillment, and the betterment of all." He patted his stomach. "Now, I'm famished, Miz Turngiddy, and in need of sustenance. As soon as possible."

"Yes . . . sir." Miz Turngiddy pressed her fingertips to her temple. Her head was splitting, and all it could do at the moment was envision orphans, farmers, and the whole of the population of Fortune's Bluff squashed under an enormous purple skyscraper. "And . . . the elephant?"

"What of it?" Neezer huffed from his doorway.

"Will it be needing water?" Miz Turngiddy clutched her

notepad in one hand, her forehead in the other. Neezer did not notice. "Or food?"

"I'll not waste one bit more of the town's food and water supply on this murderous animal. She belongs to Percival Gallant. Let Percival Gallant foot the cost of her care." He gazed down his nose at Miz Turngiddy in a way that made her feel no bigger than a bug at his shoe tip. "Don't give that monster another thought."

But, as Neezer's office door shut with an authoritative click, Miz Turngiddy *did* give Mag another thought.

Poor creature was her thought.

She glanced at Mag one last time, just as another tear plunked to the floor, then quickly looked away. The elephant would survive the night, at least, she reasoned, and by tomorrow morning, with the arrival of Percival Gallant, the elephant would no longer be her problem at all. Tomorrow morning, she would double her efforts and, perhaps at last, stop Neezer's hunger in order to save Fortune's Bluff. Yes, that was what she would do, if only her head didn't ache so. . . .

Miz Turngiddy scurried off in search of sustenance for Neezer and a cool rag for her forehead, and Mag was left alone.

ᢦᔑᢧ

Mag shuffled her feet, and the hollow rattling of her chains made her tears fall faster. Make no mistake: Mag was indeed crying.

She was crying for herself—for her hunger, her thirst, her loneliness. She was crying for the chains that bound her feet again. She was crying for the night of her trainer's accident, months past now.

She'd been bound like this when he'd come at her with the bull hook. Her flanks and heels were still raw and sore from other beatings, and each swing of the hook brought another wave of pain. She'd backed up against her circus wagon, pressing into one of its wheels. She heard the splintering of wood and felt the wheel beneath her haunch give a little. A second later, she forgot about the wheel and the wagon, because the hook was raised and sharp and painful and it was being swung directly at her chest. She raised her trunk.

Then, all at once, the hook was in her trunk and out of her trainer's hands. She held it over him. She knew what the hook would do if she brought it down with a hard *thwack* on her trainer's head. It would be as easy as splitting a tree trunk.

She only wanted to be free of that hook.

She tossed it under the wagon, out of his reach.

She didn't expect him to crawl under the wagon to look for it. She didn't expect the splintering wheel to suddenly snap, or for the wagon to come buckling to the ground with her trainer caught underneath its weight.

She knew he'd stopped breathing. His warm, pungent, alive scent disappeared, replaced by a soured, dried-leaves scent.

She still tried to help. She pulled her chains from their stakes in the ground. Using her head and shoulders, she pushed at the wagon with all her might until, with a thundering crash, it tipped over, freeing her trainer from its weight.

It was too late.

Voices shouted in the darkness, and though the words made no sense to her, their hard, cold tone made her remember and fear them. "The beast!" the cold words came. "The beast has crushed him!"

There was running and shouting and dozens of hands and whips and bull hooks in her face. It was frightening, but not nearly as frightening as the stagnant stillness of her trainer.

Nor was it as frightening as the blame they placed on her for his death.

There was no one who saw what had happened, who understood that it had been the wagon, and not Mag, that had crushed the trainer. There was no one who could speak for her. No one who understood her enough to know, with certainty, that she would never do harm no matter how she herself might be harmed.

No one until the girl—*her* girl—came along. Tonight, Mag cried for her girl, too. She wanted to be by her side to keep her safe. She wanted to be far from her to keep her safe. Her girl was all that mattered.

Mag sank to the floor. The chains dug into her ankles and forelegs, making every move painful. What she would've given to be back in the sweet-smelling barn with her girl curled into her trunk!

Mag closed her eyes. Her tears fell, one by one, in silence to the floor. Alone and frightened, Mag cried. Her great pumpkin heart was breaking.

CHAPTER TWENTY-SEVEN

In Which Escapes Are Made and Farewells Spoken

Nitty stood in the silty shadows of the Homes kitchen, watching Windle sleep. Her head and chest still ached. Her floursack dress scratched her skin, but she'd made up her mind to leave her decent clothes behind. They were from Lillah's girlhood, and she didn't feel right taking them. It felt akin to stealing, and her stealing days were over and done with. She'd stolen those green seeds from the Merrythought Windowshop. But what about all she'd hoped would come from them?

When the seeds had sprouted and grown with the froozle fruit, she'd believed in their triumph. But now Twitch was sick, so morbidly sick that he was leaving. The Homes farm was back to being lovelorn. Windle was back to being hopeless. And Mag . . . dear Mag was back in chains.

Even with her froozle fruit, her Twitch, her Windle, *her* Mag . . . nothing had triumphed except Neezer Snollygost. She'd never been one to bemoan her misfortunes, but—oh!— she bemoaned them tonight.

Windle looked so mournful, sleeping in the rocker with his chin to his chest. It was his disappointment in her, no doubt, that stooped his shoulders and sagged his mouth into its doleful horseshoe.

Nitty wished she could tell him where she was going. She wished she could tell him she was sorry she'd happenstanced into his life, that she'd only meant to bring good to him instead of all this vexation. She wished she didn't have to leave him. But she did.

She opened her Gleam Jar and took from it the daffodil-yellow button. She gently set it in Windle's open palm.

"Because you believe in luck and dreaming big," she whispered, "even though you don't always remember that you do."

She went to the door, looking back once to see a scant, sad smile cross Windle's dreaming face. Then, before her willpower could abandon her, she left.

⌒⫯⌒

The walk to Twitch's house didn't wear Nitty out as much as the sight of his pallid face through the window did.

"You look unequivocally cadaverous!" Nitty declared as she

climbed over the window ledge into his bedroom. She wrinkled her nose. "*And* you smell of camphor."

"Ma's putrid chest liniment." Twitch's voice was spoon-strumming-a-washboard hoarse, but he managed a weak smile, which brought no end of relief to Nitty. "At least she's not pouring turnip soup down my throat. Froozle soup is heaps better." He sat back against his pillows, seeming exhausted from the few words he'd spoken. "I didn't think you'd come."

"What did you think? That I'd leave you a captive?" Nitty sat down at the end of Twitch's bed, trying to smile. Smiles are difficult to keep when you're sad and scared and sitting at the sickbed of someone you love. Still, she hoped to appear stalwart, as all dependable partners should. She pulled a froozle fruit from her pocket—a small one, because only the smaller ones were left. The folks of Fortune's Bluff had harvested the rest. She'd brought several with her, having picked them on her way to Twitch's, but she needed to save some for Mag, too.

"Here." She set the froozle fruit beside Twitch. "This will do you some good. It might taste better than Mr. Moop's Cough Tonic, too."

"Might?" Twitch scoffed. "Anything tastes better than that tarlike slop."

He took a weak bite while they both giggled.

"You should've seen me skulking past your mama," she kept on. "She's outside packing the motorcar right now."

Twitch sank deeper into his pillow. His nutmeg skin had

a pearly sheen that frightened Nitty even more. "Doc Grant doesn't like me being moved at all, but he says my lungs can't take even one more duster. Ma's set on going before another comes."

"That may be." Nitty crossed her arms. "But *I'm* set on springing you. We have to close this case, once and for all. First, though, we have to rescue Mag."

Twitch's eyes widened. "What happened to Mag?"

"Neezer's got her locked up. He's giving her back to the circus." She quickly explained what had happened, and watched Twitch turn several shades paler. "I'm on my way to the Snollygost Institute right now. To rescue her. But I can't do it alone."

Twitch coughed, and Nitty thought that, for the rest of her life, nothing would ever sound as horrid as that cough. When it was at last over, Twitch lay panting and damp with fever. "This time," he finally managed, "you have to defeat the villain without me."

"No." Nitty's nerves were a jumble of sweat and vinegar. "It wouldn't be fair, seeing as how this was your case long before I came here. Besides, you can't move away. Don't you want to stay?"

"I want to stay. But I want to go, too." Twitch raised a shaking hand from the sheets. In it was a piece of paper. "It's a letter. From my pa. It came today. He's found work in California. He wants us to come to him."

"Oh." Nitty stared at the floor. Her head was suddenly throbbing again. Or it could've been that her heart's throbbing was spreading to her head. It was hard to tell. At any rate, the throbbing was relentless and terrible.

"Nitty, you'd do the same. You know you would." Twitch's eyes were dark and glassy, sorrowful and hopeful. "It's my pa."

Yes, Nitty's heart whispered to her, *you'd do the same. For your pa. For a family.*

Twitch was leaving for one family. She was running from another. And it was all to try to save them.

She nodded. "I understand. But I don't have to like it."

Twitch managed a squeak of a laugh. "I didn't figure you would."

She sighed and kicked at the dust motes floating about the toe of her shoe. "Just how am I supposed to manage Mag's liberation without you?" Before she could stop herself in time to remember how sick Twitch was, she glared at him.

Twitch squeaked again. "Nitty Luce, you're the most effervescent individual I've ever met. You rescued Mag once already. You'll do it again, to be sure."

Nitty felt a burst of bubbles rise and pop happily inside her. She wasn't used to being complimented. And "effervescent" sounded so much more pleasant than "suspicious" or "scrappy." "Effervescent" had an emerald-green feel to it, like the seeds, like the froozle field, like her own eyes. "Effervescent," she decided, was something she felt proud to be.

"Thank you," she said softly. Then, for the second time in so many hours, she opened her Gleam Jar. "I'd like you to have this." She set the cardinal-red agate marble in Twitch's trembling hand and closed her fingers over his. *Brother,* her heart whispered. "You are a true friend. I—I used to wish for a brother. A brother like you." The marble grew warm between them. "It's meant to belong to you."

Twitch rolled the marble around in the cup of his palm. Even in the sooty air, the red of the marble fought to gleam. "I'll take good care of it."

"Isn't saying goodbye an abysmal affair!" she cried then, swiping at her eyes in frustration. A trough of lonesomeness for Twitch was already being plowed through her, and he hadn't even left yet. She could feel it there—bruise tender—in her heart. If Twitch went, his dust pneumonia could clear. He could see his pa. But if Twitch went, he'd be gone from her. It was a quandary. "Why is it that caring for another soul means you want to do what's best for them, even when it's hurtful to you?" She crossed her arms and glared at him again. "By all rights I should be incensed at you."

Twitch grinned weakly. "You can't stay sore at me, Nitty Luce. It's my muddy lungs that are maddening, not me."

"Well." She huffed, thinking this over. "I can't blame you." The hotness leaked out of her anger. "If I had a pa who wanted me with him, I'd go in a blink."

"You better write to me." Twitch heaved a determined breath. "I want to hear every detail of Neezer Snollygost's come-uppance."

"You're assuming he'll have one."

Twitch nodded. "He will. Every villain does."

At that moment, Mrs. Higgler's voice sounded outside Twitch's bedroom door.

"Go! Hurry!" Twitch wheezed. "Before she comes."

Nitty scrambled off the bed and hurried to the window. Twitch rasped out her name.

He was propped up on his elbow, looking as mischievous and determined as ever, even in the midst of his trembling and coughing. "Remember: 'Ten Ways to Be a Villain, number six: Hide your Achilles' heel from those who would destroy you. The moment you expose your weakness is the moment of your downfall.'" He clutched the red marble in his fist. "Neezer has an Achilles' heel. Find it."

He sank back, exhausted, onto his pillow, just as his bedroom door flew open.

"What on earth?" Mrs. Higgler exclaimed as she took in the open window and Nitty dropping over the side of the sill. "Nitty Luce, how did you sneak in here? Angus Higgler, what do you think you're doing getting yourself into such a state in your condition?"

"Stay eagle-eyed and sure-footed, Nitty!" Twitch hollered hoarsely over Mrs. Higgler's cries of distress. "Neezer's defeat is within your grasp!"

Mrs. Higgler called after Nitty, "Where are you going? You shouldn't be out of bed! There's bound to be another duster. Nitty, come back!"

"Goodbye, Twitch," Nitty whispered as her feet pounded the dirt beneath them.

For she was already running toward Fortune's Bluff, the Snollygost Institute, and Mag, solemnly pledging, as she ran, to make Twitch proud.

CHAPTER TWENTY-EIGHT

In Which There Are Reunions, Happy and Unhappy

Nitty ran through the deserted streets of Fortune's Bluff, more disheartened with each passing second. In the hazy early light, the town looked in far worse shape than ever before. Dust drifts nearly as tall as she was covered most windows and even some doors. The brown fog blanketing Main Street made it difficult to see more than a few feet at a stretch, but still, Nitty saw plenty. Roofs were torn to pieces; windows were broken and gaping; motorcars and wagons were buried.

No one dared set foot outside for risk of not being able to find the way back home. Or, worse, for fear of getting caught in a duster so fierce a person might be buried alive. No one dared. Except Nitty Luce.

When she passed the Sigh bakery, she saw its windows

gaping, its shelves buckled. She half hoped Bernice would appear at her side, offering her help, but then decided it was better for Bernice to stay safe where she was. Crispin and the Sigh children couldn't do without her. Today, Nitty would have to face the foe alone.

As she ran, she remembered the leather graininess of Mag's skin, the warmth of her trunk wrapped around her. She remembered that this was how the two of them had begun, she and Mag, like this, under a blinding shadow of dust, each of them searching for a sympathetic soul.

It could've stayed that way, just the two of them. But they'd stumbled into a barn. They'd met Windle and Twitch. Ferdinand Klempt, and Bernice and Crispin Sigh. Where she'd wished for one sympathetic soul, Nitty had been granted Fortune's Bluff. Only now, it seemed, she would have to leave Fortune's Bluff worse off than she'd found it, instead of better. The very thought cleaved her heart in two.

When she set eyes on the Snollygost Institute, untouched by the storms, looming menacing and black against the sod-laden sky, whumping its infernal, ever-lasting *WHUMP,* Nitty's every hair stood on end.

Mag was her one thought. *I have to save Mag.*

Theirs, Nitty believed in her bones, was meant to be a great and timeless friendship. And in all great and timeless friendships, momentous rescues occur. Mag had rescued her once before, and Nitty understood that it was now her chance to return the favor.

It was this thought that pushed her forward, this thought that made her ignore the grittiness filling her lungs, this thought that made a locomotive of bravery steam through her veins. This thought that made her, without hesitation, race over the now-flattened fence of the Snollygost Institute, scale the withered vines clinging to the building, and sneak through its tallest window.

It was at this moment that Nitty found herself grateful for the Whirlybog's teeth-rattling *WHUMP*, because it was the *WHUMP* that muffled the sound of her dropping, not very gracefully, onto the sacks of flour below. She was back in the storage room, surrounded by canned foods, the sacks of rice and flour, and a pyramid of cantaloupes. There was no sign of Mag. But in the brief seconds of silence between each of the Whirlybog's *WHUMP*s, Nitty heard muffled voices.

Nitty tiptoed across the storage room toward Neezer's office, listening all the while.

WHUMP! . . . The low mumble of voices . . . *WHUMP!* . . . A whistled version of "Happy Days Are Here Again," which meant that Neezer's nose was nearby . . . *WHUMP!* . . . The wretched clank of chains dragging along the floor.

Mag. Nitty was getting closer to Mag.

Slowly, slowly, slowly, Nitty inched forward through the maze of canned goods. Then she went down on her knees, listening for the clanking, and crawled, following the sound and keeping to the shadows, hoping she'd find Mag before Neezer found her.

On the hard, cold floor a dozen feet from Neezer's office, Mag lay in a restless slumber. Her throat was parched and her stomach empty, and for these very reasons, her sleep was disturbed with nightmares involving circus wagons, bull hooks, and blame.

She was always blamed, one way or another, for many wrongs. First by her trainer. Then by her ringmaster. Now by that man who sat in his office, feasting on food that made Mag's mouth water and her stomach whine, talking in his too-loud, too-hungry voice. Occasionally he stood in the doorway of his office, simply, it seemed, to scowl at her.

She did not like the man. It was unnatural for a man to trumpet through his nose like an elephant. Yet he did trumpet. She did not trust his trumpeting, or his scowl. Both frightened her.

But it was the blame he directed at her with his accusing tone and his bitter, angry scent that frightened her most of all.

She had no defense against the blame. She could never explain it away. No one could understand her language. No one could understand her. Except her girl.

Nitty. Her girl was called Nitty.

My girl, Mag thought then. *I will dream of my girl.*

The dream was vivid. In it, her girl was by her side, whispering in her ear, calling her name.

"Mag," her girl whispered. "Mag, wake up. It's Nitty. I'm here."

Mag opened her eyes. She blinked.

Nitty was by her side, whispering in her ear, calling her name.

"Mag," Nitty whispered again. "I'm here, Mag. I'm here."

Slowly Mag raised her trunk to touch her girl's cheek, soaking up her beloved green-grass scent.

Her girl had come for her.

Her girl pulled a bunch of froozle fruit from her pocket and slipped it into Mag's mouth.

Mag chewed the pulpy fruit, swallowed, then sighed contentedly.

Her great pumpkin heart warmed, as if it were resting in a field of bright, golden sunshine. Her girl had come for her, and her heart was mending.

She lifted her head to look into her girl's eyes. What she saw, though, was not Nitty's eyes. What Mag saw was the man with the trumpeting nose, standing over them both.

⌒╬⌒

"Nitty Luce the orphan!" Neezer bellowed. "I suspected you'd come."

Miz Turngiddy hovered behind him, wringing her notebook in her hands, her expression caught in an uncomfortable tug-of-war between duty and doubt.

Nitty lifted her chin, meeting Neezer's gaze. Her locomotive of bravery was steaming on strong. "I've come for Mag."

"Of course you have." Neezer lowered his head, his nose-whistling turning shrill and insistent. "You can't possibly take her, however, because you see . . ." He waved a hand toward his office door. "Someone, in fact, has come for *you.*"

There was nothing, in that moment, that could've surprised Nitty more than the sight of Miz Ricketts standing in the doorway of Neezer's office. Her head-to-toe black dress was as dour as her expression, and her expression clearly said, *The hour of your demise has come at last.*

"I've been looking for you." Miz Ricketts clasped and unclasped her hands. "All of us at Grimsgate have been most concerned for your welfare since your hasty departure."

"That's a change, then." Mag rose to her feet, and Nitty pressed against her side, taking comfort in the steadfast thud of Mag's heart against her back. "I don't recall you showing interest in my welfare at any time at all."

Miz Ricketts clasped her hands tighter, her knuckles whitening. She stepped toward Nitty, but stopped a safe distance from Mag. "You always were a scrappy, selfish thing. With such peculiar eyes." Her own eyes narrowed hawkishly as she spoke. "Now I hear you've brought this poor town to the brink of tragedy with your reckless behavior, nearly killing a hapless boy."

Nitty shook her head. "It's not true. But it hardly matters what *you* believe about me." She understood that now. She straightened her spine and curled her arm around Mag's trunk. "You never did think I had a spot of goodness, but all it needed was a chance to grow. Away from the likes of you."

For a moment Miz Ricketts was a codfish, gasping for air.

Then, in a swift, catlike movement, she pounced on Nitty, grabbing her by the hair at the nape of her neck. Her mouth snapped down on the words "Why you—"

"Mag!" Nitty cried as Miz Ricketts and Neezer pulled Nitty away from Mag's side.

"Come now!" Neezer's voice boomed. "Struggles are so unseemly."

But Nitty struggled, thrashing against the viselike hands gripping her and steering her toward the front door of the building. Mag struggled, too, pulling at her chains, which were bolted to the cement floor. Mag trumpeted loudly enough to drown out the Whirlybog's whumping. But nothing lessened Neezer's and Miz Ricketts's hold on Nitty.

Once outside in the mustardy daylight, Nitty saw a motor-wagon waiting, black and foreboding. This made her pull even more fiercely against her captors' grasp.

"Miz Ricketts," Neezer said (with some difficulty due to the immense and impressive battle Nitty was waging against them both). "Our meeting of minds is drawing to a close." He crooked a finger at Miz Turngiddy, who had been following the threesome with hesitant steps. She was clutching a bulky envelope against her waist, her lips quivering.

Neezer stared at her. "Give the headmistress the envelope, Miz Turngiddy."

Miz Turngiddy did not move. Her hold on the envelope tightened.

"Miz Turngiddy!" barked Neezer. He wrenched the envelope from her and deposited it into Miz Ricketts's one free and outstretched hand.

Miz Turngiddy took a step backward, then another. She turned from the scene, sinking her head into her hands, while Neezer nodded to Miz Ricketts. "I am eternally grateful for your willingness to take back the child."

The headmistress's frown kinked upward unnaturally, and Nitty supposed it was the closest she could come to a smile. "And I, sir, am grateful for your donation." While Neezer clamped down on Nitty's arms, Miz Ricketts, panting with exertion, was able to slip the envelope into her pocketbook. "It will improve our meager orphanage tenfold."

Miz Ricketts brushed a damp hair from her forehead, looking increasingly weathered, and resumed her hold on Nitty. "In you go. Now," Miz Ricketts said in a low, clenched-toothed tone. "My ship's come in at last, and even *your* evil eye can't ruin it for me."

"That money in the envelope," Nitty said. "It belongs to the people of Fortune's Bluff! And *you'll* never use it to help the orphans of Grimsgate."

"Shut. Your. Mouth." Miz Ricketts raised her hand, as she had so many other times while Nitty was in her care (if "care" was what her wretched failure at guardianship could be called), and prepared to bring it down with the full force of her weight across Nitty's cheek.

This time the intended blow was blocked from its target

by a resolute fist, which wrapped itself around Miz Ricketts's hand and would not let go. The fist, Nitty stopped struggling long enough to notice, belonged to none other than Windle Homes.

"Release your hold on my daughter." Windle's voice was solid and immovable as an oak as he planted himself before Miz Ricketts.

Daughter. The word flew from Windle's mouth so easily, without a second's faltering, and as it did, a window in Nitty's heart opened to catch it.

"As *if* that feral creature could be anybody's daughter!" Miz Ricketts snapped, while Neezer clutched his sides at the hilarity of the idea. Still, because Miz Ricketts stood two feet shorter than Windle, and also because she had no wish to stoke the flames she saw in Windle's eyes into a wildfire, she released her hold on Nitty.

"Good riddance to her," the headmistress spat. After colliding with Miz Turngiddy, who blustered apologies as she handed Miz Ricketts back the pocketbook she'd dropped in the crash, Miz Ricketts hurriedly climbed behind the wheel of the motorwagon. The wagon snarled to life.

"Miz Ricketts, wait!" Neezer might've stopped her had it not been for the wagon's spray of exhaust hitting him square in his face. "We had a bargain!" he coughed.

"I have all I care to take!" Miz Ricketts waved her pocketbook out the window in farewell. Neezer watched, puffing from rage as the wagon, and the money, rattled away.

Nitty looked at Windle then and for the first time noticed that he was wearing the daffodil-yellow button, pinned to the collar of his shirt. "Windle. You bested Miz Ricketts."

"So I did," he responded. There was a certain giddy lilt to his voice, as if he'd very much enjoyed it.

Nitty grinned. "Such a display of heroic steeliness puts the *Daily Tattler* to shame!"

Windle opened his arms to Nitty. She flew to him, letting the spindly branches of his arms enfold her. *Daughter,* Nitty thought. *He called me daughter.* Of the many impressive words Nitty had tucked into the dictionary of her mind, none could ever match the splendor or comfort of that simple one. *Daughter.*

But the rapture in Nitty's soul could only last the smallest second before Neezer burst out with "The girl does not belong with you."

"She does, and so does her elephant. If the idea appeals to her." Windle looked down at Nitty with bright eyes.

"Appeal to me?" Nitty laughed. "The idea has me teeming with euphoria!"

Windle harrumphed, but simply because he was at a loss for what else *to* do with such a bombardment of emotion. "No time to waste. We have negotiations to make and an elephant to retrieve." He straightened with resolve. "First . . . I plan to have some words with Neezer."

He and Nitty glanced around and noted several things at once. The first was the ominous moan of wind heralding from the east, the second was the fortress of dust plunging toward them across the barren horizon, and the third was Neezer, or the sudden *absence* of Neezer.

The door to the institute stood open. From its yawning darkness came the ever-present, ever-loudening *WHUMP!* and a foreboding, nasal trill. Neezer's nose was whistling "Dust Can't Kill Me."

CHAPTER TWENTY-NINE

IN WHICH MACHINE BETRAYS MASTER

It took only seconds for Nitty and Windle to reach the door, but in those seconds the air turned sludgy and the wind savage. Never had any duster descended so quickly and with such ferocity. This was a duster of reckoning, of demolition, of extermination. This was a duster to end all dusters.

Inside, a dirt-pudding fog permeated the warehouse, and Nitty and Windle inched their way forward blindly. The lamentable whumping grew louder and faster.

"The Whirlybog," Nitty said between coughs. "Neezer's using it to bring on the storm." Her heart quickened. "I have to get to Mag."

"Stay with me, Nitty." Windle's voice came, choked and

muffled, from somewhere to Nitty's right. His hand had hers, holding tight. "Let Mag find us."

Nitty itched to set off on her own to search for Mag. Mag was chained and alone and in danger. Very real danger. As was the entirety of Fortune's Bluff.

But Windle had spoken the word: *daughter.* He was wearing the daffodil-yellow button. She would not let go of his hand.

So instead, as Windle and Nitty made their way toward Neezer and his Whirlybog, Nitty called to Mag.

Find us was the thought she sent out to Mag through the brown stew and deafening whumping. *Find us.*

She was still thinking this when, suddenly, the curtain of dust before them was swept aside to reveal Neezer standing before the monstrous, galumphing Whirlybog. Neezer set the Whirlybog's Dustometer to Oily Loam and then began pouring the contents of jar after jar into the machine's holding tank.

Nitty cringed. Neezer was emptying every single jar of wind into the holding tank. The tank was beginning to shake violently as a black, dangerous funnel churned inside it.

"Neezer," Windle called over the Whirlybog's frenzied whumping. "Turn off the machine."

Just then, Miz Turngiddy rushed past Windle and Nitty, scurrying to Neezer's side with a tray of food, a look of determined purpose on her face. As she did this, she nodded at Nitty to make her way toward the large red lever on the Whirlybog.

Nitty could scarce believe it. Could Miz Turngiddy be

trying to help? Miz Turngiddy gave her the answer in a pointed wink. She *was*!

Nitty took a step toward the lever while Miz Turngiddy held the platter under Neezer's nose. "Mayor Snollygost, sir, might I offer you some sustenance? Perhaps a bite of eggplant Florentine?"

Neezer looked at Miz Turngiddy. He laughed. "There are times for eggplant, Miz Turngiddy, and there are times for hegemony. You would do wisely not to confuse the two."

"Brother," Windle said to Neezer then, "won't you see reason?"

Neezer laughed again. It was not a kind laugh, but a greedy laugh. It was a laugh filled with hunger. "You choose this moment, of all moments, to call me brother again? Have you forgotten how you called me a failure and a fool?"

"It was long ago. It was wrong of me." Windle bowed his head. Given his past penchant for unbridled aspirations and sky-high cornfields, he'd never gotten into the habit of admitting wrongs. But how else can anyone make amends, except by being humble and honest? "Some words spoken can't be forgotten, I know. But can't they be forgiven? Clara would've wanted that."

At the mention of Clara's name, Neezer paused. His fingers hovered, hesitating, over the Whirlybog's Dustometer, and a wistfulness passed over his features. "Clara," he said softly. "She loved me."

Nitty paused in her advance toward the red lever, remembering

316

Twitch's words about Neezer's Achilles' heel. Might the memory of Clara weaken Neezer's resolve? She waited, watching, only to see Neezer stiffen, his face harden. "Clara loved me, and even she refused to give me what I asked for."

"What you wanted was too much," Windle said.

"Some biscuits and gravy, perhaps?" Miz Turngiddy interjected loudly. This time her suggestion was met with not even a glance in her direction.

Nitty took another tiptoe step toward the red lever.

Windle pressed on. "We wanted our farm kept the way it was—open and wild and free. Not suffocated by cement and skyscrapers."

"Suffocated . . . pish!" Neezer scowled. "It's progress, but no one here has vision for that. The people of Fortune's Bluff are the *true* fools and failures, and I've suffered them long enough! When there's nothing left in Fortune's Bluff, there will be nothing left to stand in my way."

"No!" Miz Turngiddy gave a banshee battle cry and raised her tray above her head like a catapult ready to launch. At the very moment the tray flew from Miz Turngiddy's hands, Nitty lunged for the red lever, and Neezer lunged for Nitty.

The eggplant Florentine missed Neezer's head but did, Nitty was delighted to see, hit him square in the chest, spelling disaster for his purple waistcoat. Nitty ducked from Neezer's grasp, but his elbow caught her in the shoulder, knocking her away from the red lever and clearing the path for Neezer to reach it.

Reach it he did, and he slid it upward. A thunderous roar echoed through the building.

Timbers snapped and cracked overhead, and when Nitty looked up, she saw a hole in the building's roof and shingles tearing away and fluttering into the burned-brown sky. Wind tunneled its way down through the holes in the roof, papers and bits of food flew from Neezer's desk into the air, Miz Turngiddy's notebook was whisked from her pocket, and soon a cyclone of shingles, paper, and food spun with worrying rapidity around the Whirlybog.

Neezer raised the lever several inches more. The force of the twister made Nitty's feet slide across the floor and then lifted them from it completely. She rose into the air with the ease of a feather. She might've been blown away entirely had it not been for the sudden grip of Mag's trunk, firm but gentle, about her middle.

"Mag," Nitty breathed. "You heard me."

Mag's chains were gone. Of course she'd heard her girl. Of course she'd broken her chains to get to her.

The elephant gently swung Nitty sideward and onto her neck. Relieved, Nitty discovered Windle there, too, holding on tightly, having just been saved by Mag's trunk as well.

"Do you know," Windle hollered into Nitty's ear, "sitting astride an elephant isn't nearly as uncomfortable as I believed it would be."

"Of course not," Nitty hollered back. "And it gives a person all manner of fresh perspective." Nitty looked at Neezer, whose hands gripped the red lever as the rest of him floated above it, and Miz Turngiddy, who, having paused in her battle against Neezer for fear of being blown away, had tethered herself to Mag's sturdy tail. "From up here, they seem so small and ordinary. Not villains so much as people. Plain, unhappy people who've lost their way."

"Seems all of us do," Windle said. "Lose our way. One time or another."

Nitty considered that. She considered the hours and days she'd spent at Grimsgate, staring into her Gleam Jar, contemplating the entire family she'd lost before she'd ever known them. And then more hours and days contemplating how she might get good and lost herself. There were times and reasons, she decided, for losing yourself. Not all the reasons might be sensible, worthy, or even right, but where was it ever written that humans were sensible creatures in the first place? Why, there would never have been anything at all of interest to read in the *Daily Tattler* if that were the case! It surely hadn't been sensible of Nitty to steal the green seeds or an elephant, but if she hadn't . . . well, if she hadn't lost her way, how might she have ever found her goodness?

Yes, there were times for losing yourself. But the better times—the best times of all—were when you were found. Not found by the likes of Miz Ricketts, but found by those who cared. Who wanted you, no matter how lost you were, how thieving, how greedy, how—Neezer's nose gave a whistle—adenoidal.

Nitty made up her mind then, and before Windle had the chance to grab hold of her, she slid down from around Mag's

319

neck. She'd never known anyone as lost as Neezer Snollygost. Or as greedy. But there was one thing Neezer had never had, one food he'd never tasted. Could that one thing be enough to weaken his resolve? Windle called her name, reaching for her, but Nitty, holding tight with one hand to Mag's foreleg, kept her eyes trained on Neezer and his red lever. With her other hand, she reached into her pocket for the very last piece of froozle fruit.

"Mr. Snollygost." Nitty held the fruit toward him. "You don't need to destroy Fortune's Bluff. Wouldn't you rather try some froozle fruit instead? *Really* try it, I mean?"

Neezer stared at the froozle fruit, then at Mag, and lastly at Nitty.

"You—" Neezer took one hand off the lever long enough to jab a finger at Nitty. "You and that elephant. If you hadn't come along, growing that nuisance of a crop, filling everyone's heads with notions of faith and promise and other such twaddle, this town would've bent to my will. You think you can change the course of its destiny, but you can't. Because you're nothing. You will always be nothing."

Nitty had heard such words before. They'd once stuck fast to her. She'd once—almost—believed them. Now she raised her chin. She locked eyes with Neezer. "I don't have faith in destiny. I have faith in green seeds and elephants and froozle fruit. And I am not nothing. I am effervescent."

She stretched to the limit of her reach, holding the froozle fruit out to Neezer.

Neezer, who was perspiring from the effort of holding the red lever and also from the distasteful sensation of being seen through by Nitty's unsettling green eyes, hesitated. Under his eggplant-splattered waistcoat, his stomach rumbled. *What might froozle fruit taste like?* he wondered. Would it taste like the glory of skyscrapers and cement? Or would it taste like sitting about the table with Windle and Clara so many years past, bouncing a baby Lillah on his knee and laughing?

He considered tasting the froozle fruit. He considered accepting Nitty's offering.

But how could one small piece of fuchsia fruit possibly sate him? Neezer's hunger was bottomless. It hungered for more—much more—than what Nitty and Windle and all of Fortune's Bluff could offer.

Neezer reached for the froozle fruit and, with one swoop of his fist, knocked it from Nitty's hand and into the swirling vortex. The fruit circled overhead once, twice, and then disappeared through the now-sizable hole in the roof.

With both hands on the red lever, Neezer slid it all the way upward, unleashing the full power of the Whirlybog.

Every sound after that was drowned out by the blusterous fury of the storm. The rampant wind tore and yanked and pummeled, and several things happened all at once.

Neezer's perspiring palms slipped from the red lever, and he became airborne.

Nitty's grip on Mag's foreleg loosened and then came undone entirely, and Nitty, too, shot into the air.

Miz Turngiddy screamed, Windle hollered, and Mag trumpeted, but each of their distress calls was sucked away into the gale.

Nitty's fingers scavenged the air until, suddenly, they found the Whirlybog's red lever and grasped it, hanging on for dear life. She saw Mag's form through the wind tunnel, her trunk reaching for her. She saw Neezer spiraling through the air with nothing to anchor him.

In Neezer's ogling eyes, Nitty saw bottomless hunger. She saw his true Achilles' heel. Even as he twisted and twirled, even as he lifted higher and higher toward the cavernous hole in the roof, Neezer hungered for everything he wanted and could not have, everything he longed to take that was not his for the taking. This was his downfall—that he'd give up everything for a chance at more. More upon more upon more. But in his eyes, Nitty also saw fear.

"Help!" Nitty cried.

"Help!" Neezer cried.

Mag's trunk swung up into the gusts and billows, reaching toward Nitty. Mag tried—oh, she tried—battling the wind with every muscle in her beautiful gray bulk of a body. An elephant, though, even an exceptional one, has limitations, and a trunk can only stretch so far.

The Whirlybog whumped one tremendous, final *WHUMP,* the cyclone loosed a colossal burst of wind, and Neezer shot higher into the air. At the very same moment, just as Mag's trunk brushed her heel, Nitty pulled down mightily on the Whirlybog's red lever.

The Whirlybog sputtered, then fell silent.

The whirlwind, though it slowed, was not so easily stopped. It began a bellowing ascension into the sky, taking the contents of its vortex with it.

The last Nitty saw of Neezer was the blur of his ruined waistcoat caught in the tempest, climbing higher and higher. The last she heard of him was his nose, whistling "Farewell Blues."

Neezer Snollygost was gone.

CHAPTER THIRTY

IN WHICH A TOWN IS LOST BUT JUICE IS FOUND

The Fortune's Bluff that Nitty saw upon leaving the now roof-less, wind-battered Snollygost Institute was vastly different from the one she'd passed through hours earlier. The town, if it could still be called that, was as flattened and bare as an unbut-tered, syrupless pancake, and indeed just as sorry to take in.

Nitty and Windle surveyed the damage from the slight knoll where the institute sat, and for a time, neither could muster a single word to say.

Miz Turngiddy, who still, out of a need for support or reas-surance, held tightly to the end of Mag's tail, was the first to make a sound. All she could manage was a mournful "Oh."

Nitty laid a hand on Mag's side, and then leaned in to her entirely, needing to feel the nearness of her heart. She pressed her face into Mag's neck as tears pricked her eyes. Mag's trunk curled around Nitty's shoulders and stroked her back.

Nitty couldn't bring herself to look a second time at the disaster Neezer's Whirlybog had wrought. She'd seen enough in her first glance. Crispin Sigh's bakery gone, Ferdinand Klempt's Schnurrbart Emporium gone, the Palace Nickelodeon and even the Snollygost General Store, all gone. Every store, home, and business in Fortune's Bluff had splintered into rubble. Folks were slowly climbing up from storm cellars and out from under piles of timber to stare at what was left, which, it seemed, was next to nothing.

"Behold." Windle's voice was dry and tired. "The product of Neezer's progress, betterment, and fulfillment."

Miz Turngiddy covered her face with her hands. "Betrayal!" she moaned. "Deceit! Treachery!"

"A hard truth," Windle said, his voice gentler this time. "One I wish I could've prevented. I'm as much to blame as Neezer in this."

Nitty's head sprang up at that, and she stared at Windle. "How can you say that? You tried to stop him, you tried to make amends—"

Windle held up his hand to silence her. "Too late. I tried too late. Windows for doing can open and close in a blink, and if you miss them . . ." He sighed. "I did nothing at all for far too long."

"I'm to blame more than most." Miz Turngiddy purpled with shame. "I fed him when I should've fought. I thought

325

I could curb him if I stayed close and paid attention. That I could protect and help our town. But I failed it instead."

"No." Nitty swiped at her eyes. "This is my fault. If I hadn't come here, none of this would've happened. I needed . . ." Her voice cracked and broke. "I had my mind set on saving Mag and fixing Fortune's Bluff, but I only brought ruination."

Windle shook his head and frowned, looking like he was about to argue otherwise, but then, suddenly, a rasping horn and wildly screeching tires sounded in the distance.

Nitty, Windle, and Miz Turngiddy all looked toward Fortune's Bluff, or what had *been* Fortune's Bluff. They stared, eyes agog, as Crispin Sigh's automobile—the worse for wear from dust and dents—wheezed, sputtered, and then died, swerving to a haphazard stop in the place where Main Street had once stood.

The door swung open and from it burst a landslide of dirt and then Bernice, covered head to toe in dust but grinning with ebullient pride. For one small second, Nitty bolstered herself enough to say, "That Bernice makes an entrance worthy of the best of the *Daily Tattler*'s daredevils."

Bernice started toward them but was instantly hampered in her approach by Crispin and the younger Sighs, who hurried from behind a sky-high pile of rubble and, seconds later, engulfed Bernice so entirely that all that could be seen of her was a puff of dust rising from her hair. The younger Sighs clung to Bernice's arms and legs with shrieks and hollers while Crispin bowed his head, crying in relieved silence.

When Bernice, at last, reached Nitty, it was to quip, "The rip-roaring getaway car conquers all."

"We *cannot* give it up," Nitty whispered so only Bernice could hear.

"What in blazes happened that you're driving about in the wake of a duster?" Windle demanded.

Bernice shrugged, dauntless in the face of Windle's sternness. "I snuck out, headed for your place. Before the duster hit. I . . ." She blushed. "Needed to pay a visit."

"You were worried about me and Twitch!" Nitty declared.

Bernice raised eyes to the sky. "Well. It would've been a waste to save your hides if you'd up and kicked the bucket afterward." She snorted. "Only you weren't home. Twitch either. And his house was emptied out, too."

"He's gone already then." Nitty's eyes welled fresh. "To California."

"Oh," came Bernice's forlorn reply. She frowned over this for a long moment, then nodded. "California's a sight better fate for him than what I imagined. I was sure Neezer had kidnapped you both and was about to head straight for the institute. Then the duster hit, and I had to wait at the farm for it to end."

Windle frowned. "There will be no more operating of motorcars. Under any circumstances. By any youngster. Ever." He arched an eyebrow, first at Bernice, then at Nitty.

Nitty, in turn, arched an eyebrow at Bernice, who gave an almost imperceptible nod. Oh, they'd make plans aplenty for that motorcar, Nitty understood that nod to mean. Only they'd best not inform any grown-ups of these plans for the foreseeable future.

Bernice smiled at her, and more dust rained from her hair. Then she looked back toward Crispin, who was mumbling as he held his rolling pin to his ear. Her smile quit her faster than a blink. Crispin, it seemed, had taken a turn for the worse.

"What of the farm?" Windle asked a moment later, and Bernice dropped her eyes.

"The house and barn are still standing," she said quietly as she took Crispin's hand. "But the froozle crop . . ." She shook her head solemnly.

Nitty's eyes filled. Could it be true? And if it was true, why? Why would she—all of them—have been given such a gift only to have it taken away? It didn't make sense.

Mag gave her a worried snuffle, and Nitty burrowed into Mag's great chest, pressing her face into her raisiny skin. Mag dipped her head and wrapped her trunk about Nitty in an all-encompassing elephant embrace. Nitty heard Mag's pumpkin heart resonating a deep and steady *I'm here. I'm here. I'm here.* Being held didn't make anything right, but it reminded Nitty that she wasn't alone in the wrongness of it all.

"I did salvage something," Bernice said then.

Nitty glanced at Bernice, who motioned for them to follow her to Crispin's motorcar.

Since they were at an utter loss as to what else to do at that very moment besides shed copious amounts of tears for the town and the froozle fruits that were no more, they walked down the knoll after Bernice.

Once they had picked their way across the expanse of debris to Bernice's side, they watched as she carefully removed two covered pitchers from Crispin's car.

To Nitty's questioning look, Bernice answered, "It's froozle juice!"

"The last two pitchers of it," Nitty whispered in disbelief. She'd set them on Windle's kitchen table herself, right after the froozle harvest.

"I know it," Bernice said with no small amount of pride. "And I wasn't about to let a single drop spill to a duster. My gut told me that, this being the worst duster yet, the juice might come in handy about town."

She cast a worried glance toward Crispin and slid her arm through his. Crispin, who'd given up on conversing with his rolling pin for the time being, now held a dusty fuchsia loaf of bread in his hands, mumbling, "Two parts hope, one part pain, that's the recipe for rain." Bernice's eyes turned watery as the smallest Sighs hugged her ankles and dress, seeming to shiver in unison, as if they were standing coatless in the dead of winter.

Nitty couldn't bear their sorrow, but neither could she bear to take in the despondent looks on the faces of the other folks surrounding them. Tears were flowing fast as rivers, and the air was full of whispered regrets and what-ifs.

"Should've left here long ago," one husband lamented to his wife.

"No reason to stay anymore," muttered a young mother, clutching her baby.

Mag went from person to person, snuffling at their tears with her trunk and letting the smaller children hug her legs. Ferdinand clutched fistfuls of fuchsia mustaches to his eyes, moaning, "All is lost. All is lost."

Nitty hung her head. There was simply too much sadness to swallow. "I'm not sure it's the right time for juice." Her voice quivered against her will.

At that, Bernice marched over to her, fists clenched at her sides. "Listen here. I don't know about the juice, but it's sure as spitfire not the right time for you to turn into a doomster." Her watery eyes turned flinty. "I'm not about to let Papa slip away again when he's only just come back to us. The froozle juice is near about all we have left, anywise, so might as well make use of it."

She dug through the rubble that had once been the Sigh bakery and enlisted the younger Sighs to do the same among the other piles of debris, until they'd unearthed a dozen tin cups. She shoved some at Nitty, motioning for her to fill them. Nitty hesitated, glancing back at her uncertainly. But when Bernice gave her another pummeling look, Nitty set to work alongside her. Windle, too, took up the cause, administering a sharp warning of "No lollygagging" if Nitty began to yield to sadness.

Although her heart was hurting and her faith floundering, Nitty filled the cups and passed them out to the folks of Fortune's Bluff, young and old.

"Take a sip and pass it on," she told them.

The whispered regrets and what-ifs quieted, until the only sound to be heard was the soft slosh of juice being lifted to lips and swallowed.

Then, when only one cup remained, she offered sips to Windle and Ferdinand, Crispin and Bernice and the smallest Sighs, even Miz Turngiddy. She scooped some into Mag's mouth. Finally she took the last sip for herself.

The juice touched Nitty's lips and slid down her throat with a cool, enveloping comfort. She closed her eyes. It tasted exactly like her first bite of froozle fruit. It tasted like triumph.

CHAPTER THIRTY-ONE

In Which Hope Is a Thing with Froozles

For years to come, the people who were present on the dilapidated Main Street that day would try to describe what happened in those moments as the cups were passed around. No one could ever come close to an accurate recounting.

As the froozle juice flowed sweetly down the throats of the folks of Fortune's Bluff, a change came over them. Their spirits, at first floundering, began to flutter and slowly rise. As they did, a baby's breath of a breeze blew the remaining dust from the sky, chasing away the burned-toast haze. The juice soothed the soul of every person in Fortune's Bluff and whispered, *Hope, hope, hope,* to their hearts.

Hope was what made Windle and Nitty clasp hands. Hope

was what made Mag raise her trunk to blow a long, sonorous note into the sky.

Hope was what each person tasted, sipping the froozle juice. Fortune's Bluff, which a moment before had been teetering at the edge of what surely would've been an irreversible despair, slowly began to right itself. Folks sipped and sighed, sighed and sipped. They let their gazes wander over the Fortune's Bluff ruins, they let their tears fall on the rubble, but they let their hearts linger in hope.

This hope proved especially serendipitous when, as the very last sip of juice from the very last froozle fruit was swallowed, a red-and-yellow circus wagon appeared on the horizon, the words GUSTO & GALLANT emblazoned on its side. A figure in a top hat drove the wagon, his red face determined and covered with a decidedly worn and ragged mustache.

"I'd recognize that horseshoe mustachio anywhere, even in its current calamitous state of disarray." Ferdinand Klempt stepped forward, suddenly stalwart where a few minutes before he'd been tear-sodden. "That's none other than Percival Gallant himself."

Here, thought Nitty, was another villain needing vanquishing. "He's come for Mag." She set down her cup and planted herself staunchly in front of Mag. Windle, Ferdinand, and then Crispin, Bernice, and the Sigh children did the same.

Windle took one of Nitty's hands while Bernice took the other.

Bernice narrowed her eyes at Percival Gallant, who had just

stopped the wagon and was climbing down from it with a purposeful air. "They took Papa to the asylum in a wagon like that. It's not a wagon so much as a jail."

Nitty nodded, frowning. "He means to send Mag to her death."

Mutterings stirred around her and Mag, and soon there was a circle of people surrounding them, much like the one Nitty remembered from the day Mag was meant to be hanged. This time, though, Nitty heard no utterance of "monster" or "murderer." This time, the folks surrounding her and Mag weren't jeering gawkers. This time, they were a shield.

Behind her, Nitty felt Mag shift nervously from side to side as Percival Gallant approached.

"We've been searching for you, beast," he said to Mag, tapping a bull hook against the ankle of his black boot. "Where's Mayor Snollygost?"

"Due to the unfortunate ferocity of the recent duster, Neezer Snollygost is no more." Windle's words were flat as stone.

The effect they had on the folks of Fortune's Bluff was strange. Upon hearing that the harbinger of progress, betterment, and fulfillment had disappeared, people first blinked in bewilderment. Slowly, those who'd worn earmuffs for all the livelong days of Snollygost's reign slid them from their ears. They raised their heads to the blessed quiet. They breathed in the dust-free air, and they felt the first stirrings of a long-overdue relief.

"I owed the mayor my thanks," Percival Gallant went on,

"for locating and returning what by rights belongs to me. Now if you'll excuse me, I'll take what's mine and be on my way."

Percival stepped toward Mag. The folks of Fortune's Bluff stepped toward Percival Gallant.

"She's not yours." Nitty pressed herself against Mag's chest. "She's not anybody's. But we love her, and she can stay with us as long as she likes."

Beside her, Bernice nodded her agreement, her expression resolute.

Percival chuckled. He might've patted Nitty on the head in the manner he had of patting all children on the head to illustrate how much taller and stronger he was than they. Only, Nitty was barricaded by Ferdinand Klempt, Crispin Sigh, and Windle Homes. Percival patted Bernice's head instead, for which he received a swift kick in the shin in response.

"Now see here." Percival grimaced, rubbing his shin. "That elephant is dangerous, a threat to public safety. She was meant to be disposed of some time ago. She's useless as a performer, but I might still gain a profit from her yet."

"You mean to sell tickets to her execution." Nitty glared at him. If she'd been close enough, she would've kicked Percival Gallant's other shin.

"Spectators will pay good money for the macabre." Percival shrugged, as if it were nothing to send another living creature to her death, as if *Mag* were nothing.

Nitty's hands balled into fists. "She's not going."

Percival snorted. "Little girl, you have no say in the matter."

"I do," Nitty said. "Each and every one of us has a say when it comes to what is right. I don't know what happened to her trainer, but Mag was not at fault."

Percival scoffed. "You know nothing of what happened."

"No," Nitty said. "But I know Mag. I know her heart." She looked deep into Mag's left eye then, so deep it felt as if she were gazing into the very well of Mag's soul. There she saw what she'd always felt—the gentleness of Mag's great pumpkin heart, her kindness, her love. "She didn't kill her trainer."

"Mr. Gallant." Ferdinand leveled unflinching eyes at him. "I knew this elephant's trainer. I heard him boast of breaking her, of beating her and worse. No animal deserves such cruelty. No animal can be blamed for defending itself against it either." He stepped closer to Percival, until the two of them were nose to nose. "I wonder, how often did you notice wounds on the elephant? How often did you notice and do nothing?"

Percival Gallant fell silent, but Ferdinand held his ground until, at last, Percival stepped back, clearing his throat and dropping his eyes to the ground.

"I thought as much," Ferdinand said.

Seeing Percival's sudden shame, Nitty felt the hope she'd swallowed burgeoning. There was a chance for Mag. . . . there was . . . there was . . .

"I need Mag," Nitty said then. "Fortune's Bluff needs Mag. And I say she stays."

"I do, too," said Windle.

"So do I," said Bernice.

"And I," said Ferdinand.

"And I," said Crispin.

And so it went, until every person in Fortune's Bluff had had a say in favor of Mag staying.

"This is preposterous!" Percival blustered. "The beast is Gusto and Gallant property. And there is nothing you can do to prevent my taking her."

Nitty glanced at Windle. "There has to be something we can do."

Hope, Nitty was certain, would not have led them this far for nothing. Hope was never an end, but always a beginning.

The whole of Fortune's Bluff fell silent in the next few moments, each person searching their mind for a solution. Only Ferdinand Klempt seemed distracted, suddenly paying particularly close attention to Percival Gallant's horseshoe mustache.

"Mr. Gallant." He took Percival for a stroll, arm in arm. "I can't help but notice that your mustache has—how shall I put this delicately?—passed its prime."

Percival bristled at this, his cheeks reddening. "What what?" He patted his mustache worriedly.

Ferdinand nodded knowingly. "It's looking reprehensibly dowdy. Why, there's no telling what effect a mustache in such deplorable condition would have on circusgoers. Surely a man in your profession understands the necessity of a mustache that offers as much in the way of grandeur as in comfort."

"Of course," Percival said worriedly, "but traveling on the road wreaks such havoc on mustaches, and with all the sawdust and animals—"

"Say no more!" Ferdinand was aglow with enthusiasm and confidence. "For I have, here in my pocket, some of the sturdiest, most dazzling mustaches you'll ever lay eyes on. Built to withstand hours, days, weeks—even months!—of showmanship."

Ferdinand held one of his fuchsia handlebar mustaches out to Percival, who touched it reverently. "What a striking shade. A novel shape, too."

"My own creation." Ferdinand's shoulders heightened with pride. "Inspired by the arc of a flamingo's wing."

Percival's eyes could not leave the mustache. "And such softness . . ."

"Perfectly suited to you." Ferdinand clapped him on the back. "I believe we may have a bargain to strike. What would you say to a lifetime's supply of froozle mustaches in exchange for the life of one elephant?"

༺ఝ༻

Not more than twenty minutes later, Percival Gallant and his circus wagon were shrinking specks on the horizon, carrying with them bags full of Ferdinand Klempt's Famous Froozle Flying Flamingo mustaches and a promise for more mustaches to come.

The children of Fortune's Bluff had made quick work of

salvaging mustaches from the wreckage of the Schnurrbart Emporium, and Percival Gallant had left in a state both cheery and allayed.

"The elephant would've proved more burdensome than profitable to be sure," Ferdinand had assured Percival as he climbed aboard the wagon, "but these mustaches, they'll assure your success. I guarantee it."

"But, Mr. Klempt," Nitty said once Percival and the circus wagon were beyond earshot, "the froozle crop is gone. What will you do when you run out of the froozle silk?"

Ferdinand shrugged. "Percival Gallant has enough mustaches in that trunk to last at least a decade, maybe even two. After that . . . well . . . I'll have to await an epiphany. Or"—he smiled—"I won't wait. I'll make my own epiphanies."

Nitty motioned him to lean down to her height, after which she gave him a peck on his cheek. "Thank you," she whispered.

The Gusto and Gallant wagon winked out of sight. Then, with a soft, sweet whisper, rain began to fall in Fortune's Bluff for the first time in ten years.

"Just as I said." Crispin looked with approval at the sky above. "Two parts hope, one part pain. That's the recipe for rain." The Sigh children gathered around him, and he planted kisses atop each of their heads, one by one.

"Everything was just like you said, Papa." Bernice smiled at him.

He nodded. "I knew it was. All along." He took the rolling pin from his back pocket. "And now, if Miz Turngiddy approves, I will go search the food stores at the Snollygost Institute for some flour."

"Help yourself," Miz Turngiddy said. "Most of the institute was destroyed, but some of the food stores survived. The food should have been given to Fortune's Bluff some time ago, and I intend to right that wrong straightaway."

Crispin nodded his thanks, then turned to look at the pile of lumber that had once been his bakery. "In the end, I think we'll do better without the snakeskins, don't you?" he asked Bernice.

Bernice hugged him. "Leaps and bounds better."

Then she smiled at Nitty, who was more than happy to return the smile with one of her own. Nitty felt a kinship with Bernice, after all they'd weathered together these last few days, and with Twitch gone, it struck her that she and Bernice would now be a duo in mischief and mayhem.

"Bernice," Nitty said, "I've a mind to tell you some tales from the *Daily Tattler*. How do you feel about pirates and convicts?"

"Is there pummeling involved?"

"And then some. Swashbuckling, too."

Bernice shrugged. "Sounds tolerable enough." But her grin confessed her enthusiasm, and so Nitty began a retelling of *The Countess and the Convict*.

Meanwhile, the rain kept on, wetting noses and eyelashes. It kerplunked harmoniously onto the thirsty, grateful ground. It sank beneath the dirt, far down through the rocks and prehistoric strata below, and whispered to the world, *Triumph*.

As it whispered, Nitty, along with the rest of Fortune's Bluff, turned her attention to the piles of rubble surrounding them.

This time, it was Windle who spoke first. Not Windle the curmudgeon. No. This Windle stood taller for the storms he'd weathered and more joyful for the fact that they'd now, at last, passed him by.

"This town is long overdue for a rejuvenation," he announced, and every head nodded in agreement.

"We'll rebuild," said Ferdinand. "With more mustaches."

"More bread," said Crispin.

"More Magnolious," said Nitty. Beside her, Mag trumpeted an enlivening *Brrt!* Then she scooped up some stray pieces of timber with her trunk and dropped them into a pile. Nitty laughed. "She knows what to do. She'll help."

"There is a small problem," Crispin said softly. "Neezer had every cent, every deed, we owned."

"Not so!" Miz Turngiddy scurried to the front of the crowd. "Every scrap of paper in the Snollygost Institute blew away with the duster. Therefore there are no records of debts, no loans to repay. And . . . I still have this!" From the pocket of her skirt she pulled a bulky envelope—the very same bulky envelope that Nitty had seen Miz Ricketts slip into her pocketbook.

"But Miz Ricketts took that money," Nitty said.

"I took it back when Miz Ricketts dropped her pocketbook," Miz Turngiddy announced, and then her perpetually pursed lips pulled back to reveal a proud smile—the first Nitty had ever seen her give. "The money belongs to Fortune's Bluff, and"—she blushed—"note-taking makes for nimble fingers."

"Miz Turngiddy!" Nitty laughed. "You're a proper pick-pocket!"

Miz Turngiddy winked. "I read the *Daily Tattler* on occasion. I find it offers a host of practical information." Then she sobered. "I only ever wanted to help our town." There was a drop of sadness in her voice. "And to have my far-off family come back to me. I overlooked our mayor's foibles for too long. But . . ." She held out the envelope. "I did salvage this. I suppose that's something."

"That is a commendable something." Nitty smiled at her.

"It's not much," Miz Turngiddy said, "but it's a start. And I have ideas. For new farming ways, irrigation, terraces . . ." She paused. "If anyone cares to hear."

"We do," came several voices.

Miz Turngiddy smiled as the cogs and wheels of her mind whirred joyfully at the prospect of sharing, at last, the fruits of their labors.

Then Windle clapped his hands together with a decisive bang, and everyone moved in different directions all at once, piling up rubble, searching for hammers and nails and paint cans among the debris, and talking of new businesses, new crops, and new lives.

It was some minutes, however, before Windle himself went to work. He spent those minutes pondering. He pondered that, at last, the heart-shaped freckle just below his right ear had quit itching for good. He pondered his sweet Clara, and how happy she'd be to see him restored to himself, and happy besides that he had Nitty (and, yes, her elephant, too) to keep him company in the coming years. He pondered the possibility of Lillah's return, if or when her singing brought her westward, and how she'd delight in getting to know Nitty. Mostly, though, he pondered something he'd once told Nitty—something that he now realized he'd said wrongly and unjustly. Something he needed to correct.

Now he put his arm around Nitty, as together they watched a town set to work rebuilding itself.

"Nitty, I once told you that after love comes loss. And that loss brings more unhappiness."

"Until?" Nitty looked up at him through the pitter-pattering rain, waiting. She'd known all along there had to be an "until," and she could see from the promise in Windle's eyes that he finally knew what it was.

Windle smiled. "Until more love comes along."

Yes, thought Nitty, twining her hand around Mag's trunk. Love could always be found lingering, waiting to blossom, sooner or later. And that was exactly as it should be.

CHAPTER THIRTY-TWO

In Which a Girl and an Elephant Ponder Triumphs and the Great Unknowable

Time passed, as it is apt to do, and dusters were never again seen in Fortune's Bluff. On the other hand, one particularly congenial elephant *was* seen with great regularity, always in the company of a green-eyed girl and, on occasion, some adventurous chickens.

There was still one shuddering green seed in Nitty's Gleam Jar, but she never planted it. She suspected that if she did, nothing would grow but a plain and common lima bean. Which was why, one fine summer day, when Nitty heard tell of a tinker passing through Fortune's Bluff, she bundled her last green seed into her pocket and rode Mag into town.

The Merrythought Windowshop was just as she remembered

it, charmingly cluttered with potions, perfumes, and tiny globed kingdoms.

The tinker—barely visible under a threadbare cloak—cackled upon seeing Nitty standing in Mag's great shadow. "I remember you, girl. You had such a hungry look about you, you did." The tinker leaned toward Nitty. "Not anymore, though." A single, shaded eye looked Magnolious up and down, and another cackle rose from the cloak. "Did you find what you needed, then?"

Nitty nodded. "Yes." She held out the green seed to the tinker, who accepted it with a wrinkled, craggy hand. "This belongs to you."

"And what am I to believe will come from such a small, unimportant seed as this?" the tinker asked.

"Anything. Everything." Nitty smiled as Mag's trunk tickled her palm. "It depends on the farmer. It depends on what you *need* it to grow."

Nitty climbed onto Mag's neck again then, and as she did, she could've sworn she heard the tinker laughing. Whether or not the seed would ever grow, Nitty couldn't say. But she believed, and maybe someone else, someday, would believe, too. It might be enough, just enough, to believe something wondrous—even miraculous—into being.

Riding Mag down Main Street, Nitty took in the whole expanse of Fortune's Bluff and smiled. The once-rubbled town had rebuilt itself, one timber at a time. It had taken months of hard work and patience. It had taken all the money in Miz Turngiddy's envelope. It had taken all the food and wood that was salvaged from the wreckage of the Snollygost Institute. It had taken sore muscles, tired eyes, and hungry bellies aplenty, but it had happened.

In time, Fortune's Bluff had grown into a cheerful, welcoming place once more. Thanks to Miz Turngiddy's innovative ideas on farming, fields of bounteous corn, beans, and grain sprouted, surrounding the town in a pool of green so vivid folks often had the urge to stop and sit right in the middle of it. And, of course, they did just that.

That green never left Nitty's field of vision as she and Mag lumbered down Main Street. But the green wasn't all she savored either. There was Ferdinand Klempt waving to her and Mag from the fuchsia doorway of the Schnurrbart Emporium. He was sporting an enormous mustache shaped like a bow tie.

"Stop in soon!" he called to her. "You must try my latest model: the Funambulist Funicular."

There was Miz Turngiddy posting VOTE TURNGIDDY FOR MAYOR signs in front of the new schoolhouse, her grandbabies toddling happily about her feet.

There was Crispin, with the smallest Sighs, setting freshly baked bread in the window of his bakery just as customers approached to buy it. And there was Bernice, her feet propped against the steering wheel of the parked Tin Lizzie, her nose stuck in the copy of *Great Expectations* that Nitty had lent her the day before.

Bernice paused just long enough in her reading to offer a trunk tickle to Mag and a whispered "Twitch's new case—I'll be by at sundown" to Nitty.

Nitty nodded, already antsy to hear Bernice's notions about the case. Twitch's latest letter sat in Nitty's pocket, and as Mag trundled past the freshly painted Palace Nickelodeon, Nitty read it once again.

To: Detective Nitty, Detective Bernice, and the exceptional sidekick Magnolious,

I'm investigating a case of a highly secretive nature, involving a one Miz Millicent Crottle, former traveling magician turned farmhand. Two weeks ago, she arrived here in Visalia to help with the harvesting. Since then, all manner of strange events have occurred. Horrid Mr. Vermix told a coarse joke in Miz Crottle's presence, and afterward he took sick with a twelve-hour pox! When I was grousing over taking my daily dose of Mr. Moop's Cough Tonic, Miz Crottle winked at me. The next thing I knew, the tonic had turned my tongue orange and Ma was swearing she'd never give it to me again. (Fine by me, for I haven't suffered a single cough or wheeze in months!) And just yesterday the carrot field was hot as a griddle . . . until Miz Crottle did a jig in the dirt. Not a minute later, a cloudburst cooled everybody off. I also have reason to believe Miz Crottle is harboring a white rabbit underneath her unusually large straw hat. Now I ask you:

Does Miz Crottle possess magical abilities? Does her shifty rabbit? Or am I falling prey to nothing but smoke and mirrors? I'm relying on your powers of deductive reasoning. Waste no time writing back with your hypotheses.

Your partner in sleuthing,
Detective Angus "Twitch" Higgler

Nitty thought on shifty rabbits and on Twitch's commendable nose for detecting. Hoo-wee, she missed him terribly at times! But she knew she'd see him again. She felt it in her heart, just the way she felt Mag's love, unspoken but true all the same. Until then, she had his frequent letters. Twitch, no matter the miles separating them, would always remain one of her greatest friends.

She tucked the letter away for safekeeping just as Mag reached the edge of their farm. Windle, Nitty knew, would be waiting for them in the rocker, husking corn for supper from their sky-high crop.

She climbed down from Mag and slipped off her shoes. Together she and Mag walked barefoot into the field that had once been plowed with juddering green seeds, where once had grown a crop of froozle fruit.

Nitty pressed her face against Mag's side to feel her pumpkin heart beating. She felt the world's great garden of love wriggling under her toes—seeds of friendship and family triumphing. She felt the joy of all that is great and unknowable, and the joy of all that is great and known. She felt that there was nothing better than to pass the days with an elephant she loved, who loved her in return.

Mag twined her trunk through Nitty's hand, and together through the field of emerald green they walked home.

AUTHOR'S NOTE

An elephant, a dream, and a farm. That's how this book began.

Several years ago, I was doing online research for another book and stumbled across an extremely unsettling photograph of an elephant hanging from a crane (rarehistoricalphotos.com/murderous-mary-1916). The Asian elephant, named Mary, belonged to the Sparks World Famous Shows circus, and she was publicly executed in Erwin, Tennessee, in 1916 after killing her trainer. Though there is still much uncertainty over the exact details of the events surrounding her execution, there is no doubt that her death was a painful and tragic one.

I could not tear my eyes from the horrible photograph and, for hours afterward, found myself asking how Mary's fate might have been different if she'd been better understood and loved. That same night, I dreamed of a little girl running through a town square, a mysterious stolen object in her arms. Dust was blowing fiercely all around her. The terrified girl was being chased by police officers and faceless townsfolk. She didn't know where to run, until she saw an elephant in the middle of the square. She ducked between the elephant's front legs, finding safety there.

I woke up in the morning with the dream still vivid in my mind, and I felt a sudden conviction that I needed to rewrite Mary the elephant's story, giving her a much happier fate. That was the moment when Magnolious the elephant and Nitty Luce were born. Their story is fictional, but born of my wish that we all—every one of us—foster a greater open-mindedness toward, and empathy and understanding for, one another, human and animal alike.

Elephants, as Nitty says in the story, are a "rather spectacular species." Although we don't yet know how much they comprehend of us and our language, we know they are highly intelligent and emotional beings. They can remember places, other elephants, and people they have close relationships with. They establish profound family ties within their herds and can develop strong bonds with people as well. It is not beyond the realm of possibility that Magnolious would sense Nitty's emotions through the sound of her voice and her intonation and would respond to Nitty with her own body language. In fact, recent studies have found that herds of elephants in Africa can identify potential threats simply by perceiving certain inflections in people's voices. In short, there is much we have yet to learn about the extent of elephants' intelligence and intuition, and much we can learn from them.

An elephant's trunk is incredible, too, and serves many purposes. It has the strength to uproot trees but also the finesse to turn (by using a pushing motion) the pages of this book. Elephants use their trunks for both smelling and touching, and for exploring and playing with a variety of objects, as Magnolious does.

While Magnolious and Nitty Luce were inspired by a real elephant and a dream, the Homes farm was inspired by my family's ancestral farm in Pennsylvania. The farm has been in my family for over 150 years, through five generations of farmers. It did not grow froozle fruit. It grew potatoes instead. Because I was raised in Southern California, where the hills remained brown and dry for the better part of each year, visiting my grandpa's Pennsylvania potato farm seemed like visiting the inside of an emerald. The farm was greener than anything I'd seen in California, and I loved it so much that it truly felt magical.

Though the dusters Nitty, Magnolious, and Fortune's Bluff experience have magical origins, the dusters that occurred during America's Dust Bowl were, unfortunately, very real and very destructive. They were a result of the overfarming of America's Central Plains. Native grasslands were plowed under to make way for agricultural crops, and much of the plains soil was left open and exposed on flat land. Without enough trees or hills to shield the soil from wind, when drought came, the soil blew away with the wind until it formed ominous dust storms. The Dust Bowl years, which lasted for approximately eight to ten years during the 1930s, brought suffocating storms that barreled across many states of the central United States. The storms made it nearly impossible for farmers to grow crops, and dust filled houses and even buried cars and small buildings. A number of people suffered from "dust pneumonia," as Twitch does in the story. Many people found it difficult to continue living in states affected by dusters, and some migrated westward to California in search of jobs and fertile farmland.

Because there was a shortage of food during this time as well, many songs from this period focused on hunger, dust, or food. In fact, most of the songs Neezer's nose whistles in the story are real, including "Dust Can't Kill Me," "Farewell Blues," and "I Heard the Voice of a Pork Chop." Some of these were specifically inspired by the Dust Bowl, while others were songs written in the 1920s and 1930s. Twitch's *Detective Comics,* too, were real, first debuting in the late 1930s, although the "Ten Ways to Be a Villain" are fictionalized. These comics featured some of the first "hard-boiled" detective stories, and eventually introduced some well-known superheroes, like Batman and Robin.

For a fascinating look at the bond one conservationist had with a particular herd of elephants in South Africa, consider reading *The Elephant Whisperer: My Life with the Herd in the African Wild* (Young Readers Adaptation) by Lawrence Anthony. For an in-depth and interactive exploration of the Dust Bowl years, inspired by Ken Burns's documentary film *The Dust Bowl,* visit pbs.org/kenburns/dustbowl/legacy.

In many parts of the world today, wild elephants are facing grave threats from poaching and habitat destruction. Some elephants, exploited for tourism, are also still subject to harsh treatment and poor living conditions. For more information about how to help save elephants or support elephant sanctuaries, visit these informative websites:

The Elephant Valley Project of Mondulkiri, Cambodia: elephantvalleyproject.org

Space for Elephants Foundation of KwaZulu-Natal, South Africa: spaceforelephants.com

The Elephant Sanctuary in Hohenwald, Tennessee: elephants.com

Acknowledgments

The seed for a story begins in the mind of an author, but it takes hope and heaps of helpful, encouraging, and talented people for that seed to sprout and, ultimately, to blossom into a book. My sister and best friend, Christina Howe, was the first person I told about the dream I'd had of Nitty and Magnolious running away together. When I asked her if she thought it was ridiculous for me to write a story about the girl and elephant from my dream, her answer was an immediate no. For her faith in my ideas and her faith in me when my own faith fails, and for her willingness to read (and reread *and* reread) my stories, I'm forever grateful.

My agent, Joan Paquette, enthusiastically cheered on *A Tale Magnolious* even when all she had to go on was a mere four-sentence synopsis. She's ever ready and willing to offer fortification and positivity, and without her in my corner I might never have had the stamina to persist as a writer, or the courage to continue trying out new story ideas in the face of potential failure.

My thanks go to the entire Erin Murphy Literary Agency "family" of agents, authors, and illustrators, who offer endless support and inspiration. This talented group was the first audience to hear the beginning of *Magnolious* read aloud, and their kind applause and smiles stayed with me—a vote of confidence as I continued writing the story.

I have the tremendous good fortune to have Michelle Frey as my editor and friend. Her insightful feedback made this book stronger and better. Discovering one of her smiley faces or a "Ha!" written on my manuscript felt as sweet as discovering one more Hershey's Kiss at the bottom of a supposedly empty bag. I clung to those little treasures with the sense that they were cheering me ever onward toward the finish line.

I'm thankful to the entire team at Knopf Books for Young Readers for its copyediting, proofreading, and design skills, especially Artie Bennett, Karen Sherman, Marianne Cohen, and Katrina Damkoehler. I'm also in awe of Emilia Dziubak and the truly magnolious cover and interior art she created for this book.

Natalie H. Hall, doctor of veterinary medicine, diplomate ACZM, shared with me her impressive expertise on elephants, and I'm indebted to her for her careful reading of the story, and for allowing me to ask her numerous questions about elephants and their amazing abilities.

I'm blessed to have many incredible friends in my neighborhood, who keep me supplied with ample laughter, hugs, walks, and coffee while I'm writing. To "The Fraus"—thanks for giving me perspective and keeping me sane.

I will never stop thanking the educators of my childhood and young adulthood for emboldening me to hone my writing skills, or my parents for endowing me with the bravery and persistence to pursue my dreams.

My biggest thanks go to my husband and children—Chad, Colin, Aidan, and Madeline. Chad, for your unwavering support, your commitment to our family, your goodness of heart, and your love. Colin, for your keen observations on life, your wicked chess game, your beautiful cello music, and your sense of humor. Aidan, for your adventurous spirit, your drawings, your impish smile, your empathy toward all living creatures, and your winged feet. Madeline, for your sweet hugs and kisses, your kind heart, your imagination, and your intuitive understanding of when I need peace and quiet, or chocolate. I love you all.